ALL THE COLOURS OF DARKNESS

OTHER INSPECTOR BANKS NOVELS
BY PETER ROBINSON

Gallows View
A Dedicated Man
A Necessary End
The Hanging Valley
Past Reason Hated
Wednesday's Child
Final Account
Innocent Graves
Dead Right
In a Dry Season
Cold Is the Grave
Aftermath
The Summer That Never Was
Playing With Fire
Strange Affair
Piece of My Heart
Friend of the Devil

ALSO BY PETER ROBINSON

Caedmon's Song
No Cure for Love
Not Safe After Dark and Other Stories

PETER ROBINSON

ALL THE COLOURS OF
DARKNESS

McCLELLAND & STEWART

Library and Archives Canada Cataloguing in Publication

Robinson, Peter, 1950-
All the colours of darkness / Peter Robinson.

ISBN 978-0-7710-7611-4

I. Title.

PS8585.O35176A82 2008   C813'54   C2008-901202-X

We acknowledge the financial support of the Government of Canada
through the Book Publishing Industry Development Program and that of
the Government of Ontario through the Ontario Media Development
Corporation's Ontario Book Initiative. We further acknowledge the support
of the Canada Council for the Arts and the Ontario Arts Council for our
publishing program.

Typeset in Minion by M&S, Toronto
Printed and bound in Canada

ANCIENT FOREST
FRIENDLY

This book is printed on acid-free paper that is 100% recycled,
ancient-forest friendly (100% post-consumer recycled).

McClelland & Stewart Ltd.
75 Sherbourne Street
Toronto, Ontario
M5A 2P9
www.mcclelland.com

2   3   4   5   12   11   10   09   08

To Dad and Averil

Although the world is full of suffering,
it is also full of the overcoming of it.
         – Helen Keller

For when my outward action doth demonstrate
The native act and figure of my heart
In complement extern, 'tis not long after
But I will wear my heart upon my sleeve
For daws to peck at; I am not what I am.
– William Shakespeare, *Othello*

The poison is working!
– Puccini, *Tosca*

1

Detective Inspector Annie Cabbot thought it was a great shame that she had to spend one of the most beautiful days of the year so far at a crime scene, especially a hanging. She hated hangings. And on a Friday afternoon, too.

Annie had been dispatched, along with Detective Sergeant Winsome Jackman, to Hindswell Woods, just south of Eastvale Castle, where some schoolboys spending the last day of their half-term holiday splashing in the River Swain had phoned to say they thought they had seen a body.

The river ran swift, broad and shallow here, the colour of freshly pumped beer, frothing around the mossy stones. Along the riverside footpath, the trees were mostly ash, alder and wych-elm, their leaves a pale, almost translucent green, trembling in the faint breeze. The scent of wild garlic filled the air, clusters of midges hovered over the water, and on the other side the meadows were full of buttercups, pignut and cranesbill. Tewits twittered and flitted back and forth, nervous about people encroaching on their ground nests. A few fluffy clouds drifted across the sky.

Four schoolboys, all aged about ten or eleven, sat hunched on the boulders by the water, draped in towels or damp T-shirts, strips of pale skin, white as tripe, exposed here and there, all the spirit crushed out of their joyous play. They'd told the police that one of them had chased another off the path into the woods above the river, and they had stumbled upon a body hanging from one of the few oaks that still grew there.

They had mobiles, so one of them dialled 999 and they waited by the riverside. When the police patrol officers and the ambulance crew arrived and took a look at the body, they agreed there was nothing they could do, so they stayed well back and radioed for the heavy brigade. Now it was Annie's job to assess the situation and decide on what action should be taken.

Annie left Winsome to take statements from the kids and followed the patrol officer up the slope into the woods. Through the trees to her left, she could see the ruins of Eastvale Castle high on its hill. Before long, just over the rise, she caught a glimpse of a figure hanging from a length of yellow clothesline on a low bough ahead of her, its feet about eighteen inches off the ground. It made a striking contrast to the light green of the woods because it – Annie couldn't tell yet whether the shape was a man or a woman – was dressed in an orange shirt and black trousers.

The tree was an old oak with a gnarled, thick trunk and knotty branches, and it stood alone in a small copse. Annie had noticed it before on her walks through the woods, where there were so few oaks that it stood out. She had even made a sketch or two of the scene but had never translated them into a fully fledged painting.

The uniformed officers had taped off the area around the tree, into which entry would be severely restricted. "You checked for any signs of life, I assume?" Annie asked the young constable making his way through the undergrowth beside her.

"The paramedic did, ma'am," he answered. "As best he could without disturbing the scene." He paused. "But you don't have to get that close to see that he's dead."

A man, then. Annie ducked under the police tape and inched forward. Twigs snapped under her feet and last autumn's leaves crackled. She didn't want to get so close that she might destroy or contaminate any important trace evidence, but she needed a clearer idea of what she was dealing with. As she stopped about ten feet away, she could hear a golden plover whistling somewhere near by. Farther up, towards the moorland, a curlew piped its mournful call. Closer by, Annie was aware of the officer panting behind her after their trot up the hill, and of the lightest of breezes soughing through leaves too fresh and moist to rustle.

Then there was the absolute stillness of the body.

Annie could see for herself that he was a man now. His head was closely shaved, and what hair remained had been dyed blond. He wasn't twisting at the end of the rope, the way corpses do in movies, but hanging heavy and silent as a rock from the taut yellow clothesline, which had almost buried itself in the livid skin of his neck, now an inch or two longer than it had originally been. His lips and ears were tinged blue with cyanosis. Burst capillaries dotted his bulging eyes, making them appear red from where Annie was standing. She guessed his age at somewhere between forty and forty-five, but it was only a rough estimate. His finger-nails were bitten or cut short, and she saw the cyanosis there, too. He also seemed to have a lot of blood on him for a hanging victim.

Most hangings were suicides, Annie knew, not murders, for the obvious reason that it was very difficult to hang a man while he was still alive and kicking. Unless it was the work of a lynch mob, of course, or he had been drugged first.

If it was a suicide, why had the victim chosen this particular place to end his life? Annie wondered. This tree? Did it have strong personal associations for him or had it simply been convenient? Had he ever real-ized that children might find him, and what effect seeing his body might have on them? Probably not, she guessed. When you're that close to ending it all, you don't think much about others. Suicide is the ultimate act of selfishness.

Annie knew she needed the Scenes of Crime Officers here as soon as possible. It was a suspicious death, and she would be far better off pulling out all the stops than jumping to the conclusion that nothing much need be done. She took out her mobile and rang Stefan Nowak, the Crime Scene Manager, who told her to wait and said he'd organize his team. Next, she left a message for Detective Superintendent Catherine Gervaise, who was in a meeting at County HQ in Northallerton. It was too early to determine the level of investigation yet, but the super needed to know what was happening.

Then there was Banks – Detective Chief Inspector Alan Banks, her immediate boss – who would normally be Senior Investigating Officer on something as serious as this. Should she call him? He had taken off early for the weekend, driving down to London that morning to stay with his girlfriend. Annie couldn't complain. Banks had plenty of time off due to him, and she herself had recently got back from a two-week stay with her father in St. Ives, mostly sketching and lounging around on the beach, convalescing and recharging after a traumatic period in her life.

In the end she decided that Banks could wait. It was time to get back to the river and see what Winsome had found out from the kids. Poor buggers, Annie thought as she tottered down the slope behind the patrol officer, arms out to keep her balance. On the other hand, kids were resilient, and when they got back to school on Monday morning, they'd have one hell of a story to tell their mates. She wondered whether English teachers still handed out "what I did on my holidays" assignments. If they did, they'd be in for a big surprise.

After the schoolchildren had been sent home to their parents and the uniformed officers had been sent to the car park across the river to see whether the victim had left his car there, Annie leaned against a tree in companionable silence with Winsome and watched the SOCOs, along with police surgeon Dr. Burns and crime scene photographer Peter Darby, work the scene in their disposable white oversuits. When they had finished photographing and examining the body *in situ*, they cut it down, careful to preserve the knot, and laid it on a stretcher the coroner's officer supplied.

There was something unnatural about all that morbid activity on such a beautiful day, Annie thought, as if it were merely some sort of exercise or practice run. But a man was dead; that much she knew. Counting her blessings, she realized that they had managed to get this far without reporters or TV cameras showing up.

The kids hadn't known much. About the only piece of interesting information Winsome had gleaned from them was that when they had first approached the shallows along the riverside path from Eastvale at about one o'clock, just after lunch, one of them had chased another up the slope and there had been no sign of the hanging man. It was 3:17 when the 999 call had been logged, which gave a window of just over two hours. With any luck, the SOCOs and Dr. Glendenning, the Home Office pathologist, would establish cause of death pretty quickly, and she wouldn't have to watch her weekend go down the tubes as she had so many times in the past.

Not that she had any grandiose plans, only house-cleaning, washing, lunch with an old colleague from Harkside station on Saturday. But over the last couple of months, Annie had started taking more control of her life, and she valued her hours alone. She had cut down on her drinking and started exercising more, even going so far as to join the Eastvale fitness centre. She also spent more time on yoga and meditation at home, and she was feeling so much the better for it all.

DI Stefan Nowak slipped off his face mask and goggles, ducked under the tape and walked towards Annie and Winsome over the stepping plates that now marked the common approach path to and from the scene. His pace was unhurried, but then it always was. Annie was glad that he had finally got his promotion to detective inspector and had been appointed Crime Scene Manager. Sometimes the invasion of police work by business terminology made her cynical – it seemed to be all managers, executives and vision statements these days – but she had to admit that a crime scene was a bit like a business in some ways, and it did have to be carefully managed.

Winsome whistled "Who Are You?"

Nowak rolled his eyes and ignored her. "You're in luck," he said.

"Suicide?"

"The post-mortem should verify our findings, but from what Dr. Burns and I saw, the only wound on his throat was that caused by the rope, and it was in exactly the place you'd expect it to be. Of course, there's no saying he wasn't poisoned first, and we'll certainly ask for a full toxicology report, but there are no visible signs of serious physical trauma to the body other than those that can be related to the hanging. I take it Dr. Glendenning is back on the job?"

"Yes," said Annie. "He's back. What about all the blood, if that's what it was?"

"It was. We've taken samples, of course. The only thing is . . ." Nowak frowned.

"Yes?"

"It *could* have come from the superficial scratches he got when he climbed the tree – we do have plenty of indication from the ground and

the bark that he did that alone, by the way, without the help of a lynch
mob – but there's rather a lot more blood than I would expect from a
few scratches. We can get typing done pretty quickly, even this weekend,
but, as you know, DNA and tox screens take quite a bit longer."

"Soon as you can," Annie said. "The rope?"

"Cheap nylon washing line, the kind you can buy almost anywhere."

"And the knot?"

"Perfectly consistent with the kind of knot a potential suicide might
tie. Hardly a hangman's knot. You wouldn't even have to be a boy scout.
It was on the left side, by the way, which indicates a left-handed person,
and given that he was wearing his wristwatch on his right hand . . . I'd
say all the indications we have here point to a suicide by hanging."

"Any idea who he was, a name, address?"

"No," said Nowak. "He didn't have a wallet with him."

"Keys?"

"No. It's my guess that he drove out here and left them in his car,
maybe in his jacket. He wouldn't have had any further use for them,
would he?"

"I suppose not," said Annie. "We'll have to find out who his next of
kin is. Any signs of a suicide note?"

"Not on or near him, no. Again, it's possible he left something in
the car."

"We'll check when we find it. I'd also like to know what his movements were this afternoon. As far as we know, he killed himself some
time between one and three. Suicide or not, there are a few gaps we
have to try to fill in before we go home. Most of all, we need to know
who he was."

"That's easy," said one of the SOCOs, a civilian soil expert by the
name of Tim Mallory.

Annie hadn't noticed him come up behind them. "It is?" she asked.

"Sure. I don't know his second name, but everyone called him Mark."

"Everyone?"

"At the Eastvale Theatre. That's where he worked. You know, the
restored Georgian theatre on Market Street."

"I know where you mean," said Annie. For years the local amateur
dramatic and operatic societies had put on their Terence Rattigans or

Gilbert and Sullivans at the Community Centre and in various church halls around the Dale, but the Town Council, aided by an Arts Council lottery grant and private funding from local businesses, had recently restored an old Georgian theatre, which had been used as a carpet warehouse and then left in a state of disrepair for years. For the past year and a half, it had been the centre for all thespian endeavours in town, along with the occasional folk or chamber music concert. "Are you sure it's him?" she asked.

"Certain," said Mallory.

"What did he do there?"

"He had something to do with props and scenery, that sort of thing. Backstage stuff. The wife's a member of the amateur operatic society," Mallory added. "That's how I know."

"Know anything else about him?"

"Nah, not really." Mallory flapped his wrist. "Except that he's a bit flamboyant, you might say."

"He's gay?"

"He didn't hide it. It's pretty common knowledge around the place."

"Know where he lived?"

"No, but one of the theatre crowd would."

"Any family?"

"No idea."

"I don't suppose you know what kind of car he drives, do you?"

"Sorry."

"OK. Thanks." What Mallory and Nowak had told her should certainly make her job a lot easier. Now she was beginning to believe that she and Winsome might get home before dark. She nudged Winsome. "Come on, let's get over to the theatre," she said. "There's nothing more we can do here."

Just then a young PC came trotting up the path, out of breath. "Excuse me, ma'am, but we think we've found the car. Want to see it now?"

The car was a dark green Toyota, an even earlier model than Annie's old purple Astra, and it had definitely seen better days. It stood in the tarmacked parking area beside the caravan site, between the river and the main Swainsdale road. There were only three other cars in the car park, which was how the officers had found it so quickly. They couldn't be certain it belonged to the victim yet, of course, but as soon as Annie saw the jack-in-a-box with its paint peeling off and the elephant's-foot umbrella stand on the back seat, she immediately thought of theatrical props.

And the driver's door was unlocked, the key in the ignition, which was what had drawn the attention of the uniformed officers. The inside was a mess, but it was only the kind of a mess a person makes in his or her own car, to which Annie could well attest. Maps, petrol receipts, sweet wrappers and CD cases littered the passenger seat. The CDs were mostly opera, Annie noticed, something Banks would have appreciated. In the back, along with the props, were a broken windscreen wiper, an unopened bag of pork scratchings and a roll of cling film. There was also a black zip-up windcheater.

Annie found the victim's wallet in a side pocket of the windcheater, along with a set of keys. He had forty-five pounds in notes, credit and debit cards in the name of Mark G. Hardcastle, a couple of business cards of local cabinetmakers and theatrical suppliers, a driving licence complete with photograph and an address not far from the centre of town, along with a date of birth that put his age at forty-six. As far as Annie could see, there was no suicide note. She rifled through the wallet again, then went through the pile of stuff on the passenger seat and on the floor, under the seats. Nothing. Next she checked the boot and found only a large cardboard box full of old magazines and newspapers for recycling, a flat spare tire and a few plastic containers full of antifreeze and window-washing fluid.

Annie took a deep breath of fresh air.

"Anything?" Winsome asked.

"Do you think he just happened to be carrying a length of clothes-line with him?"

"Unlikely," Winsome answered. She jerked her head towards the car. "But just look at some of the other stuff he had in there. Who knows? Maybe it was a theatrical prop."

"True enough. Anyway, I was thinking there might be a receipt. Obviously if he was planning to hang himself, and he *didn't* have any rope conveniently stashed in his car, he'd have had to buy some, wouldn't

he? We'll get Harry Potter to check the local shops. It shouldn't be too dif-
ficult to trace." Annie showed Winsome a handful of receipts from
Hardcastle's wallet. "Three of these are from London – Waterstone's,
HMV and a Zizzi's restaurant. All dated this past Wednesday. There's
also a petrol receipt from an M1 service station at Watford Gap dated
Thursday morning."

"Any signs of a mobile phone?" Winsome asked.

"None."

"What next, then?"

Annie glanced back at the car, then over the river at the woods. "I
think we'd better make a few inquiries around the theatre, if there's
anyone there at this time of day," she said. "But now that we've got his
address, we should call at his home first. God forbid there's someone
there waiting for him."

Branwell Court branches off Market Street just a hundred yards or so
south of the square. A broad, cobbled street lined with plane trees on
both sides, its main features of interest are a pub called the Cock and
Bull and the Roman Catholic church. The houses, among the oldest in
Eastvale, are all weathered limestone with flagstone roofs, cheek to jowl
but varying greatly in width and height, often with ginnels running
between them. Many have been renovated and divided into flats.

Number twenty-six had a purple door with the name MARK G.
HARDCASTLE engraved in a brass plate beside the doorbell to the upper
floor. Just in case there was somebody home, Annie rang. She could hear
the sound echo inside the building, but nothing else. Nobody came
down the stairs.

Annie tried the keys she had taken from the pocket of Mark
Hardcastle's windcheater. The third one fitted, allowing them into a
whitewashed hall leading to a flight of uneven wooden stairs. A raincoat
hung on one of the hooks behind the door. A few letters lay scattered on
the floor. Annie picked them up to examine later, then climbed the
narrow, creaking staircase, Winsome behind her.

The flat, once the upper floor of a small cottage, was tiny. There was
hardly space in the living room for the television set and sofa, and the

dining area was a narrow passage with a table and four chairs between
the living room and the kitchen, which was nothing more than a few feet
of linoleum-covered floor surrounded by countertop, tall storage cupboard, oven and fridge. The toilet was beyond the kitchen, a sort of
capsule attached to the side of the building at the back. A ladder led up
from the dining area to the converted loft with a double bed at the
centre of the claustrophobic inverted V of timber beams. Annie climbed
up. There was barely room for a bedside table and a chest of drawers.
Very quaint, she thought, but almost uninhabitable. It made her little
cottage in Harkside feel like Harewood House.

"Strange place to live, isn't it?" said Winsome, catching up with her
in the attic, standing with her head and shoulders bowed, not out of
reverence, but because she was over six feet tall and there was no way
she could stand upright there.

"Definitely bijou."

"At least there's no one waiting for him at home."

"I doubt there'd be room," said Annie.

The bed had been slept in, its flower-patterned duvet askew, pillows
used, but it was impossible to tell whether one or two people had lain
there. Winsome checked the dresser drawers and found only socks,
underwear and a few folded T-shirts. A well-thumbed Penguin Plays
volume of Tennessee Williams sat on the bedside table next to the
reading lamp.

Downstairs again, they checked the kitchen cabinets, which held a
few pots and pans and tins of mushroom soup, salmon and tuna, along
with various condiments. The fridge was home to several wilting lettuce
leaves, an almost empty tub of Flora, some wafer-sliced ham with a sell-
by date of 21 May, and a half-full carton of semi-skimmed milk. There
were two butter-and-garlic Chicken Kievs and a stone-baked margherita
pizza in the freezer. The tiny sideboard in the dining area held knives,
forks and spoons and a set of plain white plates and bowls. Three bottles
of bargain-price wine and a selection of cookbooks sat on top of it. Half
a loaf of stale Hovis almost filled the bread-box.

In the living room, there were no family photographs on the mantelpiece, and there certainly wasn't a convenient suicide note propped up
against the brass clock. In the bookcase next to the television were a few

popular paperbacks, a French–English dictionary, several historical books on costumes and a cheap complete works of Shakespeare. The few DVDs Mark Hardcastle owned centred on TV comedy and drama – *The Catherine Tate Show*, *That Mitchell and Webb Look*, *Doctor Who* and *Life on Mars*. There were also a few "Carry On" movies and some old John Wayne westerns. The CDs were mostly operas and show tunes: *South Pacific*, *Chicago*, *Oklahoma*. A search behind the cushions of the sofa yielded a twenty-pence piece and a white button. Hanging over the fireplace was an old poster for a Stoke-on-Trent repertory production of *Look Back in Anger* with Mark Hardcastle's name listed in the stage credits.

Annie scanned the letters she had left on the coffee table. The oldest was postmarked the previous week, and they were either utility bills or special offers. Still, Annie thought, that was hardly surprising. Since email, letter-writing had become a dying art. People just didn't write to one another any more. She remembered a pen pal she had once had in Australia when she was very young, how exciting it had been receiving airmail letters with the SYDNEY postmark and the exotic stamps and reading all about Bondi Beach and The Rock. She wondered whether people had pen pals these days. She wondered what hers was doing now.

"What do you think?" Winsome asked.

"There's nothing really *personal* here, have you noticed?" Annie said. "No address book, no diary. Not even a computer or a telephone. It's as if he only lived here part time, or he only lived part of his life here."

"Maybe he did," Winsome offered.

"Then let's see if we can find out where he lived the rest of it," said Annie. "Fancy going to the theatre?"

The Eastvale Theatre was a masterpiece of restoration, Annie thought, and it managed to pack a great deal into two storeys hardly more than forty feet wide. Clearly its original patrons hadn't cared much about wine bars and cafés, so they had been added on to the side of the original building in the same stone and design. Only the large, long plate-glass windows on the addition bowed in the direction of a more modern style. Beside the entrance were posters for the major production now running, the Eastvale Amateur Dramatic Society's version of *Othello*.

The foyer was far livelier than she would have imagined at that time of day, mostly because a children's matinee of *Calamity Jane* put on by the Amateur Operatic Society had just finished. Annie and Winsome went first to the box office, where an overly made-up woman sat talking on her mobile phone.

They showed their warrant cards. "Excuse me," Annie said. "Is the manager here?"

The woman held the phone against her ample bosom and said, "Manager? Do you mean the stage manager, dearie?"

"I mean the person in charge," said Annie.

A gang of children dashed by singing "The Deadwood Stage" and pretending to shoot at one another. They almost knocked Annie over. One of them apologized as he backed away, but the rest just ran on as if they hadn't even noticed her. One of them whistled at Winsome.

The woman in the box office smiled. "Kids," she said. "You should see the job our cleaning staff have to do after these shows. Chewing gum, sticky sweet wrappers, spilled Coke. You name it."

It sounded like the local fleapit Annie used to go to with her boyfriend in St. Ives. "The manager?" Annie said.

The woman excused herself, spoke into her mobile for a few moments, then ended her call. "There isn't one, really," she said. "I mean, I suppose there's the stage manager, or the director, but he's not really –"

"How about someone who works with the props, sets?"

"Ah, that'll be Vernon Ross. He's in charge of all the technical stuff." The woman squinted at Annie. "What's this about?"

"Please?" said Annie. "We're in a hurry."

"And the rest of us aren't? I've been here since –"

"If you'd just point us in the right direction, you can go home," said Winsome, smiling.

"Yes, well . . ." The woman frowned at Winsome and nodded towards the theatre entrance. "If you walk through those doors down the aisle to the stage, you should find Vernon. If he's not there, go through one of the doors beside it. They'll be clearing up, getting ready for tonight."

"OK. Thanks," said Annie.

They headed through the double doors. Both stalls and circle were fitted with restored wooden benches, cramped like pews. There were also a few boxes close to the stage for dignitaries. It might have been better if the renovators had modernized the interior, Annie thought, though she understood why they wanted to keep the authentic Georgian experience. But the seats were hard and uncomfortable. She had watched a performance of *The Mikado* there once, her only visit, shortly after the grand opening. The mayor had looked miserable in his box most of the evening, constantly shifting in his seat, his wife glowering beside him, and Annie's bum and back had ached for a week. She knew that Banks had taken Sophia to see concerts by Kathryn Tickell, Kate Rusby and Eliza Carthy there, even though Annie gathered that Sophia didn't really like folk music, but he hadn't complained. No doubt *his* bum had been floating a foot above the hard surface on a cushion of bliss. *Love.*

The house lights were on, and a group of people in jeans and old T-shirts were carrying around pieces of furniture and shifting backdrops. A young woman glanced over as Annie and Winsome approached.

"The performance is over," she said. "Sorry. We're closed."

"I know," said Annie. "I'd like to talk to Vernon Ross."

A man came down from the stage and walked towards her. Older than the rest, he had curly grey hair and a red complexion, as if the exertion had got to him. He was wearing khaki overalls and a checked work shirt with the sleeves rolled up. There were cuts on his hairy forearms. "I'm Vernon Ross," he said, extending his hand to both of them in turn. "How can I help you?"

The young woman returned to her duties, glancing back occasionally. Annie could tell that her ears were well attuned to what was going on. She shook Vernon Ross's hand. "DI Annie Cabbot and DS Winsome Jackman, Western Area Major Crimes."

Ross frowned. "Well, that's quite a mouthful," he said. "But as far as I'm aware we haven't had any major crimes around here."

"No," said Annie with a smile. "At least, we hope not."

"What's it about, then?"

"Were you a friend of Mark Hardcastle's?"

"*Was* I? We all are. Yes. Why?" His forehead creased into a frown. "What is it? Has something happened to Mark? Has there been an accident?"

Annie became aware that work had ceased on and around the stage. People put down the chairs, plates, tables or whatever they were carrying, sat on the edge and looked towards her and Ross. Winsome had her notebook out. "Do you happen to know if he has any next of kin?" Annie asked.

"My God," said Ross, "so this is serious?"

"Sir?"

"No. No," said Ross. "His parents are dead. He did once mention an aunt in Australia, but I don't think they were at all close. Why? What –"

Annie turned to face everyone. "I'm sorry to be the bearer of bad tidings," she said, "but it very much seems as if Mark Hardcastle has been found dead in Hindswell Woods." She turned back to Vernon Ross. "Perhaps you can help us identify the body, sir, after I've asked you all a few questions?"

As Annie had expected, a deep hush followed the collective intake of breath at her announcement. Vernon Ross turned pale. "Mark? But how? *Why?*"

"We don't have the answers yet," said Annie. "That's partly why I'm here. Did any of you see Mr. Hardcastle today?"

"No. He didn't come in," said Ross. "I . . . I'm sorry, but I can't quite manage to take this in right now."

"That's understandable, sir," Annie said. "Would you like to sit down?"

"No, no. I'll be all right." He rubbed the backs of his hands across his eyes and leaned against the edge of the stage. "Please, carry on with your questions. Let's get this over with."

"Very well. Excuse me if I sound as if I don't know what I'm talking about, because so far we've got practically nothing to go on. Was Mr. Hardcastle expected in to work today?"

"Well, he said he was going to try and come by. He was going down to London for a couple of days with Derek Wyman, the am dram director."

"Is Mr. Wyman here today?"

"No. He's still in London. He's due back tomorrow."

"You don't need him for tonight's performance, or this afternoon's?"

"No. *Calamity Jane* is being put on by the Amateur Operatic Society. They have their own director and cast. Quite separate." He gestured to his co-workers. "Mark and us are the only ones actually employed by the theatre – along with the box-office staff, of course. We're the only constants, you might say. And everything's in place for tonight. We can manage without Derek for a couple of nights."

"So Derek Wyman isn't employed by the theatre, but Mr. Hardcastle was?"

"That's right. Derek teaches drama at Eastvale Comprehensive. Amateur dramatics is only his hobby. Mark trained professionally in theatrical costume and set design."

"Do the actors all have other jobs, like Mr. Wyman?"

"Yes. It's an *amateur* company."

"I'll need to talk to Mr. Wyman when he gets back."

"Of course. Sally in the box office should be able to give you his address."

"When did Mark Hardcastle go to London?"

"Wednesday."

"Was he supposed to be back here this morning?"

"He said he was driving back up Thursday afternoon."

"Weren't you concerned when he didn't show up for work today?"

"Not really. As I said, Mark's our set and costume designer. His job is mostly done by opening night. We're the ones who do the donkey work. He doesn't carry lamps and bookcases around the stage – though in all fairness he helps out with the heavy stuff when we need him. Mostly he creates the vision of the production, the blueprint of how every scene and costume should appear. Along with the director, of course."

"In this case Derek Wyman?"

"Yes. For some reason, they settled on German Expressionist sets for *Othello*, so it's all big, unusual cut-out shapes, light and dark, angles and shadows. Very *Nosferatu*. That's why they went to London, why Derek's still there, actually. There's a celebration of German Expressionist cinema at the National Film Theatre."

"Do you know if Mark Hardcastle had a mobile phone?"

"No. He hated them. Used to go spare every time one went off during a performance. And that was more often than it should be, despite the warnings. What's happened to Mark? I still can't make any sense of this. You say he's been found dead. Has there been an accident? Did someone kill him?"

The others all sat on the edge of the stage listening closely. "What makes you think that?" Winsome asked.

Ross looked at her. "Well, *you're* here, aren't you? Major Crimes."

"We don't know what we're dealing with yet, Mr. Ross," Winsome said. "In all cases of suspicious death there are certain protocols to follow, certain procedures."

"So he didn't just drop dead of a heart attack, then?"

"Did he have a bad heart?"

"It was just a figure of speech."

"No, he didn't drop dead of a heart attack. Was he ill?"

"His health was fine," said Ross. "As far as we knew. I mean, he was always healthy enough, lively, full of energy and vitality. Mark loved life."

"Did he take drugs?" Annie asked.

"Not that I was aware of."

"Anyone?" Annie glanced around the room. They all shook their heads. She counted six people on the stage; that made seven including Ross. "I'll need to talk to you all individually at some point," she said. "For the moment, though, can any of you tell me anything at all about Mr. Hardcastle's recent state of mind?"

"Did he commit suicide?" asked the young woman who had been paying close attention from the start. She had a pleasant, heart-shaped face, free of make-up, and her light brown hair was tied back in a pony-tail. Like the rest, she wore jeans and a T-shirt.

"And you are?" Annie asked.

"Maria. Maria Wolsey."

"Well, Maria, why do you ask?"

"I don't know. Just the way the two of you are talking. If it wasn't an accident or a heart attack, and he wasn't killed . . ."

"Suicide is one possibility," Annie said. "Was he depressed or upset about anything?"

"He'd been a bit edgy lately," Maria said. "That's all."

"Edgy? In what way? Why?"

"I don't know why. Just . . . maybe, like there was something worrying him."

"I understand that Mr. Hardcastle was gay," Annie said.

"Mark was quite open about his sexuality," said Vernon Ross. "Open without being . . . well, without overdoing it, if you understand what I mean."

"This trip to London with Derek Wyman," Annie went on. "Anything in it?"

Comprehension dawned on Ross's face. "Good Lord, no," he said. "Derek's a happily married man. With children. Has been for years. They're just colleagues with a shared interest in theatre and film, that's all."

"Did Mark Hardcastle have a partner?"

"I think so," said Ross, clearly a bit embarrassed by the whole idea. "Maria?"

"Yes, he did. Laurence."

"Do you know his surname?"

"I don't think it ever came up."

"Were you a particularly close friend of Mark's?"

"I suppose so. I like to think so. I mean, as much as you could be. He never let you *really* close. I think things had been difficult for him. He'd had a hard life. But he was one of the best men I've ever known. Surely he can't be dead? Just like that?"

"Was this relationship recent?"

"Six months or so. Just before Christmas, I think," said Maria. "He was very happy."

"What was he like before?"

Maria paused, then she said, "I wouldn't say he was unhappy, but he was definitely more restless and superficial. He lived for his work, and I also got the impression that he was doing the rounds, you know, going through the motions, sexually, like, but that he wasn't very happy. Don't get me wrong. On the surface he was always cheerful and had a kind word for everyone. But deep down I think he was very unhappy and unfulfilled in his life until he met Laurence."

"For God's sake," said Ross. Then he turned to Annie. "You'll have to forgive Maria," he said. "She's our resident romantic."

Maria blushed, with equal parts of anger and embarrassment, Annie guessed. "I can forgive her that," she said to Ross, then turned to Maria again. "Did he talk much about this relationship?"

"Not in any sort of detail. He was just more . . . comfortable, more settled, relaxed than I'd seen him before."

"Until recently?"

"Yes."

"Did you ever meet Laurence?"

"A few times, when he came to the theatre."

"Could you describe him?"

"About six foot, handsome, a bit sort of upper class. Dark hair with a touch of grey at the temples. Slender, athletic. Very charming, but rather remote. Maybe a bit of a snob. You know, a sort of public school type, to the manor born."

"Do you know what Laurence does? What his job is?"

"Mark never mentioned anything. I think he might be retired. Or maybe he buys and sells antiques, works of art, something like that."

"How old?"

"Early fifties, I'd say."

"Do you know where he lives? We really need to find him."

"Sorry," said Maria. "I don't know. I think he's fairly well off, though, at least his mother is, so he's probably got a posh house. I know Mark was spending more and more time with him. I mean, they were practically living together."

Annie saw Winsome make a note of that. "This change you noticed in Mr. Hardcastle lately," she went on. "Can you tell me a bit more about it?"

"He'd just been a bit moody this past couple of weeks, that's all," Maria said. "He shouted at me once for putting a table in the wrong place on the stage. He never usually does that."

"When was this?"

"I don't remember exactly. Maybe about ten days ago."

Vernon Ross glared at Maria as if she were betraying state secrets. "Lover's tiff, I should imagine," he said.

"Lasting two weeks?" Annie said.

Ross gave Maria another stern look. "It didn't appear serious at the time," he said. "Maria *did* position that table in the wrong place. It was a silly mistake. It would have put the actor completely off his timing. But that was all. It wasn't *that* serious. Mark was just in a bad mood. It happens to all of us. There was nothing that would drive him to *suicide*, for crying out loud."

"If he did commit suicide," said Annie. "Do *you* have any idea what it was all about, Mr. Ross?"

"Me? No."

"Do any of you know if Mr. Hardcastle *did* have anyone he was close to, outside the theatre scene? Someone he might have talked to, shared his problems with. Other than Derek Wyman."

No one said anything.

"Anyone know where he was from?"

"Barnsley," said Maria.

"How do you know that?"

"He made jokes about it, said he had to support the local football team when he was growing up, or people would think he was a poof. Naturally, it came up when Barnsley got to Wembley for the FA Cup semi-final and everyone was talking about them beating Liverpool and Chelsea. Pity they didn't go all the way. And Mark mentioned his dad once. Said he worked down the pit. I got the impression it was a tough place to grow up gay."

"I should imagine so," said Annie, who had never been to Barnsley. All she knew about it was that it was in South Yorkshire and used to have a lot of coal mines. Certainly she wouldn't have expected most mining communities to be sympathetic towards gays.

She addressed the others. "Is there anyone else here apart from Ms. Wolsey and Mr. Ross who was close to Mark Hardcastle?"

One of the other girls spoke up. "We all felt close to Mark. He made you feel special. You could talk to him about anything. And there was nobody more generous."

"Did he talk to you about his problems?"

"No," the girl said. "But he'd listen to yours and give you advice if you wanted it. He wouldn't push it on you. He was so wise. I just can't believe it. I can't believe any of this." She started crying and took out a handkerchief.

Annie glanced at Winsome to let her know they were done, then she took some cards from her briefcase and handed them out.

"If any of you think of anything, please don't hesitate to call," she said. Then she looked at Vernon Ross again and said, "Mr. Ross, can you come to the mortuary with us now, please, if it's convenient?"

2

"**G**ot it!" said Annie, punching the air in victory. It was half past eight on Saturday morning, and she and Winsome were in the Western Area HQ squad room with DC Doug Wilson. They had called it a day at seven o'clock the previous evening, after Vernon Ross had identified Mark Hardcastle's body, and after a quick drink they had both gone their separate ways home.

Wilson had trawled the local shops and discovered that Mark Hardcastle had bought the yellow clothesline from a hardware shop owned by a Mr. Oliver Grainger at about a quarter to one on Friday afternoon. He had blood on his hands and face, and Grainger had thought he might have cut himself doing some carpentry. When he had asked about this, Hardcastle had shrugged it off. He had been wearing his black windcheater zipped up, so Grainger hadn't been able to see whether there was also blood on his arms. Hardcastle had also smelled strongly of whisky, though he hadn't acted drunk. According to Grainger, he had appeared oddly calm and subdued.

Now, while sorting through the SOCO reports on her desk, Annie discovered that a thorough search of Mark Hardcastle's car had produced a letter mixed in among the newspapers and magazines in the boot. The letter was nothing in itself, just an old special wine offer from John Lewis, but it was addressed to a Laurence Silbert at 15 Castleview Heights, and somehow it had got mixed in with the papers for recycling. Castleview Heights was nothing if it wasn't posh.

"Got what?" said Winsome.

"I think I've found the lover. He's called Laurence Silbert. Lives on the Heights." Annie got up and grabbed her jacket from the back of her chair. "Winsome," she said, "could you hold the fort here and start the interviews if I'm not back in time?"

"Of course," said Winsome.

Annie turned to Doug Wilson. With his youthful looks – which, along with the glasses, had earned him the nickname of "Harry Potter" around the station – his hesitant manner and a tendency to stutter when under stress, he wasn't the right person to conduct the interviews, but all he needed, Annie reckoned, was a bit more self-confidence, and only on-the-job experience would give him that. "Want to come along, Doug?" she asked.

Winsome gave Wilson a nod, assuring him it was OK, that she wasn't feeling slighted. "Yes, guv," he said. "Absolutely."

"Shouldn't we find out a bit more about the situation first?" Winsome said.

But Annie was already at the door, Wilson at her heels. Annie turned. "Like what?"

"Well . . . you know . . . it's a pretty posh area, the Heights. Maybe this Silbert is married or something? I mean, you shouldn't just go barging in there without knowing a bit more about the lie of the land, should you? What if he's got a wife and kids?"

"I shouldn't think he has, if Maria Wolsey was right when she said he and Mark were practically living together," said Annie. "But if Laurence Silbert *is* married with children, I'd say his wife and kids deserve to know about Mark Hardcastle, wouldn't you?"

"I suppose you're right," said Winsome. "Just tread softly, that's all I'm saying. Don't tread on any toes. A lot of people up there are friends with the Chief Constable and ACC McLaughlin, you know. You'll ring and let me know what happens?"

"Yes, Mother." Annie smiled to soften the barb. "As soon as I know myself," she added. "Bye."

DC Wilson put on his glasses and dashed out the door behind her.

Winsome was perhaps understating it when she described the Heights, as the area was known locally, as "a bit" posh, Annie thought as DC Wilson parked on the street outside number 15. It was a *lot* posh, with the reputation of being an exclusive club for Eastvale's wealthy and privileged. You wouldn't get much change from a million quid for a house up there. If you could find one on the market, and if the tenants' association and neighbourhood watch committee approved of your credentials. They must have approved of Laurence Silbert, Annie thought, which meant that he had money and status. The homosexuality would not necessarily be a problem so long as he was discreet about it. All-night raves with rent boys, on the other hand, might attract a bit of local disapproval.

Getting out of the car, Annie could see why the locals did their best to protect and preserve their habitat from the *hoi polloi*. She had been up there once or twice before during her time at Eastvale, but had almost forgotten how magnificent the view was.

To the south, straight ahead, she could see over the slate and flagstone rooftops and crooked chimneys of the terraced streets below to the cobbled market square, with its tiny dots dashing about their business. Just to the left of the Norman church tower, beyond The Maze, stood the ruined castle on its hill, and below that, at the bottom of the colourful hillside gardens, the River Swain tripped over a series of little waterfalls, sending up white spray and foam. Directly across the water stood The Green, with its Georgian semis and mighty old trees. Things got uglier after that, with the East Side Estate poking its redbrick terraces, two tower blocks and maisonettes through the gaps in the greenery, and then came railway lines. Even farther out, Annie could see all the way across the Vale of York to the steep rise of Sutton Bank.

South, past the square and the castle, on the left riverbank, she could also see the beginnings of Hindswell Woods, but the spot where Mark Hardcastle's body had been discovered came after a bend in the river and was hidden from view.

Annie breathed in the air. It was another beautiful day, fragrant and mild. DC Wilson stood waiting for instructions, hands in his pockets, and Annie turned to the house. It was an impressive sight: a walled garden with a black wrought-iron gate surrounded the gabled mansion, built of local limestone, with large mullioned windows and ivy and clematis climbing up the walls.

A short gravel drive led from the gates to the front door. Just to the right stood an old coach house, the lower half of which had been converted into a garage. The double doors were open, and inside was an extremely sleek, beautiful and expensive silver Jaguar. There would be plenty of room to hide Hardcastle's old Toyota in there, too, Annie thought. It wasn't the kind of car the neighbours would appreciate seeing parked on their street, though the houses were generally far enough apart here, and sufficiently separated by high walls and broad lawns that the people who lived in them need have as little to do with one another as possible.

So Mark Hardcastle hadn't only got lucky in love; he had also found himself a rich boyfriend into the bargain. Annie wondered how much that had mattered to him. It was a long journey for the son of a Barnsley coal miner, and it made Annie feel even more intrigued to meet the mysterious Laurence Silbert.

Annie banged the brass lion's-head knocker on the front door. The sound echoed throughout the entire neighbourhood, quiet but for the sounds of traffic from the town below and the twittering of birds in the trees. But from inside there was nothing. She knocked again. Still nothing. She turned the handle. The door was locked.

"Shall we try round the back, guv?" asked Wilson.

Annie peered in through the front windows but could see only dim, empty rooms. "Might as well," she said.

The path led between the coach house and the main building into a spacious back garden complete with hedges, well-kept lawn, wooden garden shed, flower beds and a winding stone path. On their way, Annie put her hand on the Jaguar's bonnet. Cool. In the garden, a white metal table and four chairs stood under the shade of a sycamore.

"Seems like everyone's away, doesn't it?" said Wilson. "Perhaps this Silbert bloke's on holiday?"

"But his car's in the garage," Annie reminded him.

"Maybe he's got more than one? Bloke this rich . . . Range Rover or something? Visiting his country estates?"

Wilson had imagination; Annie had to grant him that. There was a spacious conservatory attached to the back of the house, complete with rough whitewashed walls and rustic wooden table and chairs. She tried the door and found that it was open. A small pile of newspapers lay on the table, dated the previous Sunday.

The door that led through to the main house was locked, however, so she knocked and called out Silbert's name. Her attempts were met with nothing but a silence that made the hairs on the back of her neck stand on end. Something was wrong; she knew it. Could she justify breaking in without a warrant? She thought so. A man had been found dead, and a letter in his possession clearly linked him to this address.

Annie wrapped her hand in one of the newspapers and punched out the pane of glass directly above the area of the lock. She was in luck. Inside was a large key that opened the deadbolt when she turned it. They were in.

The interior of the house was gloomy and cool after the bright, warm conservatory, but as her vision adjusted and she found herself in the living room, Annie noticed that it was cheerfully enough decorated, with vibrant modern paintings on the walls – Chagall and Kandinsky prints – and paint and wallpaper in light, airy colours. It just didn't get much light downstairs. The room was empty except for a three-piece suite, a black grand piano and a series of bookcases built into the walls, mostly holding old leather-bound volumes.

They walked through to the kitchen, which was state of the art, all gleaming white tiles, brushed steel surfaces and every utensil a master chef would ever need. Everything was spotless. The cooking area itself was separated from the dining room by a long island. Clearly, Hardcastle and Silbert liked to entertain at home, and one of them, at least, probably enjoyed cooking.

A broad, carpeted staircase with gleaming banisters and wainscotting led upstairs from the hallway. As they walked up, every once in a while Annie called out Silbert's name in case he was somewhere else in the house where he hadn't been able to hear them earlier, but she was still met with that same chill and eerie silence. The dark, patterned carpet on the landing was thick, and their feet made no noise as they padded around, checking the rooms.

It was behind the third door that they found Laurence Silbert.

Fortunately, they didn't have to do anything more than stand at the threshold to see the body that lay spreadeagled on the sheepskin rug in front of the hearth. Silbert – or at least Annie assumed it was Silbert – lay on his back on the rug, arms spread out, making the shape of a cross. His head had been beaten to a pulp, and a dark halo of blood soaked into the sheepskin around it. He was wearing tan chinos and a shirt that had once been white but was now mostly dark red. The area between his legs was also bloody, whether from cuts or overspill from the head injuries, Annie couldn't tell.

She managed to drag her eyes away from the body and look around the room. Like the rest of the house, the upstairs drawing room, complete with Adam fireplace, was a strange mix of the antique and the contemporary. A framed picture that reminded Annie very much of Jackson Pollock hung over the empty fireplace. Maybe it *was* a Jackson Pollock. Sunlight poured in through the high sash window, lighting the Persian carpets, antique desk and a brown leather-upholstered settee.

Annie became vaguely aware of Wilson's grunt and the sound of him being sick on the landing before he managed to get to the bathroom.

Pale and trembling, she shut the door and reached for her mobile. First she rang Detective Superintendent Gervaise at home and explained the situation. It wasn't that Annie didn't know what to do, but something big like this, you let the boss know immediately, or things could have a nasty habit of coming back at you. As expected, Gervaise said she would call in the SOCOs, photographer and police surgeon, then she said, "And DI Cabbot?"

"Yes?"

"I think it's time we called DCI Banks back. I know he's supposed to be on holiday, but things could get very messy up here, and this *is* the Heights. We need to be seen to have a senior and experienced officer in charge. No criticism implied."

"None taken, ma'am," said Annie, who felt she could handle the situation perfectly well with Winsome and Doug Wilson. "As you wish."

As she leaned against the wall watching an ashen Wilson sitting on the stairs with his head in his hands and picked Banks's mobile number from her BlackBerry's address book, Annie thought this would certainly put the kibosh on Banks's Saturday morning shag. Then she chastised herself for having such evil thoughts and pressed the call button.

Alan Banks stretched and almost purred as he reached for the luke-warm cup of tea on the bedside table. The sun was shining, the glorious morning warmth rolling in through the slightly open window, the net curtains fluttering. Tinariwen were singing "Cler Achel" on the alarm clock's iPod dock, electric guitar weaving in and out of the Bo Diddley-style riff, and all was well with the world. The little semicircle of stained glass above the main window filtered the light red and green and gold. The first time Banks had woken up in that room he had had a bad hangover, and for a moment he had felt as if he had died and woken up in heaven.

Sophia had had to go to work, unfortunately, but just for the morning. Banks was due to meet her outside Western House and go for lunch at a little pub they liked, the Yorkshire Grey, off Great Portland Street. That evening, they were hosting a dinner party, and they would spend the afternoon shopping for ingredients at one of her favourite farmers' markets, probably Notting Hill. Banks knew how it worked. He had been with Sophia on previous occasions, and he loved to watch her choosing strangely shaped and oddly coloured fruits or vegetables, an expression of pure childlike wonder and concentration on her face as she weighed them in her hands and felt their firmness and the texture of their skin, tongue nipped gently between her teeth. She would chat with the stall-owners, ask them questions, and she always walked away with more than she intended to buy.

In the evening, he would offer to help make dinner, but he knew that Sophia would only shoo him out of the way. At best he might be allowed to chop a few vegetables, or prepare the salad, then he would be banished to the garden to read and sip his wine. The special alchemy of cooking was reserved for Sophia alone. He had to admit that she did it with exqui-site style and flair. He hadn't eaten so well in ages, *ever*, if truth be told. After the guests had gone, he would stack the dishwasher while Sophia leaned back against the kitchen counter, a glass of wine in her hand, and quizzed him about the various courses, seeking an honest opinion.

Banks put his cup down and lay back. He could smell the pillow where Sophia had lain beside him, her hair like the memory of apples he had picked in the orchard with his father one glorious autumn afternoon of his childhood. His fingers remembered the touch of her skin, and that brought back the one little wrinkle on the mantle of his happiness.

Last night, making love, he had told her that she had beautiful skin, and she had laughed and replied, "So I've been told." It wasn't the little vanity that bothered him, her awareness of her own beauty – he found that quite sexy – but the dark thought of the other men who had been close enough to tell her that before him. That way madness lies, he told himself, or at least misery. If he surrendered to images of Sophia naked and laughing with someone else, he didn't know whether he would be able to hang on to his sanity. No matter how many lovers she had had, whatever he and she did together, they did for the first time. That was the only way to think of it. John and Yoko had it right: *Two Virgins*.

Enough lounging around and slipping into dark thoughts, Banks told himself. It was nine o'clock, time to get up.

After he had showered and dressed, he made his way downstairs. He thought he would go to the local Italian café this morning, read the papers and watch the world go by, then he might just have time to drop in at the HMV on Oxford Street on his way to Fitzrovia and see whether the new Isobel Campbell and Mark Lanegan was out.

Sophia's terrace house was in a narrow street off the King's Road. She had got it as part of her divorce settlement, otherwise she would never have been able to afford such a location. It had to be worth a fortune today. It had a pastel blue façade that reminded Banks a little of the blue of Santorini, perhaps deliberate, as Sophia was half Greek, with white trim and white-painted wooden shutters. There was no front garden, but a low brick wall with a small gate stood about three feet or so from the front door, so it didn't open directly on to the street. Though it looked very narrow from the outside, the lot was deep and, TARDIS-like, the space opened up when you went inside: living room to the right, stairs to the left, dining room and kitchen at the end of the hall, and a little garden out back where you could sit in the shade, and where Sophia grew herbs and cultivated a couple of flower beds.

On the second level were the two bedrooms, one with an en suite shower and toilet, and French windows leading to a tiny wrought-iron balcony with a couple of matching small chairs, a round iron table and a few plants in large terracotta urns. They hadn't sat out for a while, either because of the rain or the never-ending and noisy renovations next door. Above the bedrooms was a converted attic area, which Sophia used as her home office.

The house was full of *things*. Spindly-legged tables inlaid with ivory or mother of pearl held artfully arranged displays of fossils, stone jars, amphorae, Victorian shell boxes, Limoges china, crystals, agates, sea-shells and smooth pebbles that Sophia had collected from all over the world. She knew where each one came from, what it was called. The walls were covered with original paintings, mostly abstract landscapes by artists she knew, and every nook and cranny was home to a piece of sculpture, contemporary in style and varying from soapstone to brass in material.

Sophia loved masks, too, and had collected quite a few. They hung between the paintings, dark wooden ones from Africa, tiny coloured bead ones from South America, painted ceramic masks from the Far East. There were also peacock feathers, dried ferns and flowers, a chunk of the Berlin Wall, tiny animal skulls from the Nevada desert, spondylus from Peru, and many-coloured worry-beads from Istanbul hung over the mantelpiece. Sophia said she loved all these things and felt responsible for them; she was merely taking care of them temporarily, and they would continue long after she was gone.

Quite a responsibility, Banks had said, which was why Sophia had installed a top-of-the-line security system. Sometimes he felt as if her house were a museum and she was its curator. Maybe he was an exhibit, too, he thought: her pet detective, to be brought out at artistic gather-ings. But that was unfair. She had never done anything to make him feel that way. Sometimes he wished he had a clearer idea of what she was thinking, though, of what drove her and what really mattered to her. He realized that he didn't really know her well at all; she was, at heart, a very private person who surrounded herself with people to remain hidden.

Banks remembered to set the security code before he left. Sophia would never forgive him if he forgot and someone broke in. Insurance was no good. None of the stuff was valuable, except perhaps some of the paintings and sculptures, but to her everything was priceless. It was also just the sort of stuff on which a burglar, irritated at finding nothing he could fence, might take out his frustrations.

Banks stopped at the newsagent's and bought the *Guardian*, which he thought had the best Saturday review section, then headed to the Italian café for his espresso and a chocolate croissant. Not the healthiest of breakfasts, perhaps, but delicious. And it wasn't as if he had a weight problem. Cholesterol was another matter. His doctor had already put him on a low dose of statin, and he had decided that that took care of the problem and allowed him to eat pretty much what he wanted. After all, he only had to be careful what he ate if he *wasn't* taking the pills, surely?

He had no sooner got his espresso and croissant and sat down to read the film and CD reviews at one of the window tables when his mobile buzzed. He pressed the answer button and put the phone to his ear. "Banks."

"Alan. Sorry to bother you on your weekend off," said Annie, "but we've got a bit of a crisis brewing up here. The super says we could use your help."

"Why? What is it?"

He listened as Annie told him what she knew.

"It sounds like a murder-suicide to me," said Banks. "For Christ's sake, Annie, can't you and Winsome handle it? Sophia's organizing a dinner party tonight."

He could hear Annie's intake of breath and the pregnant pause that followed. He knew she didn't like Sophia and put it down to jealousy. A woman scorned, and all that. Not that he had ever really scorned her, though he had sent her packing a while ago when she had come to his cottage drunk and amorous. If anything, *she* had scorned *him*. Most people were pleased for him – his son Brian and girlfriend Emilia, his daughter Tracy, Winsome Jackman, ex–Detective Superintendent Gristhorpe, his closest friend. But not Annie.

"It's not my idea," she said finally. "I don't even know why you'd think it would be. The last thing I'd want to do is spoil Sophia's dinner party by stealing you away. But it's orders from above. You know we're short-staffed. Besides, it could turn into something big and nasty. There's money involved – Castleview Heights – and the gay community. Yes, I agree, it *looks* like a murder-suicide so far, but we haven't got the forensics back yet and we don't know a great deal about the victims, either."

"And you know you won't get forensics until the middle of next week. Maybe you should have waited until then before calling me."

"Oh, bollocks, Alan," said Annie. "I don't need this. I'm only the messenger. Just get up here and do your job. And if you've got a problem with that, talk to the super."

And she left Banks listening to the silence, chocolate croissant halfway to his mouth.

Annie stood behind the crime scene tape that zigzagged across the door of the drawing room and watched Peter Darby, their photographer, go to work for the second time in two days. She was still inwardly fuming at Banks, but on the outside she was all business. She had been shaken by what she had seen and had overreacted, simple as that, but Banks could really get up her nose without trying very hard these days. Who the hell did he think he was, telling her what to do and what not to do?

Stefan Nowak was running the show for the moment. He stood beside Annie with a clipboard in his hand, checking off actions, his SOCO team kitted up and ready to go as and when required. A couple of them were working the landing, where there were bloodstains on the carpet and smears on the wall, as if the killer had brushed against it as he ran off.

The room wasn't very large, and the fewer people who were in it at one time, the better, Nowak had said, so he was restricting admission and working according to a strict hierarchy of access. Everyone going in, of course, had to wear full protective clothing, and their names were entered in the log. Even Annie and Doug Wilson were properly kitted out. Dr. Burns, the police surgeon, the on-scene forensic medical examiner, had already pronounced death and now he went back to work to glean what information he could from the body.

The whole house and gardens had been cordoned off as a crime scene, but this room was the centre of it all, and it was even more scrupulously protected. Nobody but those given the OK by Nowak would get past the door, and they'd do it in the order he decided. Luckily, Annie and Wilson had discovered the body, and neither had entered the room, so for once Nowak was pleased to find that he had as close to a pristine crime scene as he could hope for.

Annie went over to Wilson, who was still sitting on the stairs in his white oversuit, recovering, and put her arm over his shoulder. "All right, Dougie?"

Wilson nodded, glasses dangling from his hand. "Sorry, guv, you must think I'm a right girl's blouse."

"Not at all," said Annie. "Can I get you some water or something?"

Wilson pulled himself unsteadily to his feet. "I'll get it myself, if that's OK," he said. "Back in the saddle and all that." And he wobbled off downstairs. There were SOCOs working down there, too, Annie knew, and they would make sure Wilson didn't touch anything he shouldn't.

When Annie went back to the drawing-room door, Dr. Burns was just finishing his external examination. As soon as he came out, Nowak sent in the trace experts to take blood, hair and whatever other samples they could find, along with a blood-spatter analyst. To the untrained eye, the place was a shambles, but an expert like Ralph Tonks could read it like a map of who had been where, done what to whom, and with what.

Annie went in with them. She needed a closer look at the body. She didn't blame Wilson for being sick. She had seen quite a few crime scenes in her time, but this one had shaken her, too: the sheer frenzied violence of it, the blood and brains splattered everywhere, the sense of pointless overkill. Lacquered antique tables had been knocked over and broken, vases smashed, mirrors and crystal-ware shattered, along with a bottle of single malt whisky and a decanter of port, the floor strewn with bright flowers, dark stains and shards of glass. Amidst it all, now that she was closer, Annie could make out a framed photograph on the floor, its glass spider-webbed with cracks, showing Mark Hardcastle with his arm around the shoulder of the dead man. Both were smiling into the camera.

She could also see that one of Silbert's eyeballs was hanging from its socket and his front teeth ran in a jagged line, the lips torn and shrunken back. He was recognisable, but barely, and Annie wouldn't want to be the one responsible for asking a family member to identify him. DNA would be the best route to go for that.

When she peered more closely again at the framed picture on the wall that she had taken for a Jackson Pollock, she saw that it was a woodland scene sprayed with blood. In fact, it wasn't a painting at all, but a blown-up photograph, digital probably, and if Annie wasn't mistaken, it was taken in Hindswell Woods, and it showed, on the far left, the very oak tree on which Mark Hardcastle had hanged himself. She felt a shiver run up her spine.

She ducked under the tape and went back out to join Dr. Burns on the landing. He was busy making notes in a black-bound book, and she waited in silence until he had finished.

"Jesus Christ," Burns whispered, putting the notebook away and looking at her. "I've rarely seen such a vicious attack."

"Anything you can tell me?" Annie asked.

Burns was almost as pale as Wilson. "According to body temperature and the progress of rigor," he said, "I'd estimate that he's been dead about twenty to twenty-four hours."

Annie made a quick back-calculation. "Between nine a.m. and one p.m. yesterday, then?"

"Approximately."

"Cause of death?"

Dr. Burns glanced back at the body. "You can see that for yourself. Blows to the head with a blunt object. I can't say yet which blow actually killed him. It could have been the one across his throat. It certainly broke his larynx and crushed his windpipe. Dr. Glendenning should be able to tell you more at the post-mortem. It may even be the one to the *back* of his head, in which case he could have been walking away from his killer, taken by surprise. He could then have turned over when he fell, trying to struggle to his feet, so the other blows landed on the *front* of his skull and throat."

"When he was already down?"

"Yes."

"Jesus. Go on."

"There are defensive wounds on the backs of his hands, and some of the knuckles have been shattered, as if he held them over his face to protect himself."

"Is the arrangement of the body natural?"

"Seems that way to me," said Burns. "You're thinking of the cross shape, did someone arrange it that way?"

"Yes."

"I doubt it. I think when he gave up the ghost he just let his arms fall naturally the way they did. A posed body would appear far more symmetrical. This doesn't. See how crooked the right arm is? It's broken, by the way."

"Weapon?"

Burns jerked his head back towards the room. "The SOCOs have it. A cricket bat." He gave a harsh laugh. "And from what I could tell, a cricket bat signed by the entire England team that won back the Ashes in 2005. Read what you will into that."

Annie didn't want to read anything into it yet. Perhaps the cricket bat had just been lying around, the handiest weapon available? Or perhaps the killer had brought it with him? An angry Australian fan? Premeditated. That would be determined later. "What about the other wounds . . . you know . . ." Annie said. "Between his legs?"

"On a cursory examination I'd say they were also done with the cricket bat, and that the blood you see there was transferred from the head wounds."

"So that happened *after* he was dead?"

"Well, he may have still been clinging on to some vestiges of life, but it was done *after* the head wounds, I'd say, yes. Probably a lot of internal damage. Again, the post-mortem will tell you much more."

"Sex crime?"

"That's for you to decide. I'd certainly say that the evidence points that way. Otherwise why attack the genitals after the head?"

"A hate crime, perhaps? Anti-gay?"

"Again, it's possible," said Burns. "Or it could simply be a jealous lover. Such things aren't unknown, and the element of overkill points in that direction, too. Whatever it is, you're certainly dealing with some high-octane emotions here. I've never seen such rage."

You can say that again, thought Annie. "Was there any sexual interference?"

"As far as I can tell, there was no anal or oral penetration, and there are no obvious signs of semen on or around the body. As you can see, though, it's rather a mess in there, very hard to be certain of such things, so again I'd suggest you wait for the full SOCO report and Dr. Glendenning's post-mortem before forming any conclusions."

"Thank you, Doctor," said Annie. "I will."

And with that, Dr. Burns marched off down the stairs.

Annie was just about to follow him when Stefan Nowak came over, a small leather-bound book in his gloved hand. "Thought you might find this useful," he said. "It was on the desk."

Annie took the book from him and looked inside. It was an address book. There didn't seem to be many entries, but there were two that interested her in particular: Mark Hardcastle at Branwell Court, and one written simply as "Mother," with a phone number and address in Longborough, Gloucestershire. "Thanks, Stefan," said Annie. "I'll inform the locals and make sure someone goes out there to break the news." Annie also remembered Maria Wolsey saying something about Silbert's mother being wealthy, which was something to follow up on, in addition to his bank accounts. Money was always a good motive for murder.

Annie bagged the book and watched the SOCOs at work for a few minutes, then she went in the same direction Dr. Burns and Doug Wilson had gone. She needed some fresh air, and they wouldn't be finished up here for a while. In the back garden, she found Wilson sipping water and talking to Detective Superintendent Gervaise, who had just arrived. To Annie's surprise, Chief Constable Reginald Murray was also there.

"Ma'am, sir," said Annie.

"DI Cabbot," said Gervaise. "The Chief Constable is here because he was a friend of the victim's."

"I wouldn't exactly say friend," said Murray, fingering his collar. "But I knew Laurence from the golf club. We played a few holes now and then, met at some club functions. A murder on the Heights. This is a terrible business, DI Cabbot, terrible. It needs to be settled as soon as possible. I assume DCI Banks has been informed?"

"He's on his way, sir," said Annie.

"Good," said Murray. "Good. I know ACC McLaughlin thinks highly of him. The quicker we get to the bottom of this, the better." He glanced at Gervaise. "You will tell Banks . . . I mean . . . ?"

"I'll keep him on a short leash, sir," said Gervaise.

Annie smiled to herself. Everyone knew that Banks wasn't at his best around the rich and privileged. "Would you like to examine the crime scene, sir, seeing as you're here?" she asked.

Murray turned pale. "I don't think so, DI Cabbot. I have every confidence in the officers under my command."

"Of course, sir, as you wish."

Not known for his iron stomach, Murray wandered off, hands behind his back, to all intents and purposes as if he were examining the rose bushes.

Gervaise gave Annie a stern look. "That was hardly necessary," she said. "Anyway, how goes it so far? Any immediate thoughts?"

Annie handed Doug Wilson Silbert's address book and asked him to go back to the station and get in touch with the Gloucestershire police. He seemed relieved to be leaving the Heights. Then she turned to Gervaise. "Not much yet, ma'am." She summarized what Dr. Burns had told her. "The timing certainly fits a murder-suicide theory," she added.

"You think Mark Hardcastle did this?"

"Possibly, yes," said Annie. "As far as we know, he drove back to Eastvale from London on Thursday. He had a flat near the centre of town, but it looks as if he only lived there part time. Maria Wolsey at the theatre said he and Laurence Silbert were practically living together. Anyway, he could either have gone back to Branwell Court and come up here Friday morning, or he could have come straight here and stopped over Thursday night.

"All we know is that Silbert was killed between nine a.m. and one p.m. on Friday, and Hardcastle hanged himself between one p.m. and three p.m. that same afternoon. Also, the amount of blood on Hardcastle's body was inconsistent with the few scratches he might have got while climbing the tree to hang himself. Grainger, the man who sold him the rope, also said he had blood on him when he called in at the shop, and that he was oddly subdued and smelled of alcohol."

"So it may be cut and dried, after all," said Gervaise, almost to herself. She stood up. "Well, let's hope we didn't drag DCI Banks back from
his weekend off for nothing."

"Yes, ma'am," said Annie, through gritted teeth. "Let's hope not."

Getting out of London was bad enough, but the M1 was an even worse
nightmare. There were roadworks near Newport Pagnell, where the
motorway was reduced to one lane for two miles, though there wasn't a
workman in sight. Later, two lanes were closed because of an accident
just north of Leicester. The Porsche ticked along nicely, when it wasn't at
a complete standstill, and Banks was glad he'd decided to keep it. It was
shabby enough now for him to feel comfortable in it. The sound system
was great, too, and Nick Lowe's "Long Limbed Girl" sounded just fine.

Banks was still annoyed at Detective Superintendent Gervaise for
giving the order to call him back. He knew it wasn't Annie's fault, no
matter how much she seemed to have relished the task. It was true, of
course; they *were* understaffed. They didn't even have a replacement for
Kevin Templeton yet, and he'd been gone since March. It was also true
that, if nothing else, the two deaths would generate a lot of paperwork
and media interest, a lot of questions to be asked and answered. Young
"Harry Potter" showed promise, but he was still too wet behind the ears
to be trusted with something like this, and if the crime involved
Eastvale's gay community, such as it was, Detective Sergeant Hatchley
could prove more of a liability than an asset. Nick Lowe finished and
Banks switched to Bowie's *Pin Ups*.

Though Banks had met Sophia during a difficult murder case, he
realized this was the first time he had been called away from her on
urgent business since they had been together. It was something that had
happened with monotonous regularity throughout his career and marriage, and something that his ex-wife Sandra had complained of more
than once, until she had decided to follow her own path and leave him.
Even the kids had complained when they were growing up that they
never saw their dad.

But things had been quiet recently. No murders since he had met
Sophia. Not even a spate of serious burglaries or sexual assaults, just the

usual day-to-day monotony, such as stolen traffic cones. For once, Eastvale had been behaving. Until now. And it *would* be this weekend.

He had been making excellent time for a while, and just past the Sheffield cooling towers, his mobile buzzed. He turned down "Sorrow" and answered. It was Sophia calling from Western House.

"What is it?" she asked. "What's wrong? I just came out of the studio. Sorry I'm late. I got a message from Tana to call you. Where are you?"

"Just north of Sheffield," said Banks.

"What?"

"Nothing's wrong. I'm fine. I've just been called in to work, that's all."

"That's all! But I don't understand. It's your weekend off, isn't it?"

"They're not sacrosanct, unfortunately. Not in this job."

"But the dinner party?"

"I know. And I'm sorry. I promise I'll make –"

"Oh, this is too much. It's too late to cancel at this point. And Gunther and Carla are only over from Milan for the weekend."

"Why should you cancel? Go ahead. Enjoy yourselves. I'm sure I'll get another chance to meet them. Offer my apologies."

"A fat lot of good they'll do. Oh, shit, Alan! I was really looking forward to this."

"Me, too," said Banks. "I'm sorry."

There was a short pause, then Sophia's voice came back on again. "What is it, anyway? What's so important?"

"Nobody's sure yet," said Banks, "but there are two people dead."

"Serious, then?"

"Could be."

"Damn and blast your job!"

"I know how you feel. There's nothing I can do about it, though. These things happen sometimes. I'm sure I warned you."

"Couldn't you have said no?"

"I tried."

"Not very hard, obviously. Who called you?"

"Annie."

There was another pause. "Surely there are other people who can deal with it? What about her? I mean, as brilliant as you are, you're not Yorkshire's only competent detective, are you? Isn't she any good?"

"Of course she is, but it doesn't work like that. We're supposed to be a team. And we're short-staffed. Annie's doing the best she can."

"You don't need to defend her to me."

"I'm just explaining the situation."

"How long will you be gone?"

"No idea. You can still come up next weekend as planned, though, right?"

"And risk spending it by myself? I don't know about that."

"You know plenty of people up here. There's Harriet, for a start. Won't your parents be up, too? Aren't we supposed to be having Sunday lunch with them? Besides, we've got a date for the theatre."

"A weekend with my parents and Aunt Harriet isn't quite what I had in mind. Nor is a visit to the theatre by myself."

"I'm sure I'll be around. Sophia, this isn't my fault. Do you think I wouldn't rather be with you right now than on my way to work?"

She paused again, then replied rather sulkily, "I suppose so."

"You'll go ahead with the dinner?"

"I don't have a lot of choice, do I? But I'll miss you. It won't be the same."

"I'll miss you, too. Call me later?"

"If I've got time. I'd better get moving. I've got a lot to do, especially now I have to do it all by myself."

"Soph –"

But she had already ended the call. Banks cursed. No matter what she had said, she *did* blame him. A terrible sense of familiarity swept over him, all the rows with his ex-wife Sandra before she gave up on him. He knew he had warned Sophia that things like this might happen, that his job might disrupt other plans, but how seriously do people take warnings like that when everything is going blissfully well? Perhaps it was for the best that Sophia had found out about the demands of his job sooner rather than later.

He turned Bowie up again. He was singing "Where Have All the Good Times Gone?" Banks hoped it wasn't prophetic.

3

There were tea and custard creams in the boardroom of Western Area Headquarters just after five o'clock that Saturday afternoon, and the biscuits only served to remind Banks that he had missed lunch, a meal he should by all rights have enjoyed with Sophia at the Yorkshire Grey in London. Well, he supposed, tea and biscuits were better than nothing.

Four of them sat around the end of the long oval table nearest the whiteboard, pens and pads in front of them: Banks, Annie, Stefan Nowak and Superintendent Gervaise. The others had already brought Banks up to speed on the major events that had occurred in Hindswell Woods and on Castleview Heights. Annie and her team had been busy all day, while Banks had been on the road, and the whiteboard was scrawled with names, circles and connecting lines.

"It seems to me," said Banks, "that the first thing we need to do now is get the forensic results on the blood."

"What would that prove?" asked Annie.

"If the blood on Mark Hardcastle's body is Laurence Silbert's, and no one else's, then it would go a long way towards proving the murder-suicide theory."

"A long way, but not the whole way," Annie argued. "If Hardcastle found Silbert dead, his natural instinct would be to touch him, hold him, try to revive him, something like that. Maybe that's how he got Silbert's blood on him. But someone else could still have killed Silbert first.

Then we'd have a murder *and* a suicide, but we'd also have a murderer still loose."

"A good point, DI Cabbot," said Gervaise. "DCI Banks?"

"I still think forensics should be able to tell us a great deal more about what happened. Stefan?"

"True," said Nowak. "And we're working on it. We'll try to get the blood work done as soon as possible, but you know what the labs are like on weekends."

"What about fingerprints?" Banks asked.

"The only fingerprints Vic Manson's lifted from the cricket bat so far are Mark Hardcastle's. And the bat belonged in the room, by the way. There was a special stand for it by the sideboard, brass plaque and all. We also have unidentified prints from the drawing room and other parts of the house, of course, but they could take forever to eliminate. We'll be running them all through NAFIS." Nowak paused. "I hesitate to express an unsupported opinion here," he went on, "but this crime scene doesn't look like a murder committed by an interrupted burglar. In fact, it doesn't appear that the house was burgled at all. There's a great deal of valuable stuff there, original paintings and antiques in particular, even some rather expensive bottles of wine, Château Yquem and the like, but none of it seems to have been removed. Of course, without a list of everything, we can't be completely sure, but . . . Anyway, the attack on that body was emotional and deeply personal, and the only room that seems to have been damaged or disturbed in any way was the drawing room, and that's entirely consistent with a frenzied attack occurring there, which is what we have."

"Any signs of forced entry?" Banks asked Annie.

"No," she said. "Only by us. Doug and I had to break a window in the back door to get in."

"What about the neighbours? Anybody see or hear anything?"

"Uniform branch has talked to most of the people on the Heights this afternoon," Annie said, "and so far nobody admits to seeing or hearing anything. But that's hardly surprising," she went on. "The houses are detached, many are walled, and the people are insular, cautious. It's hardly the kind of community where people live in one another's pockets. Money buys you all the solitude you want."

"Yes, but they like to be vigilant, don't they?" Banks said. "Neighbourhood watch and all that."

"Not in this case," said Annie. "Though we can be pretty certain that someone would have noticed if anyone had wandered over from the East Side Estate."

"So if it *was* murder," Banks theorized, "it could well have been someone who looked as if he fitted into the community."

"I suppose so," Annie said.

"I don't suppose anyone saw a bloody figure in an orange T-shirt getting in a dark green Toyota and driving away from 15 Castleview Heights on Friday morning?" asked Superintendent Gervaise.

"No," said Annie. "Nobody saw anything. They don't want to get involved."

"Do you think someone's lying?"

"It's possible," Annie said. "We'll be talking to them all again, and there are still a couple we have yet to track down, people who've gone away for the weekend. I wouldn't hold out much hope, though. Perhaps the one bright spot is that some of the houses have surveillance cameras, so if we can get hold of the tapes. . . . Anyway, one or two reporters were sniffing around this afternoon, too, so word is spreading fast. We've tried to delay them by telling them we can't release the victim's name until next of kin has been informed – which should have been done by now – but they'll be able to work out whose house it is easily enough. We've left a couple of PCs guarding the gate and another inside."

"Good," said Gervaise. "I'll handle the press. Do we know anything about the mother?"

"Not yet," said Annie. "Not even her name. But it's something we'll be following up on. The Gloucestershire police said they'd inform her as soon as Harry Potter phoned them around lunchtime."

"Have we found anyone who actually *knew* Silbert and Hardcastle yet?"

"We're still working on that, too," Annie said, a trace of irritation in her voice. "Certainly no one we've talked to so far admits to having them over for drinks or dinner on a regular basis. The closest seem to be Maria Wolsey and Vernon Ross at the theatre, and neither of them knew Silbert well. Judging by the kitchen and dining area at Castleview Heights,

Silbert probably did a fair bit of entertaining. He was sophisticated, obviously well educated, a man of great discernment, and probably quite wealthy, though the suggestion is that his mother's the one with the money. On the other hand, Mark Hardcastle was the son of a Barnsley coal miner. Also, Hardcastle wasn't, as far as we've been able to gather, at all coy about his sexuality." Annie glanced at Gervaise. "Did Chief Constable Murray have anything to add about Laurence Silbert?" she asked. "Idle chatter at the nineteenth hole or something?"

Gervaise pursed her Cupid's-bow lips. "Not much. He said he found him a bit stand-offish. They weren't close; they simply played golf to make up a foursome from time to time and had a drink at the club. I think the CC would like to maintain a little distance on this matter. But he has other friends on the Heights, so he'll be watching over our shoulders. What do you think of all this, DCI Banks? You're the closest we've got to fresh eyes."

Banks tapped the end of his yellow pencil on the table.

"I think we just keep on asking questions while we're waiting on forensics," he said. "Try to build up a picture of Hardcastle and Silbert's life. And we work on a detailed plan of everything they did during the last two or three days."

"We've talked to Hardcastle's downstairs neighbour at Branwell Court," Annie added, "and she confirms that Hardcastle's only there from time to time. And one of Silbert's neighbours says she's noticed that a green Toyota has become something of a fixture at Silbert's house lately, too, which seems to confirm the living together bit. She didn't sound too pleased about it. The car, that is."

"Well, she wouldn't, would she?" said Banks. "Lowers the tone of the neighbourhood."

"There speaks a true Porsche owner," said Annie.

Banks smiled. "So, you think they were definitely living together?" he said.

"Yes," said Annie. "More or less. I saw a lot of Hardcastle's personal stuff when I had a quick look around the house," she went on. "Clothes, suits hanging in the same wardrobe as Silbert's, books, a laptop computer, sketchpads, notebooks. He used one of the other upstairs rooms as a sort of office."

"Why hang on to the flat, then?" Banks asked. "Hardcastle can't have been making that much money at the theatre. Why waste it on a flat he only used occasionally? And you said he still got his post there, too. Why not put in a change of address?"

"Any number of reasons," said Annie. "Insecurity. A bolt-hole. A little private space when he needed it. As for the post, as far as I could see he didn't get anything but bills and circulars, anyway. We need to do a more thorough search of both places, though, and I suggest we start with Castleview."

"You and DCI Banks can have a good poke around the house tomorrow," Gervaise said. "With DI Nowak's permission, of course."

"All right with me. I'll probably still have a couple of men working there, but if you don't get in each other's way . . ."

"See what you can dig up," Gervaise went on. "Personal papers, bank books, stuff like that. As you say, we don't even know what Silbert did for a living yet, do we, or where he got his money. What about Hardcastle? Did he have any family?"

"A distant aunt in Australia," Annie said. "A ten-pound pommie."

"Phone records?"

"We're working on it," Annie said. "Mark Hardcastle didn't have a mobile, hated them apparently, but we found one in Silbert's jacket pocket, along with his wallet. Nothing out of the ordinary on it so far. In fact, nothing very much on it at all."

"No call log, address book or stored text messages?" Banks asked.

"None."

"But he had an address book?"

"Yes. Not much in it, though."

"That's a bit odd in itself, isn't it?" said Gervaise. "I understand you talked to the cleaning lady?"

"Yes," said Annie. "Mrs. Blackwell. Highly regarded in the Heights, so we're told. She wasn't much help. Said Mr. Hardcastle was around more often than not these days, when Mr. Silbert as at home, at least. Apparently he travelled a lot. They were a nice couple, always paid her on time, sometimes with a nice little bonus, blah, blah, blah. Mostly they went out while she did her work, so they didn't hang about and chat. If she knew any deep, dark secrets, she wasn't telling. We can talk to her again if we need to."

"What brought the two of them together, I wonder," Banks said. "How did they meet? What on earth did they have in common?"

Annie shot him a cool glance. "You know what they say. Love is blind."

Banks ignored her. "Was it the theatre? Silbert didn't appear to have any real involvement in that world, but you never know. Or could it have simply been money? How rich was Silbert exactly?"

"We haven't had time to find and examine his bank accounts and holdings yet," said Annie. "Partly because it's the weekend. Maybe we'll find something on Monday, and maybe his mother will be able to tell us something when she's got over the shock of her loss. But, like I said, he must have had a bob or two to live where he did and buy some of those paintings. The car's no old jalopy, either. Which reminds me." Annie took a slip of paper sheathed in a plastic folder from her file. "We found this in the glovebox of the Jag just a short while ago. It's a parking receipt from Durham Tees Valley Airport timed nine twenty-five a.m. Friday. The car had been parked there for three days."

"So wherever he went, he went on Tuesday?" said Banks.

"So it seems."

"Have you checked the flight arrival times?"

"Not yet," said Annie. "Haven't had a chance. But from some of the restaurant receipts we found in his wallet, it looks as if he was in Amsterdam."

"Interesting," said Banks. "It should be easy enough to check on the flight passenger lists. We'll get Doug on it. So what did Silbert walk into when he got home on Friday morning? I wonder. How far are we from the airport, about forty-five minutes, an hour?"

"Forty-five minutes, depending on the traffic on the A1," said Annie. "And as far as I know, they don't service a lot of destinations directly through Durham Tees Valley. It's a pretty small airport."

"I remember," said Banks. "We flew from there to Dublin once not long ago. I also think BMI flies to Heathrow. Anyway, that would fix his arrival at Castleview Heights at around quarter past to half past ten."

"And by one o'clock he was dead," added Superintendent Gervaise.

They all sat in silence for a moment to let that sink in, then Banks said, "And Mark Hardcastle was definitely in London on Wednesday and Thursday?"

"Yes," said Annie. "He was there with Derek Wyman, the director of *Othello*. Hardcastle had a restaurant receipt in his wallet from Wednesday evening, and one for petrol dated Thursday afternoon, two twenty-six p.m. Northbound services, Watford Gap."

"On his way home, then," said Banks. "If he was at Watford Gap at two twenty-six p.m. and drove straight home, he'd be here by about half past five, maybe a bit earlier. What's the restaurant?"

"One of the Zizzi's chain, on Charlotte Street. Pizza trentino and a glass of Montepulciano d'Abruzzo. A large one, going by the price."

"Hmm," said Banks. "That would indicate that Hardcastle probably ate alone. Or he and Wyman went Dutch, or shared the pizza. Any idea where Hardcastle stayed on Wednesday night?"

"No," said Annie. "We're hoping Derek Wyman might be able to tell us. He's not back yet. I was planning on interviewing him first thing tomorrow morning."

"Any idea what Hardcastle did on Thursday evening after he got back to Eastvale?" Banks asked.

"Who knows?" Annie said. "He must have stopped in, most likely at Castleview. The downstairs neighbour at Branwell Court says she hasn't seen him since last week, and most of the letters are postmarked around that time or later. We haven't been able to find anybody who saw him go out. He wasn't at the theatre. All we know is that the next day, around lunchtime, he went into Grainger's shop, smelling of alcohol, bought a length of clothesline and went and hanged himself in Hindswell Woods. So between late Thursday afternoon and Friday morning, he'd had a few drinks, or a lot of drinks, and he possibly killed Laurence Silbert."

"Anything else of interest in Silbert's wallet?" Banks asked.

"Credit cards, a little cash, a business card, sales receipts, driving licence. He was born in 1946, by the way, which makes him sixty-two. Nothing yet to give a hint of his profession or sources of income."

"Business card? Whose? His own?"

"No." Annie slid the plastic folder over to him.

"Julian Fenner, Import-Export," Banks read. "That covers a multitude of sins. It's a London phone number. No address. Mind if I hang on to it?"

"OK by me," said Annie. "Maybe it's another lover?"

"More speculation," said Gervaise. "What we need is solid information." She rested both her palms on the table as if to push herself up to leave, but she remained seated. "Right," she said. "We'll keep at it. We still have a lot of questions to answer before we can close the book on this one. Is there much else on in Major Crimes at the moment?"

"Not much," said Annie. "Couple of gang-related incidents on the East Side Estate, a spate of shoplifting in the Swainsdale Centre – looks organized – and a break-in at the Castle gift shop. And the traffic cones, of course. They're still disappearing. DS Hatchley and CID are dealing with most of it."

"Good," said Gervaise. "Then we'll let DS Hatchley worry about the traffic cones and the shoplifting. Stefan, how long do you think it will take the lab to get the basic blood work done?"

"We can get the samples typed by tomorrow," said Nowak. "That's easy enough. DNA and toxicology will take longer, of course, depending whether we put a rush on it or not, and that costs money. I'd say by midweek, at best."

"Any idea when Dr. Glendenning might get around to the post-mortems?"

"I've spoken to him," said Annie. "He wasn't out playing golf like everyone thought. He was actually in his office at Eastvale General Infirmary catching up on paperwork. I think he's bored. He's willing to get started whenever he gets the go-ahead."

"Wonderful," said Gervaise. "He's got his wish."

"It'll have to be Monday, though," Annie said. "The rest of his staff's away for the weekend."

"I don't suppose we're in a rush," said Gervaise. "And it is the Sabbath tomorrow. First thing Monday morning will do fine."

"Just one point," said Banks. "Do you think it might make sense if Dr. Glendenning autopsies Laurence Silbert first, rather than Mark Hardcastle? I mean, everyone is pretty sure that Hardcastle hanged himself. There's no evidence of anyone else having been with him, is there, Stefan?"

"None at all," said Nowak. "And everything about that scene, including the knot and the rope marks, is consistent with suicide by hanging. Textbook case. As I've said before, it's difficult to hang someone against his will. The only questions we still have are toxicological."

"You mean, was he drugged?"

"It's a possibility. The shopkeeper said he was calm and subdued, though that's not terribly strange in someone who has made the decision to take his own life, and we do know that he had been drinking. He might have taken pills. Anyway, we'll be testing the blood samples carefully."

"OK," Banks said. "Are we working on the assumption that if Hardcastle *didn't* kill Silbert himself, then someone else did, and that Hardcastle found the body and hanged himself from grief?"

"Makes sense to me," said Gervaise. "*If* he didn't do it himself. Any objections?"

No one had any.

"In the meantime, then," Gervaise went on, "as DCI Banks suggested, we ask more questions. We try to plot out their movements, the hours leading up to their deaths. We dig into their backgrounds, family history, friends, enemies, ambitions, work, finances, previous relationships, travels, the lot. OK?"

They all nodded. Superintendent Gervaise gathered up her papers and walked over to the door. Just before she left, she half turned and said, "I'll try to keep the media at bay for as long as I can, now they've got wind of it. Remember, this is the Heights. Tread carefully. Keep me informed at every stage."

After the meeting, Banks sat in his office listening to Natalie Clein playing the Elgar cello concerto and studied his copies of the materials gathered from Silbert's wallet and Hardcastle's car. It didn't add up to a hell of a lot. He glanced at his watch. Just after 6:15. He wanted to talk to Sophia, see whether she had forgiven him, but now would be the worst possible time. The guests were due to arrive at half past seven, and she would be right in the midst of her dinner preparations.

Idly, he dialled the number of Julian Fenner, Import-Export, from the card found in Laurence Silbert's wallet. After only a few rings and several distant clicks and echoes, an automated voice came on the line to tell him that the number had been discontinued and was no longer in service. He tried again, slowly, in case he had misdialled. Same result. After a few attempts to find a matching address through reverse directories, he gave up. It appeared that the number did not exist. He called the squad room and asked Annie to drop by his office.

While he waited, he walked to the open window and gazed out over the market square. At that time of evening it was still fairly quiet. The shadows were lengthening, but Banks knew it would stay light until after ten o'clock. The market had packed up and moved on hours ago, leaving a slight whiff of rotting vegetables about the cobbled square. Most of the shops were closed, except Somerfield and WH Smith, and the only people around were those who wanted an early meal or a drink.

When Annie came, Banks sat opposite her and moved his computer monitor out of the way so he could see her properly. She was casually dressed in a russet T-shirt and short blue denim skirt, no tights. Her tousled chestnut hair hung over her shoulders, her complexion was smooth and free of all but the lightest of make-up, her almond eyes were clear, and her demeanour seemed calm and controlled. Banks hadn't had a really good talk with her since he'd taken up with Sophia. He knew she had had one or two problems to deal with from their last case together, and he hadn't exactly been a rock, but she looked as if she had managed it well. A couple of weeks down in Cornwall at her father's place had obviously done her a lot of good.

Banks turned the business card to face her. "Did you try this number?" he asked.

"No time," Annie said. "I'd no sooner got back from the Heights than Superintendent Gervaise called the meeting. Then you took it."

"It wasn't meant to be a criticism, Annie. I was just wondering."

Annie raised an eyebrow but said nothing.

Banks shifted in his chair. "It's been disconnected," he said.

"Sorry?"

"The number. Julian Fenner, Import-Export. There's no such number. And no address. I've checked. Discontinued. No longer in service."

"Since when?"

"No idea. We can put technical support on it, if you like."

"Probably a good idea. Maybe it's just really old?" Annie suggested.

"Then why would Silbert continue to carry the card? It was the only one he had."

"Don't tell me you empty your wallet out every day? Every week? Every month?"

"About as often as you empty your handbag, probably."

"Then that's hardly ever. God knows what I'd find in the bottom of *that* if I had time to rummage through it."

"Maybe you're right," Banks said. "Its just another little oddity, that's all, like the two of them being away at the same time but in different places. Hardcastle was in London with Wyman and Silbert was –"

"In Amsterdam," said Annie. "Doug looked into it. Silbert stayed at the Hotel Ambassade on Herengracht for three nights – Tuesday, Wednesday and Thursday. He checked out early Friday morning and came back on the flight from Schiphol that got in at ten past nine. And it was on time that day. He left on Tuesday at nine fifty-five a.m."

"Herengracht? Is that near the red light district?"

"No idea," said Annie. "Want me to check?"

"Later. Why would they go to different places? Why not go away together?"

"They had different business to conduct, I should imagine. They obviously didn't live in each other's pockets. Hardcastle even kept his own flat."

"I suppose so," said Banks, rubbing his temples. "Sorry, I just don't seem to be quite on the ball yet as far as this case goes."

"Mind elsewhere?"

Banks glanced sharply at her.

Annie paused. "Look, Alan, I'm sorry you got dragged back from London," she said. "But we used to work well together, remember? We were a team."

"We still are."

"Are we?"

"What's that supposed to mean?"

"I don't know. You tell me. Lately things have been a bit weird, that's all. I could have used you . . . you know, a shoulder, a friend . . . after the Karen Drew case and all. But you weren't there."

"Is that what you're holding against Sophia?"

"I'm not holding anything against Sophia. We're not talking about her."

"Don't deny that you don't like her."

Annie leaned forward. "Alan, honestly, I've nothing against her. I don't care one way or the other. It's you I'm concerned about. My friend. Maybe you're . . . I don't know . . . a bit oversensitive, a bit over-defensive? She doesn't need it, believe me. She's a survivor."

"What does that mean? What's wrong with that?"

"Nothing. There you go again."

"You said Sophia's a survivor. It's just an odd thing to say. I wondered what you meant by it."

"All I'm saying is don't get too caught up in it all. Keep some perspective."

"Are you saying I've lost my perspective? Because –"

The phone rang.

Banks and Annie glared at one another, then Banks answered it. He listened for a moment, said, "Keep her there," then hung up and turned to Annie. "PC Walters at Castleview Heights. Apparently a woman has just turned up there claiming to be Laurence Silbert's mother. Want to come along?"

"Of course," said Annie. She stood up. "I'll follow you in my car. To be continued?"

"What?"

"Our discussion."

"If you think it's worth it." Banks picked his car keys up from his desk and they left.

Laurence Silbert's mother was sitting in the driver's seat of a racing-green MG sports car outside number 15 Castleview Heights smoking a cigarette and chatting with PC Walters when Banks and Annie arrived not more than three or four minutes later. The soft evening light, after a brief shower, had turned the limestone grey-gold and softened the slate and flagstone rooftops. A few dirty grey clouds lingered in the blue sky, one of them occasionally blocking out the sun for a minute or two.

There were still plenty of media people around the area, held back by a police cordon, but Banks and Annie ignored the calls for comments and turned towards the MG.

The woman who got out had once been at least as tall as Banks, but age had given her a slight stoop. Even so, she was a commanding presence, and the grey hair drawn back tightly from her forehead, her high cheekbones over tanned, sunken cheeks, wrinkled mouth and twinkling blue-grey eyes spoke of a beauty not too long faded. In fact, she was still beautiful, and there was something vaguely familiar about her.

"Good evening," she said, offering her hand in turn. "I'm Edwina Silbert, Laurence's mother."

Banks stepped back. "*The* Edwina Silbert?"

"Well, I suppose I did attract a certain amount of notoriety at one time," she said, dropping her cigarette on the ground and stepping on it. She was wearing black high heels, Banks noticed. "But that was a very long time ago."

Annie looked puzzled.

"Mrs. Silbert started the Viva boutique chain in the sixties," Banks explained. "And it went on to become enormously successful."

"Still is," said Annie. "I shop there myself when I can afford it. Pleased to meet you."

"It used to be more affordable," said Edwina. "That was one of the novelties about it at the time. Everyone could dress like the beautiful people. We used to dream of equality for all."

"I'm very sorry for your loss," Banks said.

Edwina Silbert inclined her head. "Poor Laurence. I've been thinking about him all the way up here. It's still very difficult to take in. Can I see him?"

"I'm afraid not," said Banks.

"That bad?"

Banks said nothing.

"I'm not squeamish, you know. I saw plenty of things during the war that would turn your stomach. I was a Queen Alexandra nurse."

"Even so . . ."

"Surely I must have *some* rights? He *was* my son."

Technically, the body was both still a crime scene and the property of the coroner, so Edwina Silbert really *didn't* have any right to see it, at least not without the coroner's permission. That was usually a formality, and a relative was generally required to identify a body, but that was not the case here.

"Mrs. Silbert —"

"Edwina. Please."

"Edwina. I'll be frank with you. It would be very difficult for you to recognize your son. We think we have enough to go on to make a positive identification for the time being, and I think seeing him the way he is now would cause you far too much pain and grief. Best to remember him as he was."

She was silent for a moment or two, as if lost in the thought. "Very well," she said finally. "But there is something that might help you. Laurence has a very distinctive birthmark on his left arm, just above his elbow." She tapped the spot on her own elbow. "It's dark red in colour and shaped like a teardrop."

"Thank you," said Banks. "We'd also like to take a DNA swab. Later, when you're feeling up to it. It's just a simple mouth swab. There are no needles or anything involved."

"I've never been afraid of needles," she said. "And you're more than welcome to take your sample in any way you wish. Look, I don't know about your rules and regulations, but I've come a long way and I could do with a drink. I happen to know that there's a delightful little pub close by."

Annie glanced at Banks, who turned to PC Walters. "Phil," he said, pointing to the media phalanx. "Make sure none of those bastards follow us."

Walters swallowed and turned as pale as if he'd been asked to hold back the massed hordes of invading Huns. "I'll do my best, sir," he said.

The Black Swan, just down the street on the corner, was not one of the pubs that attracted the rowdies on a Saturday night. In fact, it attracted hardly anyone except people from the immediate neighbourhood, as it was so well hidden and the prices were too high for the yobs. Banks had never been there before, but he wasn't surprised it was so upmarket, with lots of horse brasses, framed Stubbs prints and polished brass rails around the bar. And they called the outside area the patio, not the beer garden. There was also no loud music or slot machines. The government might have banned smoking in pubs, Banks thought as he went inside, but here everyone seemed to have at least one dog. He felt his nose begin to itch. Why couldn't they ban dogs, too?

"Shall we sit outside?" Edwina Silbert suggested. "I could do with a cigarette."

"Fine," said Banks, happy for the chance to get away from the dogs. Smoke he could handle.

They found an empty bench and table on the patio. It offered a magnificent view over the town and the distant hills, dark green as the light weakened, and it was still warm enough to sit outside in a light jacket. Banks suggested they all sit down while he went back inside to pick up some drinks. Edwina wanted a gin and tonic and Annie a Diet Coke. Banks studied the pumps and chose a pint of Timothy Taylor's Landlord. The small round cost him an arm and a leg. He thought about getting a receipt for expenses, then thought better of it as he imagined Superintendent Gervaise's reaction.

He managed to secure a tray and carried the drinks back to the table. Edwina Silbert was already smoking, and she accepted the gin and tonic eagerly.

"You shouldn't have come all this way," Banks said. "We were going to drive down and see you soon, anyway."

"Don't be silly," she said. "I'm perfectly capable of driving a few miles. I set off shortly after the local bobby came round with the news this afternoon. What else was I supposed to do? Sit at home and twiddle my thumbs?"

If Silbert was sixty-two, Banks thought, then Edwina was probably in her eighties, and Longborough was two hundred miles away. She looked much younger, but then so had her son, by all accounts. Annie had told Banks that Maria Wolsey at the theatre guessed Silbert to be in his mid-fifties. Youthfulness must run in the family.

"Where are you staying?" he asked.

She seemed surprised at the question. "At Laurence's house, of course."

"I'm afraid that's not possible," said Banks. "It's a crime scene."

Edwina Silbert gave her head a slight shake. Banks could see tears glistening in her eyes. "Forgive me," she said. "I'm just not used to this. What's that nice hotel in town? I stayed there once when the house was being decorated."

"The Burgundy?"

"That's the one. Do you think I'll be able to get a room?"

"I'll check for you," said Annie, taking out her mobile. She walked over to the edge of the patio to make the call.

"She's a nice girl," said Edwina. "I'd hang on to her if I were you."

"She's not . . . I mean, we're not . . ." Banks began, then he just nodded. He didn't want to try to explain his relationship with Annie to a stranger. "Were you and Laurence close?" he asked.

"I'd say so," Edwina answered. "I mean, I would like to think we were friends as well as mother and son. His father died when he was only nine, you see, killed in a car crash, and Laurence is an only child. I never remarried. Of course, when he left university he travelled a lot and there were lengthy periods when I didn't see him at all."

"How long had you known Laurence was gay?"

"Ever since he was a boy, really. All the signs were there. Oh, I don't mean that he was effeminate in any way. Quite the opposite, really. Very manly. Good at sports. Fine physique. Like a young Greek god. It's just the little things, the telling details. Of course, he was always most discreet. Apart from the odd peccadillo at public school or Cambridge, I very much doubt that he was sexually active until his twenties, and by then it was perfectly legal, of course."

"It didn't bother you?"

She gave Banks a curious look. "What an odd thing to say."

"Some parents get upset by it." Banks thought of Mark Hardcastle's father.

"Perhaps," said Edwina. "But it always seemed to me that there's no point in trying to change a person's nature. A leopard's spots, and all that. No. It was what he was. Part of what he was. His cross to bear and his path to love. I hope he found it."

"If it means anything, I think he did. I think he was very happy these past few months."

"With Mark, yes. I like to think so, too. Poor Mark. He'll be devastated. Where is he? Do you know?"

"You knew Mark?"

"*Knew?* Oh my God, is there something you haven't told me, something I don't know?"

"I'm sorry," said Banks. "I thought you would have heard. Please forgive me." Why he had assumed that the Gloucestershire police would have told her about Mark Hardcastle, he didn't know. Unless Doug Wilson had asked them to, and he clearly hadn't.

"What happened?"

"I'm afraid Mark's dead, too. It seems he committed suicide."

Edwina seemed to shrink in her chair as if she had taken a body blow. She uttered a deep sigh. "But why?" she said. "Because of what happened to Laurence?"

"We think there's a connection, yes," said Banks.

Annie came back and gave Banks a nod. "We've got a nice room for you at the Burgundy, Mrs. Silbert," she said.

"Thank you, dear," said Edwina, reaching for a handkerchief in her handbag. She dabbed her eyes. "Excuse me, this is really very silly of me. It's just rather a lot to take in all at once. Mark, too?"

"I'm sorry," Banks said. "You liked him?"

She put her handkerchief away, took a sip of gin and tonic and reached for another cigarette. "Very much," she said. "And he was good for Laurence. I know their backgrounds were very different, but they had so much in common, nonetheless."

"The theatre?"

"I like to think Laurence got his love for the theatre from me. If it hadn't been for the rag trade, you know, I might have become an actress. God knows, he spent hours hanging about backstage with me at various theatres."

"So Laurence was interested in the theatre?"

"Very much so. That's where they met. He and Mark. Didn't you know?"

"I know very little," said Banks. "Please tell me."

"I visited Laurence just before Christmas, and he took me to the theatre here. It's very quaint."

"I know it," said Banks.

"They were doing a panto. *Cinderella*, I believe. During the intermission we got talking in the bar, as you do, and I could see that Laurence and Mark hit it off immediately. I made my excuses and disappeared to powder my nose, or some such thing, for a few minutes, you know, just to give them a little time to exchange telephone numbers, make a date or whatever they wanted to do, and that, as they say, was that."

"Did you see much of them after that?"

"Every time I visited. And they came to see me in Longborough, of course. It's so lovely in the Cotswolds. I do wish they could have enjoyed summer there." She took out her handkerchief again. "Silly me. Getting all sentimental." She sniffed, gave a little shudder and sat up as upright as she could. "I wouldn't mind another drink."

This time Annie went and came back with another round.

"How would you characterize their relationship?" Banks asked when Edwina had a fresh drink before her.

"I'd say they were in love and they wanted to make a go of it, but they moved cautiously. You have to remember that Laurence was sixty-two and Mark was forty-six. They'd both been through painful relationships and split-ups before. Strong as their feelings were for one another, they weren't going to jump into something without thinking."

"Mark hung on to his flat," Banks said, "yet it seemed they were practically living together at Castleview. Is that the kind of thing you mean?"

"Exactly. I imagine he would eventually have given it up and moved in with Laurence completely, but they were progressing slowly. Besides, Laurence has a pied-à-terre in Bloomsbury, so I should imagine Mark didn't want to feel left out in that department."

"Was he competitive?"

"He came from nowhere," Edwina said, "and he was ambitious. Yes, I'd say he was competitive, and perhaps material things meant more to him than they do to some people. Symbols of how far he'd come. But it didn't stop him from being a wonderful, generous person."

"You mentioned a pied-à-terre. Would Mark have stayed there, too, when he was in London?"

"I can't see why not."

"Would you give me the address?"

Edwina gave him an address near Russell Square. "It really is very tiny," she said. "I couldn't imagine the two of them staying there together. It would drive any couple crazy. But if you're alone, it's perfect."

"Did you ever sense any tension between them? Any problems? Did they argue? Fight?"

"Nothing that stands out," said Edwina. "No more than any other couple. Actually, they laughed a lot." She paused. "Why? You're not . . . ? Surely you can't . . . ?"

"We're not really suggesting anything yet, Mrs. Silbert," Annie said quickly. "We don't know what happened. That's what we're trying to find out."

"But that you can even believe there's a possibility of Mark's . . . of Mark's doing something like that."

"I'm afraid it *is* a possibility," said Banks. "But that's all it is at the moment. As Annie said, we don't know what happened. All we know is that your son was killed in his home, and that shortly afterwards Mark Hardcastle committed suicide in Hindswell Woods."

"Hindswell? Oh my God, no. Oh, Mark. That was their favourite spot. They took me to see the bluebells there once, back in April. They were absolutely gorgeous this year. Grief, Mr. Banks. That would be why he killed himself. Grief."

"That occurred to us, too," said Banks. "And your son?"

Edwina hesitated before answering, and Banks sensed that something had crossed her mind, something she wasn't sure that she wanted to share yet. "A burglar, perhaps?" she said. "Surely an area like this must attract them from time to time?"

"We're working on it. What we need, though, is a lot more background on your son and Mark. We know so little about them, about their pasts, their work, their life together. We're hoping you can help us with that."

"I'll tell you what I can," said Edwina. "And I'll submit to whatever tests you require. But can it wait until tomorrow? Please? I'm feeling suddenly very tired."

"I don't suppose there's any hurry," said Banks, disappointed but trying not to show it. She was an old woman, after all, and though she had managed to hide that fact for an hour or more, the mask was slipping. He wanted to get home, himself, anyway, so he was quite willing to postpone the rest of interview until the following day. They should have the blood typing back from Stefan by then, too, someone would have checked the birthmark, and Derek Wyman might be able to fill them in on some details of Mark's life.

Edwina got up to leave and Annie stood. "Can I drive you? Honest," she said, "it's no bother."

Edwina touched her shoulder. "It's all right, dear," she said. "I have to get the car there anyway. I might as well do it now. I know the way. I think I've got just about enough energy left."

And she walked away.

"Should she be driving?" Annie asked.

"Probably not," said Banks. "But I wouldn't recommend you try to stop her. She didn't get to run a multimillion-pound retail fashion empire by giving in easily. Sit down. Finish your Coke."

"I suppose you're right," said Annie. "She'll be OK. She barely even touched her second drink."

Annie shivered, and Banks offered her his jacket to put over her shoulders. He was surprised when she took it. Perhaps she was being polite. Still, he knew that he didn't feel the cold the way she did.

He could hear people laughing and talking inside the pub, and beyond the low wall, way below in the town centre, he could see tiny dots of people crossing the market square, just as Joseph Cotten and Orson Welles watched people from the giant Ferris wheel in *The Third Man*, one of his favourite films.

"So what do you think about that pied-à-terre?" Banks asked.

"I don't know," said Annie. "I suppose it was worth hanging on to if he could afford it, and if he used it often enough."

"We should probably check the place out. Hardcastle might have stayed there on Thursday night. He might have left some sort of clue behind as to his state of mind."

"I suppose we should."

"Do you think Edwina was right about why Hardcastle kept his flat?"

"Probably," Annie said. "Though I'd incline more towards the moving cautiously theory than the competitiveness. He's got one, so I have to have one, too. I'm not sure I buy that."

"Some people are like that."

Annie shrugged. "Anyway, it's not so unusual, is it? Sophia still has a cottage up here, doesn't she, as well as a house in London?"

"It's her family's," Banks said.

"Maybe Silbert's mother bought it for him?" Annie said. "We'll have to ask her about his finances tomorrow. She's certainly an interesting woman, though, isn't she? I gather she's another of your adolescent fantasies, along with Marianne Faithfull and Julie Christie?"

"That's right," said Banks. "She was quite beautiful in her day, if a little older than the rest. I remember reading about her at the time, seeing pictures of her in the papers. One of the perks of doing a newspaper round. I think she started Viva around 1965. It was on Portobello Road then. It was famous for its reasonable prices, but everyone who was anyone at the time used to shop there, too. Mick Jagger, Marianne Faithfull, Paul McCartney, Jane Asher, Julie Christie, Terry Stamp. She knew them all. All the beautiful people."

"I didn't know they were all so cheap," Annie said.

"It wasn't the prices. It was the cachet. She was right in the thick of things, party-going with all the big names, being seen at all the right clubs. She also had a brush with heroin addiction later on, and affairs with all the eligible stars. I didn't even know that she had a son. She obviously kept him well out of the limelight."

Annie yawned.

"I'm boring you."

"Long day."

"Then let's call it a night. We've got a busy one tomorrow."

"Good idea," Annie agreed, handing Banks back his jacket.

"Look, what you said earlier, about my not being there for you . . ."

"You were at first, very much so. I just . . . oh, Alan, I don't know. Take no notice of me."

"It's just that you seemed to withdraw. I didn't know how to reach you."

"I suppose I did," Annie said. She patted his arm and stood up. "Difficult times. All behind us now. Let's just move on and try to get to the bottom of this business as soon as we can."

"Agreed," said Banks, finishing off his beer and standing up. They walked to their cars, still parked outside Laurence Silbert's house, where a few diehard reporters lingered on, and said goodnight to PC Walters, then to each other. Banks watched Annie drive away in her old Astra, then started the Porsche and headed for Gratly. Cameras flashed in his rear-view mirror.

It felt like weeks since Banks had been home, but it had only been a couple of days. One night away, he realized. Only one night with Sophia. Even so, his isolated cottage greeted him with a silence that felt even more profound and oppressive than usual.

He turned on the orange-shaded lamps in the living room. There was only one message on the answerphone: his son Brian informing him that he was back in the London flat for a couple of weeks if Banks happened to be down there and fancied dropping by. Brian had recently moved into a very nice, if very small, flat in Tufnell Park with his actress girlfriend Emilia, and Banks often visited them when he was in London with Sophia. He had even taken Sophia there for dinner once, and she and Brian and Emilia had got along well – mostly because Sophia knew and liked many of the same bands as they did. For a while, Banks had felt a bit old and out of it, like a boring old sixties fart, even though he listened to a lot of new music himself. Still, as far as he was concerned, for great rock you couldn't beat Hendrix, Dylan, Floyd, Led Zep, The Stones and The Who.

A dark turquoise afterglow shot with orange and gold remained in the sky over Gratly Beck and the valley below. Banks gazed at it for a few moments, drinking in the beauty, then closed the curtains and went through to the kitchen for a glass of wine. He realized he was hungry, hadn't eaten since breakfast, unless he counted that custard cream at the meeting. The only thing remotely resembling a meal in his fridge was a carton of leftover goat vindaloo from the local takeaway, and the remains of a naan wrapped in foil. But curry wouldn't go with the red wine he was drinking. Besides, it had been in the fridge too long. Instead, he dug out some mature Cheddar, checked the bread for green spots and, finding none, made himself a toasted cheese sandwich, which he carried through along with his wine to the entertainment room.

He felt like listening to something mellow but sensuous, and, thinking about new music, he put on a Keren Ann CD. The distant, distorted guitars and eerie, hushed vocals of "It's All A Lie" that filled the room were perfect. Just what he wanted. He lounged back in the armchair and put his feet up, his mind ranging over what he knew of the Hardcastle–Silbert case so far.

It resembled a textbook murder-suicide, a crime of passion distinguished by extreme violence and overwhelming remorse. From what Banks could remember of the study he had read in Geberth's *Practical Homicide Investigation*, homosexual murders were often characterized by extreme violence directed towards the throat, chest and abdomen. In this case, the larynx had been shattered by a powerful blow. Geberth said the throat was a target because of its significance in homosexual love-making, and the violence so extreme because both parties are sexual aggressors. That sounded a bit politically incorrect to Banks, but he didn't really care. He hadn't invented the theory.

He wanted to know what Laurence Silbert had been doing in Amsterdam, a place as famous for its red light district and permissive attitudes to sex as for anything else. Perhaps Edwina would be able to help tomorrow? Her sadness over the loss of both Laurence and Mark seemed genuine to Banks, as did her absolute shock at the idea that Mark could have had anything to do with it.

Banks also wondered whether Mark Hardcastle's trip to London with Derek Wyman had played a part in the events that followed, however innocent it might have been. Was it so innocent? Had Laurence Silbert found out? Had he flown into a violent, jealous rage? Was that how the argument that led to both their deaths had started? Banks and Annie would talk to Derek Wyman in the morning and perhaps find some answers to those questions, too. It would be Sunday, but there would be no time off for Banks, not when he'd come all this way and given up his weekend with Sophia. A DCI didn't get paid overtime, nor did Annie, a DI, so the best he could hope for was a little time in lieu, then maybe he and Sophia could manage a long weekend in Rome or Lisbon. That might just make up for missing the dinner party.

It was half past eleven when the phone rang, and Keren Ann had long since given way to Richard Hawley's *Cole's Corner*, another late-evening favourite.

Banks picked up the extension beside his armchair. It was Sophia, and she sounded a little tipsy.

"How did it go?" Banks asked.

"Great," she said. "I did Thai and everyone seemed to like it. They just left. I thought I'd leave the dishes. I'm tired."

"I'm sorry I'm not there to help you," said Banks.

"Me, too. Just sorry you're not here, I mean. Is that Richard Hawley you're listening to?"

"It is."

"Yuk. So that's what you get up to when I'm not around?"

Sophia didn't like Richard Hawley, called him a yob from Sheffield with pretensions to easy listening. Banks had once countered by dismissing Panda Bear, one of her new favourites, as watered-down Brian Wilson with cheap sound effects. "A man has to have some vices," he said.

"I can think of better ones than Richard Hawley."

"I was listening to Keren Ann earlier."

"That's better."

"I think I'm in love with her."

"Should I be jealous?"

"I don't think so. But I had a drink with Edwina Silbert this evening."

"Edwina Silbert! From Viva?"

"One and the same."

"My God, what's she like?"

"Interesting. She's definitely got charisma. And she's still a very beautiful woman."

"Should I be jealous of her, too?"

"She's eighty if she's a day."

"And you prefer younger women. I know. How did you get to meet her?"

"She's the mother of one of the victims. Laurence Silbert."

"Oh dear," said Sophia. "The poor woman. She must have been absolutely devastated."

"She managed to put a brave face on it for a while," Banks said, "but yes, I think she was."

"How's the case going?"

"Slow, but we're making some progress," said Banks. "Chances are it might lead in the direction of London before too long."

"When? I've got a really busy week coming up."

"I'm not sure. It's only a possibility, but I might have to check out a pied-à-terre in Bloomsbury. At the very least we should be able to manage lunch or something. More important, what about next weekend. Are you still coming?"

"Of course I am. But *do* promise me you'll be around."

"I'll be around. Don't forget, I've got tickets for *Othello* next Saturday night. The Eastvale Amateur Dramatic Society." He didn't want to tell her that the case was connected to the theatre; he had got the tickets well before Mark Hardcastle's suicide, well before he had ever heard of Hardcastle.

"An amateur production of *Othello*," said Sophia with mock enthusiasm. "Wow! I can hardly wait. You sure know how to treat a girl well, Detective Chief Inspector Banks."

Banks laughed. "Drinks and dinner before at one of Eastvale's finest establishments, of course."

"Of course. The fish and chip shop or the pizza place?"

"Your choice."

"And after . . . ?"

"Hmm. Remains to be seen."

"I'm sure we'll think of something. Don't forget your handcuffs."

Banks laughed. "I'm glad you called."

"Me, too," Sophia said. "I wish you'd been here, that's all. It's just so not fair, you being up there, me down here."

"I know. Next time. And I'll do the cooking."

It was Sophia's turn to laugh. "Egg and chips all round?"

"What makes you think I can cook an egg? Or make chips?"

"Something more exotic?"

"You haven't tasted my spag bol yet."

"I'm going to hang up now," Sophia said, "before I collapse in an unstoppable fit of giggles. Or is that a fit of unstoppable giggles? Anyway, I'm tired. Miss you. Goodnight."

"Goodnight," said Banks. And the last thing he heard was her laughter as she put down the phone. Richard Hawley had finished and Banks drained the last of his wine. He didn't really feel like listening to anything else as the waves of tiredness rolled over him. The only sounds left were the hum of the stereo and the wind moaning down the chimney. Banks felt more alone and farther away for having just talked to Sophia than he had before her call. But it was always like that – the telephone might bring you together for a few moments, but there's nothing like it for emphasizing distance. He hadn't told her missed her too, and he wished he had. Too late now, he thought, putting the glass down and heading for bed.

4

D erek Wyman's household at half past ten on Sunday morning reminded Banks of his own before Sandra and the kids had left. It
wasn't far away from his old semi, either, just off Market Street about
half a mile south of the town centre. In the spacious living and dining
area, pop music was blasting out from a radio or stereo, a teenage boy
lay on his stomach on the carpet in front of the television playing games
that involved killing futuristic armour-clad soldiers with a great deal of
noise and gouts of blood, while his shy, skinny sister chatted away on her
mobile, face completely hidden by hair. The smell of bacon lingered in
the air as Mrs. Wyman cleared away the breakfast table by the bay
window. Outside, the wind lashed sheets of rain across the street. On
the opposite wall stood a large bookcase full of theatrical texts, an
edition of Chekhov's plays, the RSC *Complete Works* of Shakespeare,
BFI screenplays and big paperback novels in translation – Tolstoy,
Gogol, Dostoevsky, Zola, Sartre, Balzac.

Derek Wyman had clearly been sitting in his favourite armchair
reading the *Sunday Times* Culture section. How he could concentrate
with all the noise going on, Banks had no idea, though he supposed he
must have done it himself at one time. The front section of the newspaper lay on the chair arm beside him, open to the news of the apparent
murder-suicide in Eastvale. It wasn't much of a story. Laurence Silbert
hadn't been named, Banks knew, because his body hadn't been identified. Mark Hardcastle's had, by Vernon Ross. At least the birthmark

Edwina had told them about confirmed Silbert's identity in Banks's mind.

"So much for the fine weather," said Wyman, after Banks and Annie had shown him their warrant cards. He nodded towards the paper. "I suppose this is about Mark?"

"Yes," said Banks.

"Quite a shock to come home to, I must say. Dreadful business. I'm finding it very hard to take in. I would never have expected anything like that of him. Please, sit down." Wyman cleared away some magazines and discarded clothes and offered them the sofa. "Dean, Charlie," he said, "why don't you go up to your rooms and play. We need to talk. And turn that damn music off."

With slow, drawn-out movements, both kids gave their father a long-suffering look and dragged themselves upstairs, Dean switching off the radio on his way.

"Teenagers," Wyman said, rubbing his head. "Who'd have 'em? I spend most of my days with them at school, and then I come home and have to deal with two of my own. Must be a masochist. Or mad."

Complaining was usually staffroom routine for teachers, Banks knew, a way of fitting in and pretending they didn't really love what they did and deserve their long holidays. In fact, Wyman seemed like a man with the energy and patience necessary to deal with teenagers on a daily basis. Tall, thin, wiry even, with a closely cropped scalp and an elongated bony face with deep-set, watchful eyes, he taught games as well as drama. Banks remembered that his own English teacher had also been a PE instructor and was particularly good at importing the plimsoll from one class to the other, where he swung it hard and frequently at his pupils' backsides. At least he didn't say, "This is going to hurt me more than it hurts you," the way the divinity teacher did every time he slippered someone. Still, there was no slippering in schools these days.

A few framed photographs graced the mantelpiece, mostly of Wyman and his wife and kids, and the children's school photos, but Banks noticed one in which a slightly younger Wyman stood next to an older man in a uniform outside a train station, the man's arm draped over his shoulders. "Who's that?" he asked.

Wyman saw where he was looking. "Me and my brother," he said. "Rick was in the army."

"Where is he now?"

"He's dead," said Wyman. "Killed in a helicopter accident on manoeuvres in 2002."

"Where did it happen?"

"Afghanistan."

"Were you very close?"

Wyman glanced at Banks. "He was my big brother. What do you think?"

Banks hadn't been at all close to his big brother, not until it was too late, but he understood. "I'm sorry," he said.

"Well," said Wyman, "that's what you sign up for when you join the bloody army, isn't it?"

Mrs. Wyman finished clearing the dishes away and sat at the table. She was an attractive brunette with a button nose, in her late thirties, a little careworn, but she obviously worked at keeping her figure and preserving her smooth complexion. "You don't mind me being here, do you?" she asked.

"Not at all," said Banks. "Did you know Mark Hardcastle?"

"I met him a few times," she said, "but I wouldn't say I *knew* him. Still, it's terrible, what's happened."

"Yes," Banks agreed, turning back to her husband. "I understand you were in London with Mark just last week?"

"Yes," said Wyman. "Briefly."

"Do you visit there often?"

"Whenever I can get away. Theatre and film are my passions, so London's the place to soak it all up. The bookshops too, of course."

"Mrs. Wyman?"

She smiled indulgently at her husband, as if rather pleased that he had a childish enthusiasm to fire him. "I'm more at home with a good book," she said. "A Jane Austen or Elizabeth Gaskell. I'm afraid the dazzle of the footlights and the smell of greasepaint are a bit rich for my sensibilities."

"Carol's a bit of a philistine," said Wyman, "though she's not lacking in education." He had a noticeable Yorkshire accent, but he didn't use many Yorkshire idioms or contractions in his speech. Banks thought that was probably because he'd been to university and spent plenty of time away.

"Do you teach, Mrs. Wyman?" Banks asked.

"Good Lord, no. I don't think I could handle any more adolescent angst," she said. "And the little ones would be too wild for me. I'm a part-time receptionist at the medical centre. Would you like me to make some tea?"

Everyone thought that sounded like a good idea. Seeming pleased to have something to do, Mrs. Wyman went through to the kitchen.

"Were many of these London trips made with Mark Hardcastle?" Banks asked Wyman.

"Heavens, no! This was the first. And I wasn't really *with* him."

"Can you explain?"

"Of course. Ask away."

"When did you go down?"

"Wednesday morning. I took the twelve-thirty train from York. It arrived at about a quarter to three. On time, for once."

"Was Mark with you?"

"No. He drove down by himself."

"Why was that? I mean, why didn't you travel together?"

"I like the train. We were leaving at different times. Besides, I assume Mark had other things he wanted to do, perhaps other places to go. He needed to be mobile, and I didn't want to be dependent on him. I'm quite happy travelling by tube and bus when I'm in London. In fact, I rather enjoy it. I can get some reading done, or just watch the world go by. I don't even mind when they're late. I get even more reading done then."

"You should be doing adverts for National Express," Banks said.

Wyman laughed. "Oh, I wouldn't go that far. But the thought of driving down the M1 in a car . . . well, frankly, it terrifies me. All those lorries. And driving in London . . . Then there's the congestion charges."

Banks didn't enjoy driving in London much himself, though he had got more used to it since he had started seeing Sophia. Sometimes he took the train for a change, and she occasionally did the same when she came up north, though she had a little Ford Focus runaround and drove up now and then. "And the purpose of the trip was?"

"The German Expressionist Cinema retrospective at the National Film Theatre."

"For both of you?"

"Well, we were both interested in it, certainly, but as I said, Mark may have had other things to do. He didn't say. We didn't spend that much time together."

"Can you tell me what you actually *did* do together?"

"Yes, of course. We met for a bite to eat at Zizzi's on Charlotte Street that first evening, about six o'clock, before the showing. It was a pleasant evening, and we managed to get a table on the pavement out front."

"What did you have to eat?" If Wyman was puzzled by the question, he didn't show it.

"Pizza."

"Who paid?"

"We went Dutch."

"Do you still have your receipt?"

Wyman frowned. "It might be in my wallet somewhere. I can check, if you like?"

"Later will do," said Banks. "And after dinner?"

"We went to see the films. *The Cabinet of Dr. Caligari* and a very rare showing of Dmitri Buchowkhi's *Othello*, a German Expressionist version of Shakespeare. It's very interesting, but ultimately not among the best. You see, I'm directing –"

"Yes, we know about that," said Banks. "What about afterwards?"

Wyman looked a little sulky at being denied his directorial bragging rights. "We had a quick drink in the bar, then we went our separate ways."

"You weren't staying in the same hotel?"

"No. Mark's partner owns a small flat in Bloomsbury. I should imagine he was staying there."

"But he didn't say so?"

"Not specifically, no. But why pay London prices when you've got somewhere you can stay for free?"

"Why indeed?" Banks agreed. "And what about you?"

"I stayed at my usual bed-and-breakfast near Victoria Station. Cheap and cheerful. It's not the most spacious room on the face of the earth, but it does all right for me."

"Do you have the address?" Banks asked.

Wyman seemed puzzled by the question, but gave Banks an address on Warwick Street.

"You mentioned Mark's partner," Annie said. "Did you know Laurence Silbert well?"

"Not well. We met a couple of times. They came to dinner once. They reciprocated, and we went to their house. The usual."

"When was this?" Annie asked.

"A couple of months ago."

"Did Mr. Hardcastle appear to be living there at the time?" Banks asked.

"More or less," said Wyman. "He practically moved in the day they met. Well, wouldn't you? Bloody big house on the hill."

"You think it was the grandeur that attracted him?" Banks said.

"No, I don't really mean that. Just being facetious. But Mark certainly appreciated the finer things in life. He was one of those working lads who've gone up in the world, done right well for themselves. You know, more your Château Margaux and raw-milk Camembert than your pint of bitter and a packet of cheese-and-onion crisps. They were a well-matched couple, despite their difference in background."

Mrs. Wyman came back in with the tea at this point, and the inevitable plate of biscuits. They all helped themselves from the tray. Banks thanked her and resumed the questioning. "What about the next day, Thursday?"

"What about it?"

"Did you see Mark?"

"No. He said he had to go home. I was staying until Saturday, as you know. I wanted to fit in a few exhibitions, too, while I was down there. Tate Modern. The National Portrait Gallery. And some book shopping. There were also a couple more films and lectures I attended at the NFT. *Backstairs. Nosferatu.* I can give you the details if you like."

"Ticket stubs?"

"Yes, probably." He frowned. "Look, you're questioning me as if I'm a suspect or something. I thought –"

"We just want to get the details clear," said Banks. "As yet there aren't any suspects." Or anything to suspect, he might have added. "So you stayed in London until when?"

Wyman paused. "Yesterday. I checked out of my B and B about lunchtime, had a pub lunch, did a bit of book shopping and went to the

National Gallery, then I caught the five o'clock train back to York last night. Got home about . . ." He glanced towards his wife.

"I picked him up at the station around quarter past seven," she said.

Banks turned back to Wyman. "And you're sure you didn't see Mark Hardcastle after he left the bar on Wednesday evening?"

"That's right."

"Was he driving?"

"No. We took the tube from Goodge Street after dinner."

"To Waterloo?"

"Yes."

"And going back?"

"Actually, I walked along the Embankment path and over Westminster Bridge. It was a lovely evening. The view across the river was absolutely stunning. Houses of Parliament all lit up. I'm not especially patriotic, or even political, but the sight always stirs me, brings a lump to my throat."

"And Mark?"

"I assume he caught the tube."

"Did he say where he was going?"

"Back to Goodge Street, I suppose. He could easily walk to Bloomsbury from there."

"So that's where he went?"

"That would be my guess. I didn't go with him, so obviously I can't say for certain."

"What time was this?"

"About half ten, quarter to eleven."

"Where had he left his car?"

"No idea. Outside the flat, I suppose, or in the garage, if he had one."

"What did you talk about over your drinks?"

"The films we saw, ideas for sets and costumes."

"What kind of state of mind would you say he was in?"

"He was fine," said Wyman. "Same as usual. That why I can't under-stand –"

"Not depressed at all?" Annie asked.

"No."

"Bad tempered, edgy?"

"No."

Banks picked up the questioning again. "Only, we've been given to understand that he'd been a bit moody and irritable over the last couple of weeks or so. Did you notice any signs of that?"

"Maybe whatever it was, he'd got over it? Maybe the trip to London did him good?"

"Perhaps," said Banks. "But let's not forget that the day after he got back to Eastvale he went out and hanged himself in Hindswell Woods. We're trying to find out what might be behind that, if there was any direct cause, or if it was simply a build-up of depression."

"I'm sorry I can't help you," said Wyman. "I didn't know he was depressed. If he was, he hid it well."

"Did you get any sense that he and Laurence might have had some sort of falling out?"

"He didn't talk much about Laurence on the trip. He rarely did, unless I asked after him. Hardly, anyway. Mark was almost pathologically secretive about his private life. Not about the fact that he was gay or anything, he was very up front about that, just about who he was sharing his life with. I think he'd had relationships before that had gone bad, and he might have been a bit superstitious about it. You know, like if you talk about liking something or someone too much, it's bound to go wrong."

"I don't mean to be indiscreet here," said Banks, "but did Mark ever make a pass at you or show any undue interest in you? Anything other than companionship and shared interests, that is?"

"Good Lord, no! Mark was a colleague and a friend. He knew I was married, heterosexual. He always respected that."

"Did you socialize often?"

"Not very often, no. We'd go for a drink now and then, mostly to discuss some theatrical matter."

"Was he a jealous person?"

"Well, I got the impression once or twice that he felt a bit insecure."

"In what way?"

"I think he had a jealous nature – this is just an impression, mind you – and I reckon he sometimes felt that Laurence was a bit out of his class, kept thinking the bubble would burst. I mean, a Barnsley miner's son and a wealthy sophisticate like Laurence Silbert. Go figure, as the

Yanks say. His mother started the Viva chain, you know. Quite the celebrity. You have to admit it's a bit of an odd pairing. I can understand where he was coming from. I'm from pretty humble origins myself. You never forget."

"Are you from Barnsley, too?"

"No. Pontefract, for my sins."

"Was Mark jealous about anyone in particular?"

"No, he didn't mention any names. He just got anxious if Laurence was away or something. Which happened quite often."

"I understand that Mr. Silbert was in Amsterdam while you were in London?"

"Yes. Mark did mention that."

"Did he say why?"

"No. Business, I assumed."

"What was his business?"

"Retired civil servant. He'd worked for the Foreign Office, travelled all over the place. Maybe it was some sort of reunion or something? Embassy staff. Or is it consulate? I never did know the difference between them. All I know is that Laurence was in Amsterdam and Mark was a bit worried about the nightlife there, you know, the red light district and all that. Amsterdam does have a bit of a reputation. Anything goes."

"Indeed," said Banks. "So Mark *was* anxious?"

"I didn't mean it like that. It was just part of his nature to worry. He even joked about it. I told him he could always go to Soho or Hampstead Heath if he wanted a bit of fun himself."

"How did he react to that?" Annie asked.

"He just smiled and said those days were over."

"So nothing out of the ordinary happened on this trip you and Mark Hardcastle made to London?" Banks said.

"No. Everything happened exactly as I said it did."

"Had you noticed anything unusual about Mark's behaviour over the past while?"

"Nothing at all."

"Mrs. Wyman?"

"No," she said. "Not that I noticed. I mean, I haven't seen him for a few weeks."

"Had you and Mark done anything like this before?" Annie asked Wyman.

"Like what?"

"You know. A few days away together."

Wyman leaned forward. "Look, I don't know what you're insinuating, but it wasn't like that. There was nothing untoward between me and Mark Hardcastle. And we didn't go away for 'a few days together.' We travelled separately to London and back, and as far as I know he was only there for one night. Christ, all we did was share a meal and go to the pictures."

"I was only wondering if you'd done it before," Annie said.

"Well, no. I told you. This was the first time."

"And absolutely nothing occurred that night that could have set in motion the events of the next two days?" Banks asked.

"No. Not that I know of. Not while I was around. Who knows what he got up to after he left me?"

"Got up to?" said Banks.

"It's just a figure of speech. Bloomsbury isn't far from Soho, is it, and there are plenty of gay clubs there, if you like that sort of thing. Maybe he met a friend? Maybe he and Laurence had an arrangement and did their own thing when they were apart? I don't know. All I'm saying is that I've no idea where he went after he left me, straight to the flat or somewhere else."

"I thought you said he told you those days were behind him?" Annie said. "Was Mark in the habit of being unfaithful to Laurence Silbert?"

"I've no idea. Like I said, he didn't confide in me about his love life. But remember, Laurence was in Amsterdam. If you want my honest opinion, no, I don't think Mark was the type for a bit of hanky-panky on Hampstead Heath, cottaging, or whatever they call it. Or in the back room of a Soho club, for that matter. That's why I could joke about it easily. But what do I know? It's not a world I belong to."

"I don't suppose it's much different from anyone else's," said Banks, "when you get right down to it."

"I suppose not," Wyman agreed. "But the point remains that I don't know what he did, what he liked to do, or with whom."

"Is there anything else you can tell us?" Banks asked.

"Not that I can think of," said Wyman.

His wife shook her head. Banks had been watching Carol Wyman's face from time to time throughout the interview, checking for telltale signs of concern, or the knowledge that her husband might be lying when the matter of Hardcastle and him being away together came up, but she hadn't shown anything other than polite interest and vague amusement. She obviously had no fears on that score and was liberal enough in her outlook not to mind too much if her husband met up with a gay friend in London. There was nothing more to be learned from Derek Wyman right now, Banks thought, so he gave Annie the sign that they should leave.

Banks and Annie managed to grab an early lunch at the Queen's Arms, already busy with earnest people in waterproof walking gear that warm, wet Sunday in June. The rain had stopped when they left Wyman's house, and the sun was breaking through gaps in the cloud.

Banks snagged a dimpled, copper-topped table for two in the corner near the Gents, while Annie went to the bar and ordered roast lamb and Yorkshire pudding for Banks and veggie pasta for herself. Conversations buzzed around them, and the pretty blonde schoolgirl, working her weekend job as waitress, was rushed off her feet with orders. Banks eyed his grapefruit juice with disdain and raised his glass to clink with Annie's Diet Coke. "Here's to working Sundays."

"It has been a while, hasn't it?"

"I think we've got a pretty good head start, at any rate," Banks said. "What did you think of Derek Wyman?"

"A bit of a trainspotter, really, isn't he? An anorak."

"You always say that about someone with a passion or a hobby."

"Well, it's true, isn't it? Hobbies are so naff."

"When I was a kid, everyone had a hobby. You had to have. There were clubs at school. Stamp-collecting, making model aeroplanes, playing chess, collecting tadpoles, growing watercress, whatever. I used to have hobbies."

"Like what?"

"You know, collecting things. Coins. Cigarette cards. Birds' eggs. Writing down car number plates."

"Car number plates? You're not serious?"

"Sure. We used to sit on the wall by the main road and write down as many as we could."

"Why?"

"No reason. It was a hobby. That's the point about hobbies; you don't need a reason."

"But what did you do with them?"

"Nothing. When I'd filled one notebook, I started another. Sometimes I tried to jot down the make of car, too, if I recognized it and was quick enough. I tell you, it would make our job a lot easier if there were more people doing that today."

"Nah, we don't need it," said Annie. "We've got CCTV everywhere."

"Cynic."

"What about the birds' eggs?"

"Well, you had to blow them, or they went bad and started to smell. I found that out the hard way."

"*Blow* them? You can't be serious."

"I am. You made little holes in each end with a pin and –"

"Yuk," said Annie. "I don't think I want to know."

Banks studied her. "You asked."

"Anyway," she went on, making a dismissive gesture, "that was probably when you were about ten or eleven. Derek Wyman's in his forties."

"Theatre's a valid passion. There's nothing anoraky about it. And it's a bit more cerebral than trainspotting."

"Oh, I don't know," said Annie. "Don't you think there's something rather heroic and romantic about standing there in your anorak in the wind and rain at the end of the platform, open to the elements, writing down the numbers of the diesels that zoom by?"

Banks studied her expression. "You're winding me up again."

Annie smiled. "Maybe just a little bit."

"All right. Very funny. Now what *do* you think about Wyman? Do you think he was telling the truth?"

"He had no real reason to lie to us, did he? I mean, he knows we can check his alibi. And he got all those receipts and stubs for us before we left, didn't he?"

"Yes," said Banks. "They turned out to be very handy indeed."

"They were just in his wallet. Exactly where you'd put something like that."

"Cinema stubs, too?"

"People do."

"I know."

"So what is it?"

"Nothing," said Banks. "Just my bloody scar's itching, that's all."

"How *did* you get that scar?"

Banks ignored her. "Do you think there was something going on between them? Wyman and Hardcastle?"

"No, not really. I think he was telling the truth about that. And his wife didn't react. If she had her suspicions, I think she would have found it hard to hide them. Not all gays are promiscuous, you know, no more than all heteros are."

"Most blokes I know fancy plenty of women other than their wives."

"That proves nothing," said Annie. "Except that most blokes are bastards and your mates have probably never grown up."

"What's wrong with fancying? With looking?"

Annie turned away. "I don't know," she said. "Ask Sophia. See what she says."

Banks was silent for a moment, then he said, "What about Derek Wyman and Laurence Silbert?"

"What about them?"

"You know."

"Doubt it," said Annie. "It doesn't sound as if Silbert was much of a mixer."

"Then what, for crying out loud, are we missing?"

Their food came and the waitress was in such a hurry that she almost dropped Banks's lunch on his lap. She blushed and dashed away while he dabbed at the few spots of gravy that had landed on his trousers. "I swear Cyril's help is getting younger every week."

"It's hard to keep them," Annie agreed. "No kid wants to go to school every day and then work here on weekends. The pay's rubbish, for a start, and nobody tips them. It's no wonder they don't last long."

"I suppose so. Anyway, back to Derek Wyman."

"I thought he was OK," said Annie. "I don't think we're missing anything. Like I said, he's a bit of an anorak, that's all. He can probably name every gaffer and best boy on every film he's seen, but I doubt that makes him a killer."

"I didn't say he was a killer," Banks argued after a bite of lamb. "Just that there's something niggling me about this whole murder-suicide business, that's all."

"But that's just what it is: a murder-suicide. Don't you think maybe we're just taking it all a little bit too seriously? You're annoyed because you got dragged away from your romantic weekend, and you can't find a good mystery to make it worthwhile."

Banks shot her a glance. "Wouldn't you be?"

"I suppose I would."

"It's all so inconclusive," said Banks. "I mean, was Hardcastle upset or wasn't he? Some of the people he worked with said he was. Maria Wolsey, for example. Wyman said he wasn't, but that he was generally insecure and jealous with regard to Silbert's travelling. I don't know. There are just too many questions." Banks put his knife and fork down and started to count them off on his fingers as he spoke. "Why did Silbert travel so much if he'd retired? Had Hardcastle and Silbert had a fight, or hadn't they? Did either, or both, of them play away or not? Who's Julian Fenner, and why doesn't his phone number connect? What was Silbert up to in Amsterdam?"

"Well, when you put it like that . . ." Annie said. "Maybe Edwina can help?"

"People don't just beat their lovers to death then hang themselves for no reason."

"But the reason could be insignificant," Annie argued. "If Hardcastle did it, then it could have been because of something that flared up right there and then. You know as well as I do that some of the most inconsequential of things can spark off the worst violence in people. Burning a piece of toast, breaking a valuable ornament, taking the piss at the wrong moment. You name it. Maybe Hardcastle had had too much to drink, and Silbert chastised him for it? Something as simple as that.

People don't like being told they've had too much to drink. Maybe Hardcastle was a little pissed, already aggressive, and before he knew it Silbert was dead? We know from Grainger's statement that he'd been drinking when he called at the hardware shop for the clothesline."

"Or someone else did it," Banks said.

"So you say."

"Look at the number of blows to Silbert *after* he was dead, the blood," said Banks.

"Heat of the moment," argued Annie. "Hardcastle lost it. Saw red. Literally. When he stopped and saw what he'd done he was horrified. That calmed him down, so when he bought the washing line off Grainger he seemed distant, resigned, his mind already made up. Then he went to the woods and . . ."

"But what about the damage inflicted on Silbert's genital area? Doesn't that suggest to you a sexual motive?"

"Perhaps." Annie pushed her half-empty plate aside. "It's nothing we haven't seen before, though, is it? If there's sexual jealousy involved, the killer will go to the area that symbolizes it. Maybe they argued about Hardcastle going to London with Wyman, or about Silbert going to Amsterdam? We might never know. It still doesn't mean that someone else did it. Whatever the motive – jealousy, infidelity, criticism of drinking habits, some antique Hardcastle might have broken – the result's the same: an argument turned violent and one man was left dead. The survivor couldn't bear what he'd done, so he committed suicide. There's nothing sinister or unusual about that at all. Sad to say, but it's very commonplace."

Banks put his knife and fork down and sighed. "I suppose you're right," he said. "Maybe I am just trying to justify losing my weekend. Or maybe *you* want to get this sorted quickly so we can concentrate on something really important, like all those police cones that have gone missing from the market square lately?"

Annie laughed. "Well, at least you're thinking along the right lines."

"Come on," Banks said. "Let's go have a shufti around Silbert's house. The SOCOs should be pretty much done there by now. Then we'll have another word with Edwina at the Burgundy. I get the impression that she's got something else on her mind, too. We'll see if we can find out something to shed a little more light on these matters."

"Sounds like a plan to me," said Annie.

A couple of SOCOs were collecting the remaining trace evidence in Silbert's upstairs drawing room when Banks and Annie arrived there early on Sunday afternoon, but apart from them, the place stood empty.

"We've had a good look around," Ted Ferguson, one of the SOCOs, told them, "and there are no hidden safes or compartments anywhere in the house. The only rooms with any personal stuff and papers in them are this one and the study down the hall." He handed them some latex gloves from the crime scene bag on the floor near the door. "We've got a few more things to do downstairs, but we're done up here for now. We'll leave you to it. Wear these."

"Thanks, Ted," said Banks, opening the seal and slipping on the gloves.

The SOCOs went downstairs, and Banks and Annie stood on the threshold and took stock.

Even though the body and the sheepskin rug it had lain on were gone, the blood spatter left on the walls and the traces of fingerprint powder on every surface now marked it as a crime scene. The photo in the shattered frame still lay on the floor. It showed Mark Hardcastle smiling, standing next to Silbert. Banks picked it up carefully, brushed off some of the fingerprint powder and studied Silbert's face. Handsome, certainly, cultured, slender and fit, and seeming much younger than sixty-two, he had a strong cleft chin, a high forehead and clear blue eyes. His dark hair had thinned just a little at the temples, and showed traces of grey above his ears, but it suited him. He wore a light blue cashmere jumper and navy chinos.

Annie pointed out the framed blow-up of Hindswell Woods on the wall. Most of the blood had been wiped off, though a few drops had smeared here and there. "Not a bad effort," said Banks. "Whoever took it had an eye for a picturesque woodland scene. The way the light filters through the leaves and branches is beautiful."

"That's the tree Mark Hardcastle hanged himself on," Annie said, pointing out the oak. "It's very distinctive."

They both gazed at the picture for a few moments, Banks remembering what Edwina Silbert had said the previous night about walks in woods full of bluebells. Then they started the search.

Silbert's computer showed nothing out of the ordinary on a cursory examination, carried out by Annie, but it would have be checked thoroughly by technical support if the evidence pointed towards a killer other than Mark Hardcastle. The desk drawers held only stationery, holiday snapshots and a few files full of business receipts, along with telephone and utility bills.

A set of keys in the middle drawer opened a locked antique wooden cabinet on the floor beside the desk. Inside, Banks and Annie found the deeds to the house, bank statements, chequebooks and all the other papers they needed to discover that Silbert had been in the millionaire-plus bracket. His civil service pension certainly didn't account for it, but regular cheques from Viva and its various subsidiaries did. There were also a few large transfers from foreign bank accounts, Swiss mostly, the nature of which remained unclear, but on the whole, the mystery of Silbert's wealth was solved. There was no will, so Silbert had either left one in the keeping of his solicitor, or he hadn't made one, in which case his fortune would go to his mother.

On the bottom shelf of the cabinet, Banks found a small bundle of personal letters held together by a rubber band. The first was dated 7 September 1997, and was from someone called Leo Westwood at an address in Swiss Cottage. Banks read through it quickly, Annie looking over his shoulder. It was written in a neat, sloping hand, with a fountain pen, judging from the varying thickness of the ink strokes.

Most of the content dealt with the death of the Princess of Wales and its aftermath. Westwood seemed to have little patience for Diana's brother's attack on the Royal Family in his funeral oration the previous day, finding it "inappropriate and ill-advised," or for the general outpouring of grief from "the hoi-polloi, who love this sort of thing almost as much as they love *Coronation Street* and *East Enders*." Banks wondered what he would make of the recent inquiry and the accusations flying around about Prince Charles, the Duke of Edinburgh and MI6.

There were also references to an afternoon's antique hunting, a George I card table with an inlay pattern that Silbert "would simply have adored," and a delicious meal, including foie gras and sweetbreads, with "Gracie and Sevron" at a Michelin-starred restaurant in the West End, where they saw one of Tony Blair's cabinet ministers dining with an out-of-favour colleague.

· The letter, like the rest, had been sent to Silbert, as diplomatic post, at the British embassy in Berlin. Banks wondered whether it had been read by censors. Gossipy as it was, there was nothing seditious in it, nothing calculated to bring the wrath of HMG down on Westwood or Silbert, and the only overt political reference was to Egon Krenz's recent conviction for a shoot-to-kill policy on the Berlin Wall. All in all, it was chatty, well-informed, snobbish and affectionate. The writer was, no doubt, aware that his words would probably be read by people other than the intended recipient, so if he had been Silbert's lover at the time, he had shown remarkable restraint. When Annie had finished reading it, Banks put the letter back in its envelope and returned it to the pile.

"Do you think these could have caused a row?" Annie asked, tapping the pile of letters.

"It's possible," Banks said. "But why now? I mean, they've probably been lying around since the late nineties."

"Maybe Hardcastle did a bit of prying on Thursday evening or Friday morning while Silbert was still away in Amsterdam?"

"Maybe," said Banks. "But surely he'd had plenty of opportunities to pry before? Silbert travelled quite a bit. Why now?"

"Jealousy got the better of him?"

"Hmm," said Banks. "Let's go have a look down the hall."

The room was clearly Hardcastle's study, and it was much less tidy than Silbert's. Most of what they found related to Hardcastle's work at the theatre and his interest in set and costume design. There were notes, sketches, books and working scripts marked up with different coloured inks. On his laptop was a computer program for generating various screenplay formats, along with the beginnings of one or two stories. It appeared as if Hardcastle himself had been interested in writing a movie script, a ghost story set in Victorian England, judging by the first page.

In the top drawer of the desk, on the latest copy of *Sight & Sound*, lay a memory stick of the type most commonly used in a digital camera.

"That's odd," Annie said, when Banks pointed it out to her.

"Why?"

"Hardcastle has a digital camera. It's over here on the bottom book-shelf." She picked up the small silver object and carried it over to Banks.

"So?" said Banks.

"Don't be such a Luddite," Annie said. "Can't you see?"

"Yes, I can see. Digital camera, memory card. I still say, 'So what?' And I'm not a bloody Luddite. I've got a digital camera of my own. I know what memory cards are for."

Annie sighed. "This is a Canon camera," she said, as if explaining to a five-year-old. Though a five-year-old, Banks thought, would probably have known what she was talking about already. "It takes a compact flash card."

"I know what you're going to say," said Banks. "This thing here isn't a compact flash card."

"Bingo. It's a memory stick."

"Won't it fit in that camera?"

"No. It's for Sony digital cameras."

"Isn't there an adapter?"

"No. Not for the camera. I mean, technically, I suppose, someone could probably do it, but you just wouldn't. You'd buy the right kind of memory. You can get card readers, and a lot of computers will accept different kinds of cards – Hardcastle's laptop there does, by the way – but you can't put a Sony memory stick in a Canon Sure Shot camera."

"Maybe it was just meant for the computer, not the camera? You said most computers have card readers."

"Possibly," Annie said. "But I still think that's unlikely. Mostly people buy those cheaper USB smart drives when they want portable computer memory. These little thingies are made for cameras."

"So the question is, what's it doing here?"

"Exactly," said Annie. "And where did it come from? Silbert didn't have a Sony, either. He's just got an old Olympus. I saw it in his study."

"Interesting," said Banks, eyeing the small, wafer-thin stick. "Should we check it out?"

"Fingerprints?"

"Damn." Banks went to the landing and called one of the SOCOs, who came up, examined and dusted the stick, then shook his head. "Everything's too blurred," he said. "It's almost always the case with things like that. You might get something from the memory stick itself, if you're lucky, but usually people tend to hold them by the edges."

"This isn't the stick?" Banks said, puzzled.

"I forgot to explain," said Annie. "The stick fits into an adapter, a kind of sheath, so you can slot it in the computer."

"OK. I see." Banks thanked the SOCO, who went back downstairs. "Let's have a look at it, then," Banks went on. "If it's protected by the sheath, we can't do it any harm, can we?"

"I suppose not," said Annie, sitting down at the laptop. Banks watched her slip the stick into a slot in the side of the computer and heard it click into place. A series of dialogue boxes flashed across the screen. Within seconds, he was looking at photographs showing Laurence Silbert with another man sitting on a park bench. In the background was a magnificent cream-coloured, two-domed building. Banks thought they were in Regent's Park, but he couldn't be certain.

Next, the two men were pictured from behind walking down a narrow street past a row of garages on the right, each a different colour painted in a series of distinctive white-bordered square panels, like a chessboard. Above the garages were gabled houses, or apartments, with white stucco fronts.

The final shot showed them entering through a door between two of the garages, which clearly led to the living space above, the unknown man in profile, his hand resting lightly on Silbert's shoulder. It could have been a simple gesture of courtesy, the man ushering Silbert into the house first. To a jealous lover, though, it could conceivably have appeared as a sign of affection, especially if the lover knew nothing about such a meeting.

Whoever the man was, he certainly wasn't Mark Hardcastle. Maybe he was Leo Westwood, Banks thought. Whoever he was, he looked about the same age as Silbert, perhaps a year or two younger, given Silbert's access to the elixir of youth, and about the same height. Judging by the light and shadows, it was early evening. Beyond the garages, the rest of the houses on the street were brick with cream stucco ground floors and steps leading down to basement entrances. The photos were dated the Wednesday before last.

"OK," said Banks. "Can we get these printed up back at the station?"

"No problem," said Annie. "I can do it myself."

"Let's call back there first, then. We'll show them to the people we've already talked to, starting with Edwina Silbert. And I've got a pal in technical support who might just be able to identify the street name if he can enhance the image enough. You can see the sign on the wall in the far background. There's obviously a damn good reason that memory stick was there. It didn't belong to either Silbert or Hardcastle, and you tell me that neither could have used it in their cameras. I don't think it was there by coincidence. Do you?"

"No," said Annie.

Banks pocketed the letters and Annie took the memory stick out of the slot and turned off the laptop. They were just about to head back to the station when Annie's mobile rang. She answered it immediately. Banks glanced around the room again as she dealt with the call, but saw nothing he thought of any significance.

"Interesting," said Annie, putting her phone away.

"Who was it?"

"Maria Wolsey, from the theatre. She worked with Mark Hardcastle."

"What does she want?"

"Wants to talk to me."

"About what?"

"She didn't say. Just that she'd like to talk to me."

"And?"

"I said I'd drop by her flat."

"OK," said Banks. "Why don't we go get the photos printed first, then you can talk to her while I have another chat with Edwina Silbert."

Annie smiled. "Alan Banks, if I didn't know any better, I'd say you fancied her."

5

The morning's rain was long gone by the time Banks got to the Burgundy Hotel. Edwina Silbert was taking a gin and tonic and a cigarette in the small, quiet courtyard, once the stables, at the back of the building. Banks got the impression that it wasn't her first drink of the day. She had one of the Sunday newspaper style supplements open before her, photos of skinny models in clothes you never saw anyone wearing, but it was clear that she wasn't really paying attention to it; her gaze was fixed on the line of the distant hills framed by a gap in the buildings.

Banks pulled up a chair and sat opposite her. "Comfortable night?" he asked.

"As well as could be expected," she said. "Do you know, there's absolutely no smoking anywhere in the hotel? Not even in my own room. Can you believe it?"

"Sign of the times, I'm afraid," said Banks, ordering a lemon tea from the hovering white-coated waiter. Edwina was looking her age this morning, he thought. Or closer to it. She was wearing a black woollen shawl over her shoulders, a sign of mourning, an indication that she felt cold, or perhaps both. Her grey-white hair and pale dry skin stood out in stark contrast.

"Where's that pretty girlfriend of yours today?" she asked.

"DI Cabbot isn't my girlfriend."

"Then she's a damn fool. If I were twenty years younger . . ."

Banks laughed.

"What? You don't believe me?"

"Edwina, I believe you."

Her expression turned serious. "Anything new to report?" she asked.

"Not much, I'm afraid," said Banks. "I just called in at the station and discovered that your son's blood type is A positive, along with about thirty-five per cent of the population, and that the only blood types we found on Mark's person were A positive and B positive, which is much rarer, and happens to be his own."

"So you're saying it looks more and more as if Mark killed Laurence?"

"We've a long way to go to be certain of that yet," said Banks, "but blood typing certainly supports the theory."

Edwina sat in silence. Banks felt that she might be debating with herself whether to tell him something, but the moment passed, and when nothing was forthcoming after a minute or so, he slipped the photos Annie had printed out of their envelope and pushed them over to her. "We found these in Mark's study," he said. "Any idea who the other man is?"

Edwina took some reading glasses from a brown leather case beside her and studied the photos. "No," she said. "Never see him before in my life."

"It's not Leo Westwood?"

"Leo? Good Lord, no. Leo's far more handsome than the man in this photograph, and not quite so tall. A little stockier, even, with tight, dark curls. Rather cherubic, actually. How do you know about Leo?"

"We found some letters."

"What kind of letters?"

"From Leo to Laurence. Nothing . . . shocking. Just letters."

"They'd hardly be shocking," Edwina said. "The Leo I knew was definitely not the sort to let it all hang out."

"When were they together?"

"About ten years ago. Late nineties until the early two thousands."

"Do you know what happened?"

She stared at the distant patterns of drystone walls. "Whatever usually happens to split people apart. Boredom? Someone new? Laurence didn't tell me. He was broken-hearted for a while, then he got over it and got on with his life. I assume Leo did the same."

"Do you know where Leo is now?"

"I'm afraid not. We lost touch after he and Laurence split up. He might still be living in the same place, I suppose. It's on Adamson Road, Swiss Cottage." She gave Banks a street number. "I had dinner with them there on several occasions. It was a nice apartment and an interesting neighbourhood. Leo liked the place, and he did own it, so if he didn't have to move for any practical reason, the odds are that he's still there."

"Their relationship was serious?"

"I would say so, from what I saw of it, yes."

"Were there any others?"

"Lovers or serious relationships?"

"Serious relationships."

"I'd say Leo was the only one until Mark came along, except perhaps for his first love, but that was many years ago, and I can't remember the young man's name now. I'm sure Laurence would have done, though. One never does really forget one's first love, does one? Anyway, Leo was the only one I knew about, at any rate, and I think I would have known. There were casual lovers, of course."

"Have you ever heard Laurence mention a man called Julian Fenner?" Banks asked.

Edwina frowned. "Fenner? No, I can't say I have."

Banks's lemon tea arrived. He thanked the waiter and took a sip. Refreshing. Edwina took the opportunity to order another gin and tonic. Birds twittered in the shrubbery. The sun felt warm on the back of Banks's neck. "We've also been thinking," he went on, "that Mark may have had suspicions regarding Laurence's faithfulness, or lack of it. Laurence might have been having an affair. Mark could have found out about it."

"I wish I could help you," said Edwina, "but I certainly wasn't privy to all Laurence's comings and goings. I would very much doubt it, though. While Laurence could be as promiscuous and unfaithful as the next man when his feelings weren't engaged in a relationship, well . . . when he was in love, it was a different matter. He took that sort of thing seriously."

"What about the man in the photo?" Banks said. "They're touching."

"I shouldn't think that means anything, would you?" Edwina said. "It's just a natural gesture when you usher someone through a door before you. I mean, it's hardly sexual, or even sensual, is it?"

"But a jealous person might see it that way."

"True. There's no accounting for the way some people interpret things."

"Might Mark have seen it that way?"

"He could have. I wouldn't have said he was *that* jealous, mind you. Just a little insecure. When you think you've landed such a wonderful catch you're understandably nervous about losing it. I'm not boasting about my son here. All these things are relative."

"I understand," said Banks, thinking that no matter how often the analysts claimed the class system had disappeared, there was always plenty of evidence to the contrary. "What about Laurence's business interests?" he asked. "I gather he was a retired civil servant?"

Edwina paused. "Yes," she said.

"But he also helped you with Viva, didn't he?"

She almost spilled her gin and tonic. "What? Where on earth did you get *that* idea?"

"But I thought that might explain some of his frequent trips to London and elsewhere, if he worked as a sort of business consultant."

"Good Lord, no. You *have* got it all wrong, haven't you?"

"Have I?"

"Office space in London is far too expensive. Our head office is in Swindon. Well, outside Swindon. One wouldn't want to actually *be* in Swindon, would one?"

Banks cursed himself. They should have checked. It wouldn't have been that difficult to find out where Viva's head office was. "When I found out who you were, I just assumed that was perhaps why Laurence went to London so often, to help you take care of Viva."

"Laurence? Viva? You must be joking. Laurence has no head for figures, no business acumen at all. *Laurence*? If I'd let him run things we'd be bankrupt or unemployed by now. I gave Laurence a percentage share in the business. That's where his money comes from. He never played any actual part in the running of the company."

"There were also a number of transfers from Swiss bank accounts we've been unable to account for. Would they have anything to do with Viva?"

"I very much doubt it," Edwina mumbled, tapping out another cigarette and lighting it. "Though I should imagine that someone in the employ of the foreign service for as many years as Laurence was would have squirrelled a certain amount away, wouldn't you?"

"Expenses?"

She looked away, up at the hills again. "Expenses. Contingency fund. Mad money. Escape hatch. Call it what you will."

Banks's head was beginning to swim. Edwina seemed to have wrapped herself in a cloud of verbal smoke, as well as the real stuff, and her answers were vague and slow to come. He felt that the interview was suddenly slipping away from him, and he didn't know why. "Do *you* know why he went down to London so often, then?"

"I'm afraid not."

"Or why he'd go to Amsterdam? He was there from Tuesday until Friday morning last week."

"I have no idea. Old friends, perhaps? Contacts. He had them all over the world. They were his life's blood."

"What do you mean? I don't understand you."

When she gazed at him, he sensed a guarded look in her eyes. "It's perfectly clear," she said. "Laurence had no business affairs. Whatever he did down in London after he retired, it certainly wasn't business. I would guess that he was meeting old colleagues, talking shop, playing golf, perhaps, visiting casinos, lunching at various clubs. Who knows?"

"Could it have had anything to do with his job? The civil service job he retired from."

"Oh, I should imagine so. One never really retires fully from that sort of thing, does one, especially in times like these?"

"I wouldn't know," said Banks, feeling his scar begin to itch. "What do you mean? What was it exactly that he did?"

Edwina sipped her gin and tonic and remained silent.

"Edwina," Banks said in exasperation. "You're keeping something from me. I can tell. You were doing it last night, and now you're doing it again today. What on earth is it? What are you holding back?"

Edwina paused and sighed. "Oh, very well. It *is* naughty of me, isn't it? I suppose you'd find out sooner or later, anyway." She stubbed out her cigarette and looked Banks in the eye. "He was a spy, Mr. Banks. My son, Laurence Silbert. He was a spook."

Maria Wolsey's flat reminded Annie of where she had lived when she was a student at Exeter. She glimpsed an unmade mattress on the floor in the bedroom, and the bookcases in the living room were made of planks separated by bricks. Posters of the Arctic Monkeys and the Killers vied for space with playbills for the RSC and the Eastvale Theatre on the walls. The armchairs they sat in needed reupholstering and the mugs they drank their coffee from were chipped and stained.

Maria, it turned out, had left the University of Bristol, where she had studied drama, only a year ago. Eastvale was her first job, and she hoped to use it as a stepping-stone to move on to higher and better things. As with Mark Hardcastle, her interest was in theatre history, costume design and set production.

"You could say Mark was a sort of mentor to me," she said, cradling her mug against her chest. The dark-rimmed glasses she had on made her look both older and more of an intellectual. She wore a loose, off-the-shoulder top, and her straight brown hair hung over her pale skin. She sat in the chair with her legs crossed, feet bare below the frayed hems of her jeans. In the background, a girl with a wispy voice was singing and playing guitar on the stereo.

"Did the two of you spend much time together?"

"Quite a bit, yes. Usually after work, or on a lunch break, you know. We'd go for a drink or a bite to eat."

"So you were close? Is that why you rang me?"

Maria's brow furrowed. She put her mug down on the arm of the chair. "I didn't want to talk in front of everyone. And Vernon acts like he's the boss, you know. He's always putting me down. I think he feels threatened by a competent woman."

"What about a competent gay man?"

"Come again?"

"Vernon. How did he feel about working for Mark?"

"Oh, that. I see. Vernon's like a lot of men. He thinks he's OK with it, but really he's a homophobe. The whole idea of it terrifies him, threatens his manhood."

"What's he doing working in the theatre, then?"

Maria laughed. "Only job he could get. He's not a bad carpenter, but there's not a lot of demand for his skills elsewhere around here."

"Did he get along all right with Mark?"

Maria twirled a stand of hair as she thought for a moment. "I guess so. I mean, basically Vernon's a do-as-you're-told-and-get-on-with-your-work sort of bloke. Salt of the earth, as they say. He was just uncomfortable sometimes, that's all."

"Did Mark make him feel that way?"

"Not deliberately, just by what he was."

"Can you give me an example? Did Mark tease him or anything like that?"

"No, nothing like that. It was just . . . like, Mark was a great mimic. He could take off just about anyone. You wouldn't believe how funny he was when he got going. You should have heard his Kenneth Williams, or seen him do his gay John Wayne or his effeminate Barnsley coal miner. Talk about laugh."

"Did Vernon find this amusing?"

"No. I think it embarrassed him when Mark started doing his outrageously gay routines. I mean, most of the time he was just . . . you know . . . ordinary. Well, I don't mean ordinary, because he was a great bloke, really special, but he didn't have any affectations or exaggerated mannerisms."

"I think I understand," said Annie. "Was Vernon at the theatre all Friday afternoon?"

"We all were."

"During the *Calamity Jane* matinee?"

"Yes."

"But could somebody have slipped away?"

"I suppose so. I just don't believe it, that's all."

"Don't believe what."

"That Vernon would hurt Mark. I mean, it's one thing to be a bit uncomfortable around gays, but quite another to go and kill one."

Annie wasn't thinking of Mark, but she didn't need to tell Maria that. "I'm not suggesting he did," she said. "We have no evidence so far that Mark did anything other than take his own life. I'm just trying to get everything clear, that's all. What about the morning? Were you all at work then?"

"We didn't start until noon."

So Vernon Ross *could* have killed Laurence Silbert, Annie thought. Maybe it was an unlikely scenario, but it was worth keeping in mind. "What about Derek Wyman?" she asked. "He and Mark went to London together last week."

"The way I understand it, they really didn't go together," said Maria. "Derek told me they were meeting up down there to see some films. He sounded quite excited about it."

"What did Mark say?"

"I didn't get to talk to him about it. He was too busy."

"Did you ever get the feeling that there was anything between Derek Wyman and Mark?"

"Good Lord, no. Derek's not gay. I can tell you that for sure."

"How do you know?" Annie asked.

"I can't really explain it. Gay-dar. No vibe."

Annie realized that Maria was right. Often a woman *could* tell. "But they'd never done anything like this before?"

"No. To be honest, it came as quite a surprise to me. I mean, it wasn't as if they were best of friends or anything."

"You mean they didn't get along?"

"No, I'm not saying that. I think Mark just got frustrated with Derek sometimes, that's all."

"Why?"

"Because Derek kept trying to do *his* job, tell him how the production should look and all that. I mean, he *is* the director, but Mark was a professional. He'd done courses and everything. We were lucky to have him here."

"I thought they were agreed on the German Expressionist set?"

"Well, they were. But it was Derek's idea, and he wasn't always receptive when Mark brought fresh perspectives to it. It was as if he expected

Mark just to do what he was told, to follow the plans, get the sets built and the costumes made and shut up. But that wasn't Mark's way. He was really creative, and he saw a production as more of a collaboration. Between all of us, really. He was always asking our opinions on things. The actors, too. Derek just gave orders. I don't mean to give the impression that they didn't like each other or anything. I mean, I know they met socially occasionally, too."

"Artistic differences, then?"

"Yes. And they're both from working-class backgrounds, you know, only Mark tried to play down his roots – he even talked a bit posh – while Derek, well, he's one of those blokes who wears his working man's club membership card on his sleeve, even though he's never been to a working man's club in his life, if you know what I mean."

"I think I do," said Annie. "Did Mark talk about himself much?"

"Sometimes. Not a lot. He was a great listener, though, was Mark. You could talk to him about anything. When I split up with my boyfriend in February I must have talked his ear off, but he didn't complain. And it helped me."

"You said he'd been a bit strange the past couple of weeks. Do you have any idea why?"

"No. We didn't really have chance to get together for a chat or anything during that period, what with one thing and another. Not that he would have told me, anyway."

"Did he ever tell you if something was bothering him?"

"There were a couple of occasions when he let his guard down." She put her hand to her mouth to stifle a giggle. "Usually when we'd had a bit too much to drink."

"And what did he talk about on these occasions?"

"Oh, you know. Life. His feelings. His ambitions."

"Can you tell me more?"

"Well, you know about his background, don't you? Barnsley and all that?"

"A bit."

"It was something he was very uncomfortable about. He was an only child, you see, and he didn't turn out to be exactly the sort of son his father wanted. His father was a miner and very macho, apparently, played rugby and all that. Mark wasn't very good at sports. Worse, he wasn't even interested. He did well at school, though."

"What about his mother?"

"Oh, Mark *adored* her. That's one thing he would go on about. But she broke his heart."

"How?"

"She was so beautiful and so artistic, so sensitive and tender, or so he said. She acted with the am drams, read poetry, took him with her to classical concerts. But his father used to mock everything they liked to do, called Mark a mummy's boy. It sounds as if he was a drunken brute. In the end, she couldn't take it any more, so she left them. Mark was only ten. He was devastated. I don't think he ever got over it. Even when he told me about the day she left he was crying."

Annie could hardly believe it. "She left her son with a brutal, drunken father?"

"I know. It sounds terrible. But there was another man in her life, apparently, and he didn't want any children hanging around. They ran off to London. I didn't get the full story, but I know it tore Mark apart. He loved her so much. He couldn't stop loving her. But he hated her for leaving him. And I think after that he found it really hard to trust anyone, to believe that anyone he started to care about wouldn't just up and leave him at a moment's notice. That's why it was so lovely to see him making a life with Laurence. They moved slowly, mind you, but it seemed to be working."

"Go on," said Annie. "What happened after his mother left?"

"Well, Mark was left with his father, who apparently just sank even deeper into the booze and became more and more angry and vicious as time went on. Mark lasted till he was sixteen, then he hit him with an ashtray and ran away from home."

"He hit his father with an ashtray?"

"It was in self-defence. His father beat him regularly, usually with a thick leather belt, Mark said. The kids at school used to tease him and bully him, too, spit on him and call him a sissy. His life was hell. That one time, he told me, it just all came surging up in him and couldn't control himself any more. He lashed out."

"What happened to his father?"

"Mark didn't hang around to find out."

"And he never went back?"

"Never."

Annie took a moment to digest this. She could see why Maria had not wanted to talk about it in front of the others. If Mark Hardcastle had shown an inclination towards violence, poor anger control, then it certainly supported the theory that he had killed Laurence Silbert in some sort of jealous rage and was then overcome with remorse. The blood typing that she and Banks had just found out about also agreed with this view.

On the other hand, there was the redemptive image of the relationship that Maria painted, and which Edwina had touched upon the previous evening: Mark loved Laurence Silbert, had practically moved in with him, was making a life with him. Annie knew well enough that the presence of love doesn't necessarily rule out murder, but she also *wanted* to believe in the positive view of the two of them.

"He did very well for himself, then," Annie said. "But it sounds as if he had a lot of inner demons to overcome."

"And prejudice. Don't forget that. We might think we're living in an enlightened society, but as often as not you'll find it's only skin deep, if that. People might know the politically correct responses and attitudes and trot them out as and when required, but it doesn't mean they believe them, any more than people going to church means they're really religious and believe in God."

"I know what you're saying," said Annie. "Hypocrisy's everywhere. But it doesn't sound as if Mark suffered a great deal from anti-gay prejudice here, at the Eastvale Theatre. I mean, you say that Vernon was uncomfortable, but he didn't actively harass Mark, did he?"

"Oh, no. I didn't mean to imply that. You're right. It was a great place for him to work. And he had such great ideas. He was going to make so many changes."

"What do you mean?"

"The theatre. Well, you know what it's like. It's quite new, and they do the best they can. We get some good acts, but on the theatrical side, well . . . between you and me, the Amateur Dramatic Society and the Amateur Operatic Society aren't exactly the cream of the crop, are they?"

"What do you mean?"

"Well, they're amateur. I'm not saying they're not enthusiastic, even talented, some of them, but it's just a sideline for them, isn't it? With people like Mark and me it's *everything*."

"So what was he going to do?"

"He had a vision of starting the Eastvale Players."

"A rep company?"

"Not strictly speaking, no, but with some similar elements. It would be made up of some of the best local actors along with jobbing actors. The idea was that Eastvale would be their home base, but they'd tour and we'd have reciprocal visits from other groups of players. Mark would be the artistic director and he said he'd put in a good word for me with the board, so I could have the job he's got now. Had. Like he was grooming me. I mean, I've got the qualifications, but it's not just what's on paper that counts, is it?"

"This would be a professional company, then?"

"Oh, yes. Absolutely. They'd be paid and everything."

"And Vernon?"

"He'd do the same as he's doing now."

"But wouldn't he be upset if you became head of set and costumes? You'd be *his* boss then."

"I don't see why it should bother him. Vernon's not ambitious. He'd still be paid, wouldn't he? Nothing would change for him."

How little you know about people, Annie thought. Maria was being rather naive, given that she had mentioned earlier on how Vernon seemed to have problems working with competent women, let alone *for* one. "What about the amateur groups?" she asked.

"They'd do what they were doing before, I suppose, put on plays in the community centre and church halls."

"And Derek Wyman?"

"He'd still be their director."

"I know, but it'd be a bit of step down for him, wouldn't it, after working at the real theatre?"

"But it's not as if it's his life, is it? Or even his real job. He's a school teacher. The theatre's just a hobby for him."

Try and tell that to Derek Wyman, Annie thought, remembering her talk with him that morning. "And who was going to finance this little venture?" she asked.

"Laurence Silbert, Mark's partner, was going to help us get started, then the idea was that it would mostly pay for itself, maybe with a little help from the Arts Council lottery money every once in a while. We were sure the board would go for it. Laurence was on the board, anyway, and he thought he could convince them."

Vernon Ross had never mentioned this, Annie thought. But he wouldn't, would he, if it was something that angered him or made him look bad? "Interesting," she said. "Just how far had all this got?"

"Oh, it was still only in the planning stages," Maria said. "That's another reason this is all so tragic. It couldn't have come at a worse time. Now nothing will change. If I want any sort of future in the theatre, I'm going to have to look for another job. I don't even think I have the heart to stay here without Mark being around."

"You're young," said Annie. "I'm sure you'll do fine. Is there anything else you can tell me?"

"Not really," said Maria. "That was about all I had to say. I can offer you another cup of instant coffee, though, if you want?"

Annie looked at the cracked, stained mug and with the grey-brown sludge in the bottom. "No, thanks," she said, standing up. "I really have to be going. More reports to write. Thanks for your help, anyway."

"Think nothing of it," said Maria, seeing her to the door. "Just don't tell Vernon what I said about him being homophobic and all that. I'm sure he thinks he's the very model of tolerance."

"Don't worry," said Annie. "I won't."

Edwina's statement hung in the silence, ready to burst like a piece of overripe fruit on a tree. Banks had had his suspicions that Silbert was up to *something* clandestine, but he would have guessed that it was sexual, or perhaps even criminal. Not this. Not espionage. He knew that it changed the whole balance and focus of the case, but it was too early to say exactly how. At least he could start by getting as much information out of Edwina as he could, though she seemed immediately to have regretted her little confidence.

"I shouldn't have told you," she said. "It'll only muddy the waters."

"On the contrary," said Banks. "You should have told me the first time we talked to you. It could be important. How long had this been going on?"

"What do you mean?"

"The spying."

"Oh, all his life. Well, ever since he graduated from university." Edwina sighed, sipped her gin and tonic and lit another cigarette. Banks noticed the yellow stains ingrained in the wrinkles of her fingers. "His father, Cedric, worked for military intelligence during the Second World War. I don't think he was very good at it, but at least he survived, and he still had the contacts, people he kept in touch with."

"Did he pursue it as a career?"

"Good Lord, no. Cedric was far too selfish to serve his country for any longer than he had to. He involved himself in a number of ill-advised business ventures. One after the other. I'm afraid, Mr. Banks, that, charming rogue as he was, my late lamented husband wasn't much good at anything. His main interests in life were fast cars and even faster women. We stayed together for appearances' sake, as married couples did then, but God knows how long it would have lasted if it hadn't been for his accident. The woman he was with walked away without a scratch." Edwina gazed directly at Banks. "I always hated her for that, you know," she said. "Not that I wished it had been the other way around. I just wished they had both died."

She must have noticed Banks's look of mingled curiosity and horror because she went on quickly. "Oh, I didn't do it. Really. I didn't fix the brakes or anything. I wouldn't know how. Don't think this is a murder confession. It was just the end of something for me, and it would have been an even more perfect end if his silly little whore had died with him. You can hardly imagine how miserable my existence was then. This was in late October 1956, well before Viva and the swinging sixties. In fact, it was right at the height of the Suez Crisis, and I think Cedric was involved in the oil business then. Suez was the main tanker route, of course. Typical of him to be putting his money in quite the wrong place at the wrong time. Anyway, things were very difficult all around. The only bright spot in my life was Laurence."

Banks noticed the tears in her eyes, but with a supreme effort of will she seemed to absorb them back into the ducts. He could feel the warm sun on his cheek and his shirt was sticking to his back. "The spying," he said gently. "How did that come about?"

"Oh, yes, that. Would you believe it but Dicky Hawkins – an old war colleague of Cedric's – actually *asked* me for permission to recruit Laurence? This was in his last year at Cambridge, 1967. He'd shown a remarkable facility for modern languages – German and Russian in particular – and a keen grasp of contemporary politics. He was good at sports, too. Not for Laurence The Beatles, marijuana and revolution. He was about as dyed-in-the-wool blue as you could get. While other kids were out buying *Sgt. Pepper's Lonely Hearts Club Band*, Laurence was running around the hills playing soldiers with the army cadets and collecting military memorabilia. And he didn't buy it to sell it to hippies on Carnaby Street later, either. Somehow all that just passed Laurence by."

"They must have had a few reservations about taking him on, though," Banks said. "Given your . . . well, your lifestyle at the time."

Edwina laughed. "It was still early days for me, remember, but yes, I was starting to make a name for myself, and I was mixing with a rather heady crowd. Most people think the sixties didn't start until the Summer of Love in 1967, but for those of us who were there at the beginning, in London, at any rate, it was all over by then. Nineteen sixty-three, 1964, 1965. *Those* were the years. All the people I knew wanted to change the world – some from the inside, some through art or Eastern religion, some by violent revolution. But wasn't that a wonderful bonus?"

"You mean Laurence spied on you and your friends?"

"I'm quite sure nothing slipped by him. But Dicky and his pals weren't really interested in all that. They didn't take that scene the least bit seriously. Not here, at any rate. I mean, everyone sang and talked about revolution, but nobody actually did anything. Dicky's lads knew who the real dangers were. And where. It was overseas they were interested in. Mainland Europe was the hotbed of terrorism back then, or starting to be. Germany. France. Italy. Cohn-Bendit, Baader-Meinhof and the Red Army Faction. We had our moments in little old Britain, mostly courtesy of the IRA or the Angry Brigade, but in comparison with the rest of the world we were still something of a sleepy backwater."

"So you told this Dicky Hawkins that it was all right to recruit Laurence?"

"The question was a mere courtesy. It clearly didn't matter what my answer was. Anyway, I can't say I was happy about the idea, but I told him he was welcome to give it a try, that I wasn't Laurence's keeper and wouldn't stand in his way. I wasn't quite sure whether he would succeed or not, but he did. The next thing I knew Laurence was off on training courses for a couple of years, learning how to drive fast in city centres and God knows what else, and I didn't see much of him. After that, he changed."

"In what way?"

"It was as if he'd taken a part of himself, cut it off and hidden it away where no one could ever see it. It's hard to describe, because on the surface he was as charming and funny and witty as ever, but I *knew* that he couldn't tell me most of what he'd been doing since I'd seen him last. And I probably suspected that I didn't want to know, either."

"So what did you do?"

"What could I do? I accepted it and life went on. I'd lost part of my son, but not all of him. Whatever they did to him, they didn't kill his love for his mother."

"Do you know which branch of the intelligence services he worked for?"

"MI6. His facility for languages sealed it. That's why he spent a good part of his time undercover overseas. East Germany, Russia. Czechoslovakia. I remember his first real assignment was in Prague in 1968. I don't know what he was supposed to do there, but I assume he had to mingle with the students and help make things difficult for the Russians, or report on developments there. After that . . . who knows? I do gather that some of the assignments he handled were not without danger."

"He never told you any details?"

"One thing Laurence could do better than anybody I have ever known was keep a secret." She noticed that her glass was almost empty and swirled the dregs around the bottom.

"Want another?" Banks asked, spotting the waiter hovering on the fringes.

"I've had enough."

Banks gestured to the waiter that they didn't require any more drinks. He went away. "Where was Laurence living during this period?"

"Oh, it varied. We're talking about quite a long time, you know. Forty years – 1964 to 2004. Though after the Wall came down, he spent less and less time abroad. He had a beautiful house in Kensington. He lived there for over twenty years, when he was in the country."

"What happened to it?"

"He sold it when the market was good. That was what enabled him to buy the large house in Yorkshire and the little pied-à-terre in Bloomsbury."

"I thought you said he had no business acumen?"

"Well," she said with a hint of a smile, "he did get a lot of help."

"You?"

"He's my only son. Money soon came to mean nothing to me. I don't mean that quite the callous way it sounds, but it just kept on rolling in, and it didn't seem to matter whether I worked hard or not. What was I going to do with it all? It was one thing I could do for him."

"What about the Swiss bank accounts?"

"I wouldn't read too much into all that. I doubt it was a huge amount. Naturally, I don't know the reality of it, but Dicky once let slip that when you do the sort of job Laurence did, there's often loose money around – pay-offs, bribes, hush money, blackmail, God knows what. Most of it's not recorded in any books or bank accounts, and sometimes it's just, well, just *there* at the end of a job, and nobody else knows anything about it. When all one has to look forward to is a government pension, there's naturally a tendency to feather one's nest rather than the alternative."

"Which is?"

"Hand it over to the government, of course."

Banks smiled. "I can certainly understand why he wouldn't want to do that. Anyway, we very much doubt that your son was killed for his money. We're just curious to know how he came to acquire such wealth."

"Well, that's how. Me and his job."

"Did Mark know about his past?"

"I would imagine so. They would have had to have him vetted."

"Others?"

"I very much doubt it. As I said, Laurence could keep a secret. As far as everyone else was concerned, he simply worked for the Foreign Office. A boring old civil servant."

Banks finished his lemon tea. It was cold and bitter. "What are you going to do now?" he asked.

"Hang around here for a couple of days, try to sort out Laurence's affairs, then head back to Longborough. Have you any idea when I might be able to make plans for the funeral?"

"Not yet," said Banks. "It depends on the coroner. There can sometimes be delays if there's likely to be a trial and the defence requests a second post-mortem."

"In this case?"

"I honestly don't know," said Banks. "But I promise I'll keep you informed."

Edwina looked at him, a ghost of a smile playing across her lips. "Just give me back twenty years," she said.

"Why didn't you tell me about Laurence before?" Banks asked.

Edwina looked away. "I don't know. Habit of secrecy? It didn't seem relevant?"

"You know that's not true. You know a hell of a lot more than you're saying. It was the first thing you thought of when we told you what had happened."

"Are you a mind reader, too? Maybe your colleague's better off without you. I'd hate to be living with a man who can read minds."

"Cut the crap, Edwina."

Edwina laughed and swallowed the dregs of her drink. "My, my, you are a direct young man, aren't you?"

"Why didn't you tell me?"

She lowered her head and whispered, "Why are you asking me this when you know what the answer is already?"

"Because I want to hear it from you."

Edwina paused for a moment, then she looked around the court-yard before she leaned forward and grasped the edge of the table with talon-like hands. Her voice was dry and sibilant. "Because I'm not convinced that Laurence had completely retired, and because I'm not sure I trust the people he was working for. There, how's that for you?"

"Thank you," said Banks, standing up to leave.

"There's something else," Edwina said, relaxing in the chair as if she had exhausted all her energy. "If you're going to proceed with this business, then I'd advise you to be very careful indeed and to watch your back. These are not nice men you're dealing with, and they don't play by your rules. Believe me. I know."

"I'm sure you do," said Banks. "And I'll remember that." He shook her limp hand, said goodbye and left her to stare out at the hills, lost in memories.

6

The East Side Estate had been built in the sixties and had steadily declined ever since. Now it could give some of the Leeds or Newcastle estates a run for their money. Certain areas were a wasteland of burned-out cars and abandoned supermarket trolleys, uncontrolled dogs running rife and a population suspicious of all strangers, especially the police. Annie Cabbot had come across plenty of people there who were simply decent folk trying to make an honest living, but she had also met more than her fair share of others – deadbeat, drug-addicted or absentee parents, kids who had had little schooling and no chance of a worthwhile job, who had given up on the future by the age of thirteen or fourteen, searching only for the quick thrill of crystal meth, ecstasy or whatever new concoction or cocktail the amateur chemists had come up with that week. And, increasingly, the oblivion of heroin.

A row of uniformed police officers held the crowds back at about half past ten on Wednesday evening, just after dark. Nobody was pushing or struggling; they were just curious and perhaps a little frightened. One or two troublemakers were trying to whip up a frenzy by shouting insults at the police, and someone even threw a half-brick at the ambulance crew, but the others mostly just ignored them. They were used to this sort of behaviour. The street lights created rainbow halos in the haze, and the ambulance lights spun blue in the humid night air near the mouth of what the locals called "Glue-Sniffers' Ginnel." It was more like "Meth Poppers' Alley" or "Skunk Smokers' Snicket," these days,

Annie thought. Solvents were way out of style as the underprivileged had become more affluent and the drug prices had dropped as cheap stuff flooded the market.

One of the kingpins in the north estate dealing operation, a fifteen-year-old boy called Donny Moore, lay bleeding on a gurney from stab wounds as the paramedics hovered over him. Annie and Winsome had been called to assess the situation for Major Crimes.

"What's the damage?" Annie asked the first paramedic, as they manoeuvred the gurney into the back of the ambulance.

"Hard to tell at this point," he said. "Three stab wounds. Chest, shoulder and abdomen."

"Serious?"

"Stab wounds are always serious. Look," he said, moving closer and lowering his voice, "don't quote me on this, but I think he'll live. Unless we find extensive internal bleeding or damage, it doesn't appear as if the weapon severed any major arteries or sliced up any essential organs."

"Thanks," said Annie. "When will we be able to talk to him?"

"Not until tomorrow at the earliest, depending how soon they manage to stabilize him. Check with the hospital. I have to go now." He climbed into the back of the ambulance, shut the doors and they sped away.

The man who had reported the incident, Benjamin Paxton, paced beside his modest grey Honda, clearly anxious to get away. His wife was still sitting in the car with the windows rolled up and the doors locked. She stared straight ahead, ignoring the crowd and the police activity around her, perhaps in the hope that they would just disappear.

"I did my duty as a citizen," said Paxton, eyeing the crowd anxiously as Annie asked him to tell her what had happened while Winsome took notes. "I reported the incident and waited here till the police arrived, as I was asked to do. Isn't that enough? My wife is really upset. Her nerves are bad. Can't we just go home?"

"Where's home?"

"We're renting a cottage near Lyndgarth."

"So you don't live in the area?"

"God, no! We live in South Shields. This is supposed to be a walking holiday."

Annie glanced around at the dilapidated red-brick terraced houses and the rusted cars on blocks out front. "Not a very good place for that sort of thing, I shouldn't have thought," she said. "Unless you're into urban blight."

"Not *here*. Around Lyndgarth."

"What brought you down here, then?"

"We got lost, that's all. We had dinner at a pub we read about in the guidebook and took the wrong road. We're on our way back to Lyndgarth. We didn't expect to run into this sort of thing in the Yorkshire Dales."

"Which pub?"

"The Angel Inn, Kilnwick."

Annie knew the place. They poured a decent pint of Sam Smith's there. The story made sense. It would have been easy to get lost on the way back through Eastvale from the village of Kilnwick, and end up on the East Side Estate. After all, it wasn't as if there was a wall or a barbed-wire barricade around the place, though sometimes Annie felt there should be, given the number of tourists who complained about getting mugged there.

"Can you tell me exactly what happened, sir?" she asked.

"We were driving down the street and Olivia thought she saw something moving on the waste ground at the end of that passage under the railway lines there. I . . . well, I wasn't going to stop, quite frankly, because I didn't like the look of the place, but it was unmistakable. A person. The white T-shirt. There was somebody on the ground there, rolling, you know, as if he was in pain. At first, of course, we thought it might have been a woman who'd been attacked and raped. There's such a lot of it around these days."

"So you stopped to help?"

"Yes. I got out and . . . well, as soon as I saw the blood I got straight back in the car and phoned the ambulance and police on my mobile."

"Did you see anyone else around?"

Paxton paused. "I'm not really sure. I mean, it was quite dark, even then."

"But?"

"Well, I thought I saw a dark hooded figure running up the passage."

"Dark as in . . . ?" asked Winsome.

"Oh, no," Paxton said. "No. I'm sorry, I didn't mean to imply . . . no. Just that it was in shadow."

"Male or female?" Annie asked.

"Male, I think."

"Could you give a description?"

"I'm afraid not. It *looked* like a largish figure, but I think that might perhaps have been exaggerated by the shadows and the tunnel. But, really, it was too dark to make anything out clearly."

"I understand," said Annie. "Did you see anyone else?"

"There were a couple of people walking up that cross-street, about a hundred yards away. A man walking his dog. And I got the most fleeting impression . . . I don't know, just before we got there and saw the figure on the ground, that there was a group of people sort of scattering."

"Scattering?"

"Yes. All going in different directions, disappearing around corners and down passageways."

"Could you describe any of them?"

"No. They were either in the shadows or wearing those hoods like they do these days so you can't make out their faces."

"Hoodies?"

"Is that what you call them?"

There were two gangs, if you could call them that, operating on the East Side Estate, Annie had learned, one to the north, centred around the two tower blocks, and the other here, to the south, hanging out around "Glue-Sniffers' Ginnel." Though ASBOs abounded on both sides, they had never caused any serious problems outside the odd scrap, graffiti, shoplifting in the Swainsdale Centre and threatening behaviour. But the mood had been changing lately; knives had arrived, baseball bats, and there were rumours of heavier drugs coming in from down south and from Manchester.

Paxton's description of the people he had seen "scattering" from the scene fitted with the kind of uniform the gang members wore, and Donny Moore, the victim, was right up there with them. Most of their names were on file, so they shouldn't be hard to track down. Whether the police would get anything out of them was another matter. People on the East Side Estate were notoriously close-mouthed when it came to talking to the police.

"Did you see anything else?" she asked.

"No," said Paxton. "I went back to the car and waited. The ambulance was quick. The boy was very still. I thought he was dead."

"And you saw no one else?"

"That's right."

"OK," said Annie. "You can go home now. Leave an address with DS Jackman here and we'll be in touch about a formal statement. It's just a formality." She turned to go and talk to the officers on crowd control. The citizens were getting restless for information.

"Thank you," said Paxton.

As Annie walked away, she heard him ask Winsome, "Er . . . do you think you could possibly tell me the way to Lyndgarth?"

Annie had to smile. If you want to know the way, ask a policeman. She turned and winked at Winsome, who took the address and gave Paxton directions.

Since his talk with Edwina Silbert, Banks had found himself thinking a lot about the fact that Laurence Silbert had been a spy. He didn't know very much about the intelligence services, which was probably the way they liked to keep it, but he knew enough to be aware that Silbert might have got up to some pretty nasty business and made himself some serious and lasting enemies. And that was just on his own side.

The whole espionage business had changed a lot since the Cold War, Banks knew, and these days you were more likely to get the head of MI5 sending secret memos to CEOs of banks and oil companies about Chinese Internet espionage than anything else. But it wasn't that long since people had been risking their lives to climb over the Berlin Wall. If Laurence Silbert hadn't travelled much for the past ten or fifteen years, as his mother had indicated, then he had probably done most of his overseas operations before all the major changes in Germany and the former USSR.

Banks decided he might as well read up on it and find out as much as he could, so on Tuesday he had gone to Waterstone's and bought Stephen Dorril's *MI6* and Peter Hennessy's *The Secret State*. He had read Hennessy's *Having It So Good* a few months earlier and liked his style.

On Wednesday evening, Banks was in the kitchen in his jeans and an old T-shirt, putting together an Ikea storage unit, now that his collection of CDs and DVDs was getting close to pre-fire proportions again, cursing because he had got the top on the wrong way around and wasn't sure he could get the back off to fix it without ruining the whole thing.

Stanford's "Symphony No. 2" was playing in the background, and the agitated movement he was listening to at the moment echoed his frustration with Ikea. When he heard the knock at the door and got up off his knees to go and answer it, he realized that he hadn't heard a car. That was odd. His cottage was isolated, even from the village it belonged to, at the end of a long driveway that ended with the beck-side woods beyond, and nobody walked there except the postman. The music hadn't been playing so loudly that he wouldn't have heard.

Banks answered the door and found a slightly stooped man of around sixty, with thinning grey hair and a neat grey moustache, standing there. Though it was a warm evening, and the sun hadn't gone down yet, the man was wearing a light camel overcoat on top of his suit. His shirt was immaculately white, and his tie looked like old school, or old regiment, the emblem of a castle keep dotted between its maroon and yellow stripes.

"Mr. Banks?" he said. "Detective Chief Inspector Banks?"

"Yes."

"I'm sorry to bother you at home. My name is Browne, with an 'e.' Er . . . may I come in?"

"I don't mean to be rude," said Banks, "but I'm busy. What's it about?"

"Laurence Silbert."

Banks paused for a moment, then stood aside and gestured for Mr. Browne to enter. He did so, glanced around the front room and said, "Cosy."

"I was working in the kitchen."

"Ah," said Browne, and followed him through.

The media storage unit lay on the floor, the untreated edge of wood that formed its top plain to see. "You've got the top the wrong way around," said Browne.

Banks grunted. "I know."

Browne grimaced. "Quite a job to put it right. I know. I've done it myself. It's the back that's the problem, you see. Flimsy stuff. I suppose you've already nailed it on?"

"Look, Mr. Browne," said Banks, "much I as appreciate your advice on constructing Ikea products, I do know the problem I'm facing. Please, sit down." He gestured to the bench at the breakfast nook. "Would you like a drink?"

"Thank you," said Browne, wedging himself into the corner. He hadn't taken off his overcoat. "A small whisky and soda wouldn't go amiss."

Banks found a bottle of Bell's in the booze cupboard and added a touch of soda. He poured himself a small Macallan eighteen-year-old with the merest threat of water. He used to be a confirmed Laphroaig drinker, but a bad experience had put him off, and he was only recently starting to enjoy whisky again. He found that he couldn't take the peat, seaweed and iodine taste of the Islay malts any more, but he could handle the richer, more caramel tones of the old Highland malts in small quantities. Mostly, he still stuck to wine or beer, but this seemed an occasion for whisky.

Browne raised his glass as Banks sat down opposite him. "*Slainte*," he said.

"*Slainte*."

"Stanford, eh?" Browne said. "I knew you were a big classical music aficionado, but I would have thought Stanford was very much out of fashion these days."

"If you know that much about me," Banks said, "then you must also know that I've never been very concerned about what's in or out of fashion. It's good music to build storage units to, that's all." As he took a sip of whisky the desire for a cigarette flooded his being. He gritted his teeth and fought it off.

Browne studied the rough edge of the top. "So I see," he said.

"I'm happy to banter about storage units and Charles Villiers Stanford for a while," Banks said, "but you told me you came about Laurence Silbert. Whose interests do you represent?" Banks had a damn good idea of exactly who Browne was, or at least who he worked for, but he wanted to hear it from the horse's mouth, so to speak.

Browne played with his glass, swirling the amber fluid. "I suppose you could say that I represent Her Majesty's government," he said finally, then nodded. "Yes, that would be the best way of looking at it."

"Is there another?"

Browne laughed. "Well, there's always another point of view, isn't there?"

"You're one of Laurence Silbert's old bosses?"

"Please, Mr. Banks. Surely even you must know that MI6 doesn't operate on British soil. Haven't you seen *Spooks*?"

"MI5, then," Banks said. "I stand corrected. I suppose seeing some identification is out of the question?"

"Not at all, dear chap."

Browne took a laminated card out of his wallet. It identified him as Claude F. Browne, Home Office Security. The photo could have been of anyone of Browne's general age and appearance. Banks handed it back. "So what is it you want to tell me?" he asked.

"Tell you?" Browne sipped some more whisky and frowned. "I don't believe I mentioned wanting to tell you anything."

"Then why are you here? If you don't have anything to say relevant to the case under investigation, you're wasting my time."

"Don't be so hasty, Mr. Banks. There's no need to jump to conclusions. We can work together on this."

"Then stop beating about the bush and get on with it."

"I was simply wondering what point your ... er ... investigation has reached."

"I can't tell you that," said Banks. "It's not our policy to discuss active investigations with members of the public."

"Oh, come on. Technically speaking, I'm hardly a member of the *public*. We're on the same side."

"Are we?"

"You know we are. All I'm interested in is whether we are likely to encounter any potentially embarrassing situations, any unpleasantness."

"And how would you define that?"

"Anything that might embarrass the government."

"A trial, for example?"

"Well, I must admit, that wouldn't exactly be a welcome outcome at this juncture. But there's very little likelihood of that happening. No, I was asking if there might be any, shall we say, *fallout* we should be worried about?"

"What did Silbert do?" Banks asked. "Put Strontium 90 in someone's tea?"

"Very funny. I'm afraid I can't tell you what he did," said Browne. "You know I can't. That information is classified, protected by the Official Secrets Act."

Banks leaned back and sipped some Macallan. "Then we're at a bit of an impasse, aren't we? You can't tell me anything and I can't tell you anything."

"Oh dear," said Browne. "I was hoping it wouldn't be like this. Some people get so very agitated at the mere idea of a secret intelligence service. We *are* on the same side, you know. We have the same interests at heart, the protection of the realm. Our methods may differ somewhat, but our ends are the same."

"The difference is," said Banks, "that you work for an organization that believes the ends justify the means. The police try to operate independently of that, of what various governments need to get done on the quiet so they can stay in power."

"That's a very cynical assessment, if I might say so," said Browne. "And I'm more than willing to bet that you've taken a short cut or two in your time to make sure someone you *knew* to be guilty got convicted. But that's by the by. Like you, we're mere civil servants. We also serve a succession of masters."

"Yes, I know. I've seen *Yes, Minister.*"

Browne laughed. "Surprisingly accurate. Did you see the one about the hospital without patients?"

"I remember it," said Banks. "My favourite."

"Wouldn't that be the perfect world? Schools without pupils, universities without students, doctors without patients, police without criminals? Then we could all get on with the *real* work."

"A secret service without spies?"

"Ah, yes, that would be a good one." Browne leaned forward. "We're not so different, you and I, Mr. Banks." He gestured vaguely towards the source of the music, which still played quietly in the background. "We both like Stanford. Elgar, too, perhaps? Vaughan Williams. Britten – though he did have a few dodgy habits and left these shores for the United States at a rather inconvenient time. The Beatles, even, given today's perspective? Oasis? The Arctic Monkeys? I can't say that I have ever listened to any of these, but I know your tastes in music are somewhat eclectic, and they *are* British. Whatever you think of The Beatles, even *they* represented traditional British values in their heyday. The four lovable moptops. And sometimes one has to stand up and fight for those values, you know. Sometimes one even has to do things that go counter to what one would deem right."

"Why? That's what I said about the ends and the means, isn't it? Is that what Silbert did? Was he a government assassin? Did he betray people?"

Browne finished his drink and edged out of his corner to stand by the kitchen door. "You're letting your imagination run away with you. It's not at all what the fiction writers say it is, you know."

"Isn't it? I always thought Ian Fleming aimed for realism."

Browne's lip curled. "I don't think this is a very productive discussion, do you?" he said. "I'm not sure what it is that's got you up on your moral high horse, but we still have a very real world to deal with out there. Take the Litvinenko business. That set us back years with the Russians. Do you know that there are as many Russian spies operating in Britain today as there were at the height of the Cold War? I came here seeking some sort of reassurance that, for the good of the country, your investigation into the death of Laurence Silbert wasn't likely to cause any . . . any further ripples that might embarrass the service or the government. That it could be swiftly and neatly concluded, and you could head off back to Chelsea to see your lovely young girlfriend."

"As far as I remember," said Banks, feeling a chill crawl up his spine, "Lugovoi denied that he had anything to do with murdering Litvinenko. Didn't the Russians claim that MI6 did it?"

Browne chuckled. "I wouldn't have taken you for a fan of conspiracy theories."

"I'm not," said Banks. "One just hears these rumours."

"Well, I hope you realize that's as ridiculous as the claim that MI6 had something to do with the death of Princess Diana," he said. "Not to mention naive. As Sir Richard Dearlove said under oath, MI6 does not sanction or involve itself in assassination. Of course the Russians denied it. Of course they made a counter-accusation. That's what they always do. Andrei Lugovoi left a trail of Polonium 210 that practically glowed in the dark and led the police to his front door."

"The police? Or you?"

"As I said before. We're on the same side."

"Are you telling me that Silbert was somehow connected with Russia? With the Litvinenko affair, even? Do you think there's something about his murder that could stir things up internationally? Is there a terrorist connection? A Russian mafia connection? Or maybe he was involved in the conspiracy over Princess Di's death? Was he a double agent? Is that where the Swiss bank accounts come in?"

Browne stared at Banks and his eyes narrowed, turned hard and cold. "If you can't give me the assurances I seek, then I'll have to seek elsewhere," he said, and turned to leave.

Banks followed him through the living room to the front door. "As far as I know," he said, "it looks like a simple murder-suicide. Happens more often than you think. Silbert's lover, Mark Hardcastle, killed your man, then he killed himself out of grief."

Browne turned. "Then there's no need for a messy investigation, is there, no chance of an awkward trial, of anything uncomfortable slipping out into public view?"

"Well, there probably wasn't," said Banks. "Not until you turned up, that is. I only said that's what it *looks* like."

"Goodnight, Mr. Banks, and grow up," said Browne. He shut the door firmly behind him. Banks didn't hear a car engine start until a few minutes later, far away, at the end of the lane. He went back to the kitchen and stared at the mess he had made of the storage centre. Suddenly he didn't feel like dealing with it any more. Instead, he topped up his whisky, noticing that his hands were shaking a little, and carried it through to the TV room, where he replaced Stanford with Robert Plant and Alison Krauss, cranked up the volume on "Rich Woman" and thought about Sophia. Now, how on earth did Browne know about *her*?

On Thursday morning, Detective Superintendent Gervaise called a meeting in the boardroom, at which Banks, Winsome, Annie and Stefan Nowak were in attendance. Banks had told her about Mr. Browne's visit beforehand, but she didn't seem either particularly surprised or interested.

After tea and coffee had been sorted, everyone turned to Stefan Nowak for his forensic summary. "I suppose I should note first of all," Nowak said, "that I just got the DNA results this morning, and on the evidence of the birthmark on the victim's arm and the DNA comparison with the mother, we can definitely state that the identity of the deceased found at 15 Castleview Heights is Laurence Silbert. According to Dr. Glendenning's post-mortems, Hardcastle died of ligature strangulation – the yellow clothesline he hanged himself with – and Silbert was killed by a series of blows to the head and throat from a hard, flat object – which we've matched to the cricket bat found at the scene. The first blow was to the back of the head, the left side, so he was moving away from his killer at the time."

"That would make sense," Banks said. "Silbert was supposed to be pretty fit, and he might have been able to put up more of a fight if he'd seen it coming."

"But does it fit with the idea of a lover's tiff?" Gervaise asked.

"I don't see why not," said Banks. "People turn away from one another in rows sometimes. Silbert must have misjudged the depth of Hardcastle's rage. And the cricket bat was in its stand right by his side. But it could also fit other possible scenarios."

"We'll leave those for the moment," said Gervaise. She turned to Nowak. "Go on, Stefan."

"At that point we think Mr. Silbert turned as he fell to his knees, and his assailant hit him on the right temple and in the throat, breaking the hyoid bone, crushing the larynx and knocking him backwards into the position in which we found him. It was one, or a combination, of those blows that killed him. After that . . . well, there was a series of other blows. Post-mortem."

"And Mark Hardcastle was left-handed," said Annie.

"Yes," said Nowak, glancing at her. "Given that the only fingerprints we found on the cricket bat belonged to him, I'd hazard a guess that he's your man. As I told you after blood typing earlier this week, the odds were very good that the only blood at the Silbert crime scene belonged to Silbert himself. DNA analysis has now verified that beyond a doubt. The same with the blood we found on Hardcastle's clothes and person. All Silbert's, according to the DNA, with a small amount of Hardcastle's own, most likely caused by scratches as he climbed the tree."

"Well," said Superintendent Gervaise, glancing from one to the other, "I'd say we've got our answer, haven't we? You can't argue with DNA. What about toxicology?"

"Nothing but alcohol in Hardcastle's blood," said Nowak. "Neither Hardcastle nor Silbert was drugged."

"Was there evidence of anyone else at the scene?" Banks asked Nowak.

"Not at the scene specifically, no. Just the usual traces. You know as well I do that there's always evidence of whoever's been in the room – friends, cleaners, dinner guests, relatives, what have you – and strangers a victim may have been in contact with, brushed up against. Trace evidence is all over the place – and don't forget both victims had recently been in big cities – London and Amsterdam. Silbert had also been at Durham Teesside and Schiphol airports, too."

"I think it's time you put your curiosity to bed," said Gervaise to Banks. "Other people had obviously been in the room at one time or another, just as they've been in my room and yours. Silbert and Hardcastle had brushed against people in the street or in a pub or at an airport. That makes sense. You've heard DS Nowak. There was no evidence of any blood at the scene other than Silbert's."

"Begging your pardon, ma'am," Annie said, "but that really doesn't prove anything, does it? I mean, we know that Silbert was beaten to death with a cricket bat, so we'd expect to find *his* blood at the scene, but the fact that we haven't found Hardcastle's simply means that he didn't shed any at the house. And if *he* didn't shed any –"

"– then another killer might not have shed any. Yes, I can see where you're going with this, DI Cabbot," said Gervaise. "But it won't wash. While we do have a lot of evidence to suggest that Mark Hardcastle killed Laurence Silbert and then hanged himself, we have none whatsoever to suggest that someone else did it. No one was seen entering or leaving the house, and no other suspects have suggested themselves. I'm sorry, but it sounds very much like case closed to me."

"But someone from the theatre might have had a motive," Annie said. "I've already reported on the conversation I had with Maria Wolsey. She reckons –"

"Yes, we know all about that," said Gervaise. "Vernon Ross or Derek Wyman might have had a motive if Hardcastle and Silbert got their new players' group together. I read your report."

"And?" said Annie.

"I just don't believe that either Ross or Wyman would have had the ability to kill Silbert and make it look as if Hardcastle had done it."

"Why not?" Annie protested. "They're both theatrical types. They're used to manufacturing illusions."

"Very clever, but I'm sorry, I don't believe it. Surely someone would have seen them coming or going? And then they'd have had to get rid of their bloody clothing. I just don't see it, that's all. What about the CCTV cameras?" Gervaise looked towards Nowak.

"We've checked all the footage, and there's nothing out of the ordinary," he said. "Too many blind spots, for a start, and number fifteen wasn't covered directly."

"It's a very insular neighbourhood," said Banks, "so it doesn't necessarily mean anything that no one was seen entering or leaving. I'll bet you the secret intelligence services are very good at moving about unnoticed, even under surveillance cameras. Maybe the locals would notice a yob or a tramp, or some kid in a hoodie, but not someone who fitted in with the neighbourhood, drove the right car, blended in. I agree with DI Cabbot. Hardcastle could have gone out, and while he was gone, someone else – Ross, Wyman, some spook – could have entered and killed Silbert. When Hardcastle returned and found the body he became distraught and committed suicide. He could have picked up the cricket bat then, after the murder, after the real killer had wiped it clean. Hardcastle would have been in shock. Given that we have a photograph from an unknown source of Laurence Silbert in London with an unknown man, that Silbert was known to be an MI6 agent and that they're pretty good in the dirty tricks department –"

"That's neither here nor there," snapped Gervaise. "I don't suppose you've identified this mystery man in the photograph, have you?"

Banks glanced towards Annie. "We've shown it around to a few people," she said, "but nobody admits to recognizing the unknown man."

"And there were no fingerprints on the memory stick itself," added Nowak.

Gervaise turned to Banks. "Have you learned anything yet about the location in the photographs?"

"No, ma'am," said Banks. "I'm pretty certain the first two were taken in Regent's Park, but I haven't heard back from technical support on the others. Or on Julian Fenner's dodgy phone number, either."

"It seems as if you're getting nowhere fast, doesn't it?" Gervaise commented.

"Look," said Banks, "I don't think it's irrelevant that Silbert was a spook or that Mr. Browne, if that's his real name, came to see me last night and basically told me to lay off. You know as well as I do that we've run into a brick wall every time we've tried to find out anything about Silbert this week. The local police said they'd handle the Bloomsbury pied-à-terre business, and the next day they phoned us back, said they'd checked it out, and all they told us was that there was nothing out of the ordinary. What does that mean, for crying out loud? And can we trust them? Perhaps if there was something out of the ordinary they made it disappear? We all know how Special Branch and MI5 have been pecking away at us from the top lately, picking off tasks and turf for themselves. Terrorism and organized crime have given the government their excuse to do what they've been wanting to do for years anyway, to centralize and consolidate control and power and use us as an enforcement agency for unpopular policies. You've all seen the results when that's happened in other countries. How do we know that the police who checked out Silbert's flat weren't influenced by them in any way? How do we know they weren't Special Branch?"

"Now you're being paranoid," said Gervaise. "Why can't you just accept that it's over?"

"Because I'd like some answers."

Nowak cleared his throat. "There is one more thing," he said. He wouldn't meet Banks's gaze, so Banks knew it was bad news.

"Yes?" said Gervaise.

"Well, perhaps we should have done this earlier, but . . . things being the way they were . . . anyway, we ran Hardcastle's and Silbert's finger-prints through NAFIS and we got a result."

"Go on," said Gervaise.

Nowak still didn't look at Banks. "Well, ma'am, Hardcastle's got form. Eight years ago."

"For what?"

"Er . . . domestic assault. The man he was living with. Apparently Hardcastle flew into a jealous rage and beat him up."

"Serious?"

"Not as bad as it could have been. Apparently he stopped before he did too much damage. Still put the bloke in hospital for a couple of days, though. And got himself a six-month suspended sentence."

Gervaise said nothing for a few moments, then she regarded Banks sternly. "What do you have to say about that, DCI Banks?" she asked.

"You said you ran Silbert's prints through NAFIS, too," Banks said to Nowak. "Find anything there?"

"Nothing," said Nowak. "In fact, as you pointed out, most inquiries connected with Laurence Silbert have run up against a dead end."

"Well, they would, wouldn't they?" said Banks. "He was a spook. He probably didn't even officially exist."

"Well, he certainly doesn't now," said Gervaise. "That's it. I've had enough of this. I'll be talking to the coroner. Case closed." She stood up and slammed her Silbert–Hardcastle folder shut on the table. "DCI Banks, could you stay behind a moment, please?"

When the others had left, Gervaise sat down again and smoothed her skirt. She smiled and gestured for Banks to sit, too. He did.

"I'm sorry we dragged you back from your holiday for this business," she said. "I don't suppose we can always tell when something's going to be a waste of time, can we?"

"It would make out lives easier if we could," said Banks. "But with all due respect, ma'am, I –"

Gervaise put her finger to her lips. "No," she said. "No, no, no, no. This isn't a continuation of the meeting. This isn't about your theories or mine. As I said, that's over. Case closed." She laced her fingers together on the table. "What plans do you have for the next week or so?"

"Nothing in particular," Banks said, surprised at the question. "Sophia's coming up tomorrow. We're going to see *Othello* on Saturday. Lunch with her parents on Sunday. Nothing special."

"Only I was feeling guilty," Gervaise went on. "About dragging you back up here for nothing on the evening of your big dinner party."

Christ, Banks thought, she wasn't going to invite them for *dinner*, was she? "It wasn't for nothing," he said. "But that's all right. Water under the bridge."

"Only I know how much trouble this job can cause a couple sometimes, and it must be really hard when you're just starting out."

"Yes, ma'am." Just where on earth was she going with this? Banks had learned that it was sometimes best not to ask too many questions, just to let Gervaise talk her own way around to her point. If you tried to nail her down too soon, she tended to get slippery.

"I hope we didn't put too much strain on your relationship."

"Not at all."

"And how is the lovely Sophia?"

"Thriving, ma'am."

"Good. Good. Excellent. Well, I suppose you're wondering why you're here?"

"I'll admit to a touch of mild curiosity."

"Ah-hah," said Gervaise. "Ever the wit. Well, seriously, er . . . Alan . . . I'd like to make it up to you. How does that sound?"

Banks swallowed. "Make what up, ma'am?"

"Make up for calling you back, of course. What did you think I was talking about?"

"Thank you," said Banks, "but that's not really necessary. Everything's fine."

"It could always be better, though, couldn't it?"

"I suppose so."

"Right. Well, I'd like you to pick up your holidays where you left off. As of this weekend. A week, shall we say?"

"Next week off?"

"Yes. DI Cabbot and DS Jackman can handle the East Side Estate business. They've got young Harry Potter to help them. He's coming along quite nicely, I think, don't you?"

"He'll be fine," said Banks. "But –"

Gervaise held up her hand. "But me no buts. Please. I insist. No reason you shouldn't enjoy the rest of your leave. You're owed it, after all."

"I know, ma'am, but –"

Gervaise stood up. "I told you. No buts. Now bugger off and enjoy yourself. That's an order."

And with that she walked out of the boardroom and left Banks sitting alone at the long polished table wondering just what the hell was going on.

7

"**S**o what do you think?"

It was hot and crowded in the theatre bar at intermission. Banks felt the sweat prickle on his scalp as he stood by the plate-glass window with Sophia looking out at the evening light on the shops across Market Street. A young couple walked by holding hands, a man walking his dachshund stopped to pick up its leavings in a plastic Co-op bag, three girls in miniskirts wearing Mickey Mouse ears and carrying balloons teetered on high heels on their way to a hen night. Banks glanced at Sophia. She was wearing her hair loose tonight, over her shoulders, and its lustre framed her oval face, the olive skin and dark eyes showing her Greek heritage. Not for the first time in the past few months, he felt like a very lucky man.

"Well," said Sophia, taking a sip of red wine, "it's hardly Olivier, is it?"

"What did you expect?"

"The lighting's good, all that chiaroscuro and whatnot, but I'm not convinced about the whole German Expressionist idea."

"Me neither," said Banks. "I keep expecting Nosferatu to jump out from behind one of those big curved screens and flash his fingernails."

Sophia laughed. "And I still think those Georgians must have been tiny."

"With well-padded bums," Banks added.

"Lord, they must have looked funny waddling around the place. Seriously, though, I *am* enjoying it. It's a long time since I've seen *Othello*.

Come to think of it, it's a long time since I've seen *any* Shakespeare play on stage. It takes me back to my student days."

"You studied Shakespeare?"

"Long and hard."

"We did *Othello* for O-level English."

"Pretty tough when you're only sixteen. It's a very grown-up play."

"Oh, I don't know. I think I could understand jealousy even then." Banks thought of the other night, down in Chelsea: Sophia saying, "*So I've been told.*"

"But that's not what it's really – oops, damn!"

Someone had accidentally jogged Sophia's arm, and she spilled a little red wine on her roll-neck top. Luckily, it was a dark colour.

"Sorry," the man said, turning to her and smiling. "There *is* a bit of a crush in here, isn't there?"

"Good evening, Mr. Wyman," said Banks. "Haven't seen you for a while."

Derek Wyman turned and noticed Banks for the first time. It might have been Banks's imagination, but he sensed a cautious expression come into the man's eyes. Still, that often happened when people found themselves confronted with a policeman. We've all got some guilty secret we don't want the law to know about, Banks thought – a motoring offence, a couple of joints at uni, a touch of adultery, a false income tax return, an adolescent shoplifting spree. They were all the same in the mind of the guilty. He wondered what Wyman's was. A bout of buggery?

"It's all right," Sophia was saying.

"No, let me get some soda," Wyman said. "I insist."

"Really, it's all right. It was only a drop. And you can't even see it now."

Banks wasn't sure he appreciated the way Wyman was staring at Sophia's chest, almost as if he were going to pull out a handkerchief and start dabbing at the barely visible wine stain. "I'm surprised you've got time to mingle with the punters," Banks said. "I would have thought you'd be backstage giving the cast a pep talk."

Wyman laughed. "It's not like a football match, you know. I don't go into the dressing rooms and yell at them during half-time. Anyway, why should I? Do you think they need one? I thought they were doing a fine job." He turned to Sophia again and held his hand out. "I'm Derek Wyman, by the way, director of this modest little effort. I don't believe we've met."

Sophia took his hand. "Sophia Morton," she said. "We were just talking about how much we're enjoying the play."

"Thank you. Inspector Banks, you didn't tell me you had such a charming and beautiful, er . . . companion."

"It just never came up," said Banks. "How are the wife and children?"

"Thriving, thank you, thriving. Look, I must dash. I –"

"Just a minute, while you're here," Banks said, pulling out the photograph that had become a fixture in his pockets. "We haven't been able to track you down during the week. Teaching duties, they told me. Do you recognize the man with Laurence Silbert, or the street where this was taken?"

Wyman studied the photograph and frowned. "No idea," he said. "I don't know why you'd expect that I should." He seemed anxious to get away.

"Just that you were in London with Mark Hardcastle, that's all."

"I've already explained all about that."

"When were you there previously? London."

"About a month ago. It isn't easy to get time off school. Look, I –"

"Do you own a digital camera?"

"Yes."

"What make?"

"It's a Fuji. Why?"

"A computer?"

"Dell desktop. Again, why?"

"Did you have any idea that Laurence Silbert had worked for MI6?"

"Good Lord, no. Of course not. Mark never said. Now I really must go. They'll be starting again in a minute."

"Certainly," said Banks, edging back as much as he could to let Wyman by. "The pep talk, after all?"

Wyman brushed past him without a word.

"That wasn't very nice of you," said Sophia.

"What do you mean?"

"Well, the poor man was only trying to be nice. You didn't have to interrogate him in the theatre bar."

"You call that interrogation? You should see me when I really get going."

"You know what I mean."

"He was flirting."

"So what? Don't you ever flirt?"

"I never really thought about it."

"Of course you do. I've seen you."

"With whom?"

"That blonde Australian barmaid in the wine bar, for one."

"I wasn't flirting. I was just . . . buying drinks."

"Well, it took you an awfully long time, and it seemed to involve a lot of back-and-forth chat and a few saucy smiles. I hardly think you were talking about rugby prospects, or the Ashes."

Banks laughed. "Point taken. I'm sorry. About Wyman, I mean."

"Are you *always* working?"

"These things have a way of getting their hooks into you."

Sophia glanced at Wyman's retreating back. "I think he's rather attractive," she said.

"For crying out loud," said Banks, "he's wearing an earring, and he's got a red bandana tied around his neck."

"Still . . ."

"There's no accounting for taste."

Sophia looked at him. "Obviously not. You don't think he's guilty of something, do you? A murderer?"

"I doubt it," said Banks. "But I wouldn't be surprised if he was mixed up in it somehow."

"Mixed up in what? I thought there was no case. You said they'd dragged you back from London for nothing."

"That's what *they* say," said Banks. "That's how they want it to appear. Only I'm not so sure."

"But officially?"

"The matter has been dropped."

"Good. Let's hope it stays that way."

The bell started ringing to announce that the performance was due to recommence. Banks and Sophia knocked back the rest of their wine and headed for the theatre entrance.

"There's something funny about that new bookcase you've got your CDs in," said Sophia, relaxing on the sofa in Banks's entertainment room while he flipped through his collection, trying to find something suitable for the late hour and the post-*Othello* mood. The rule was that when they were in his house, he chose the music, and when they were in Chelsea, Sophia chose. It seemed to work, for the most part. He enjoyed the music she played and had discovered all kinds of new singers and bands; she was a bit more finicky, and there were things he knew he had to avoid, such as Richard Hawley, Dylan, opera and anything that sounded too folksy, though she was happy to attend the occasional folk concert at the theatre. She said she liked music that pushed at the boundaries. She liked his sixties collection, though, and most of the classical stuff, along with Coltrane, Miles, Monk and Bill Evans, so that usually gave him plenty of leeway. In the end, he decided that Mazzy Star would do nicely and put on *So Tonight That I Might See*. Sophia said nothing, so he assumed that she approved.

"The bookcase, yes," he said. "I messed it up. It's the top. It's the wrong way around. I can't get the damn flimsy back off without ruining it, so I thought I might stain the edge. I just haven't got around to it yet."

Sophia put her hand to her mouth to stifle her laughter.

"What?" Banks said.

"Just the thought of you on your knees with an Allen key in your hand cursing to high heaven."

"Yes, well, that's when Mr. Browne turned up."

"Your mysterious visitor?"

"That's the one."

"Forget him. From what you said, I very much doubt that he'll be back. Surely you've got real criminals to catch, not just spooks and shadows?"

"Plenty," said Banks, thinking of the East Side Estate. "Trouble is, most of them are underage. Anyway, enough of that. Enjoy this evening?"

"It's not over yet, is it?"

"Certainly not." Banks bent over and kissed her. A taste of things to come.

Sophia held her glass out. "I'll have one more glass of that spectacular Amarone before you sit down," she said, "then I think it'll be bedtime."

Banks poured the wine from the bottle on the low table and passed her the glass. "Hungry?" he asked.

"For what? Leftover chicken chow mein?"

"I've got some nice Brie," said Banks. "And a slab of farmhouse Cheddar, extra old."

"No thanks. It's a bit late for me to start eating cheese." Sophia pushed back a stray lock of hair from her cheek. "Actually, I was thinking about the play."

"What about it?" Banks asked, filling his own glass and sitting beside her.

Sophia turned to face him. "Well, what do you think it's about?"

"*Othello*? Oh, jealousy, betrayal, envy, ambition, greed, lust, revenge. The usual stuff of Shakespearean tragedies. All the colours of darkness."

Sophia shook her head. "No. I mean, well, yes, it *is* about all those themes, but there's something else, a subtext, if you like, another level."

"Too deep for me."

Sophia slapped his knee. "No it's not. Listen. Do you remember at the very beginning, when Iago and Rodrigo wake up Desdemona's father and tell him what's going on?"

"Yes," said Banks.

"Well, did you notice anything about the language Iago uses?"

"It's very crude, what you might expect from a soldier, and a racist, something about a black ram tupping a white ewe and making the beast with two backs. Which, by the way –"

"Stop it." She brushed his hand away from her knee. "It's also very powerful language, very visual. It plants images in the hearer's imagination. Remember, he also talks about Desdemona being *covered* by a Barbary horse. That's the language of the stud farm. Just imagine what sort of images it must have put into her father's mind, how unbearable it must have been to think of, to *see*, his daughter that way."

"That's how Iago works," said Banks. "He plants ideas, pictures, lets them grow, bides his time." Banks thought of Sophia saying, "*So I've been told*" and the images it created in *his* mind.

"Exactly. And why?"

"Because he feels slighted in his career and he thinks Othello has slept with his wife."

"So most of the poison comes from within himself. Thwarted ambition, cuckoldry?"

"Yes, but he spews it out on others."

"How?"

"Mostly in words."

"Exactly."

"I know what you mean," Banks said, "but I still don't see what you're getting at."

"Just what we've been saying. That it's a play about the power of language, about the power of words and images to make people *see*, and what they see can drive them insane. Iago uses exactly the same technique on Othello later as he did on Desdemona's father. He presents him with unbearable images of Desdemona's sexual activities with another man. Not just the idea of it, but *images* of it, too. He paints pictures in Othello's mind of Cassio fucking Desdemona. I mean, what real evidence does Othello have of his wife's unfaithfulness?"

"There's the handkerchief," said Banks. "But that was fabricated, planted evidence. Verdi made rather a lot of it, too, mind you. And Scarpio does the same thing with the fan in *Tosca*."

Sophia gave him a look. Verdi and Puccini were out of her purview. "Other than the damn handkerchief?"

"Iago tells him that Cassio had a dream about Desdemona, said things in his sleep. Did things."

"Yes, and that in this dream, he – Cassio – tried to kiss Iago, and get his leg over, thought he *was* Desdemona. Othello's already half crazed with jealousy by then, and bit by bit Iago feeds him even more unbearable images until he's over the edge. And he kills her."

"Of course," Banks said, "you could also argue that Othello did the same thing with Desdemona, too. He even admits to winning her over by telling her stories of battles and exotic places and creatures. Putting pictures in her mind. Cannibals. *Anthropophagi*. Those things with their heads below their shoulders. Real life and soul of the party."

Sophia laughed. "It worked, though, didn't it? It got Desdemona all steamed up. And you're right. Othello benefited by the same technique. As chat-up lines go it can't have been such a bad one. It works both ways. Language can impress and it can inflame the passions. In this case jealousy. Othello must have been a man who was *used* to possessing things. Even women. It's a play about the power of stories, language, imagery."

"For good *or* for evil."

"Yes, I suppose you could say that."

"Well, it *did* get Othello laid."

Mazzy Star were singing "So That I Might See" now, the last track on the CD, with its slow, hypnotic beat and distorted guitars. Banks sipped the last of his rich, silky Amarone. "And in the end," he said, almost to himself, "Iago succeeds in talking Othello into murdering Desdemona and killing himself."

"Yes. What is it, Alan?"

"What?" Banks put his glass down. "Just a glimmer of an idea, that's all." He reached out for her. "But then a better one came along. How would you like to hear a story about a particularly grisly murder I solved once?"

"Well, you certainly know how to get a girl in the mood, don't you?" Sophia said, and came into his arms.

Sunday morning dawned clear and sunny, the sky as blue as the grass was green, a perfect early summer day. After an early breakfast, Banks and Sophia drove to Reeth in the Porsche, parked on the village green, then headed past the Buck Inn and the bakery towards the old school and turned up Skelgate. At the top, they went through the gate on to open moorland and walked high along the dale side below Calver Hill. Curlews soared above the moors making their curious piping calls. There were rabbits everywhere. Families of grouse bobbed in and out of the tufted grass. Once in a while, Banks or Sophia would approach too close to a tewit's ground nest, and the birds would start to panic, twittering and flying nervously back and forth, defending their territory.

Across the dale, on the rising green slopes of the other side, pale grey drystone walls formed the shapes of milk churns and teacups. The path was muddy in places, but the ground was drying quickly.

They turned a sharp bend and walked down a steep curving hill, hand in hand, then passed through the hamlet of Healaugh, the limestone cottages with their tiny, well-tended gardens of bright-coloured flowers, a profusion of red, yellow, purple and blue, where bees droned lazily, and then back along the riverside, under the shade of the alders, to the small swing-bridge, which they crossed, continuing by the riverside, turning on to the old Corpse Way into Grinton.

They didn't see another human being until they passed St. Andrew's church on the lane, where a woman in a red polka-dot summer dress and a white broad-brimmed hat was putting flowers on a grave.

Banks had a sudden and ominous feeling of apprehension, of impending disaster, that this would be the last good day for a long time and that they should go back to Reeth, start the walk again. This time they should make sure that they savoured every moment even more than they had the first time, store up the beauty and tranquillity they felt against future loss and adversity. In days to come, he thought, he might cherish and cling to the memory of that morning. Was it T.S. Eliot who said something about shoring fragments against his ruins? Sophia would know. The feeling passed, and they crossed the road to The Bridge.

Sophia's parents were already waiting in the bar when they got there. They had taken a table by the window, settling themselves on the comfortable padded bench. Banks and Sophia sat in the cushioned chairs opposite them. They could see St. Andrew's across the road through the low bay window. The woman in the hat was just leaving through the lychgate. St. Andrew's, a beautiful, small twelfth-century Norman church with its square tower and arched door porch, was where the Corpse Way ended, Banks remembered.

Before Muker church was built in 1580, St. Andrew's had the only consecrated ground in Upper Swaledale, and people had to carry their dead in large baskets all the way from Muker or Keld sometimes, along the Corpse Way to Grinton. At some of the bridges on the way, there were old flat stones that used to act as resting places, where you could put down the coffin for a few moments and have a bite to eat and a spot of ale. Some of the travellers were no doubt drunk in charge of a coffin when they finally got to Grinton, and perhaps even one or two coffins got dropped along the way. There was a famous book about a journey with a coffin, but he couldn't remember its title. Another question for Sophia. He asked her, and she did know. It was Faulkner's *As I Lay Dying*. Banks made a mental note to read it. She also knew about the T.S. Eliot quote. It was from *The Wasteland*, she told him. She had written a long essay about it at university.

"We haven't ordered yet," said Victor Morton, Sophia's father. "Just got here ourselves. Thought we'd wait for you." He was a fit, slim man in his early seventies, not an ounce of fat on him, and judging by the fancy, adjustable, sprung walking sticks by the table – more like ski poles than walking sticks, Banks thought – the Mortons had also been for a walk before lunch. His face glowed from exercise.

"Let me order," said Banks. "Everyone know what they want?"

The choices were fairly predictable for a Sunday pub lunch – roast beef and Yorkshire pudding for Banks and Victor, roast lamb for Sophia and pork for her mother, Helena. It was easy to see where Sophia got her looks, Banks thought, glancing at Helena as he went to the bar to order. She must have been quite a beauty in her day, and Victor was no doubt a dashing, handsome young diplomatic attaché. Banks wondered how much parental resistance they had encountered. After all, a Greek waitress in a taverna and a young Englishman with a shining civil service career ahead of him . . . It can't have been easy. Banks got along perfectly well with Helena, but he sensed Victor's disapproval and suspicion of him. He wasn't sure whether it was the age difference, his job, his background, the fact that he was divorced, or simple paternal possessiveness, but he felt it.

Sophia helped him carry the drinks back. Beer for Victor and himself, white wine for the women. At least they had some fairly decent wine at The Bridge, and the young landlord was also a keen fisherman who sometimes put his catch of the day on the dinner menu.

Banks sat back and enjoyed his drink through the small talk. Somehow, nothing tasted quite as good as a pint of well-kept ale after a long walk. Victor and Helena had walked west along the river to Marrick Priory and back, and they were also ready for a hearty lunch.

When the food came, they all ate in silence for a few moments, then Victor looked up at Banks and said, "Very good meal. Nasty business, that Hindswell Woods and Castleview Heights. You involved?"

"I was," said Banks, with a sideways glance at Sophia, who had told him exactly what she thought of his pursuit of chimeras.

"Funny chap, Laurence Silbert."

Banks paused, glass halfway to his mouth. "You *knew* him?"

"Well, yes, sort of. Not in Eastvale, of course. Didn't even know he lived there. Years ago. Bonn. Back in the old days, before the Wall came down." He nodded towards Sophia. "She was still at school," he said, then turned back to Banks as if his words were some sort of accusation or challenge.

Banks said nothing.

Sophia looked at her mother, who said something in Greek. The two of them started chatting quietly.

Victor cleared his throat and went on between mouthfuls of food. "Anyway, I say I knew him, but it was more by reputation than anything. I believe I only met him the once, in passing. But you hear things, you know, and things happen. Embassies, consulates, pieces of home ground abroad, a sort of sanctuary, hallowed ground. The soil in the vampire's coffin, so to speak. People come and go at all times of the night and day, in a hell of a state, some of them. I often wondered why we didn't employ a full-time doctor. We didn't like it, of course. All that cloak-and-dagger sort of thing is supposed to be kept out of sight. Not supposed to be happening at all, most of it, but . . . what can you do? A fellow country-man in pain, trouble or danger. And there were documents, of course. Diplomatic bags. Sometimes you couldn't help but see their contents. Why people feel compelled to keep written records of even the worst things they do is beyond me. Lucky for you they do, I suppose, though, isn't it?" He went back to his meal.

"Sometimes," said Banks, who had often wondered the same thing himself. "When did you meet him? Do you remember?"

"Remember? Of course I do. I might be going a bit deaf, but I'm not senile yet, you know."

"I wasn't –"

Victor waved his fork. "It was the eighties, eighty-six or eighty-seven. Not too long before the Wall came down, at any rate. The embassy was in Bonn then, of course, not West Berlin. Bonn was the capital. Interesting times." He lowered his voice and leaned forward conspiratorially as he spoke. He needn't have worried about people overhearing, Banks thought; the pub was noisy with family conversations, laughter and the shrieks of children. There was a man at the bar, Banks had noticed, who looked out of place and kept glancing over, but he wouldn't be able to hear their conversation.

"Were you involved in intelligence work?" Banks asked.

"No, not at all. And I'm not just saying that because it's classified or anything. We weren't all spies, you know. A lot of us were just your basic office workers. Some of us were genuine diplomats, attachés, consuls, vice-consuls, under-secretaries, what have you, not like the Russians. Spies to a man, that lot. No, in fact, I tried to keep as much distance as possible . . . you know. But one hears things, sees things, especially in heady times like those. I mean, we didn't stand around with our heads buried in the sand. There was gossip. The lifeblood of the diplomatic service, I sometimes thought, gossip."

Banks slipped the photograph out of his pocket and discreetly showed it to Victor. "Do you recognize this man with Silbert?" he asked.

Sophia shot him an annoyed glance, but he ignored it and she went back to talking to her mother.

Victor studied the photo and finally shook his head. "No, I've no idea who he is," he said.

Banks hadn't expected him to know, really. It had been a long shot, a reflex action. "Why do you remember Laurence Silbert in particular?" he asked.

"Well, it's funny you should mention that. His reputation, I suppose. I was just thinking about him a little while ago when all that stuff about Litvinenko hit the fan. *Plus ça change* and all that. We used to call Silbert 007 around the office, just between yourselves, you understand. A little joke. Bit of a James Bond. Not the girls, of course, he never was interested in that direction, but he had the good looks, the coldness, ruthlessness, and he was tough as nails."

"He killed people?"

"Oh, I'm sure he did. Not that I ever had any evidence, mind you. Just rumour. But he worked on the other side a lot, so he's bound to have faced danger and . . . well, I'm sure you can imagine what it was like."

"Yes," said Banks.

Sophia kept glancing at Banks sideways, and he could tell from her expression that she was half annoyed and perplexed that he was talking shop with her father, but also pleased that they were getting along, not reduced to the usual monosyllabic grunts that had become their excuse for conversation lately. He turned and smiled at her while Victor was cutting off another lump of Yorkshire pudding, and she smiled back. "Shall I get more drinks?" she asked.

"I'll have one, please," Banks said. "Victor?"

Victor picked up his empty glass. "Please, dear."

Sophia went up to the bar to get another round. Victor watched her go and turned his watery grey eyes back on Banks. He seemed on the verge of saying something about the relationship, but first Banks asked, "How long were you in contact with Silbert?"

Victor gave Banks the kind of look that indicated he might have headed trouble off at the pass for the moment, but there'd be another pass and another opportunity later, and next time he might not be so lucky. "Oh, it wasn't real contact," he said. "As I told you earlier, I had nothing to do with that sort of thing. Then the Wall came down and things changed. We moved to Berlin, for a start – '91, I think that was. Of course, that was never quite the real end of things, as some people think, more the symbolic one, which was the face presented to the world."

"But did you know anything about what Silbert did, what operations he was involved in?"

"No, nothing like that. As I said, I only knew him by reputation, really."

Sophia came back with two of the drinks. Banks apologized for not going to help her with the rest, but she said she was fine and went back to the bar for the other two. They had all finished their meals by now, and Sophia and her mother were studying the list of sweets.

"Now then, Helena, dear," said Victor, "would you be so kind as to pass me the dessert list. I rather fancy something hot and sticky with lashings of custard."

Banks could read an 'end of discussion' signal as well as the next man, and he turned to Sophia, asking her had she enjoyed her meal and was she going to have a sweet. Then Helena joined in, and the conversation moved on to her and Victor's travel plans for the winter, which included a three-month visit to Australia. Soon it was well into the afternoon and the lunchtime crowd was thinning out. Time to go. Sophia had to drive back to London that evening for a full day of work the next day, and Helena and Victor were staying in the Eastvale flat. Banks had no plans other than to stay in and perhaps see about staining the top edge of the bookcase.

Victor said he would drop them off at their car by Reeth village green. As they picked up their bags and walking sticks, Banks couldn't get Victor's story out of his mind. It was a bygone age, or so it seemed to him, the world he knew about only from reading Le Carré and Deighton. But Laurence Silbert had lived it. *James Bond. 007*. He wished Victor had known more details. He remembered the mysterious Mr. Browne telling him that there were still as many Russian spies in the UK as there were during the height of the Cold War, and he wondered who they were spying on, what they wanted to know. Of course, the Americans were still here; there were early-warning systems and satellite spy stations at Fylingdales and Menwith Hill and countless other places. No doubt there were still places like Porton Down, conducting their scientific experiments into germ and chemical warfare. Could Laurence Silbert's, and by extension Mark Hardcastle's, death be in any way connected with that clandestine world? And if so, how on earth could Banks find out about it? It seemed he not only had the secret intelligence services against him in this, but also his own organization. He was convinced that Superintendent Gervaise had been got at.

Before they left through the back door to cross the little beck over to the car park, Banks glanced at the man at the bar reading a *Mail on Sunday* and sipping a half-pint of ale. The man looked up as they passed and gave them a vague smile. Banks went to The Bridge fairly often and knew most of the regulars, but he hadn't seen this man before. Still, that didn't mean much. He didn't know everyone, and lots of tourists dropped in on Sundays, although not usually alone, and not wearing a suit. There was just something about him. He certainly wasn't dressed for walking, and he wasn't one of the local farmers. Banks put it out of his mind as Victor drove them the half-mile or so to Reeth, back to the car, and he and Sophia said goodbye to her parents.

"Well," said Sophia, as she settled into the Porsche. "Even a simple family lunch becomes quite an adventure with you."

"Anything to stop him getting on to the age difference and my job prospects."

"I was doing my A-levels."

"What?"

"The period Dad was talking about. I was at an English school in Bonn doing my A-levels. Sometimes we used to go to Berlin and I'd hang out in underground bars dressed in black, with transvestites and coke dealers, listening to David Bowie and New Order clones."

"What a chequered life you've led."

She gave him an enigmatic smile. "If only you knew the half of it."

They took the minor roads home, winding south over the moors back to Gratly, Cherry Ghost singing "Thirst For Romance" on the iPod. It was an unfenced road crossing high moorland of gorse and heather, beautiful and wild, where the sheep roamed freely. Only the occasional burnt patch of ground and warning signs to watch out for red flags and slow-moving tanks reminded Banks that the landscape they were driving across was part of a vast military training range.

8

Annie Cabbot wondered what Banks wanted with her as she slipped out of the squad room at four o'clock on Monday afternoon and headed for the Horse and Hounds, which had become the secret getaway for anyone who wanted to avoid Superintendent Gervaise and enjoy a contemplative pint during the day. It was almost knocking-off time, anyway, barring any unusual occurrences in the next hour or so.

She was in good spirits, as she had enjoyed a teetotal weekend, got all her washing done, exercised, meditated, worked out at the fitness centre and spent a few pleasant hours in the open air painting a Langstrothdale landscape from a vantage point above Starbotton. The only bad moments had come on Saturday night, when she had had another nightmare about the end of her last case. Fragmented, bloody images and fear made her heart beat fast, and floods of pity and pain surged through her. She had awoken crying, drenched in sweat, at about half past two, and had been unable to get back to sleep. After making a cup of tea, finding some quiet music on the radio and reading her Christina Jones novel for an hour or so, she had felt better and finally drifted off just as the sun was coming up.

Most of her working time had been taken up with the East Side Estate business, especially as it seemed that Superintendent Gervaise had kicked the Silbert–Hardcastle case into touch. Annie had spoken briefly with Donny Moore at the hospital on Friday. His injuries weren't life-threatening, but he claimed to remember nothing of what happened the night he was stabbed, except that he was just innocently walking along the street when a big bloke in a hoodie came at him. Benjamin Paxton, the man who had reported finding Moore, had also mentioned a largish bloke heading away, so it was definitely worth following up. Winsome and Doug Wilson had tracked down most of the gang members they suspected had been present and, as expected, discovered nothing. None of them was particularly large, all of them being just kids, but Winsome had nonetheless noted that one or two of them merited a follow-up visit, and Annie intended to be in on that over the week.

Annie had also gone for a radical haircut on Saturday, swapping her tumbling masses of auburn waves for the short, layered style, She had been shocked to find a few traces of grey, but her hairdresser had applied the right chemicals and, *voilà*, all was well. She wasn't sure whether she liked it yet, worried that it perhaps made her appear older, emphasized the crow's-feet around her eyes, but she also thought it made her seem more professional and businesslike, which couldn't be a bad thing for a detective inspector. She would have to get rid of the jeans and red boots, though, she decided, as they undermined her general air of competent authority. But she liked them. One thing at a time, perhaps.

Anyway, there was no way she was having a pint with Banks, she thought, walking into the dim interior. Whatever he drank, she would have a Britvic orange. As expected, Banks was in the little windowless room, which had become a sort of home from home, a copy of the *Independent* spread on the table in front of him and a full pint of Black Sheep Bitter in his hand.

He folded up the newspaper when he saw her. "Are you alone?" he asked, glancing towards the doorway behind her.

"Of course I am," she said. "Why? Who else are you expecting?"

"You weren't followed?"

"Don't be silly."

"Drink?"

Annie sat down. "Britvic orange, please."

"Sure?"

"Certain."

Banks went to the bar. She got the feeling he went to check out who was in there as much as to buy her a drink. While he was gone, Annie studied the hunting prints on the wall. They weren't bad, if you liked that sort of thing, she thought. At least the horses were quite realistically portrayed, their legs in the right positions, which was a difficult thing to achieve. Usually horses in paintings looked as if they were floating an inch or two above the ground and their legs were about to fall off. She was quite proud of her Langstrothdale landscape, even though there were no horses in it. It was the best thing she'd painted in ages.

Banks came back with her drink and settled down opposite her.

"What's all this about me being alone, not being followed?" Annie asked.

"Oh, it's nothing," Banks replied. "Just that you can't be too careful these days."

"The walls have ears and all that?"

"I always preferred the poster I saw in a book once, the one with the sexy blonde and the two servicemen leering over her."

"Oh?"

"The caption reads, 'Keep mum, she's not so dumb.'"

"Sexist pig."

"Not at all. I like blondes."

"So why all the cloak-and-dagger stuff?"

"Well, Laurence Silbert worked for the Secret Intelligence Service, which is more commonly known as MI6, so it makes sense, doesn't it?"

"You're getting in character? You're playing a game? Alan, I hate to tell you this, but it's over. Superintendent Gervaise said so the other day. You're on leave, remember? Whatever Laurence Silbert did or didn't do for a living, or for his country, it had nothing to do with his death. Mark Hardcastle killed him and then hanged himself. End of story."

"That may be the official version," said Banks, "but I don't I think it's as simple as that."

Annie could hear the drone of voices from the bar. The barmaid laughed at one of her customer's jokes. "All right," she said. "Humour me. Tell me what you do think."

Banks sat back in his chair. "Have you ever read *Othello*?"

"Years ago. At school. Why?"

"Seen the play, the movie?"

"I saw the Laurence Olivier version once, yes. Again, it was years ago. What are you —"

Banks held his hand up. "Bear with me, Annie. Please."

"All right. Go on."

Banks sipped some beer. "What do you remember most about the play?"

"Not much, really. Is this an exam or something?"

"No. Try."

"Well, there was this . . . this Moor called Othello, and he was married to a woman called Desdemona, but he got jealous and killed her, strangled her, then he killed himself."

"What made him jealous?"

"Someone told him she was playing away. Iago told him. That's the one."

"Right," said Banks. "Sophia and I went to see it at the Eastvale Theatre on Saturday night. The one Derek Wyman directed and Mark Hardcastle did the German Expressionist sets for."

"How was it?"

"The sets were crap, a real distraction. It looked like it was taking place in an aircraft hangar or somewhere. Anyway, the acting was pretty decent, and Derek Wyman has a fair grasp of things thespian, anorak or not. But that's not the point. The thing is, Sophia and I were talking later —"

"As you do," said Annie.

Banks glanced at her. "As you do. Anyway," he went on, "she pointed out that the play was more about the power of words and images than it was about jealousy and ambition, and I think she's right."

"That's what an English Lit. degree will do for you. I can't say we ever got much further than ambition and jealousy at my school. Oh, and the animal imagery. I'm sure there was animal imagery."

"There's always animal imagery," Banks agreed. "But if you think about it . . . well, it really makes sense."

"How? What?"

"Let me just get another drink first. Remember, I'm on holiday. You?"

"I'm fine with this." Annie tapped her Britvic orange.

Banks went out to the bar and Annie thought about what he was saying, still not sure where he was going with it. She remembered bits of the Olivier movie, how strange he appeared in blackface, a big fuss about a handkerchief, a young Maggie Smith as Desdemona singing a sad song about a willow tree before Othello strangled her. Frank Finlay's persuasive Iago. Just fragments. Banks came back with another pint and set it next to his paper. Briefly, he tried to explain what Sophia had said about the use of language to create unbearable images in the mind.

"OK," Annie said, "so Sophia says that *Othello*'s about the power of language. She may be right. And being such a manly man, he decides on the flimsiest of evidence that the only sensible thing to do is to strangle his wife?"

"Now's not the moment for feminist criticism of Shakespeare."

"I'm not criticizing. I'm only saying. Besides, I hardly think it's especially feminist to point out that strangling your wife isn't a good thing to do, whether she's had an affair or not."

"Well, Desdemona hadn't. That's the point."

"Alan, this is all very stimulating and all, and I do love a literary discussion late on a Monday afternoon, but I've got ironing to do at home, and I still don't see what this has to do with us."

"It got me to thinking about the case," Banks went on. "About Hardcastle and Silbert. Everyone's pretty much decided how it happened, that no one else came in and bumped off Silbert while Hardcastle went out for a while, right?"

"That's the general thinking."

"Even though you pointed out that the absence of anyone else's blood other than Silbert's didn't really prove anything."

"Right," Annie agreed.

Banks leaned back against the wainscoting, pint in his hand. "I think you're right," he said. "I don't think Hardcastle did go out, and I don't think anyone else *did* break in. I think it happened exactly as Superintendent Gervaise and Stefan say it did. Mark Hardcastle beat Silbert to death with a cricket bat then went out and hanged himself out of grief."

"So you agree with the official version?"

"Yes. But I also don't think that's the point."

"What is, then?"

"Listen." Banks leaned forward, elbows on the table. Annie saw that gleam in his piercing blue eyes she always associated with his fanciful theories. Sometimes, though, she had to admit they were right, or at least close to the mark. "Hardcastle and Silbert hadn't been together all that long. Six months. By all accounts, they were very much an item, practically living together and everything, but the relationship was probably still a bit fragile, vulnerable, and we know Mark Hardcastle was a bit insecure. Both kept other apartments, for one thing. Also, as Stefan pointed out, Hardcastle's got form for assaulting a previous lover, which may mean he has a short fuse. What if someone worked on him?"

"Worked on him? On Hardcastle?"

"Yes," said Banks. "The way Iago worked on Othello. Plagued him with unbearable images of Silbert's infidelity."

"So you're saying that someone goaded him into this?"

"I'm saying it's a possibility. But it would be bloody difficult to prove. It's a hands-off murder. Murder from a distance, murder by proxy."

"I very much doubt that you could call it murder, even if it did happen that way," said Annie. "And I'm not saying it did."

"We'll find a charge."

"But why do it?"

"To get rid of Silbert."

"Any idea who would want to do that?"

Banks sipped his beer. "Well," he said, "I suppose there are plenty of possibilities. Means and opportunity are obvious and easy enough, so it would simply be a matter of looking for a motive. Anyone who was close to one or both of them could have done it, really. Vernon Ross or Derek Wyman, for example. Maybe even Maria Wolsey had a motive she's not telling us about. Or Carol, Wyman's wife. There's no shortage of possibilities." Banks paused. "On the other hand, it could have been someone acting for one of the secret intelligence services. It's just the sort of labyrinthine plot they would come up with."

"Oh, come off it, Alan! That's a bit far-fetched, even for you, don't you think?"

"Not necessarily."

"But hold on a minute," Annie argued. "You're raising an awful lot of new questions here."

"Like what?"

"Who could have known that Silbert was seeing someone else, if he was?"

"It doesn't matter. If information like that hadn't somehow fallen or been dropped into the killer's lap, he could have made it up. After all, that's what Iago did."

"And how could someone know about Hardcastle's previous form for violence against a partner?"

"Maybe he let something slip? Or more likely the people we're talking about have methods of getting hold of whatever information they want, access to criminal records. I'll bet you MI6 knew about it. They must have vetted Hardcastle. It obviously didn't merit his being put on their out-of-bounds list – it didn't make him a security risk – but I'll also bet they tipped Silbert off, too, told him to be careful, even though he'd officially retired."

"Well, he wasn't, was he? OK, let's assume all that, for the sake of argument. One big stumbling block still remains: how could they ever be certain of the result?"

Banks scratched his temple. "Well, you do have a point there," he said. "I've been grappling with that one. The previous form helps a bit. Hardcastle had a temper and it had got him into trouble with a partner before."

"Even so, there could be no guarantee he'd do it again. Maybe he'd learned his lesson? Taken anger management courses?"

"Push someone far enough and their reactions can be pretty predictable. People resort to patterns they've followed in the past. You see it all the time with abusers and the abused."

"I know," said Annie, "but I'm still saying that as a method of murder, it sucks."

"But why?"

"Because you can't be sure of the outcome, that's why. Even if Hardcastle had turned violent, even if that was predictable, he hadn't killed before, and there could be no guarantee that he would kill this time. Maybe they'd have just had a row? There's no way anyone could depend on Hardcastle killing Silbert. I'm sorry, Alan, but it just doesn't make sense. It's not reliable."

"I know that," said Banks. "I can see it's a flawed hypothesis. But I still think there are a lot of possibilities in it."

"OK, then," said Annie. "Let's assume for a moment that you're right. Then we come to the matter of motive. Why?"

Banks sat back on the bench and sipped some beer before he spoke. "Well, that one's easy enough," he said. "It goes right along with who."

"I know what you're going to say, but they just don't –"

"Hear me out, Annie. This Mr. Browne with an 'e' comes to see me and basically tells me to lay off, that any publicity around the Silbert murder would be unwelcome. What sort of disaster? I ask myself. Now we know Silbert was an MI6 agent, and Lord knows what sort of things he got up to in his heyday. What if the government wanted rid of him for some reason? Say he knew too much? Something embarrassing? I'm sure they've got a good line in psych ops. They could have made *certain* that the information about Hardcastle's temper resulted in the violence it did. I'll bet they even have drugs that don't show up on our tox screens."

"But they'd only act if he threatened to talk, surely? And we've no evidence at all that he would do that. Most don't."

"Well, let's say he posed some sort of threat to them. I don't know what."

"That's an awful lot to suppose."

"Hypothetically, then."

"OK, hypothetically he posed a threat to MI6."

"Or the present government's credibility."

"Assuming they have any left."

"Anyway, it's not as far fetched as it sounds, Annie. These things come home to roost. The people who were your enemies yesterday are your friends today, and vice versa. Often the only thing you have in common to start with is that you're united against the same enemy. Alliances change and shift with the wind. Germany. Russia. Iraq. Iran. The bloody United States, for all I know. They've been known to get up to some pretty dirty tricks in their time. Maybe he's got evidence they engineered terrorist attacks in the UK to keep us involved in the Iraq war. God knows. I wouldn't put anything past any of them. Silbert could have been involved in something that shows MI6 and the government, or a friendly foreign government, in a bad light, and with an election coming up . . ."

"They'd stop at nothing?"

"Something like that. If they felt threatened."

"I still don't swallow it, Alan. OK, so the victim was a spook. When these people want rid of one another don't they just stab them with poisoned umbrellas or slip them a dose of radioactive isotopes or something? They'd hardly be likely to go for such an unreliable method as trying to make Silbert's partner jealous and just hope he does their job for them when they could just . . . well, push him under a bus or off a bridge."

Banks sighed. "I know there are holes in the theory," he said. "It's still a work in progress."

Banks seemed deflated, but Annie didn't feel like giving any quarter. "Holes big enough to drive a lorry through," she said. "And not much progress, if you ask me. No, I'm sorry, but it won't wash."

"Have you been got at?" Banks asked. "Has someone got to you?"

Annie's jaw dropped. "I resent that. Have I ever given you any reason to think I wasn't on your side? Don't we play devil's advocate as a matter of course? How could you even *think* something like that?"

"I'm sorry," said Banks. "It's just . . . maybe I am getting paranoid. But look what happened. The day after Mr. Browne's visit, Madame Gervaise says the case is closed, keeps me back after school and tells me to take some leave owing. Are you saying she hasn't been got at? And I thought someone was watching me in the pub at lunchtime yesterday. I've also had the feeling I'm being followed more than once over the past few days, since Browne's visit. Things are just . . . confusing."

"Well, *I* haven't been got at. I'm just trying to take a rational perspective on some of the half-baked ideas you're coming up with."

"Can't you at least accept that it *might* have happened the way I just outlined it?"

"I don't know that I can. OK, I'll accept your *Othello* theory up to a point. Maybe somebody *did* stir things up for Hardcastle. Or perhaps it's true that Silbert was having an affair. Maybe he was being blackmailed, then he told the blackmailer to bugger off, so the evidence – the memory stick – found its way to Hardcastle. But I don't swallow all this spook junk, and I don't care what you say about people falling back on previous patterns of behaviour. *Nobody could have predicted what would happen next.* That's the point I'm making."

"We've found no evidence of blackmail."

"We've found no evidence of *anything* except what forensics bears out and we all agree happened."

"That's not true. We *know* that Silbert worked for MI6. We found the memory stick and the business card with a non-existent phone number on it. Mr. Browne came to visit me and made veiled threats. He also knew a hell of a lot about me and my private life, by the way. And now everyone suddenly wants to drop the whole thing like a hot potato. I don't call that nothing. And I don't like it, Annie. I don't like it one bit."

"Put like that, I suppose you've got a point." Annie gave a little shudder. "I wish you wouldn't put it like that, though. You're giving me the creeps."

"So you believe me?"

"Are you really being watched?"

"Since Browne's visit, yes, I think so."

"Well, I suppose you did send him away with a flea in his ear. They must think you're something of a loose cannon."

"My lot in life. He even knew about Sophia."

"Who? Browne?"

"Uh-huh. He knows where she lives. He said something about my lovely young girlfriend in Chelsea."

Annie said nothing for a moment. Somehow, the image of Sophia's loveliness got in the way of their discussion and distracted her, rolled over her as a wave of dissatisfaction with herself, her appearance, weight, everything. Christ, Banks hadn't even noticed her new haircut. "So what are you going to do?" she asked.

"I still need a couple more pieces of information," he said, "then I think I'll head down to London, check out the pied-à-terre for myself, dig around, see what I can find. I've still got a few days' holiday left."

"Chasing shadows, tilting at windmills?"

"Maybe."

"I don't know," said Annie. "It could be dangerous. I mean, if you're right and they *are* capable of knocking off one of their own, they'd hardly think twice about killing a troublesome copper, would they?"

"Thank you," said Banks. "I was trying not to think of that. Anyway, what else can I do?. Madame Gervaise has closed the case. I can't expect any support there."

"I think you should be very careful."

"I will be."

"I suppose you'll be staying with Sophia?"

"I suppose so. If she's not too busy."

"Oh, I doubt that she'll be too busy for you. It's just that . . ."

"What?"

"Well, are you sure you should be involving her in all this?"

"I'm not involving her. Besides, they already know about her."

"Listen to me. You've got me as paranoid as you are."

"That's all right. It's good of you to be concerned. But don't worry, I'll be careful. For both me and for Sophia."

Annie tore the edge of her beer mat. "So what is it you want from me?"

"I'd like you to be my eyes and ears up here while I'm away. Keep a lookout for anything out of the ordinary. And if I need any information, some record tracked down, another chat with Wyman and the theatre people, fingerprints running through NAFIS, any sort of information I can't get my hands on, I'd like to think you might help."

"Might as well be hanged for a sheep as a lamb," said Annie. "Anything else, while you're at it?"

"Yes. Could you water the plants?"

Annie gave him a playful slap on the arm.

"I'll be buying a new mobile as soon as I get down there," Banks went on. "Pay-as-you-go, throwaway. I don't want my calls traced, or any troublesome records kept. I'll ring you and let you know the number."

Annie frowned at him. "Just like a criminal. You're really serious about all this cloak-and-dagger stuff, aren't you?"

"You didn't meet Mr. Browne. And there is one more thing before we go."

"What's that?"

"What did you do with your hair? It looks great."

Though Banks didn't expect any further visits from the likes of Mr. Browne, he nonetheless kept his door locked, his alarm system on and his ears open at home that evening. After a Marks and Spencer's beef Wellington washed down with a 1998 Eight Songs Shiraz, he decided to give up on the bookcase and settled down to an evening of reading Stephen Dorril's book about MI6 instead, with John Garth's cello concertos playing quietly in the background.

The fire had been over three years ago now, Banks recalled, and the rebuilding, with the addition of the entertainment room, extra bedroom and conservatory, had taken the best part of a year. Whereas before he had lived in the kitchen or the front room, occasionally enjoying an evening on the wall by the beck, now he spent most of his time in the conservatory at the back, or in the entertainment room, using the kitchen mostly just for cooking – reheating might be more accurate – and the front room as a kind of study-cum-sitting-room, where he kept his computer and a couple of battered old armchairs.

MI6's history proved to be complicated and tough going, hardly like the Ian Fleming novels he remembered from his teenage years, and after a couple of chapters, he wasn't sure that he knew much more than when he had started. He also still had many chapters to cover to get up to the present.

The phone rang shortly after half past nine. It was Sophia. He was more than relieved for the interruption to his reading.

"Have a good journey home?" Banks asked.

"Fine. Just boring, that's all. I think I'll take the train next time. At least then I can get some work done, read a book."

He thought he could hear her stifle a yawn. "Tired?"

"Long day. Sometimes I think there's just one arts festival after another."

"How's your week shaping up?"

"More of the same. Lots of interviews. A fifteen-minute special on that new James Bond book by Sebastian Faulks, including a few comments from Daniel Craig."

"Don't tell me he's coming to the studio."

"Don't be an idiot. But a girl can always dream."

"Hmph. Right. Well, I hope to be down your way in a day or so.

Could you maybe give Daniel Craig a raincheck and find a bit of room in your busy schedule to fit me in? I can easily get a hotel, if . . ."

"Of course I can, you idiot. You've got a key. Just come over. It'll be great to see you. If nothing else, at least we'll get to sleep together."

Banks couldn't help but feel his heart glow at the genuine pleasure in her voice. "Great," he said. "I'll ring you."

"Is this trip business or pure holiday?" Sophia asked.

"A bit of both, really."

"What sort of business?"

"Same as before."

"That murder-suicide case?"

"That's the one."

"The one you were quizzing Dad about, with all the spooks?"

"One of the victims was an MI6 agent, that's all."

"How exciting," Sophia said. "With you around, who needs Daniel Craig? Bye."

Always, at the end of their telephone conversations, Banks was tempted to say, "I love you," but he never did. The "L" word hadn't been mentioned yet, and Banks got the feeling that it would only cause complications at this point. Best go on as they were and see where it led. There would be plenty of time for the "L" word later.

He kept the receiver off the hook a bit longer than usual, listening for that telltale click he had heard so often in spy movies. Then he chastised himself for being such a fool and put it down. With today's technology, you could be damn sure a tapped telephone didn't go "click" when you finished your call. Besides, he should have thought of that earlier. He would have to be more careful what he said over the landline from now on.

When he hung up, he turned on the TV for *News at Ten*, poured another glass of wine and sat through the usual lead stories on greedy politicians caught out in a lie, the upcoming American elections, a twelve-year-old schoolgirl gone missing on her way home from a piano lesson, famine and genocide in Africa, war in the Middle East and more trouble in the old Russian satellite states. His ears pricked up at a story about the Hardcastle–Silbert case.

The presenter stopped short of announcing that Silbert had worked for MI6, mentioning only that he was Edwina Silbert's son, had been a civil servant, and that he lived with his gay lover, "the son of a West Yorkshire coal miner," in an "exclusive" and "desirable" residential suburb of Eastvale. Typical southern nonsense, Banks thought. As if Eastvale had *suburbs*. And Barnsley was in *South* Yorkshire, not West.

The segment also stressed that police were satisfied it was a tragic case of murder-suicide, and then went on to refer to details of similar cases over the past twenty years or so. At the end, Detective Superintendent Gervaise appeared on camera looking cool and professional. She assured the interviewer that police were satisfied with the result, stressing that forensic evidence had borne out their investigative conclusions, and there was no need for a further investigation which, she added, would simply cause more grief to the victims' families. That was a load of bollocks, Banks thought. Edwina Silbert could probably take anything the world could throw at her, and Hardcastle had no family except for the distant aunt. Well, whoever had assembled that story had certainly done a good job of assuring anyone who might be concerned that the business was well and truly over. We'll see about that, Banks thought.

After the news, Banks had a sudden urge to play some more music and go outside to sit on the wall beside Gratly Beck. This was one of his favourite spots, and though he didn't use it as often as he had before, he still enjoyed it when the weather was warm enough. His cottage was isolated, a little quiet music in the background wouldn't disturb anyone, even late at night, and it was only half past ten. Before he could pick out a CD from his collection, though, the phone rang again. Thinking it might be Sophia phoning back, Banks hurried and picked it up.

"DCI Banks?"

"Yes?"

"It's Ravi here. Ravi Kapesh. Technical support."

"Oh, Ravi. Sorry, I didn't recognize your voice. It's a bit late for you to be working, isn't it?"

"Par for the course these days if you want to get ahead," said Ravi, resignedly. "Anyway, I think I might have something for you. You did say to ring as soon as I got anything."

Banks felt a tremor of excitement. "Absolutely. You do? Great. Look, I know this might sound a bit weird, but can you call me back on my mobile?"

"Sure. When?"

"Right now. I'm hanging up." Banks didn't know whether his mobile was likely to be any more secure than his landline, but he thought it might be. He would certainly feel a lot less paranoid when he bought the pay-as-you-go. The thing to remember about mobiles was to keep them switched off when you were not using them, or you might as well stand on the top of the nearest large building and shout, "I'm here!"

"OK, let's have it," he said, when the mobile rang.

"I managed to enhance the street sign enough to get a name," said Ravi. "It's a little street called Charles Lane, off the High Street in St. John's Wood. Ring any bells?"

"None," said Banks, "but I can't say I expected it to. Thanks a lot, Ravi. Got a house number, by the way?"

"Sorry. You can tell which one it is from the photo, though."

"Of course. Ravi, you're a genius."

"Think nothing of it. Talk to you later."

"What about the phone number? Fenner."

"Drew a blank. According to all my efforts it's a number that has never actually been assigned in the UK. Maybe it's for somewhere overseas?"

"Maybe," said Banks, "but I doubt it. Just one more favour."

"Yes?"

"Keep it under your hat, OK?"

"OK," said Ravi. "My lips are sealed."

"Bye." Banks hung up. St. John's Wood. Well, that was a posh enough area. So what was it all about? Banks wondered. A fancy man? One of Kate Moss's parties? Sharing government secrets with the other side? Whatever it was, Banks felt sure it had contributed to Silbert's death.

Perhaps Annie was right in that the Iago method couldn't absolutely guarantee results, but if it didn't work, the would-be assassin could always try something a bit more direct. If it did work, however, he would have brought off the perfect murder. A murder that wasn't even murder. And it fitted right in with the sneaky, underhanded way he assumed the secret intelligence services of the world worked. After all, who else outside the realm of fiction would think of using a poisoned umbrella or a radioactive isotope to murder someone?

Banks picked up his wine, put on Sigur Rós's *Hvarf-Heim*, then took his drink outside, leaving the door open just a crack so that he could hear the strange, eerie music. It harmonized naturally with the sounds of the beck making its way down the terraced falls, and the occasional cry of a night bird fitted right in, almost as if the band had planned for it and left a little space between their notes.

It was after sunset, but there was a still a glow deep in the cloudless western sky, dark orange and indigo. Banks could smell warm grass and manure mingled with something sweet, perhaps flowers that only opened at night. A horse whinnied in a distant field. The stone he sat on was still warm and he could see the lights of Helmthorpe between the trees, down at the bottom of the dale, the outline of the square church tower with its odd round turret, dark and heavy against the sky. Low on the western horizon, he could see a planet he took to be Venus, and higher up, towards the north, a red dot he guessed was Mars. Above, the constellations were beginning to become visible. Banks had never been very good at recognizing them. The Big Dipper and Orion were about as far as he got, and he couldn't see either of them tonight.

Banks thought he heard a sound from the woods, and he had the odd sensation that he was being watched. It was probably just some nocturnal animal, he told himself. After all, he heard them often enough. There were badgers, for a start, and plenty of rabbits around. He mustn't allow his nerves to get the better of him. He shook off the feeling and sipped some more wine. The water flowed on, here a touch of silver as it parted around a rock, there a flurry of white foam as it dropped a few feet over a terrace, and everywhere else shifting shades of inky blue or black.

It was nothing, Banks told himself, nothing but the wind through the trees, the Icelandic music and a sheep, frightened by a fox or a dog, baaing on a distant dale side. Like the streets, the woods were full of shadows and whispers. After a while, even those sounds ended and he was left in a silence so profound that all he could hear was his own heart beating.

9

The fine weather had brought out the crowds by Wednesday lunchtime, and Oxford Street was clogged with the usual array of tourists, street vendors, shop workers and people handing out free newspapers or flyers for language schools. Banks had taken an indirect route to Sophia's, and he was pretty sure he hadn't been followed. Not that it mattered. Mr. Browne had known enough about Sophia that he probably knew where she lived, too.

Banks had parked his car – a Porsche was hardly out of place on a Chelsea side street, and he was also legal there – left his grip in the house, then headed for Tottenham Court Road by tube, stopping to look in a shop window every now and then on his way. There were so many people about, however, that he had soon realized there was no way he would be able to pick out someone who was following him, especially if that person was well trained. Still, it was best to make caution a habit.

He had worked undercover for varying periods in his twenties and early thirties, and he still had the rudiments of tradecraft. Also, one of the reasons he had done so well at it was that most people said he didn't look like a policeman, whatever that meant. He could blend into the crowd. In Waterstone's, just down the street from the tube station, he bought an AA street atlas of London, not willing to trust his memory of years ago, then he called in at one of the electronics shops on Tottenham Court Road and bought a cheap pay-as-you-go mobile, paying cash. It would need charging, but that could wait. He wasn't in a hurry. He had spent all of Tuesday gathering most of the information he needed to do what he had to do in London.

As he walked along Tottenham Court Road he was overwhelmed by memories. The last time he had been in London doing detective work alone had been when his brother Roy disappeared. And look how that had turned out. Still, there was no reason to think that this time would turn into a disaster of similar proportions. He put his hand in his pocket and touched the spare key to Laurence Silbert's Bloomsbury flat. He knew it was the right one because it had been marked with a neat label when he found it in Silbert's study drawer that morning. He remembered seeing it when he and Annie had carried out their search. The rules called for Banks to get in touch with the local police, let them know he was on their patch and ask permission to visit the house, but he hadn't done so. No sense inviting trouble, he thought, or paperwork. Besides, he was on holiday.

He turned up Montague Place between the British Museum and the university and found the street he wanted off Marchmont Street on the other side of Russell Square. He was in the heart of the University of London campus area, now, and there was also a healthy sprinkling of hotels for the tourists. The house he wanted was divided into flats, and the names under the brass number plates still listed an L. Silbert in flat 3A. It was a well-appointed building, not dingy student accommodation, as he would have expected for a man in Silbert's position, with dark, thick-pile carpets, flocked wallpaper, framed Constable prints on the landings and a hovering scent of lavender air-freshener.

Banks didn't know what he hoped to find, if anything, after the local police, and probably Special Branch, had turned over the place. He certainly didn't expect any messages scrawled in invisible ink or written in a fiendish code. He told himself that he was there more to get a feel for Silbert and his London habitat than anything else.

The door opened into a tiny vestibule, hardly bigger than a hall cupboard. There were three doors leading off, and a quick check told him that the one on the left led to a small bedroom, just big enough for a double bed, wardrobe and chest of drawers, the one on the right to a bathroom – new-looking walk-in shower, toilet and pedestal washbasin, toothpaste, shaving cream, Old Spice – and the door straight ahead led to the living room with a tiny kitchenette. At least there was a view of sorts through the small sash window, though the narrow alley it looked out upon wasn't much, and the buildings opposite blocked out most of the sunlight.

Banks started in the bedroom. The blue-and-white duvet was ruffled and the pillows creased. On impulse, Banks pulled the duvet back. The linen sheets were clean but wrinkled, as if someone had slept on them. More than likely, Mark Hardcastle *had* spent his night in London here.

There were a few clothes in the wardrobe, sports jackets, suits, shirts, ties, a dinner jacket and trousers, designer jeans creased along the seam. Banks found nothing hidden on the top or at the back of the wardrobe.

A copy of Conrad's *Nostromo* lay on the chest of drawers beside the bed, a bookmark sticking out about three-quarters of the way through. The top drawer held folded polo shirts, T-shirts and underwear. In the middle drawer was an assortment of odds and ends, like his grandmother's old rummage box, which he used to love to root around in when he visited her. None of it was of much interest: old theatre ticket stubs and programs, restaurant and taxi receipts from earlier in the year, a tarnished cigarette lighter that didn't work, a few cheap ballpoint pens. No diary or journal. No scraps of paper with telephone numbers on them. No business cards. The room had a spartan feel about it, as if it were somewhere merely functional, a place to sleep. The restaurant receipts also indicated an appetite for fine food: Lindsay House, Arbutus, L'Autre Pied, The Connaught, J. Sheekey and The Ivy. Clearly more Silbert's than Hardcastle's tastes. The bottom drawer held only socks and underwear, nothing sinister hidden among them.

The bathroom held no surprises and the living room was every bit as neat and clean as the bedroom. There was a small bookcase, mostly Conrad, Waugh and Camus mixed in with a few Bernard Cornwells and George MacDonald Frasers and a selection of hardcover biographies and histories, along with the latest Wisden. The small stack of CDs showed a predilection for Bach, Mozart and Haydn, and the magazines in the rack dealt mostly with antiques and foreign affairs. In the kitchenette Banks found an empty Bell's whisky bottle and an unwashed glass.

He heard a noise outside and stood by the window watching the street cleaners go by at the end of the alley. There was nothing here for him, he decided. Either Silbert had been very careful or someone had already removed anything of interest.

Just before Banks left, he picked up the phone and pressed redial. Nothing happened. He tried again and got the same result. In the end, he concluded that it either wasn't working properly or it had been erased – most likely, he thought, the latter.

Annie took Winsome with her when she went to talk to Nicky Haskell after school that Wednesday afternoon. She felt more than one pair of eyes following them as she drove along the winding main street of the estate past some of the better-kept terrace houses to Metcalfe House. Building permission had been granted for only two tower blocks, despite the bribes and kickbacks to local politicians that were rumoured to have exchanged hands. If Eastvale had been within the boundaries of the Yorkshire Dales National Park, there would have been no question of such atrocities going up, even though they were only ten storeys high, but it wasn't. And the maisonettes that surrounded the tower blocks were just as ugly.

Metcalfe House had one of the worst reputations of any area on the estate, and Nicky Haskell had a reputation for antisocial behaviour. He was already on an Anti-Social Behaviour Order, which was more of a badge of honour in his circles than the stigma or hindrance to criminal activity it was supposed to be.

One problem was that often the parents hadn't been around much while their kids were growing up – not because they went to work, but because they were doing much the same then as their children were doing now. They were often products of the Thatcher generation, who had also had no jobs and no hope for the future, a legacy they passed on to their children. Nobody had come along with that magic fix to reverse the damage. Like the homeless, they were far easier to ignore, and the drugs that helped to take the pain away demonized them even more in the eyes of society.

Nicky Haskell's parents were a good case in point, as Annie well knew. His mother worked on the check-out at the local Asda, and his father, well known to the police, had been on the dole since the day he got thrown out of school for threatening his physics teacher with a knife. The idle days and hours that followed had left him plenty of time to indulge in his favourite pastimes, which included drinking enormous quantities of strong lager, smoking crack cocaine and having the occasional night at the dogs just to get rid of any surplus money he might have left over from his other habits. It was up to his wife to supply food, clothing, rent and utilities on her own meagre salary.

It was soon clear that they needn't have waited for the end of the school day.

"Got a cold, haven't I?" Nicky said, turning his back after letting them in. His lank greasy hair hung over his collar.

"I don't know," said Annie, walking into the living room behind him. "Do you? You sound fine to me."

Nicky sank back on the battered sofa he had probably been lying on all day, if the empty crisp packets, loud television, overflowing ashtray and can of lager were any indication. The room smelled as if he had been lying in it all day, too. The apple hadn't fallen too far from the tree in this instance. "My throat hurts," he said. "And I ache all over."

"Want me to call a doctor?"

"Nah. Doctors ain't no use." He popped a couple of pills and drank Carlsberg Special Brew from the can. The pills could have been paracetamol or codeine for all Annie knew, or cared. Well, she did care, but she wasn't out to change society single-handedly, or even with Winsome's help; she was on yet another futile mission for information. He reached for his cigarettes.

"I'd prefer it if you didn't drink or smoke in our presence," Annie said. "You're underage."

Haskell smirked and put the cigarettes down next to the lager. "I can wait till you're gone," he said.

"Mind if I turn the TV down?" Annie asked.

"Knock yourself out."

"*Midsomer Murders*," Annie said as she turned the volume down. "I wouldn't have thought that was your cup of tea."

"It's soothing, innit? Like watching paint dry."

Annie quite liked the program. It was so far removed from the real policing she did that she accepted it for what it was and didn't even find herself looking for mistakes. She and Winsome sat on hard-backed wooden chairs because they didn't like the look of the dark stains on the armchairs. "Where are your parents?" Annie asked.

"Mum's at work, Dad's at the pub."

Technically, as he was only fifteen, they weren't supposed to talk to him unless his parents were present. But as he wasn't a suspect – Donny was one of his crew, after all – and most likely he wasn't going to say anything that would prove useful in court, Annie wasn't inclined to worry much about that.

"We been over all this before," said Haskell before she even started. "It's over and done with. Time to move on."

"Someone stabbed Donny," Annie reminded him, "and we're not moving on until we find out who it was."

"Well, I don't know, do I? It wasn't me. Donny's me mate. He's all right, isn't he?"

"He'll be fine. And we know he's your mate. That's why we thought you might be able to help us. You were there."

"Says who?"

"Nicky, we know there was a scuffle down by the waste ground next to Glue-sniffers' Ginnel. We know you and your mates, including Donny Moore, hang out there every night, and we know you wouldn't take kindly to Jackie Binns and his crew muscling in, but we know they did. So why don't you make it easy for us and just tell us what happened?"

Haskell said nothing. He might have thought he was looking tough and defiant, Annie thought, but she could see the slight trembling of fear in his lower lip. She turned to Winsome, who picked up the questioning. Sometimes just a simple change of voice and tone worked wonders.

"What did you see that night, Nicky?" Winsome asked.

"I didn't see nothing, did I? It was dark."

"So you *were* there?"

"I might have been somewhere around," Haskell mumbled. "It don't mean I saw nothing, though."

"What are you scared of, Nicky?"

"Nothing. I ain't scared of nothing."

"Did you see a large hooded figure running away, down the ginnel?"

"I didn't see nothing."

"If this is some sort of code of honour about not ratting on –"

"There's no code of honour, bitch. I told you. I ain't scared of nobody or nothing. I didn't see nothing. Why you don't just chill and leave me alone?"

Winsome glanced at Annie and shrugged. It was, as expected, a wasted journey. "I don't know why you bother to come talking to me, anyway," Haskell went on, a sneer of a smile on his face. "Didn't you ought to be spending your time taking care of those rich folk up on Castleview Heights? They be the ones doing all the murder and shit these days, seems to me."

"Cut it with the black talk, Nicky," said Winsome. "It's really bad." Like so many of his contemporaries, Haskell occasionally tried to emulate the black urban street talk he heard on television programs like *The Wire*, but it came out sounding lame. Haskell glared at her for a moment. He obviously thought he'd got it down pat.

"What do you know about Castleview Heights?" Annie asked.

"You'd be surprised," Haskell said, tapping the side of his nose and grinning.

"If you know something, you should tell me."

"You were asking me about Donny Moore and that rat-shit Jackie Binns. Not about them two shirt-lifters on the Heights. What you got for me?"

"What if I were to ask you about Laurence Silbert and Mark Hardcastle?" Annie went on, intrigued by his mention of Castleview Heights. "What would you be able to tell me about them?"

"That Mark Hardcastle, he the one from the theatre?"

"That's right," Annie said.

"I been there. School trip, few months ago." Nicky eyed them defiantly, as if to say that he *did* go to school sometimes, when the mood took him. "Some Shakespeare shit, man. *Macbeth*. Dudes speaking some weird kind of language and offing each other all over the stage. That man, that Hardcastle, he answered some questions after the play, him and Mr. Wyman and some of the actors. That's why I knew him when I saw him the next time."

"Where did you see him the next time?" Annie asked.

"Like I say, what you got for me, bitch?"

Annie felt like saying that she had a clip around the ear for him if he didn't tell her what he knew, but he would only laugh at that, and she wouldn't do it. Instead, she reached for her purse and pulled out a five-pound note.

Nicky laughed. "You must be joking. That don't buy shit these days."

Annie put the five back and pulled out a ten.

"Now we talking the same language, bitch," said Nicky, and reached for it.

Annie held it away from him, so that he would have to get up from his supine position on the sofa to grab it. As she expected, he didn't. "Two things before you get this," she went on. "First, you tell me where and when you saw Mark Hardcastle for the second time."

Haskell nodded.

"And second," Annie went on, "you don't ever call me bitch again. In fact, you don't even use the word in my presence. Got it?"

Haskell glowered, then grinned. "OK. You got a deal, sweetheart."

Annie sighed. "Go on."

"Was in a pub, wasn't it?"

"You were in a pub? But you're only fifteen."

Haskell laughed. "They don't care about that in the Red Rooster. Long as you pay the price."

"The Red Rooster? Down in Medburn?"

"That's the one."

Medburn was a village about two miles south of Eastvale, a short distance off the York Road, not far from the A1. A cluster of ugly stone-clad houses around an overgrown green, it had never been likely to win the prettiest village of the year award. And there was one pub, the Red Rooster. They had live music on weekends and karaoke on Thursdays, and the place had a bit of a reputation for rowdiness and the occasional fight, not to mention the sale of drugs. A lot of young squaddies from Catterick camp went there.

"When was this?" Annie asked.

"Dunno. Maybe two or three weeks before he offed himself. I saw his picture on the TV the other day."

"What was he doing when you saw him?"

"That's why I noticed him, man. I was just there having a quiet drink, you know, chillin' with my friends, and then I see my fucking teacher and I have to get out real fast, or he'll bring all kinda shit down on me."

Annie frowned. "Your teacher?"

"Yeah. Mr. Wyman."

"Let me get this straight," Annie said. "You saw Derek Wyman in the Red Rooster with Mark Hardcastle a short time before Hardcastle died?"

"That right. You got it." He glanced at Winsome. "Hey, give the lady a prize."

Winsome returned Annie's puzzled gaze. "What were they doing there?" Annie went on.

"Well, they wasn't doing none of that fag stuff, if you know what I mean."

"So what *were* they doing?"

"They just talkin', man. Just chillin' and talkin'."

"Did you see Mr. Wyman hand Mr. Hardcastle anything?"

"Huh?"

"Did anything change hands?"

"Nope. This wasn't no drug deal, if that's what you're thinking."

"Were they looking at anything? Photographs or anything?"

"You mean, like *porn*? Pictures of men sucking –"

"Nicky!"

"No, they didn't look at nothing."

"And there was nothing on the table in front of them?"

"Only drinks."

"Was anyone else with them? Or did anyone join them?"

"Nope. Can I have my money?"

Annie gave him the ten-pound note. She wanted to ask whether there was anything intimate about the meeting, any closeness, touching, whispering, meaningful glances, that sort of thing, but somehow she didn't think Nicky would be attuned to such subtleties. She asked anyway.

"Don't know nothing about all that stuff, man," Nicky said, "but that Hardcastle, he sure seemed angry. Mr. Wyman had to cool him down."

"Wyman was calming Hardcastle down?"

"That's what I said."

"Did they appear to be arguing?"

"Arguing? No. Like they were friends."

"What happened next?"

"I got out of there, man. Before he saw me. Like I say, he can bring a whole lotta shit down on a person, Mr. Wyman can."

"Is there anything else you can tell me?"

Haskell waved the ten-pound note at her. "Your time up on this, b –"

Annie spoke between her teeth, with menacing softness. "I said is there anything else?"

Haskell held his hands up. "No. Hey. Chill out. They nothing else. Like I tole you, Mr. Wyman say something and got Hardcastle all upset, then he chill him right down again."

"Mr. Wyman upset Hardcastle in the first place?"

"The way it look. They was in the other bar, in the corner, so I figure they couldn't see me, but I wasn't taking no chances. Plenty more places a dude can get a drink. Why'd I want to hang around a pub where my teacher's drinking, man?"

"Nicky, the amount of time you spend in school, he probably wouldn't even recognize you," Annie said.

"Ain't no need to be sarcastic. I do OK."

Annie couldn't help but laugh, and Winsome laughed with her. They got up to leave. "Back to Jackie Binns and Donny Moore for a minute," Annie said at the door. "Are you certain you can't tell us anything more about what happened? Did you see Jackie Binns with a knife?"

"Jackie didn't have no knife, man. You got that all wrong. Jackie didn't do nothing. I didn't see nothing." He turned away, picked up the remote control and turned up the volume on the television set. "Now look what you gone and done," he said. "You made me lose track of the plot."

The lifts hadn't been working when Annie and Winsome had arrived, and they still weren't working. It was easier to walk down the six floors, but the smell wasn't any better. Mostly stale urine with the occasional piece of rotting garbage dropped by a dog or a cat. Around the third floor, a hooded figure came bounding up the stairs and brushed past them, bumping into Annie's shoulder, knocking her against the wall, and carried on without a word of apology. She caught her breath and checked her handbag and pockets. All there. Even so, she was relieved to get down to the concrete forecourt. She had felt claustrophobic in the stairwell.

When they got to the car, Annie was happy to find it was still there, and that nobody had spray-painted PIG BITCH all over it. She checked her watch. Going on for five o'clock. "How about a drink?" she suggested to Winsome. "On me. The sun's over the yardarm and I could certainly do with one."

"Anything to get the taste of this place out of my mouth."

"How about the Red Rooster?" Annie suggested.

As it was such a beautiful evening, Banks decided to follow Silbert's route and walk through Regent's Park to St. John's Wood. He took the paved path that parallelled the Outer Circle around the southern edge. There were quite a few people around, mostly joggers and dog-walkers. Soon he came to the bench in the photograph, where Silbert had met his boyfriend, or contact, just opposite the boating lake. Soon after, the path ended, and Banks had to walk past the Central Mosque to Park Road and make his way through the crowds on their way to evening prayers. At the roundabout opposite the little church, he turned on to Prince Albert Road and crossed over to walk past the prep school and the graveyard along St. John's Wood High Street. The houses opposite were the kind that always made him think of confectionery, about six storeys high, red brick with lots of fancy white trim like piping on cakes. Some of the flats had balconies with hanging baskets and big plant pots.

He found Charles Lane easily enough. It was a secluded mews, in some ways similar to where his brother had lived in South Kensington. From the High Street, it looked as if it ended at a brick house with a narrow white façade, but that was just a little dog-leg, and beyond it he came to the garages in the photograph. He realized this must have been the corner where the photograph was taken from, using the zoom function. The door he wanted was between the sixth and seventh garages along, one painted in green panels with white outlines, the other white panels with black edging.

Before anyone could find his loitering suspicious, he strolled down the street, crossed to the house in question and looked up at the lace-covered windows above a window box full of red and purple flowers.

There was only one thing to do. Banks took a deep breath, walked up to the front door and rang the bell.

After about thirty seconds, a woman opened the door on its chain and peered at him. He reached for his warrant card. She made him hold it close to the narrow strip that was all the chain allowed and spent so long studying it that he thought she wasn't going to let him in. Eventually the door closed, and when it opened again, it opened all the way, revealing a neatly dressed grey-haired woman in her sixties.

"You're a long way from home, young man," she said to Banks. "You'd better come in and explain yourself over a cup of tea."

She led him upstairs into a small, cluttered living room above the garage, where a man of about her age sat in an armchair reading the newspaper. He was wearing a suit, complete with white shirt and tie. It certainly wasn't the man in the photograph. He carried on reading his newspaper.

"It's a policeman," the woman said to him. "A detective."

"I'm sorry to intrude like this," Banks said, feeling awkward.

"No matter," said the woman. "I'm Mrs. Townsend, by the way. You can call me Edith. And this is my husband Lester."

Lester Townsend looked over his newspaper and grunted a quick hello. He seemed less than happy to be disturbed.

"Pleased to meet you," said Banks.

"Sit yourself down," Edith said. "I'll just go and put the kettle on. Lester, put your newspaper away. It's rude to sit and read when we have guests."

Edith left the room and Townsend put his newspaper down, staring suspiciously at Banks before reaching for a pipe on the table beside him, stuffing it with shag and lighting it. "What is it we can do for you?" he asked.

Banks sat down. "Can we wait until your wife comes back with the tea?" he said. "I'd like to talk to both of you."

Townsend grunted around his pipe. For a moment, Banks thought he was going to pick up his newspaper again, but he just sat there smoking contemplatively and staring at a spot high on the wall until his wife returned with the tea tray.

"It's not often we get visitors," she said. "Is it, darling?"

"Hardly ever," her husband said, glaring at Banks. "Especially policemen."

Banks was beginning to feel as if he had wandered on to a film set, a period piece of some kind. Everything about the place was old fashioned, from the flower-patterned wallpaper to the brass andirons. Even the teacups with their tiny handles and gold rims reminded him of something from his grandmother's china cabinet. Yet these people were only perhaps ten or fifteen years older than he was.

"I really am sorry for interrupting your evening," Banks said, balancing the teacup and saucer on his lap, "but this address has come up in connection with a case I'm working on back up in North Yorkshire." It wasn't entirely true, but the Townsends weren't to know that Superintendent Gervaise had technically closed down the investigation and sent him packing.

"How exciting," said Edith. "In what way?"

"How long have you lived here?" Banks asked.

"Ever since we were married," her husband answered. "Since 1963."

"Do you ever rent out the house?"

"What a strange question," Edith said. "No, we don't."

"Do you rent any of the rooms or floors as flats or bedsits?"

"No. It's our home. Why would we rent any of it?"

"Some people do, that's all. To help pay the bills."

"We can manage all that perfectly well by ourselves."

"Have you been on holiday recently?"

"We took a Caribbean cruise last winter."

"Other than that?" Banks asked.

"Not recently, no."

"Did you use a house-sitter?"

"If you must know, our daughter drops by every other day and takes care of the place. She lives in West Kilburn. It's not far away."

"You haven't been away even for only a few days over the past month or so?"

"No," she repeated. "Lester still works in the City. He should have retired by now, but they say they still need him."

"What do you do, Mr. Townsend?" Banks asked.

"Insurance."

"Might anyone else have, er . . . used your house, say while you were out one evening?"

"Not to our knowledge," Edith answered. "And we don't often go out in the evenings. The streets are so unsafe these days."

Banks put his cup and saucer down on the table beside his chair and reached for the envelope in his pocket. He took out the photographs and passed them first to Edith. "Do you recognize either of these men?" he asked.

Edith examined the photos closely and passed them to her husband. "No," she said. "Should I?"

"You, sir?" Banks asked Townsend.

"Never seen either of them in my life," he answered, handing the photographs back to Banks.

"You do agree it's this house, don't you?" Banks asked.

Edith took the photo of the mews again. "Well, it certainly *looks* like it," she said. "But it can't be, can it?"

She passed the photograph to Townsend, who turned to Banks without even re-examining it and said, "What on earth is all this about? What's going on? You come barging in here upsetting my wife and showing us pictures of . . . of I don't know what, asking damn fool questions."

"I'm sorry, sir," Banks said. "I didn't mean to upset anyone. One of our technical support officers was able to enhance the digital photograph I just showed you and read the street name. This street name. As you can see, the façade in the photo also resembles this house."

"Couldn't he have made a mistake?" Townsend said, handing the photo back. "After all, it's a bit blurred and you can't just blindly trust *all* modern technology, can you?"

"Mistakes *are* made," said Banks. "But not this time. I don't think so."

Townsend stuck his chin out. "Then what's your explanation? Eh?"

Banks put the photographs back, pocketed the envelope and stood up to leave. "I don't know, sir," he said. "But one way or another I'll get to the bottom of it."

"I'm sorry we couldn't be any more help," said Edith, as she led Banks to the door.

"Have you ever heard of a man called Julian Fenner?" Banks asked. "He works in import-export?"

"No."

"Laurence Silbert? Mark Hardcastle?"

"No, I'm afraid neither of those names is familiar to me."

"Do you have a son?" he asked. "Or any other close relative who might have used the house in your absence?"

"Only our daughter."

"Can I talk to her?"

"She's away. In America. Besides, I can't imagine why she would think of coming here unless we asked her to. I'm afraid you'll have to leave now. We can't tell you anything more."

And Banks found himself standing on the doorstep scratching his head.

Medburn wasn't much more than a post-war council estate with a pub, a post office and a garage clustered around the green, where bored kids lounged on the benches and scared off the few old folks who lived there. The Red Rooster had been there first, at the crossroads, and it was one of those ugly sprawling pubs with a brick-and-tile façade that had recently been taken over by a brewery chain and tarted up a bit – long bar, family area, children's playroom, a bouncy castle in the garden, brass numbers screwed to every table to make ordering easier. And woe betide you if you forgot to memorize your table number, or it somehow slipped your mind as you waited at the bar for half an hour to order, because there was usually only one person serving, and it always seemed to be his first day on the job.

This one's name tag identified him as Liam, and he didn't look old enough to be serving in a pub, Annie thought. Luckily, the place wasn't too busy around half past five on a Wednesday afternoon – it was the kind of pub that filled up later, after dinner, when the quizzes or karaoke started, and at lunchtimes on weekends – and Annie and Winsome had no trouble getting a couple of drinks and putting in an order for table 17.

"What's all this about, then?" Winsome asked, when they had sat down with their drinks, a pint of Abbots for Annie and a glass of red wine for Winsome. "I thought the Hardcastle business was over and done with. Superintendent Gervaise said so."

"It is," said Annie. "At least officially." She debated whether to bring Winsome into the picture. If she could trust anyone else in Western Area HQ it was Winsome, but she could also be prudish and judgemental, and she tended to do things by the book. In the end, Annie decided to tell her. Even if Winsome disapproved, at least she wouldn't go telling Superintendent Gervaise or anyone else.

"So DCI Banks is in London following this up instead of on leave?" Winsome said, when Annie had finished.

"Yes. Well, he's officially on leave, but . . . he's not convinced."

"And you?"

"Let's just say I'm intrigued."

"And he wants you to help at this end?"

"Yes."

"And that's why we're sitting in this lame pub in this gross village waiting for some naff food."

Annie smiled. "That's just about it, Winsome."

Winsome muttered something underneath her breath.

"Want in?" said Annie.

"It looks like I'm stuck here, doesn't it? You've got the car keys."

"There's always the bus."

"On the hour every hour. It's five past six."

"Maybe it'll be late."

Winsome held her palm up. "OK, all right, enough. I'm in. Unless you start crossing any serious boundaries."

"What's a serious boundary?"

"One you know when you're crossing it."

Annie paused for a moment as their food arrived, a beefburger and chips for Winsome and a mini pizza margherita for her. She had strayed a little from her vegetarianism lately, to the extent of a coq au vin and a potted-meat sandwich, and she was also finding that she enjoyed fish more often. On the whole, though, she tried to stick with it, and she certainly avoided red meat. Their knives and forks were tightly wrapped in serviettes and bound with a strip of blue paper. Winsome's knife was spotty from the dishwasher.

"What did you think of Nicky Haskell this time?" Annie asked as she picked up a slice of pizza with her fingers. "It's the third time we've talked to him and his story hasn't changed. The mention of Hardcastle was the only thing that was new, and he'd obviously just seen something about that on TV by accident. Not a newspaper reader, our Nicky, I shouldn't think."

"Dunno," said Winsome around a mouthful of burger. "It was on the news the night before last. Silbert and Hardcastle." She dabbed her lips with the serviette. "Did he seem more scared to you this time?"

"He did," Annie said. "And he's such a tough nut himself that I really don't think he'd be scared of Jackie Binns or his mates."

"So what is it? Misguided loyalty? Instinctive aversion to talking to the police?"

"Could be either or both," Annie said. "Could also be that there's someone else involved he really is scared of."

"Now *that* would be an interesting development."

They ate their meals in silence for a while, each pausing occasionally for a sip of beer or wine. When she had finished about half her pizza, Annie asked casually, "Got a boyfriend at the moment, Winsome?"

"Nah. There was . . . there was someone from technical support, but . . . you know, his hours, my hours, it just didn't work out."

"Do you want a husband and kids?"

"No way. Least, not for a while, not for a long while. Why? Do you?"

"Sometimes I think so," Annie said, "and then sometimes I feel the same way you do. Trouble is, my biological clock's running out and yours has got plenty of time left on it."

"What about . . . you know, DCI Banks?"

Annie rolled her eyes. "He's in lo-ove." Then she burst into laughter.

Winsome laughed, too. "Seriously, what you were saying before, this theory of his about the Hardcastle–Silbert case."

Annie pushed her plate aside with one piece of pizza left and sipped some Abbots. "Yes? What about it?"

"Does DCI Banks really think the Secret Intelligence Service goaded Hardcastle into bumping off Silbert for some sort of twisted government reason?"

"Well," said Annie, "government reasoning is usually pretty twisted, as far as I can make out, so he might not be far wrong. Thing is, though, what Nicky Haskell just told us changes things."

"It does? Derek Wyman?"

"Well, yes. Think about it. If it was Wyman did the Iago bit, then it might have had nothing to do with Silbert's MI6 career. Wyman probably didn't even know about that, or even if he did it wouldn't necessarily mean anything to him. He did, however, stand to lose his position at the theatre if Hardcastle got his new group of players going, and Hardcastle needed Silbert's backing for that."

"So why did this Browne bloke pay DCI Banks a visit, then?"

"A fishing expedition? To see which way the wind was blowing? They're bound to be interested if it was one of their blokes who copped it, aren't they? Silbert probably knew all kinds of secrets, did all sorts of nefarious deeds that could bring down the government, or at least bring about a clean sweep of the intelligence services, if they became public. They're running scared. Only natural they'd be worried about that, isn't it?"

"But you're saying that may not be the case?"

"I don't know," Annie said. "But if Wyman was the one stirred up the hornet's nest, the motivation might be a whole other thing, mightn't it? Professional jealousy. Revenge."

"Maybe they were having a . . . you know . . . a thing?"

Annie smiled. Winsome always got flustered when she was dealing with matters of sex, whether gay or straight. "You mean an affair? A fling?"

"Yeah," said Winsome.

"Who?"

"Wyman and Hardcastle. They were in London together. They were the ones Nicky Haskell said he saw having a tête-à-tête."

"He said he thought he saw Wyman say something to upset Hardcastle, then calm him down. It certainly fits."

"They could have met on some other occasion, later, and Wyman could have given him the memory stick."

"But when and how did Wyman get the photos? He couldn't be running off down to London every time Silbert did. How did he know where to look, for a start?"

"I don't know," said Winsome. "It's just a theory. Wyman was pally with Hardcastle, and he knew about the flat in London. Maybe he followed Silbert from there on one of his trips and got lucky?"

"And if Wyman and Hardcastle were having an affair, why would Wyman want Hardcastle to kill Silbert and then himself?"

"He wouldn't," said Winsome. "I mean, maybe that wasn't what he wanted. Maybe he just wanted to turn Hardcastle against Silbert so he could have him for himself."

"It's possible," Annie said. "And it backfired. Hardcastle overreacted. Finished?"

Winsome drained her glass. "Uh-huh."

"Let's have a quick word with young Liam on the way out. He doesn't seem too busy."

Liam turned when Annie called his name and immediately assumed a serious air when she showed him her warrant card. At the same time, he could hardly stop looking at Winsome. He was a gawky lad with slightly bulging eyes, rubbery lips and a gentle face, so easily flustered and excited, so easy to read, he wouldn't have made a good poker player.

"How long have you been here?" Annie asked.

"Since ten this morning."

"No. I mean how long have you been working here?"

"That. Oh, sorry. Stupid of me. Six months. Give or take."

"So it's not your first day."

"Come again?"

"Never mind." Annie fanned out photographs of Hardcastle and Silbert on the bar. She didn't have one of Wyman and regretted that now. Maybe she could get one later. "Recognize either of these men?"

Liam pointed immediately to the photograph of Mark Hardcastle. "I recognize him. He's the bloke who hanged himself in Hindswell Woods. Nasty business. I used to like to go for walks there. Peaceful sort of place." He gave Winsome a soulful look. "You know, somewhere you can *really* just be alone and think. But now . . . well, it's ruined, isn't it? Spoiled."

"Sorry about that," Annie said. "Bloody inconsiderate, most suicides." Liam opened his mouth to say something else, but Annie bulldozed on. "Anyway, have you ever seen him in here?"

"He's been here once or twice, yes."

"Recently?"

"Past month or so."

"How often would you say?"

"Dunno. Two or three times."

"Alone or with someone else?"

Liam blushed. "With another bloke." Liam gave a quick description that resembled Derek Wyman. "I know what it said about them, on the telly, like, but this isn't that sort of a pub. We don't have any of that sort of shenanigans here." He gave Winsome a manly glance, as if to establish his hetero-cred. "Nothing went on."

"That's good to know," said Annie. "So they just sat there and stared into space?"

"No. I don't mean that. No. They had a drink or two, never more than two, and mostly they just talked."

"Ever see them arguing?"

"No. But the bloke that hanged himself, Hardcastle, got a bit agitated once or twice and the other bloke had to calm him down."

It was exactly as Nicky Haskell had described them on the one occasion he had seen Wyman and Hardcastle together. "Did they ever come with anyone else, or did anyone else join them?" Annie asked.

"Not when I was on duty."

"Did you ever see anything change hands?"

Liam drew himself up to his full height behind the bar, which was still a few inches less than Winsome's. "Never. That's something else we don't countenance in this establishment. Drugs." He spat out the word.

"I'm impressed," said Winsome, and Liam blushed.

"Ever see them looking at photos?" Annie asked, hoping she wasn't going to get the same response she had from Haskell.

"No," Liam said. "But they were usually here when we were pretty busy. I mean, it's not as if I was keeping an eye on them or anything." He began to get flustered and looked at Winsome again. "But if you want me to, I can keep my eyes and ears open. You know, if they come in again. I mean, I know Hardcastle can't, like, he's dead, right, but the other one, whoever he is, and I'll certainly –"

"It's all right, Liam," Annie said, though Liam seemed to have forgotten her presence. "We doubt very much that he'll be back. Thanks a lot for your help."

"What you might do," Winsome said before they left, leaning forward on the bar, so she was closer to Liam and a little shorter than he was, "is keep an eye open for underage drinkers. And drugs. We've had a few reports . . . you know. It would be a great help. Wouldn't want you to get into any trouble, mind you."

"Oh, God, no. I mean, yes, of course. Underage drinkers. Yes. Drugs. I'll do that."

They were laughing as they went out of the door. "'Countenance in this establishment,' for crying out loud," said Winsome. "Where's he get that from?"

"Good one, Winsome," Annie said. "You got him all flustered. You know, I think he fancies you. You might be in with a chance there."

Winsome nudged her in the ribs. "Get away with you."

Banks met Sophia in their local wine bar on the King's Road just after eight o'clock that evening. It was always crowded by then, but they managed to get a couple of stools at the bar. The place always reminded Banks a bit of their first night together. The Eastvale wine bar was a bit smaller and less upmarket, of course, its wine list perhaps not quite so comprehensive, and certainly lighter on the wallet, but it had a similar ambience: curved black bar, bottles on glass racks against a lit mirror behind the work area, soft lighting, candles floating among flower petals on the black circular tables, chrome chairs, padded seats.

That first night Banks hadn't been able to take his eyes off Sophia's animated face as they talked, and without his even being aware of it, he had somehow forgotten everything else in his life and broken through his natural reserve, found his hand reaching out for hers across the table, not another thought in his mind at that moment but her dark eyes, her voice, her lips, the light and shade of the flickering candle playing on the smooth skin of her face. It was a feeling that he knew would stay with him forever, no matter what happened. He felt his breath catch in his chest even as he thought about it now, sitting next to her, rather than opposite, in a place where they could barely hear one another speak, and whatever the music that was playing, it certainly wasn't Madeleine Peyroux singing "You're Gonna Make Me Lonesome When You Go."

"He was *terrible*," Sophia was saying, finishing a story about an interview she had produced that afternoon. "I mean, most crime writers are nice enough, but this bloke came on like he was Tolstoy or someone, proceeded to ignore the questions he was asked, pontificated about navel-gazing literary fiction and complained about not being nominated for the Man Booker. If you even hinted that he wrote crime novels, he'd snarl and practically go apoplectic. And he swore all the bloody time! And he *smelled*. Poor Chris, the interviewer, stuck there in that little studio with him."

Banks laughed. "What did you do?"

"Well, let's just say the technician's a friend of mine, and thank God it wasn't live," said Sophia with a wicked smile. "And you can't smell someone over the radio." She knocked back a healthy draught of Rioja and patted her chest. Her face was a little flushed, the way it got sometimes when she was excited. She prodded Banks gently in the chest. "So tell me about your day, Mr. Superspy."

Banks put his finger to his lips. "Ssshhh," he said, glancing towards the bartender. "'Keep mum, she's not so dumb.'"

"You think the Rioja's bugged?" Sophia whispered.

"Could be. After today, I wouldn't be surprised."

"What happened today?"

"Oh, nothing happened. Not really."

"Am I going to see much of you while you're down here, or are you going to be slinking among the shadows and darkness?"

"I hope not."

"But are you going to be running out at all hours of the night on mysterious missions?"

"I can't guarantee nine to five, but I'll do my best to be home by bedtime."

"Hmm. So tell me what happened today."

"I went to this house in St. John's Wood today, a house we had evidence that Laurence Silbert and an unknown man entered together about a week before Silbert died . . ." And Banks proceeded to tell Sophia about Edith and Lester Townsend. "Honestly," he said, "I felt as if

I'd walked right into the world of one of those strange fantasy novels. Or fallen down a rabbit hole or something."

"And they said they were there all the time, that no one else lived there or had rented from them, and they didn't know either of the men in the photo?"

"That's about it."

"How very *North by Northwest*. Are you sure your technical support people didn't make a mistake?"

"I'm sure. It's the same place. You can see that as soon as you stand outside."

"Well, they must be lying, then," said Sophia. "It stands to reason. It's the only logical conclusion. Don't you think?"

"So it would seem. But why?"

"Maybe they've been paid off?"

"Possibly."

"Perhaps they run a gay brothel?"

"A little old lady like Edith Townsend? In St. John's Wood?"

"Why not?"

"Or maybe they're simply a part of it all," Banks said.

"A part of what?"

"The plot. The conspiracy. Whatever's going on." He tossed back the rest of his drink. "Come on, let's go for that meal and talk about something else. I'm sick of bloody spooks already. It's doing my head in. And I'm starving."

Sophia laughed and reached down for her handbag. "Talking about doing your head in," she said, "if we hurry, Wilco are playing at the Brixton Academy tonight, and I can get us in."

"Well, then," said Banks, standing and holding out his hand for her. "What are we waiting for? Have we got time for a burger on the way?"

10

Sophia left for work early on Thursday morning while Banks was still in the shower trying to wake up. The Wilco concert had been great, and they had had a drink afterwards with some of Sophia's friends, which had made for a late night. At least Banks had remembered to charge his new mobile, and as soon as he'd dressed and had some coffee, he planned on phoning Annie to let her know his number.

He wasn't sure whether to revisit the Townsends again that day. Probably not. He didn't really see much point. On the one hand, the taciturn Mr. Townsend would be at work, and his wife might be more forthcoming if her husband wasn't around. On the other hand, she would probably be terrified, refuse to open the door and ring the police as soon as she saw Banks on her doorstep.

If they were involved, it meant they were part of the intelligence service, or paid by them to run a safe house or some such thing, and if that were true, they were hardly going to give anything away. If, as Sophia had suggested, they ran a gay brothel, then it was clearly an elite one, and the same code of silence probably applied. Charles Lane was most likely a dead end in the investigation.

Banks's only consolation was that perhaps what had happened there didn't really matter. The important thing was that Silbert had gone there with a man, and photographs of that visit had ended up in the possession of Mark Hardcastle, who had either misconstrued the whole business or been right on target. Perhaps the identity of the man wasn't as important as the identity of the photographer.

Humming "Norwegian Wood" for some odd reason, Banks dried himself and dressed. He thought he heard someone at the door, but when he went down and opened it, there was nobody there. Puzzled, he went through to the kitchen and blessed Sophia for leaving some coffee in the pot. He poured himself a cup, put a slice of wholemeal bread in the toaster and sat on a stool at the island. It was a small kitchen, especially given how much Sophia loved to cook, but it was organized and modern, with various high-quality pots and pans hanging from hooks above the island, a brushed-steel gas oven and burners and just about every kitchen gadget you could want, from a set of J.A. Henckel knives and a multi-speed mixer to a cheap plastic carrot-peeler you wore on your finger like a ring.

The toast popped out and Banks spread it with butter and grapefruit marmalade then had a quick look through that morning's copy of the *Independent* which Sophia had left behind. The Hardcastle–Silbert case seemed to have slipped from their radar entirely, and there wasn't much else of interest. Amy Winehouse was in trouble over drugs again. It was a shame, Banks thought, as it made people pay less attention to her amazing talent. Or perhaps it got her name across to a wider audience. Billie Holiday had had much the same problems – and she did go to rehab – yet she had made wonderful music. A lot of musicians had trouble with drugs, and Banks worried perhaps more than he should about Brian. The only great detective with a drug problem Banks knew of was Sherlock Holmes, and he had been pretty good at his job. Pity he wasn't real.

Banks shut the newspaper and pushed it aside. He had to work out his day. What he needed was information about Laurence Silbert, and it wasn't going to be easy to get. Sophia's father had come across him in Bonn in the mid-eighties. At that time Silbert would have been about forty, and given his condition when he died, probably at the height of fitness. What had he been doing in Germany? Most likely the same as everyone else in his line of work had been doing then – getting defectors over the Berlin Wall, penetrating the Eastern bloc for information about scientific, military, industrial and political goings-on, perhaps even carrying out the occasional, unofficial assassination. The whole business was such a complex jumble of espionage and counter-espionage, single, double and triple agents, that it was probably impossible for an outsider and layman to know where to start. In addition, much of the information on the shady activities of those times had been lost or buried. Only the Germans seemed determined to reassemble their old Stasi files, even going so far as to invent a computer program that could put together shredded documents in the blink of an eye. Everyone else just wanted to forget the dirty deeds they had done.

There was, however, one place he could start.

Banks washed his breakfast dishes, made sure the coffee-maker was turned off and that he had everything he needed in his briefcase. At the front door, he paused and set the alarm system, then he headed up to the King's Road and turned left towards Sloane Square tube station, cursing not for the first time that it was served only by the District and Circle lines, which meant that he would either have to go all the way round to Baker Street or change at both Victoria and Green Park. But he wasn't in a hurry, and it wouldn't take long to get to Swiss Cottage and find out whether Laurence Silbert's old lover Leo Westwood still lived there.

Annie was no stranger to Detective Superintendent Gervaise's office and had no hesitation in accepting the offer of tea, which Gervaise immediately sent for. The last time Annie had sat in this chair, she had been facing a lengthy torrent of both praise and censure for the way her last major case had turned out. She could understand that. Crimes solved was a good thing; dead bodies as part of the solution were not. In the end, she was lucky to come out without any serious black marks against her. It was possible that Gervaise had gone easy on her because of her fragile emotional state at the time, but then Gervaise wasn't known for making such allowances. On the whole, Annie felt that she had been fairly treated.

"How are things going?" Gervaise asked, making small talk while they waited for the tea. "That's a nice new hairdo, by the way. It suits you."

"Thank you, ma'am," said Annie. "Everything's going fine." What else was she going to say? Besides, things *were* going fine. A little dull at times, but fine.

"Good. Good. Nasty business, this East Side Estate. Any ideas? What do you think about this Jackie Binns character?"

"He's a waste of space," Annie said. "Nicky Haskell is actually quite bright, once you get past the posturing and the imitation gangbanger-talk. Despite his aversion to school, he might actually make something of himself. But Binns is a lost cause."

"I'm not sure that it's healthy to regard members of our community in such a negative way, DI Cabbot, particularly *downtrodden* members."

"I'm sure it's not, ma'am," said Annie with a smile. "Just put it down to copper's instinct."

"Did he do it?"

"You mean did Jackie Binns stab Donny Moore?"

"That's what I'm asking."

"I'm not sure," said Annie. "I don't think so. I was talking with DS Jackman about that very thing and we agreed that Haskell is scared, and we don't think he'd be that scared of Binns. They have a history, more a bit of mutual, grudging respect than anything else. They've had a couple of scraps. Thing is, it's not like Binns to take a knife to a kid like Donny Moore. I'm not saying he's honourable or anything. It's just . . ."

"Not his style?"

"That's right."

"Who says he did?"

"Nobody. That's the problem. That's what we're trying to get someone to tell us. He's certainly the leader of the south estate gang and if he felt Haskell and Moore were encroaching on his territory he'd probably feel he had every right to take action. He could have delegated the task. But no one has admitted to seeing anything yet."

"So if not him, who?"

"No idea, ma'am. But we're still investigating it. At least there haven't been any more incidents or reprisals."

"That's a good thing," said Gervaise. "Don't want to upset the tourists, do we?"

"I doubt if any of them have even heard of the East Side Estate, unless they got lost like the Paxtons did the other night. They won't forget it in a hurry."

"Even so . . . we don't want gangs bringing their problems into the town centre. We've got enough problems already with weekend binge drinking."

Despite the rape and murder of a young girl after an evening's binge drinking a few months ago, the problem hadn't abated much, Annie thought. Now it was almost a test of mettle among the kids involved to go walking around the Maze, that labyrinth of alleys beyond the other side of the market square where the girl was killed. Still, they had caught the killer quickly enough, and there had been no more attacks.

The tea arrived, along with a couple of Penguin biscuits. Gervaise poured, added milk and sugar and passed a teacup and saucer over to Annie, who helped herself to a biscuit.

"I'm glad you have the situation under control," Gervaise went on. "But that's not really what I wanted to talk to you about."

"No, ma'am?"

"No. You probably know that, on my advice, DCI Banks has taken a few days of leave owing."

"Yes. Well deserved, I'd say."

"No argument with that. I'm just wondering if . . . well, I can't say that I sensed any real, true *closure* on his part regarding this other business."

"Is there ever really true closure?" Annie said.

"Oh, please, DI Cabbot. Spare me the philosophical digressions. Do you really think that's likely to throw me off course?"

"Sorry, ma'am."

"I should think so." Gervaise gripped her teacup, her little finger sticking out, and sipped daintily. "You do know what I'm talking about?" she said as she put the cup down.

"I assume you're referring to the Hardcastle–Silbert business?"

"Yes. Two *solved* cases. Looks good in the crime figures. And the Chief Constable is happy."

"What are you asking me, ma'am?"

"What's your opinion?"

"Of what? The case?"

"No. There is no case. Of DCI Banks."

"Well," said Annie. "He does have a new girlfriend, and he *was* called away from her in rather a hurry the other weekend. I should imagine he wants to finish what he started, maybe treat her to a few days at the seaside or somewhere and make up for lost time."

"That's what you really think?"

"Yes, ma'am."

"Bollocks, DI Cabbot. Would you be surprised to hear that Banks was asking questions of an elderly couple called Townsend in St. John's Wood late yesterday afternoon? They phoned the local police as soon as he'd left. Scared out of their wits. He'd shown them his warrant card and they were able to let us know his name. As far as the locals were concerned, DCI Banks shouldn't have been trespassing on their patch in the first place without letting them know."

"No, ma'am, I didn't know."

"So what do you have to say to that, DI Cabbot? There's no seaside near St. John's Wood as far as I remember."

"It was just a figure of speech, ma'am," said Annie. "DCI Banks's girlfriend lives in London. Perhaps –" Annie's mobile went off. It no longer played "Bohemian Rhapsody" but had the simple, straightforward bell tone of an old-style telephone. For once, Annie was glad of the interruption.

"Answer it," said Gervaise. "It might be important."

Annie answered. Banks's voice came on. "I'm sorry," she said. "I can't talk now. I'm in a meeting."

"Gervaise?"

"Yes, that's right."

"Does she know?"

"I think I can manage that, Winsome. Bye."

"DS Jackman?" asked Gervaise.

"Yes, ma'am. She wants me to meet her at Eastvale Comprehensive to talk to Nicky Haskell's teachers." This was something they had arranged earlier, so Annie didn't feel that she was really lying, simply altering the order of the facts. And she *was* going to the comprehensive as soon as she got out of Gervaise's office.

"And here's me thinking it might have been DCI Banks."

"He's on holiday, ma'am."

"Sounds like a busman's holiday to me, going around questioning people." She rested her arms on the table. "Annie, I like DCI Banks, I really do. I respect his abilities and I'd hate to lose him. I can't always get through to him, myself, but you sometimes seem able to manage it. God knows how."

"I don't –"

Gervaise waved her hand in the air. "Please. Hear me out. I don't like this any more than you do. As a criminal case, this Hardcastle–Silbert business was relatively easy to crack. The one killed the other, then killed himself. There are, however, complications. The people involved, or one of them, at any rate, happens to have some very strong connections with the secret intelligence services and, well, to make no bones about it, with the Chief Constable himself. I've been advised in very strong terms from the highest level that there is *no* investigation to be pursued and that neither I nor the Chief Constable can be responsible for the consequences to any of our officers who choose, foolishly, to pursue such an avenue. Do I make myself clear?"

"What are they going to do?" Annie asked. "Kill him?"

Gervaise banged her fist on the desk. "Don't be flippant, DI Cabbot. These are serious matters of state we're dealing with here. Things that people like you and DCI Banks can't just go meddling in willy-nilly. It's not only your heads on the block here, you know."

The violent gesture had shocked Annie. She had seen Gervaise in many moods but hadn't seen her lose her cool like that before. Someone must have really got to her. "I don't know what you think I can do," she said.

"I think you can let me know if DCI Banks gets in touch with you at all, and if he asks you for help in any way you can refuse and come immediately to me. Let him know that if he chooses to pursue this business he's on his own."

"You want me to act as an informant?"

"I want you to consider your career and DCI Banks's career. I want you to grow up. I want you to turn your back on this one and report any anomalies to me. Do you think you can do that?"

Annie said nothing.

"DI Cabbot?"

"I'm not involved," Annie lied.

"Then keep it that way." Gervaise made a gesture for Annie to leave. When Annie got to the door, Gervaise called out after her, "And by the way, DI Cabbot. If I find that you have been involving DS Jackman or any other of my officers in this affair, I'll not only have you tossed out on your arse, but them too. Got it?"

"Loud and clear, ma'am," said Annie, and shut the door gently behind her, heart pounding, hands shaking.

Banks had picked up the Gervaise alert clearly enough when he phoned Annie, so he killed half an hour in a Starbucks on Finchley Road drinking a latte with a double shot of espresso then phoned her back. This time she told him she could talk; she was walking down King Street on her way to meet Winsome at the comprehensive.

"So what is it?" Banks asked.

"Storm clouds gathering," said Annie. "You're definitely *persona non grata* around these parts."

"And all those who sail in her?"

"Exactly."

Annie sounded a bit breathless, as if she'd had a shock. She was walking, Banks realized, but the comprehensive was *downhill* on King Street, past the infirmary, and she was too young and fit to be out of breath. It made him feel nervous, too. He glanced around, but nobody was paying him undue attention. But they wouldn't, would they; they were too clever for that. Holding his paranoia in check, he asked, "What happened?"

"She knows where you were yesterday, who you talked to."

"The Townsends?"

"Yes."

That surprised Banks. He hadn't expected them to call the police. When he thought about it, though, it made perfect sense if they were connected with the security services. Another possible way of getting him called off and put back in his cage before he did any real damage.

Or perhaps they had told their masters and it was they who had phoned the police. Either way the result was the same. "What's the bottom line?" he asked.

"What do you think? I'm to stay out of it if I value my career and let Gervaise know if you get in touch. Then I'm supposed to let you hang out to dry. Why don't you just take Sophia to Devon or Cornwall for a few days, Alan, make everyone's life a bit easier, including your own?"

"*Et tu*, Annie?"

"Oh, sod off, you idiot. I didn't say I was going to do what she asked, did I? I was just outlining the sensible solution again. Only to have it shot down, as usual."

"She's a devious one, Madame Gervaise," Banks said. "Besides, the sensible solution isn't always the best one."

"They'll put that on your tombstone. Anyway, I'm almost at the school and I've got something to tell you before I have second thoughts. It might change things."

Banks's ears pricked up. "What?"

"Nicky Haskell mentioned seeing Mark Hardcastle drinking with Derek Wyman in the Red Rooster a couple of weeks ago."

"The Red Rooster? That's a kids' pub, isn't it? Karaoke and bad Amy Winehouse impersonations?"

"More or less," Annie said.

"So why would they go there?"

"I have no idea. Unless it's the sort of place where they didn't think they'd be noticed."

"But Wyman told us he had a drink with Hardcastle every now and then. There's nothing odd about that, except their choice of location."

"There's more." Banks listened as Annie went on to tell him about Wyman calming Hardcastle down.

"But nothing changed hands?" Banks said. "No pictures, no memory stick or anything?"

"Not that Nicky Haskell saw. Or Liam, the bartender."

"Maybe you could ask again? Find someone else who was there. Who was Nicky with?"

"His mates, I suppose. The usual suspects."

"Try them. One of them might have seen something. If Gervaise is watching you'll just appear to be following up on the East Side Estate stabbing."

"I am following up on the stabbing."

"Well, there you go. A couple of extra questions won't do much harm, then, will they?"

"I'm at the school driveway now. I have to go."

"You'll ask around?"

"I'll ask around."

"And Annie?"

"Yes?"

"Rattle Wyman's cage, too, if you get the chance."

According to what Edwina Silbert had told Banks, Leo Westwood had lived in a third-floor flat on Adamson Road, near the Swiss Cottage tube station. There was a row of farmers' market stalls at the top of Eton Avenue, just opposite the Hampstead Theatre, and Banks thought he might pick up some Brie de Meaux, chorizo sausage and venison pâté on his way back. Sophia would appreciate the gesture, and he was sure she would know what to do with the chorizo. Left to himself, Banks would probably just put it between two slices of bread with a dollop of HP Sauce.

Adamson Road branched off to the left, with the Best Western Hotel to the right, a tree-lined street of older, imposing three-storey houses with white stucco façades, complete with porticos and columns. They reminded Banks of the houses on Powys Terrace in Notting Hill. There were plenty of people on the streets and on the porches chatting; all in all, it looked like a lively neighbourhood. According to the list of tenants, Leo Westwood still lived there. Banks pressed the bell beside the name and waited. After a few seconds, a voice crackled over the intercom. Banks identified himself and the reason for his visit and found himself buzzed up.

The halls and landings had clearly seen better days, but there was a kind of shabby elegance about it all. The Axminsters may have been a little worn, but they were still Axminsters.

Leo Westwood stood at the door of his flat. He was a short, pudgy man with silky grey hair and a smooth ruddy complexion, somewhere in his early sixties, wearing a black polo-neck jumper and jeans. Banks had expected an antique-laden apartment, but inside, beyond the hallway, the living area was ultra-modern, all polished hardwood floors, chrome and glass, plenty of open space, a fine bay window, and a state-of-the-art music and TV system. The flat had probably been reasonably inexpensive when Westwood bought it years ago, but now would be worth somewhere in the region of half a million pounds or more, Banks guessed, depending on how many bedrooms there were.

Westwood bade Banks sit on a comfortable black leather-and-chrome armchair and offered coffee. Banks accepted. Westwood disappeared into the kitchen and Banks took the opportunity to look around. There was only one painting on the wall, in a simple silver frame, and it drew Banks's eye. It was abstract, a combination of geometric shapes in various colours and sizes. There was something calming about it, Banks found, and it fitted the room perfectly. On a small media storage unit beside the sound system was a mix of books – mostly architecture and interior design – several DVDs ranging from recent cinema hits like *Atonement* and *La Vie en Rose* to classics by Truffaut, Kurasawa, Antonioni and Bergman, along with numerous opera boxed sets.

"I like to keep the space relatively uncluttered," Westwood said from behind him, putting a silver tray bearing a cafetière and two white cups down on the glass coffee table before them. He then sat at a right angle to Banks. "We'll give it a minute, shall we?" His voice had a slight lisp, and his mannerisms were a little fussy and effeminate. "I was sorry to hear about Laurence," he said, "but you must realize it was a long time ago. Ten years."

"You were close then, though?"

"Oh, yes. Very. Three years. It might not sound like long, but . . ."

"If you don't mind my asking, why did you part?"

Westwood leaned forward and poured the coffee. "Milk? Sugar?"

"Just black, please," Banks said. "It could be relevant, what I'm asking."

Westwood passed him the cup. "I'm afraid I can't take it without a little sweetener, myself," he said, adding some powder from a pink sachet. He leaned back in his chair. "I'm sorry, I wasn't trying to avoid your question. I just find that if you leave the coffee brewing too long it takes on a bitter flavour that even the sweetener won't overcome."

"It's fine," said Banks, taking a sip. "Excellent, in fact."

"Thank you. One of my little luxuries."

"You and Laurence?"

"Yes. I suppose it was his work, really. I mean, he was always heading off somewhere and he couldn't tell me where. Even when he got back I'd no idea where he'd been. I knew that sometimes his missions involved danger, so I would lie awake and worry, but I rarely got a phone call. In the end . . ."

"So you knew what he did?"

"To a degree. I mean, I knew he worked for MI6. Beyond that, though . . ."

"Was he unfaithful?"

Westwood considered carefully before answering. "I don't think so," he said finally. "He could have been, of course. He was away often enough. A one-night stand, a weekend affair in Berlin, Prague or St. Petersburg. It would have been easy enough. But I think I would have known. I do believe that Laurence truly loved me, at least as well as he could love anyone."

"What do you mean by that?"

"There was a large part of his life that he kept secret from me. Oh, I understand it was his job, national security and all that, but nevertheless it still meant that I only got a small part of him. The rest was shades of darkness, shadows, smoke and mirrors. Ultimately, you can't live with that day in, day out. Sometimes it felt as if he was all surface when he was with me, and I had no idea what was underneath, what he was really thinking about."

"So you wouldn't be able to give me any idea of his personality?"

"I'm afraid I never knew. He was a chameleon. When we were together, he was charming, attentive, kind, considerate, sophisticated, extremely intelligent and cultured, politically leaning to the right, an atheist, a man of exquisite taste in art and wine, an antique lover . . . oh, I could go on with the list. Laurence was many things, but you still felt you were hardly scratching the surface. And you couldn't pin him down. Do you know what I mean?"

"I think so," said Banks. "That's what this case feels like, these people."

"What people?"

"The ones Laurence worked for."

Westwood sniffed. "Oh, them. Yes, well, you would feel that way about them."

"When did you last see him?"

"Years ago, when we split up. He went off on one of his trips and I never saw him again."

"Did you meet any of his colleagues?"

"No. They didn't exactly have office parties. I tell a lie, though. I was vetted, of course, and interviewed. They came here once. Two of them."

"What did they ask you?"

"I can't really remember. Nothing very probing. Of course, a few years earlier a homosexual relationship like ours would have been out of the question because of the possibilities for blackmail it opened up, but that was no longer an issue. They asked me about my job, what sort of people I worked for, how I felt about my country, about the USA, about democracy, communism, that kind of thing. I assumed they got most of the information about me they needed from elsewhere. They treated me with the utmost respect and politeness, but there was an edge, you know. There was a veiled threat. 'We'll be watching you, mate. Any funny business and we'll have the electrodes on your balls before you can say shaken not stirred.'" He laughed. "Well, something like that. But I got the message."

Hardcastle had probably got the same treatment, Banks imagined, especially when they found out about his conviction. "What is your job?" he asked.

"I'm an architect. Back then I worked for a small firm, but I'm on my own now. I work from home, which is why you found me in. I can't say I do very many jobs these days. I get to pick and choose. I'm lucky. I don't need to work full time. I've made a fair bit of money over the years, and I'm a saver. I've also made some good investments, even in these troubled times, and I've got enough to see myself out in reasonable style."

"Did you ever see these people after you split up with Laurence?"

"No. I suppose they lost interest in me after that."

"Have you heard of someone called Fenner? Julian Fenner."

"No, I can't say I have."

"What about a couple called Townsend?"

"No, again the name doesn't ring a bell."

Banks showed him the photographs of Silbert with the man in Regent's Park and at the door on Charles Lane, but apart from reacting a little emotionally to the image of his ex-lover, he said it didn't mean anything to him.

"Can you answer me just one question?" Westwood asked.

"Perhaps."

"How did you find out about me?"

"Edwina mentioned you, and we found some old letters from you in Mr. Silbert's safe."

"Ah, I see . . . do you think, perhaps, when this is all over . . . ?"

"I'll see what I can do," said Banks. He noticed a tear glisten in Westwood's right eye. He didn't think there was anything more to be gained from talking to him. If Westwood *had* known Fenner or the Townsends, they had probably gone under different names then. They probably changed their names as often as most people changed their underwear. He finished his coffee, thanked Westwood and stood up to go. It seemed that every time he thought he was taking a step closer to Laurence Silbert or Mark Hardcastle he was actually moving farther away from them. It was like trying to grasp a handful of smoke.

"They're waiting for us in the staff room," Winsome said, when Annie arrived at the front entrance of Eastvale Comprehensive. Some of the pupils running back and forth from classrooms shouting and laughing paused and gawked at them, Winsome in particular, and more than a few giggles and wolf whistles echoed in the high corridors.

They found the staff room close to the administration offices. Three teachers, one of them Derek Wyman, sat on battered sofas and armchairs around a low table littered with the day's newspapers, the *Daily Mail* open to the puzzle page. Someone had done the crossword and sudokus in ink. The walls were painted day-care-centre yellow, and there was a big corkboard with notices and memos pinned to it. There was also a small kitchen area with sink, coffee urn, electric kettle, microwave and fridge. Yellow Post-it notes clung to every surface, telling you to wash your hands, don't touch other people's items in the fridge, throw away your rubbish, use only your own mug, clean up after yourself, remember to pay your coffee money. Annie couldn't imagine that even the pupils needed more rules spelled for them out than the teachers did. It was very quiet in the room, though, as if it had been soundproofed from the noise outside, and Annie imagined that must be one of its great appeals, even after her short walk along the corridor.

"So you've found our secret lair," said Wyman, standing up.

"I phoned. The school secretary told me where you were," said Winsome.

"I can see you're not a detective for nothing," said one of the other teachers.

Winsome and Annie exchanged glances.

Wyman obviously noticed their reaction. "I apologize for my colleague," he said. "He spent all morning with year ten, and he hasn't recovered yet."

"That's all right," said Annie, positioning herself so she could see them all and take control of the interview. Winsome sat next to her and took out her notebook. "This shouldn't take long," Annie went on. "We don't want to keep you from your duties."

They laughed at that.

"You're here because you all teach at least two of the pupils we think might be involved in the stabbing of Donny Moore on the East Side Estate last week. We're still trying to form a picture of exactly what happened that night, and you might be able to help us. Can you start by telling us who you are and what you teach?"

"Well, you know who I am," said Wyman. "I teach drama and games, for my sins."

The man next to him, the one who had made the bad joke, said, "I'm Barry Chaplin and I teach physics and PE."

The third was a woman. "I'm Jill Dresler," she said, "and I teach arithmetic and algebra. No sports."

"And you all know Nicky Haskell and Jackie Binns?" Annie asked.

They nodded. "When he can be bothered to come to class," Jill Dresler added.

"Yes, we know about his poor attendance record," Annie said. "But he does appear on occasion?"

"Just enough to avoid getting suspended," said Barry Chaplin.

"And Jackie Binns?" Annie asked.

"About the same," Wyman answered, glancing at the others for agreement.

"Probably a bit more often," said Chaplin. "But not much."

"And what about the victim?" Annie went on. "Donny Moore."

"Donny isn't a bad student," said Dresler. "He's more of a follower than an instigator. You know, he drifted in with Haskell's crowd just to belong. He's harmless enough. The quiet one."

"Not a scrapper?"

"Not at all," said Chaplin. "Not like Haskell."

"So Nicky Haskell likes to fight?" Annie pressed on.

"Well," said Chaplin, "I wouldn't say he picks fights, as such. I mean, he's not a bully. But people sometimes pick on him because he's a bit shorter than the rest and they usually get a hell of a surprise."

"So people underestimate his strength?"

"Yes. He's good at games, too," Wyman added. "Strong, fast, quick-witted, good coordination. I'd go as far as to say he could make a damn good football player if he put his mind to it."

"But he doesn't?"

"Oh, he's interested. But it takes more than that. It takes dedication. Haskell's a bit of a dreamer."

"Well, he's young yet," said Annie.

"So's Matthew Briggs," Wyman answered.

"Right. Anyway, we believe that Haskell might be a witness, but he's not talking."

"That figures," said Chaplin. "I mean, he wouldn't, would he? He'd lose face. These kids don't rat out each other, even their worst enemies."

"It's just that he seems scared."

"Of Binns?" said Chaplin. "I don't believe it. I've seen them tangle on the football field and Haskell has never shown any fear of him. What would you say, Derek?"

"I agree. He's tough. And strong. Enjoys boxing and wrestling as well as football. As Barry says, it's the lack of discipline that drags him down, not ability."

"So you don't think he would lie out of fear of what Jackie Binns might do to him if he did?"

"Absolutely not," said Chaplin. "Binns isn't that tough. He's all bluster."

"Haskell just wouldn't split on anyone," said Wyman. "He strikes me as the kind who stays loyal to his mates."

Annie remembered Nicky Haskell telling her that he wasn't obeying some stupid code about not splitting on his pals, and she wondered how true that was. If he wasn't telling because he was scared of Binns, which was beginning to sound unlikely, or because he felt he shouldn't betray Binns, then there had to be some other reason. Something they didn't know. She would have to make a note to talk to some of the others involved again. Haskell and Binns were the leaders. Both dealt drugs, mostly ecstasy, weed, crystal meth and LSD. Binns was known to carry a flick-knife, though he usually only used it to show off and scare people, and Donny Moore hadn't been stabbed with a flick-knife.

"Is there anything else you can tell us?" Annie asked.

"I don't think so," said Jill Dresler. "I know what you probably think, but they're not bad kids, really. Not all of them. I mean, OK, so they do break the law and sell drugs, but they're not big-time dealers, and they don't really have organized gangs, and you don't have to shoot anyone to belong or that sort of thing."

"I suppose we ought to be thankful for small mercies," Annie said, getting to her feet.

"I know how it sounds," Dresler went on, "but Binns isn't a killer, for crying out loud."

"Luckily," said Annie, "nobody's dead yet."

"Yes," said Dresler, running her hand through her lank hair. "Of course. I'm just saying . . . you know . . . they're not monsters. That's all."

"Point taken," Annie said. "And I appreciate your defence of your kids. I know they're not monsters. But somebody's lying, and until we find out the truth we can't get to the bottom of this. Things are getting a bit tense on the estate, as I'm sure you can imagine. People are scared to go out on the streets alone. What do you want us to do, send in the troops? Occupy the East Side Estate like it was a military zone? We don't have any no-go areas in Eastvale, and we don't want them. That's why I'm asking questions." She reached in her bag. "So if you do think of anything that might help us, here's my card. Don't hesitate to phone. Mr. Wyman, a word please."

"Of course. I'll walk to the door with you," said Wyman.

Once they were out in the noisy corridor, Annie let Winsome get a few feet ahead, remembering Superintendent Gervaise's warning about not involving anyone else, then turned to Wyman. "Can you tell me what you were doing in the Red Rooster with Mark Hardcastle a couple of weeks ago?"

Wyman seemed surprised, but he answered quickly. "Having a drink. I told you, we got together for a drink every now and then to talk about theatre business."

"Yes," said Annie. "But the Red Rooster isn't really the sort of place you go for a quiet drink, and it's hardly just around the corner."

"It was quiet enough when we were there."

A laughing boy being chased by his friends bumped into Annie as he dodged his pursuers. "Watch where you're going, Saunders!" Wyman yelled after him.

"Yes, sir. Sorry, sir," said Saunders, and kept on running.

"Sometimes I wonder why I bother," Wyman complained.

"The Red Rooster?"

"Well, the food's OK, and the beer's not bad."

"Look, Mr. Wyman," said Annie. "It's out of the way – at least two miles from Eastvale, where there are plenty of nice pubs – and it's mostly a young kids' pub. The beer might be passable, but the food's crap. Anyone would think you didn't want to get away from the kids once in a while, or that you went there because you didn't want to be seen."

"Well, to be quite honest," said Wyman, "knowing the way tongues start wagging around these parts, and given Mark's, er . . . sexual inclinations, I will admit that somewhere a little out of the way seemed more suitable."

"Come off it, Derek. Your pupils drink there. And you went to London with Mark. You told us you met up for a drink every now and then. You said you don't care whether a person's gay or straight, and your wife wasn't at all put out by your relationship with Mark Hardcastle, either. You expect me to believe that you went –"

"Now, you look here." Wyman stopped in his tracks and turned to face her. "I don't like this one bit. I don't see why I have to explain to you why I drink where I do. Or who with. Or justify myself in any way."

"What was Mark Hardcastle upset about?"

Wyman turned away and carried on walking. "I don't know what you're talking about."

Annie caught up with him. "Something you said upset him. Then you calmed him down again. What was it?"

"That's rubbish. I don't remember anything remotely like that happening. I don't know who's been telling you this, but someone's spreading vicious rumours."

"Don't you?" said Annie. She was at the door, and Wyman stopped again. He clearly wasn't coming any farther. "Funny, that," she went on. "Other people remember it very well." She pushed the door and walked out towards Winsome, who was waiting on the steps. "Bye, Mr. Wyman," she said over her shoulder. "I'm sure we'll talk again soon."

11

After a quick burger and chips and a pint of Sam Smith's at Ye Olde Swiss Cottage, a rambling pub with wooden balconies, which did look rather like a large ski chalet stuck in the cleft of busy traffic between Avenue Road and Finchley Road, Banks made his way to the tube station and negotiated his route to Victoria. The carriage was hot, and several of the people he found himself crushed up against clearly hadn't bathed that morning. It brought back memories of going to work on hot days in London, the way you'd get all kinds of deodorant and perfume smells in the morning, while the evening rush hour was dominated by sad and wrung-out-looking people smelling of sweat. He gave his underarm a surreptitious sniff as he left the station and was relieved to find that his anti-perspirant was still holding its own.

Banks found Wyman's bed-and-breakfast hotel easily enough about five minutes' walk from the Underground, off Warwick Way. A sign in the window offered vacancies from £35 per night, which sounded remarkably cheap to Banks. He realized how money could be a problem for Wyman, with a wife who only worked part-time and two teenage children with appetites to match. A teacher's salary was reasonable, but not extravagant. No wonder he stayed in places like this and ate at Zizzi's.

Inexpensive as it was, the bed-and-breakfast turned out to be quite charming. The entrance was clean and the decor lively and fresh. The man who answered Banks's ring was a rotund Pakistani with a moustache and a shiny head. He was wearing a pinny and seemed in the midst of vacuuming the hallway. He turned off the vacuum, introduced himself as Mohammed and asked with a smile what he could do for the gentleman. A vague aroma of curry spices wafted from the back and made Banks's mouth water, despite the hurried burger. Maybe he would suggest to Sophia that they go out for a curry dinner or get a takeaway.

Banks took out his warrant card and Mohammed scrutinized it. "No trouble, I hope?" he said, a worried expression corrugating his brow.

"Not for you," Banks said. "It's just information I'm after really." He described Wyman and the dates he said he had last been staying there. It didn't take long before Mohammed knew exactly whom Banks was talking about.

"Ah, yes, Mr. Wyman," he said. "He's one of my regulars. Very fine gentleman. Educated. He's a schoolteacher, you know." Mohammed spoke with a trace of South London accent.

"Yes, I know," said Banks. "Was he here on the dates I mentioned?"

"It was quite recent, I do remember that. Please, let me check for you." Mohammed went behind the small reception desk and thumbed through a large book. "Yes, here it is. He arrived on Wednesday afternoon the week before last, and he left on the Saturday."

"Was he any different than on previous visits?"

"In what way?"

"I'm not sure," said Banks. "Excited, depressed, on edge, anxious?"

"No, none of those things. Not that I noticed. He seemed quite . . . pleased with everything, quite happy with life."

"What time did he leave?"

"Check-out time is eleven o'clock."

That squared with what Wyman had told them when they talked to him. He said he had gone for a pub lunch then done some book shopping and visited the National Gallery before catching his train home. His wife Carol had met him at York station at about a quarter past seven. "Do you have any idea where he went or what he did while he was here?"

Mohammed frowned. "I don't spy on my guests, Mr. Banks," he said.

"I understand," said Banks. "But you must have noticed him coming in or going out at certain times. Did he sleep here every night?"

"As far as I know. His bed was always slept in and he was always down for breakfast."

"I don't suppose you know what times he came and went?"

"No. He usually went out after breakfast, about nine o'clock, and he might call back at some point for an hour or so in the middle of the afternoon, perhaps to rest, and then he would go out again at teatime. We don't do any other meals, you see. Only breakfast. He was just like any other tourist."

"Was he late back at night?"

"Not that I know of. I saw him come in about eleven a couple of times. I was usually making sure everything was tidy and shipshape for morning by then."

"Did he have any visitors?"

"We don't encourage visitors in the rooms. As I told you, I don't keep a watch on my guests, and I'm not always here, so I suppose he *could* have sneaked someone in the room if he'd wanted. All I'm saying is that I don't think he did, and he never had before."

"Mr. Wyman is a regular here, right?"

"He likes to come down for the theatre, the art galleries and the NFT, he told me. But it's hard for him to get away. Schoolteachers get many holidays, but not always when they want to take them."

My heart bleeds, thought Banks, who was supposed to be on holiday right now. Still, it was his own fault that he wasn't.

"Mr. Wyman is a model guest," Mohammed went on. "He never makes any noise. He never complains. He is always polite."

"Good," said Banks. "This might sound like an odd request, but is there any chance I might have a look at the room he stayed in the last time he was here?"

Mohammed stroked his moustache. "That is indeed a very unusual request," he said. "But as it happens, Mr. Wyman always prefers the same room, if it's available. The prices of the rooms here vary, you understand, depending on the level of accommodation offered, but he didn't mind the shared toilet and bathroom, or the noise from the street."

"Your cheapest room?"

"Yes, as a matter of fact."

"And he always got it?"

"Most times. And you're in luck. It's empty now. Though what you hope to find there I have no idea. Other guests have stayed since

Mr. Wyman, you know, and everything has been cleaned and washed. I can vouch for that. My wife does the cooking and I take care of the cleaning myself."

"Did you find anything odd or interesting when you cleaned the room after Mr. Wyman left last time?"

"No. I . . . Wait a minute," said Mohammed, stroking his moustache. "It had slipped down the back of the radiator. It's always difficult to clean behind there. There's not enough space."

"What was it?" Banks asked.

"Just a business card. I wouldn't have noticed, but there's a special attachment for the vacuum cleaner. The card was too big to go down the tube so it got stuck over the end by the suction, and I had to remove it by hand. I remember thinking it must have fallen out of the top pocket of his shirt when he took it off to go to bed. Mr. Wyman was usually a most tidy guest."

"Do you still have it?"

"No. I put it in with the rest of the rubbish."

"I don't suppose you can remember what the card said, can you?"

"Oh, yes," said Mohammed. "It was the name, you see."

"What about it?"

"'Tom Savage.' Wouldn't you remember that?"

"I suppose I probably would," said Banks.

"And," Mohammed went on, beaming, "you would certainly remember it if it said 'Tom Savage Detective Investigations.' Like 'Magnum P.I.' or 'Sam Spade.' I'm a fan of the American detectives, you see."

"Could it have been dropped there before Mr. Wyman came to stay?"

"No," said Mohammed. "I'm most thorough. I clean every nook and cranny between guests."

"Thank you," Banks. "I'm very glad of that. Was there anything else about it?"

"The top left corner was indented, as if it had been attached to something by a paper clip."

"I don't suppose you remember an address or telephone number?"

"I'm sorry."

"That's OK," said Banks. "It should be easy enough to find out."

"Do you still want to look at the room?"

"Yes, please."

"Very well. Follow me."

Mohammed took a key from a hook on the wall and came out from behind the reception desk. He led Banks up three flights of carpeted stairs and opened a door off the landing. Banks's first impression was of how small the room was, but everything else about it was clean and in order, the striped cream wallpaper giving it a cheerful air. He spotted the radiator. A hard-backed chair stood right next to it. It was close to the bed and seemed a natural place to lay out one's clothes for the morning, or to hang trousers and a casual jacket over the back. Easy for a card to slip out of a pocket and flutter behind the radiator.

There was no television set and only a single bed, but there was a small armchair by the window, which overlooked the street. Banks could hear the traffic and imagined it could be noisy, even at night – there was no double-glazing here to dampen the sound – but Wyman must be a good sleeper. All in all, if Banks found a room so snug and comfortable in London at that price he would probably stay there himself. Most of the places he had ever stayed in around Victoria had been dives.

"It's charming," he said to Mohammed. "I can see why he liked it."

"It's very small, but clean and cosy."

"Is there a telephone?"

"There's a payphone in the hall."

"Mind if I have a look around?"

"Please. There's nothing here."

Banks could see what he meant. A quick glance under the bed revealed nothing, not even the dustballs one might usually expect to find there. Mohammed was not lying when he said he was thorough. The wardrobe, too, was bare apart from the coat hangers that rattled when he opened it. On the small desk, there was a note about breakfast times on the table, along with a writing tablet and a ballpoint pen. The ubiquitous Gideon's Bible lay all alone in the top drawer of the bedside table.

"I'm sorry to have troubled you," Banks said.

"It's all right. Have you finished now?"

"Yes, I think so. Thanks a lot for answering my questions and for letting me see the room."

Banks followed Mohammed down the stairs and stopped at the public telephone on the lower landing. There were no phone numbers scribbled on the wall and no directory. "Do you know if he made or received any phone calls while he was here?" Banks asked.

"I don't think so. He could have done. I wouldn't necessarily have known. I do hope Mr. Wyman isn't in any trouble."

"So do I," said Banks, taking Mohammed's card, smiling and shaking hands as he left. "So do I."

The detective agency looked like a one-man operation housed in a non-descript sixties office tower on Great Marlborough Street, between Regent Street and Soho. Banks had got the address easily from the Yellow Pages. A group of casually dressed young men and women stood around outside the building, smoking and chatting to bicycle couriers. It was about the only place they could smoke now outside of their own homes.

Banks took the jerky lift up to the fifth floor and found the door marked "Tom Savage Detective Investigations," followed by "Please Press Bell and Enter," which he ignored. When he walked into the room, he was almost expecting a rumpled, hungover, smart-mouthed tough with a bottle of Scotch in his filing cabinet, though he had met plenty of private investigators before and none of them had matched that partic-ular stereotype. Savage had a receptionist, but she wasn't sitting behind her desk polishing her nails; she was actually stuffing papers in folders in a filing cabinet. She had to bend over to do it, too, and her low-slung tight jeans didn't leave much to the imagination.

On hearing Banks arrive, she stood up, smoothed her jeans and blushed. She knew exactly what he'd been looking at. "Yes?" she chal-lenged him. "I didn't hear you ring. Can I help you?"

"I didn't ring," said Banks. "Mr. Savage in?"

"Do you have an appointment?"

"I'm afraid not."

"Then, I'm sorry –"

Banks pulled out his warrant card and showed it to her.

She gave him a sharp glance and said, "Why didn't you say?"

"I just did," said Banks. "Does it make any difference?"

She read the card again. "Are you . . . Alan Banks . . . You're not? . . . Are you Brian Banks's father?"

"Yes. Why?"

"Oh my God!" She put her hands to her cheeks. Banks thought she was going to jump up and down. "You are. You're Brian Banks's father!"

"I'm sorry," said Banks. "I don't . . ."

"I just *love* the Blue Lamps. I can't believe it. I only saw them a couple of weeks ago. Your Brian was terrific. I play a bit of guitar myself and write my own songs. Just an amateur band, like, but . . . When did he start playing? How often did he practise?"

"In his mid-teens, and way too often, when he should have been doing other things," said Banks. "Like homework."

She managed a quick smile. It really lit up her face, which was very pretty, a pale oval with good cheekbones, clear, direct emerald eyes and a smattering of freckles framed by straight blonde hair down to her shoulders. "I'm so sorry," she said. "What must you think of me, acting like a silly schoolgirl?" She stuck out her hand out. "Tom Savage. Pleased to meet you. Actually it's Tomasina, but somehow I don't think that would go down very well in this business, do you?"

Banks tried not to show his surprise. "And the Savage?"

"My real name."

"Lucky you. How did you know who I was?"

"I read an article about the band, an interview, and your son mentioned that his father was a detective chief inspector in North Yorkshire. There can't be that many called Banks. I'm sorry. I didn't mean to gush. It was just the shock."

"That's OK," said Banks. "I'm very proud of him."

"So you should be. Let's go through to the main office. It's more comfortable in there." She gestured around the reception area. "It's a one-woman show at the moment, I'm afraid. I really do have to do all the filing myself. I don't have any client appointments today, hence the casual wear. It's office clean-up day."

"I know what you mean," said Banks, following her into the office and sitting opposite her. The walls looked flimsy and thin, and there was no view. There wasn't even a window. Her desk was uncluttered, and a slim Mac Air sat in front of her.

"My only extravagance," she said, patting the sleek laptop. "I noticed you looking at it."

"I wish I could afford one," said Banks.

"So," Tomasina said, resting her palms on the desk. "What can I help you with?"

"Maybe nothing. I found your card in a hotel room that may have been used by a murder suspect." Banks was embellishing the truth, but he thought it might be the best way of getting her to talk.

"And what?" She pointed at her chest and blinked. "You think I . . . I mean, you think he hired *me* to kill someone?"

"No doubt he picked you on the basis of your name in the telephone directory. It sounds tough, like the sort of person who'd be capable of anything."

"But if he'd known I was Tomasina?"

"Exactly," said Banks. "Anyway, I'm not accusing you of murder."

"Well, thank the Lord for that."

"I just want to know if you accepted an assignment from a man called Derek Wyman, and if you did, what exactly it consisted of."

She picked up a pencil and started doodling. "You know," she said, looking down as she spoke, "that there are issues of confidentiality involved here. When people come to me, they come to a *private* investigator, not someone who'll shout out their business to the world, or the police."

"I understand that, and I have no intention of shouting out your business to the world."

"Even so," she said, "I can't tell you who my clients are or what they want me to do. None of it's illegal. I can assure you of that."

"I'm sure it's not." Banks paused. "Look, you can really help me here. I'm going out on a limb on this and I need to know if I'm right. If I'm not, then . . . well, I don't know. But if I am . . ."

"It could lead to a court case in which you'd expect me to testify for the Crown?"

"It won't come to that."

"Yeah, and you'll still respect me in the morning."

"You're very cynical for one so young."

"I'm only trying to protect my interests." She gave him a direct look. "As you can see, the place isn't exactly crawling with clients – despite the tough, sexy name. In fact, I'm hard pushed to make ends meet from one week to the next if truth be told. Now you expect me to throw away my reputation because of some limb you're out on."

"Why not try another career? A more lucrative one?"

"Because I like what I do. And I'm good at it. I started out with a big agency, and I did my ABI training and got my Advanced Diploma. Then I decided I wanted to go out on my own. I've done all the courses. And passed them with flying colours. I'm twenty-seven years old, I've got degrees in law and criminology, and I've had five years' on-the-job experience with the big boys before I set up my own firm. Why should I search for another career?"

"Because you don't have any clients and you can barely pay the rent?"

She glanced away, her cheeks flushed. "They'll come. It just takes time, that's all. I'm just starting out."

"I'm sorry," said Banks. "I'm not trying to browbeat you or any-thing. I'm really just asking for your help. To be honest, I'm rather in the same boat as you on this one."

"You mean this isn't an official investigation?"

"Not exactly."

"You're acting on your own? Oh, that's prize, that is." She dropped her pencil. "Not only do you come in here pushing me to give you con-fidential information, but it's not even part of a sanctioned police inves-tigation. Why don't you stop wasting my time?"

"Because it seems to me you've got plenty to waste. Or would you rather get back to your filing?" Banks could swear he saw her eyes begin to shine with tears, and he felt awful. She was the kind of person you wanted to make happy, wanted good things for. If you could hurt someone like Tomasina, he thought, you really were a shit. Then he told himself not to be such a soft bastard; she had to be tough to be in the business she was in, and if she wasn't tough enough, it was better she found out sooner rather than later. But she didn't cry. She was tougher than she looked, and he was glad of that.

"Why?" she said. "So you can have a good ogle at my arse again? Don't think I didn't notice."

"It's a very nice arse."

She glared at him, and for a moment he thought she was going to throw something, the heavy glass paperweight that held down what looked like a heap of bills on her desk, for example, but instead she leaned back in her chair, linked her hands behind her head and started to laugh. "Oh, you're a prize specimen, you are," she said.

"Does that mean you'll help me?"

"I know the rules," she said. "I know I'm supposed to co-operate with the police if the situation merits it. But I don't know anything about this situation."

"It's hard to explain," Banks said.

"Try. I'm bright and I'm a good listener."

"Have you read or seen anything about the two deaths in Eastvale recently?"

"The two gay guys? Sure. Murder-suicide, wasn't it?"

"So it would appear."

"But you don't believe it?"

"Oh, I believe that Mark Hardcastle beat Laurence Silbert to death with a cricket bat and then hanged himself. I just don't believe he did it without help. A rather unusual form of help."

"I'm listening."

Banks tried to explain his *Othello* theory, aware of how absurd it sounded every time he did so. By the end he was having a hard time believing it himself. Instead of laughing at him or scoffing, though, Tomasina sat with her brow furrowed and her hands meeting in a steeple on the desk for a full minute or so after he'd finished. And that's a long time.

"Well?" Banks said, when he could wait no longer.

"You really believe that? That that's how it happened?"

"I think it's likely, yes."

"But what evidence do you have?"

"None." Banks wasn't going to bring the Secret Intelligence Service into his discussion with her. He had already decided on that.

"Motive?"

"None that I'm aware of right now, other than professional jealousy."

"So the only thing even approaching evidence you have is that this Wyman character was directing *Othello*, that he met up with Hardcastle in London the day before the killing, that they had some professional differences and that they have been seen drinking and talking together in a pub a couple of miles out of town?"

"And that he may have had a memory stick with pictures of Silbert with another man. Neither Hardcastle nor Silbert had a digital camera that took such a card."

"What about Wyman?"

"He didn't have one, either. His is a Fuji."

"And that's all you've got?"

"Yes. I suppose if you put it like that . . ."

"What other way *is* there to put it?"

"That when you add it all up together it's damn suspicious, that's what. Why go two miles to a grotty teens' pub when there are plenty of good pubs in Eastvale? A group of his bloody fifteen-year-old pupils was in there, for crying out loud. And how did he get Hardcastle upset and then calm him down? Why?"

"There's no way anyone could have known what effect playing Iago would have on two people."

"That's what Annie said."

"Annie?"

"DI Cabbot. We were working on it together."

"And now?"

"Well, officially, we're off it. Orders from above."

"Why?"

"I don't know. We were just told to drop it. Anyway, aren't I the one supposed to be asking the questions here?"

She smiled that radiant smile again, the one that made you feel you had to maintain her happiness at all costs. "I told you, I'm good at my job. That was one of my best marks, interviewing techniques. Along with surveillance and research. She's right, though, your partner."

"I know that. Maybe it went wrong?"

"Then it wasn't murder. A very bad practical joke, perhaps. Some sort of malicious trick backfiring. But not murder. I suppose you know

that, don't you? At the most, you'd be able to charge him with harassment or incitement, that's if you can prove that he did indeed incite
anyone to a criminal act."

"It doesn't matter," Banks said. "The result's the same. Two men are
dead. And very nastily, brutally dead, I might add. One beaten to a pulp
and the other hanging from a tree near a beauty spot where children
were playing."

"You can't intimidate me with the graphic horror of it all. I've seen
dead bodies. I've even seen *Saw IV* and *Hostel Part II*."

"Well, what *will* work with you?"

Tomasina studied him again for what felt like another long time,
then she said, "I took those photos."

"What?"

"The photos you're talking about. On the memory stick. I took
them."

Banks's jaw must have dropped. "Just like that?"

"Well, it wasn't quite that easy. I had to stay out of sight."

"No, I mean, you're admitting it just like that. I appreciate what
you're doing, really I do."

Tomasina shrugged. "When a cute man – and the father of my rock
hero, no less – says nice things about my arse, I can't very well hold out
on him, can I?"

"I'm sorry about that. It just sort of slipped out."

She laughed again. "It's all right. I'm only teasing. But you'd better
be careful. Some women might not appreciate it as much as I do."

"I know. You're one in a million, Tomasina." Sophia certainly
wouldn't appreciate it, though she might say "I know" or "So I've been
told," Banks thought. Or Annie. In fact, just about every woman he
knew would have given him shit for a comment like that. What the hell
had he been thinking of? Sometimes he would just slip from the politically correct world everyone inhabited these days back to the primeval
slime without warning. Perhaps age was lowering his guard? But he
wasn't *that* old, he told himself. And he was *cute*. "Will you tell me about
it?" he asked.

"There's not much to tell, really."

"But Derek Wyman did come to you?"

"Yes. And he was surprised, as most people are. But not because I wasn't some sort of tough guy. He didn't want me to do any strong-arm work or anything like that. Anyway, I managed to convince him I could do the job."

"What was this job?"

"Simple surveillance. Well, as simple as surveillance can be if you don't want to be spotted. I'm sure you've been there."

Over the years, Banks had spent many hours in cold cars with only a water bottle to pee in. But not for a long time. Surveillance was a young man's job. He wouldn't have the patience now. And the bottle would fill up a lot faster. "Do you remember when Wyman first came to you?"

"I could find out. Hang on."

Tomasina got up and walked back out to her filing cabinets. In a moment she was back carrying a buff folder, which she consulted. "It was the beginning of May."

"That long ago," Banks mused. "What did he ask for?"

"He gave me an address in Bloomsbury, described a man, and asked me if, on certain occasions – he would phone me first – I would watch it, follow the man who left, find out where he went and take photos of him with anyone he met."

"Did he tell you why he wanted to do this?"

"No."

"And you just assumed it was all above board?"

"He seemed all right. I thought, you know, maybe he was gay and he thought his lover was having an affair. It's happened before. All he wanted was photos. It wasn't as if he was asking me to hurt anyone or anything."

Images of Silbert and Hardcastle in the mortuary flashed through Banks's mind. "There's more than one way of hurting someone."

Tomasina flushed. "You can't blame me for what happened. You can't do that."

"It's OK. I'm sorry. I'm not blaming you. I'm just saying that in the wrong hands photos can be as deadly as a gun. Maybe they were intended for blackmail? Didn't you think of that?"

"To be honest, I didn't. It was just my job to take them. Like I said, he seemed nice enough."

"You're right," said Banks. "It wasn't your fault. You were simply doing your job."

She was studying his face, he felt, looking for signs so that she could be certain he was telling the truth and not winding her up. In the end, she reached her decision and relaxed visibly. "It was easy enough," she said. "In the early evening, seven o'clock, the man in question would walk up to Euston Road, then across Regent's Park. Always he would stop and sit on a bench by the boating lake and another man would join him."

"How many times did you follow him?"

"Three."

"He met the same man every time?"

"Yes."

"OK. Go on."

"They didn't talk, but they'd get up and walk together to St. John's Wood. You know, the High Street where the cemetery is."

"I know it," said Banks. "And from there they would walk to Charles Lane and enter a house together."

"Yes. You know all about it?"

"We identified the house and street from one of your photos."

"Of course," said Tomasina. "My, my, you do have all the resources, don't you?"

"Taxpayers' money at work. How long did they stay?"

"Almost two hours every time."

"And then?"

"When they came out they parted ways. My man usually walked to the tube on Finchley Road."

"Usually?"

"Yes. Once he walked all the way back to Bloomsbury the same way he came."

"And the other man?"

"I never followed him. It wasn't required."

"But which direction did he head in?"

"North. Towards Hampstead."

"On foot?"

"Yes."

"When they got to the house on Charles Lane, who had the key?"

"Nobody," said Tomasina.

"Do you mean they just walked straight in? The door was open?"

"No. They knocked and someone answered."

"Did you actually see this person?"

"Not really. She was always in the shadows, back from the open door, and she didn't really show on the photos."

"She?"

"Oh yes, it was definitely a woman. An elderly woman, I'd say. Grey-haired, maybe in her sixties. I could see that much. I just couldn't describe her features. I had to stand around the corner and use the zoom to avoid being seen. But she was quite small, smartly dressed."

"Edith Townsend," said Banks.

"Do you know her?"

"In a way. Did you ever see a man?"

"No. Just the woman."

Lester was probably sitting in the living room reading his *Daily Telegraph*, Banks thought. So they *had* been lying to him, as he suspected, which meant they were something to do with Mr. Browne and the spooks. Or the other side. What had Silbert been up to? It wasn't an affair, Banks was almost certain of that, but were the photos enough to convince Hardcastle that it was? The friendly hand on the shoulder? With the added Iago-style innuendos and rhetoric, perhaps they were, as Hardcastle was insecure and jealous to begin with. Perhaps Silbert was working part-time, involved in some special project run, or fronted, by the Townsends? "Did your client ask you to investigate further when you gave him the memory stick?"

"No. All he seemed interested in was the photos of the two men together. I mean, I didn't get the impression that he really cared what they were doing, why they were meeting."

"When did you give him the memory stick?"

"Wednesday afternoon. The end of May. Two weeks ago."

"Did you give him prints, too?"

"Yes. Do *you* know what it's all about?"

"Not really," Banks said. "I have a few vague ideas, but that's all they are."

"Will you tell me, or is this a one-way street?"

Banks smiled at her. "It's a one-way street for the moment, a cul-de-sac, too, as far as I can see."

"So that's it? You come here and use me up and then simply discard me?"

"'Fraid so. Don't take it so hard, Tomasina. It's a tough business you're in. Look on the bright side. You've done the right thing. Talked to the police."

"Yeah, sure. I've talked to one policeman who's already been warned off. OK, forget it. Is this it, then? You walk out of here and I never see you again?"

"This is it." Banks stood up. "But if you need to get in touch, you can call this number." He scribbled down his new mobile number on the back of his card, handed it to her and walked over to the door.

"Wait," she called out behind him. "Will you do just one teeny little thing for me?"

Banks paused at the door. "It depends on what it is."

"The Blue Lamps. Can you get me a ticket for their next show? And will you introduce me to Brian?"

Banks looked back at her. "I'll see what I can do," he said.

12

By late Thursday afternoon, Annie had had quite enough of Eastvale Comprehensive and the East Side Estate's problems. She didn't want a drink, but she did want a bit of peace and quiet, so she bought a Britvic orange and hid herself away in the back room of the Horse and Hounds. As usual, there was no one else around but her. It was dim and cool, the perfect place to collect her thoughts and perhaps have another quiet chat with Banks on her mobile.

Though she still wasn't convinced by Banks's wild theories, she was beginning to believe that there was something odd about Derek Wyman and his whole relationship with Mark Hardcastle. What had he got out of it? Was it really just a matter of two film and theatre buffs having a drink and a chat every now and then? A couple of anoraks together? Or was there something more ominous behind it? If Wyman really were concerned about Hardcastle's plan for a professional acting group, then why did he act as if they were the best of friends?

It might be worth having a word with Carol Wyman alone, Annie thought. Better not get caught, though. Superintendent Gervaise wouldn't take kindly to her moonlighting for Banks. They'd be tarred by the same brush, if they weren't already. And for what? A half-baked theory based on a Shakespeare play that, even if it were true, couldn't lead to any criminal charges that she was aware of. Still, Annie had to admit that she was intrigued by the whole business, and there were enough niggling doubts in her mind to make her willing to take the occasional risk.

The first item on the agenda, though, was to phone Banks, if he was available. Annie found his last call in the log and pressed the call button. It rang. When Banks answered, she could hear traffic in the background.

"Where are you?" she asked. "Are you driving? Can you talk?"

"I can talk," said Banks. "I'm just entering Soho Square. Hang on a minute. I'll sit on the grass." There was a short pause, then he came back on the line. "That's better. OK, what is it?"

"I just thought we should get up to date, that's all. I talked to Derek Wyman in the school staffroom. We were asking him about Nicky Haskell and the stabbing, but on the way out I let him know he'd been seen with Mark Hardcastle in the Red Rooster."

"And?"

"He got very stroppy indeed. Told me I should mind my own business and he had a right to drink anywhere and with anyone he wanted. Well, words to that effect."

"The strain's showing?"

"I'd say that, yes. Assuming you're right about this, the Iago business and all that – and I'm not saying you *are* right – but let's say something along those lines did happen."

"I'm still with you. I think."

"Well, have you thought how it changes things?"

"In what way?"

"If Derek Wyman did poison Mark Hardcastle against Laurence Silbert –"

"There's no 'if' about it, Annie. He did. I just found the private detective he hired to follow Silbert and take the photos."

Annie practically dropped her phone. "He did what?"

"He hired a private detective. Which is quite a luxury on his part, because he wasn't exactly rolling in money. You should have seen the B and B he stayed at in Victoria. Definitely cheap and cheerful. But I imagine he had no choice. With school duties and everything, he couldn't get down to London as often as he would have liked. And I'll bet he didn't want to be recognized, either. Remember, he *had* met Silbert once or twice at dinners."

"So what happened?"

"This woman followed Silbert from the Bloomsbury pied-à-terre to Regent's Park, where he met a bloke on a bench, then the two of them carried on to the house in St. John's Wood. Wyman wasn't interested in what they were doing together, apparently, or in anything other than the photos. That's all he wanted, Annie. Photos of Silbert with another man. Evidence."

"So it could have been completely innocent?"

"I doubt it. The pictures are ambiguous, to say the least. They meet on a park bench, walk and go into a house. There's no hand-holding or anything. The only time they touch is when Silbert precedes the other man into the house. But I'd say with Iago's powers of persuasion they made pretty good icing on the cake."

"So what were Silbert and his pal up to?"

"My guess is that they were probably working on something together. Some intelligence service project or other. I've been to that house and the old couple who own it are definitely dodgy. The sweet little old lady lied to me through her teeth, which leads me to believe she's one of them, too, rather than the madam of a posh shag-pad."

"So he was still spying? He hadn't retired?"

"Something like that. Or he was working for the other side, whoever that is. But imagine what it would seem like to Hardcastle, Annie, especially with the help of Wyman's sly innuendos and graphic images."

"The point I was trying to make," Annie went on, "was that if – or because – Wyman poisoned Hardcastle against Silbert, there's no reason to believe that Silbert was the intended victim. Wyman hardly knew him. He *did* know Hardcastle quite well, though."

"So you're saying Mark Hardcastle was the victim?"

"I'm saying he could have been. And you still have to consider the simple but significant fact that Wyman could *not have been certain of the effects of his actions.*"

"I agree he couldn't have known that Hardcastle would kill Silbert, then himself."

"Well, thank the Lord for that."

"But he did know he was stirring up a volatile situation, and that someone might get hurt."

"True. Even if only emotionally, even if his only intention was to split them up."

"Is that what you're suggesting?"

"It makes sense, doesn't it? Isn't it what you'd expect if you convinced someone his partner was being unfaithful, rather than bloody murder and suicide? And Wyman had plenty of reason to be upset with Hardcastle over developments at the theatre. Not enough to kill him, obviously, but perhaps enough to want to do a bit of mischief."

"Perhaps," said Banks.

"In which case," Annie went on, "all this spooks business is beside the point. What happened wasn't anything to do with the security of the realm, terrorists, the Russian mafia, or any of that claptrap."

"What about Mr. Browne?"

"You pissed in his swimming pool, Alan. For God's sake, we'd be swarming around quickly enough if it was one of our blokes died that way."

"Julian Fenner, Import-Export, the mysterious phone number that doesn't ring?"

"Tradecraft? Part of what Silbert was up to when he was in London? How he contacted the man in the photo? I don't know."

"And us being warned off?"

"They don't want publicity. It does so happen that Silbert was a member of MI6, and he'd probably been involved in a fair bit of dirty business over the years. Probably still was, judging by what you were telling me. They don't want to take the slightest chance that any of that might come out in the press or in the courts. They don't want their dirty laundry washing in public. It was all neatly wrapped up. Murder-suicide. Sad but simple. No need for any further messy investigations. And then you come along sticking your chest out and waving your fist in the air crying foul."

"Is that how you see me?"

Annie laughed. "A bit, I suppose."

"Charming. I thought I was more of a knight on a white charger tilting against windmills and throwing a spanner in the works."

"Now you're *really* mixing your metaphors. Oh, you know what I mean, Alan. Bloke stuff. Pissing contest."

"I'm still not convinced."

"But you admit that I could be right, that it was all about Hardcastle, not Silbert?"

"It could be. Why don't you nose around into Wyman's and Hardcastle's backgrounds a bit more deeply, see if you can find anything? Who knows, maybe you'll find the missing link somewhere in all that? It's also possible that someone else was involved, that someone put Wyman up to it. Paid him, even. And I know you don't like to consider the spook stuff, but it's also possible that someone in that line of work who wanted to hurt Silbert put Wyman up to it, too. Not as likely, I admit, because the outcome was far from certain, but not entirely out of the question."

"But we concentrate on the Wyman–Hardcastle angle for the time being rather than . . . Oh, shit!"

"What is it, Annie?"

Annie looked up at the slight but commanding figure of Detective Superintendent Gervaise standing in the doorway, a pint in her hand. "Ah, DI Cabbot," Gervaise said. "So this is your little hideaway. Mind if I join you?"

"No problem, ma'am," Annie said loudly enough for Banks to hear, then she pressed the end-call button.

Banks wondered how Annie would talk herself out of being caught in the Horse and Hounds by Superintendent Gervaise, who had probably also heard that remark about following the Wyman–Hardcastle angle. No doubt she would tell him as soon as she could. He got up and brushed the grass off his trousers. It was a fine evening, and the little park in the centre of Soho Square was filling up: a couple lying together on the grass stroking and kissing, a student sitting by her backpack reading a book, a shabby old man eating sandwiches out of greaseproof paper. Office workers cut through on their way to or from Oxford Street and Tottenham Court Road tube station. Already a few young people had gathered around the fringes of the park to prepare for that night's concert at the Astoria, tight jeans, straight dyed hair and T-shirts bearing band logos. Banks remembered he had been to see Brian's band there a couple of years ago and had felt very ancient and out of it. He passed the odd little gardener's hut at the park's centre, and the statue of King Charles II, then crossed Oxford Street and continued on Rathbone.

The pubs were filling up, smokers crowding the pavements outside. On Charlotte Street the patios were mostly full already – Bertorelli's, Pizza Express, Zizzi's – the streets packed with people searching for somewhere to eat. The high-end restaurants with their discreet façades, like Pied à Terre, would be filling up later, but for now, in the early evening light, people wanted to be seen. Most of them were tourists, and Banks heard American accents along with couples speaking German and French.

Not quite sure what he was going to do, Banks made a quick dash when he saw someone leaving one of the outside tables at Zizzi's, getting there before a couple of Americans, who had also had their eye on it. The woman glared at him, but her husband tugged her sleeve and they walked away.

Banks hadn't made any firm arrangements for dinner with Sophia, wasn't even sure what time she'd be home or whether she would have stopped off for a bite, so he decided he was hungry and he might as well have a pizza and a glass of wine, rather than the curry he had been fancying earlier. He was only taking up a table for two, so he didn't get such a dirty look from the waitress when she finally arrived and took his order. The wine soon arrived, a nice large glass, and Banks settled back to sip and watch the pageant.

This was much what Derek Wyman and Mark Hardcastle must have seen when they sat out here about two weeks ago, Banks thought. Mostly pedestrians, some just walking back and forth until they found somewhere to eat, a few beautiful people in evening dress piling out of taxis and limos to some special event in the club next door. Pale pretty blonde girls in jeans and T-shirts carrying backpacks. Grey-haired men wearing powder-blue polo shirts and white trousers walking next to impossibly skinny, tanned women with faces sewn and stretched tight over their skulls, and angry, restless eyes.

What had they been talking about? By then, Banks now guessed, Derek Wyman would have picked up the memory stick and prints of the digital photographs it contained from Tom Savage. Had he given them to Hardcastle here? Perhaps even at this very table? And what had Hardcastle's reaction been? Had they simply gone off to the cinema as planned, or was that another lie? Hardcastle had probably gone and got pissed that night. Banks would have. He knew that Silbert was away in Amsterdam and wouldn't be back until Friday, so he had been in no hurry to get back to Castleview Heights. He had driven up the next day, no doubt drank some more, examined the photos again, brooded over them, got angry, and by the time Silbert got home he had reached breaking point.

Tom Savage had told Banks that she gave Wyman the memory stick on the Wednesday afternoon at about four o'clock, so it would have been fresh in his possession around six when he met Hardcastle here for an early pizza before the film. He must have removed Tomasina's business card, which was probably paper-clipped to the photos, and put it in the top pocket of his shirt and forgotten about it. Perhaps he didn't want Hardcastle to know the source of the photos so he wouldn't be able go around asking questions himself.

When the waitress reappeared with his pizza diavola, Banks asked her whether she had a spare moment. She was clearly busy, but the sight of his warrant card, discreetly shown, drew a curt nod, and she leaned closer.

"Do you work here regularly?" Banks asked.

"Every day."

"Were you working on Wednesday two weeks ago? This same shift?"

"Yes. I work every day same shift."

"Did you notice two men sitting outside at one of these tables about six o'clock?"

"There were many people," she said. "Very busy. Long time ago." Banks thought he detected an Eastern European accent. She glanced over her shoulder, apparently worried that her boss was watching her.

Banks hurried on. "Two men together. One gave something to the other. There might have been an argument or a fuss of some sort."

She put her hand to her mouth. "The man who tear the photographs?"

"What?" Banks said.

"I was delivering order to other table, over there, and this man – I think he dye his hair blond – he look at some photographs and then he get angry and tear them up."

"Did you see the other man give him the photos?"

"No. Very busy. I just notice he tear them."

"Was this two weeks ago today?"

"I no know. Not sure. Maybe. I must go."

It was hardly likely, Banks thought, that two such incidents had occurred in the past couple of weeks. "Did they leave then?" he asked.

"They pay me. Separate bills. Very strange. Then he leave, the one who tear the photographs."

"And the other?"

"He gather up the pieces and stay longer. I must go."

"Thank you," Banks said. "Thank you very much."

The waitress scurried away and Banks sipped some more wine and began to eat his pizza. So Wyman had given Hardcastle the photos at the restaurant, and he had reacted by tearing them up. Which was why they hadn't been found at Castleview Heights. Hardcastle had taken the memory stick, though. Wyman must have asked for two separate bills. No doubt he didn't want to seem so friendly that he had bought dinner for Mark Hardcastle, even at Zizzi's. So it was all a tissue of lies. Banks very much doubted that Hardcastle had rejoined Wyman to go to the National Film Theatre after seeing the photographs. More likely, he went off in a state and got drunk, slept at the Bloomsbury flat, where he had probably polished off the whisky, then drove home the next day to brood and drink until Silbert came back from Amsterdam.

Banks thought further on his conversation with Annie and realized that she could very well be right in that Hardcastle, not Silbert, had been the intended victim, and that left the whole espionage business on the sideline. He also realized that he had *wanted* to be right, wanted it to be something to do with grey men doing dark deeds in the shadows, with or without government approval. He had probably watched and read far too many fictional espionage tales – from *The Sandbaggers* and *Spooks* on television to *The Spy Who Came in from the Cold* and *The Ipcress File* between the covers of a book. Not to mention James Bond. No doubt the reality wasn't like that at all.

On the other hand, one heard rumours. Assassinations had certainly been carried out, elected governments undermined, not only by the CIA in South America, and rival spies or double agents had been murdered in the street. You couldn't forget Philby, or Burgess and Maclean, if you had grown up when Banks had. The Profumo affair, too, had its own very definite whiff of the Cold War in the form of Ivanov, the naval attaché at the Soviet embassy, despite the pleasurable distractions of Christine Keeler and Mandy Rice-Davies. More recently, there were the Bulgarian killed by the poisoned umbrella and Litvinenko poisoned with a radioactive isotope that left a trail halfway across London.

No, it was a shady and much misunderstood world, but it existed, all right, and Banks had apparently become fixed on its radar. The real problem was that, while they could always find you when they wanted to, you could never find them. He could hardly go knocking at the door of Thames House or Vauxhall Cross and ask for Mr. Browne. There was one person he could talk to, though. Detective Superintendent Richard 'Dirty Dick' Burgess had been working with some elite counterterrorism liaison squad for a while now. Even their acronym was so secret that if you heard it you had to die, he had joked. Burgess was a cunning old bastard, but he and Banks went back a long time, and there was a chance he might know some of the people involved, let slip a morsel or two. Phoning him was an option, at any rate.

As Banks finished his wine and decided to leave the last slice of pizza, he was convinced that the young couple who had just passed by again on the opposite side of the street had not had to walk up and down Charlotte Street six times in the past hour, as they had done, simply to find an outside table at a restaurant. Who was it who said that paranoia simply means being in possession of all the facts? Banks gestured to the waitress and reached for his wallet.

"Drink, DI Cabbot?" said Superintendent Gervaise as she plonked her pint down on Annie's table.

Annie glanced at her watch. Just after six.

"You're officially off duty, aren't you? Besides, a senior officer is asking you to have a drink with her."

"OK. Thank you, ma'am," said Annie. "I'll have a pint of Black Sheep, please."

"Good choice. And there's no need to call me ma'am. We're just a couple of colleagues having a drink after work."

Somehow, that sounded more ominous to Annie than Gervaise had probably intended. Though she wasn't sure about that. She still hadn't quite got a grasp on the superintendent yet. Gervaise was tricky. You had to be careful. One minute she could come on like your best friend, and the next she was all business again, the boss. Then just when you started to think she was a careerist, straight from university and training school to a desk upstairs, she would surprise you with a story from her past, or take a course of action that could only be described as reckless. Annie decided it was best to remain as passive as possible and let Gervaise lead the way. You never quite knew where you were with her. The woman was unpredictable, which was an admirable quality in some, but not in a superintendent, and sometimes when you went away from a meeting with her, you weren't always quite sure what had transpired or what you had agreed to do.

Gervaise came back with the Black Sheep and sat opposite Annie. After raising her glass for a toast, she looked around the small room, its dark, varnished panelling glowing in the soft light, and said, "Nice here, isn't it? I always think the Queen's Arms is just a little too noisy and busy at times, don't you? I can't say I blame you for coming here instead."

"Yes'm . . . Yes," said Annie, just collecting herself in time. *Two colleagues having a drink after work.* So the game was up. Gervaise knew about the Horse and Hounds. Pity. Annie liked the place, and the beer was good. Even the Britvic orange was good.

"Was that DCI Banks you were talking to just now?"

"I . . . er . . . yes," said Annie.

"Having a nice holiday, is he?"

"So he says."

"Any idea where he is?"

"London, I think."

"Still? So he hasn't got as far as Devon or Cornwall yet?"

"Apparently not."

"But he does have his mobile with him?"

Annie shrugged.

"Funny, that, because I can't seem to get hold of him at all."

"I don't suppose he has it turned on all the time. He *is* on holiday, after all."

"Ah, that must be it. Anyway, did I hear a mention of some sort of Wyman–Hardcastle connection?"

"You might have done, yes. Just a bit of harmless theorizing, you know . . . as one does . . ."

Gervaise put on a puzzled expression. "But that can't be, surely? According to my files, there is *no* Hardcastle case. And I'm supposed to be in charge, aren't I? I believe the coroner even filed a verdict of suicide."

"Yes, ma'am."

"I told you. Skip the formalities. It *is* all right if I call you Annie, isn't it?"

It felt odd, but Annie wasn't going to argue at the moment. She needed to find out where Gervaise was going, and you could never tell from her opening gambits. "Of course," she said.

"Look here, Annie," Gervaise went on. "I like you. You're a good copper. You appear to have your head screwed on the right way, and at a guess I'd say you're fairly ambitious, am I right?"

"I like to do a good job and be recognized for it," said Annie.

"Exactly. Now nobody can fault you on that last business you were involved in on detachment to Eastern Area. One might argue that you acted rather hastily at the end, went off half-cocked, but there was no way you could predict how things were going to turn out. As it happened, you acquitted yourself very well. It's always a pity when blood is shed, but it could have been worse, a lot worse, if you hadn't kept your head and your wits about you."

Annie didn't feel that she had kept her head at all, but you didn't throw such praise back in the face of the person who gave it to you. Especially Superintendent Gervaise. "Thank you," she said. "It was a difficult time."

"I can well imagine. Anyway, that's behind us now. As, I thought, was the Hardcastle and Silbert business."

"It's just a few loose ends," Annie said. "You know, dotting i's, crossing t's."

"I see. And just what, once you've done all that, does it spell out?"

"Murder-suicide?"

"Exactly. Now the Chief Constable himself has taken a personal interest in this whole business, and he thinks it's in the best interests of all concerned – his very words – that we toss the file in the solved cabinet – he really thinks we have such a thing, you know – and put it out of our minds, deal with the situation on the East Side Estate before it escalates. This *is* tourist season, you know."

"And let's not forget the traffic cones," said Annie.

Gervaise gave her a disappointed look. "Yes, well. My point is that if you were doing your job, if you were following instructions, if you were –"

"I *am* working on the Donny Moore stabbing."

"I know you're working on it, Annie, but I'm not convinced you're giving it your full attention. Now I catch the tail end of a telephone conversation you're having with DCI Banks, who's supposed to be on holiday, about a business that not only I, but also our Chief Constable, want to forget about. What am I to think? You tell me."

"Think what you like," said Annie. "He just wants to tidy up a few loose ends, that's all."

"But there *aren't* any loose ends. The Chief Constable says so."

"And who told him?"

Gervaise paused and regarded Annie coolly for a moment before replying, "Someone even higher up the tree than he is, no doubt."

"But don't you feel used when the intelligence services start muscling in on our territory?" Annie asked.

"Tut-tut," said Gervaise. "That's not the way to think of it. Not the way at all. This is co-operation. We're all fighting a common battle here, a united front against the forces of evil. They're not 'muscling in,' they're offering us their expertise and helping us find our direction, and in this case they've directed us to a brick wall."

"Like my satnav usually does," said Annie.

Gervaise laughed. They both drank more beer. "Let me tell you a story," she went on. "A few years ago when I was working on the Met, we sometimes had to work a lot more closely than we would have chosen with Special Branch and MI5. You're right, Annie, they can be arrogant and devious bastards, and they usually have the ultimate argument-crusher on their side, don't they, whether it's 9/11 or the July bombings. There's not much you can say when someone brings that up. Fancy another drink?"

"I shouldn't," said Annie.

"Oh, come on."

"OK. But it's my shout." Annie got up and went to the bar. Where the hell was Gervaise going with all this, she wondered as she ordered two more pints of Black Sheep. The pub was filling up now with its usual mix or locals and tourists, some of the latter carrying large rucksacks and walking gear, enjoying their first pint after a ten-mile hike. The pub music system was playing 10CC's "I'm Not in Love." Annie had always liked the song. One of her old boyfriends, an English graduate, had used it to point out to her the difference between irony and sarcasm. She still hadn't gone to bed with him, and when she had quoted "I Get Along Without You Very Well" back at him, she hadn't meant it ironically at all.

Ready for the next instalment, she carried the drinks back to the old snug.

The tube was hot and crowded again, and Banks was relieved to get off at Sloane Square. He walked down the King's Road in the evening light past the big drab Peter Jones department store and Habitat to where the street narrowed and the posh boutiques and jewellery shops took over. As he walked, instinctively slowing down every now and then to look in a shop window and check for anyone who might be following him, he mulled over everything he had discovered that day, from Tomasina's revelation about the photos and Hardcastle's behaviour at Zizzi's to what Annie had told him about Nicky Haskell seeing Wyman arguing, or remonstrating, with Hardcastle at the Red Rooster, and Wyman's reaction to her mention of it.

He hoped Annie was OK. She was usually pretty good at talking herself out of difficult situations, but Gervaise could be tenacious, not to mention wily. There was a part of him that wanted to tell the superintendent that the evidence was bearing out his theory about the Hardcastle–Silbert case, and that Derek Wyman was in it up to his neck, but he didn't trust her that much. There was no glory to be got from this one, and it had already been made perfectly clear to him that MI5, MI6 and Special Branch didn't want him anywhere near the Silbert case.

Sometimes Banks longed for the old days with Gristhorpe in charge. You knew where you were with Gristhorpe, as plain-speaking a Yorkshireman as you could find. There was also a chance that he would have stood up to the powers that be. Gristhorpe had been nobody's puppet, always his own man. Which was perhaps why he had got no higher than detective superintendent. That reminded Banks that he hadn't visited his old boss and mentor in quite some time. Another thing to put on his must-do-soon list.

He turned into Sophia's street and tried to put the case out of his mind. If Sophia was home, perhaps they would have a glass of wine and then go to the cinema, or to a concert, as they had the other night. Even spending the evening at home together would be perfect as far as Banks was concerned. If she wasn't home, then she would probably have left a phone message arranging to meet him somewhere later. When he got to the steps he noticed that the living-room light was on, which meant she was in.

Banks and Sophia had agreed that each should come and go from the other's house as if it were their own, so he put his key in the lock and was surprised when the door opened at his touch. It hadn't been locked. That wasn't like Sophia. He checked the handle and lock for any signs of forced entry and found none. The alarm system should have taken care of anything like that, anyway.

Calling out Sophia's name, Banks turned right from the hall into the living room and stopped dead on the threshold. She was so still, with her head hanging on her chest, that at first he feared she was dead. But when he called her name again, she lifted up a tear-stained face to him and he could see that she was physically unharmed.

She was sitting on the floor, leaning back against the sofa, her long legs stretched out into the heap of broken things piled at the centre of the carpet. *Her* things. Banks couldn't tell exactly what was there. It looked like a random selection of her cherished possessions taken from various places in the room: a slashed landscape painting that had hung on the wall above the stereo; an antique table on which she had displayed various objects, its spindly legs splintered, mother-of-pearl inlay smashed; a broken Eskimo soapstone sculpture; a shattered ceramic mask; scattered beads from broken strings; a cracked painted Easter egg; dried ferns and flowers tossed willy-nilly over the whole mess like a parody of a funeral.

Sophia sat clutching a piece of exquisite gold-rimmed pottery in her hand, her palm bleeding from how tightly she had clutched it. She held it out to Banks. "This belonged to my mother. Her grandmother gave it to her. God knows how long she'd had it or where she got it." Then she suddenly flung the shard at Banks. It hit the door jamb. "You bastard!" she screamed. "How could you?"

Banks made to move over to her but she held up her hands, palms out. "Don't come near me," she said. "Don't come near me or I don't know what I'll do."

She had her mother's eyes when she was angry, Banks noticed. "Sophia, what is it?" he asked. "What happened?"

"You know damn well what happened. Can't you see? You forgot to set the alarm and . . ." She gestured around the room. "*This* happened."

Banks crouched across the heap from her. His knees cracked. "I didn't forget to set the alarm," he said. "I've never forgotten to set it."

"You must have. There's no other explanation. The alarm never went off. I came home as usual. The door hadn't been broken open or anything. And this was what I found. How else could it have happened? You forgot to set the alarm. Someone just walked in."

Banks didn't see the point in questioning her logic – regarding how anyone could have known if he *hadn't* set the alarm, for example – because she was clearly in no state for that sort of thing. "Did you check the back?" he asked.

Sophia shook her head.

Banks walked down the passage to where the back door opened off the kitchen. Nothing. No sign of forced entry, no sign of any kind of entry. For good measure, he went out into the garden and saw that nothing had been disturbed there, either. The back gate was padlocked, as usual, though anyone could have climbed over it. They would still have had the alarm system to reckon with, though, as it covered the whole house.

He went back to the living room. Sophia hadn't moved. "Have you called the police?" he asked.

"I don't want the bloody police. What can the bloody police do?"

"Even so," he said. "They might be able –"

"Oh, just go away. Why don't you just go away?"

"Sophia, I'm sorry, but this isn't my fault. I set the alarm as usual this morning."

"So how do you explain all this?"

"Was anything taken?"

"How should I know?"

"It could be important. You should make a list for the police."

"I told you, I don't want the police here. What can they do?"

"Well, the insurance company –"

"Bugger the sodding insurance company! They can't replace any of this."

Banks stared at the heap of broken treasures and knew she was right. Everything here was personal, none of it worth a great deal of money. He knew that he *should* call the police, but he also knew that he wouldn't. And not only because Sophia didn't want him to. There was only one explanation for all this, Banks knew, and in a way it *did* make him guilty. There was no point calling the police. The people who had done this were shadows, will-o'-the-wisps, to whom fancy alarm systems were child's play. Mr. Browne had known where Sophia lived, all right. Banks knelt down beside the wreckage. Sophia wouldn't meet his gaze. "Come on," he said, sighing, "I'll help you clean up."

"Thank you," said Gervaise when Annie came back with the drinks. "Where was I?"

"September 11 and the London bombings."

"Ah, yes. My little digression. Anyway, I'm sure you get the picture. Work around these people long enough and you get to think like them. One of the lads on our team, let's call him Aziz, was a Muslim. His family came from Saudi Arabia, and he'd grown up here, spoke like an East Ender, but they still went to the local mosque, said their prayers, the whole thing. This was all in the wake of the July London bombings and the unfortunate shooting of that Brazilian on the tube. Tempers were a little frazzled all round, as you can imagine. Anyway, Aziz made some criticism of the way our local Special Branch–MI5 liaison officer handled a situation at a mosque, said something to indicate that he thought we were all being a bit heavy-handed about it all, and the next thing you know he's got a file as thick as your wrist. They'd fitted him up with a legend. It was all in there, the training camps in Pakistan, the meetings with terrorist cell leaders, all documented, photographs, the lot. Personal friend of Osama bin Laden. I'm sure you get the picture, anyway. And every word, every image of it, was a lie. Aziz had never left England in his life. Hardly even left London. But there it was, in glorious Technicolor, the life of a terrorist. We all knew it was crap. Even MI5 knew it was crap. But they had a point to make and they made it."

Gervaise paused to drink some beer. "They talk about giving their field agents legends," she went on. "Aliases, alternative life histories, complete with all the proof and documentary evidence anyone could ask for. Well, they gave Aziz this, without his even asking for it or needing it. Of course, they searched his flat, interrogated him, told him they'd be back, pestered his friends and colleagues. This was something that could happen to any one of us who stepped out of line, they were saying. Aziz just happened to be dark skinned, happened to be a Muslim, but we weren't immune just because we were white police officers. You might think I was being paranoid, Annie, but you weren't there."

"What happened to Aziz?"

"His career was over. They took back all the files about training camps and stuff, of course – that was all for effect – but they'd made their point as to what they *could* do. A week later Aziz jumped off an overpass on the M1. I mean, I don't suppose it's fair to blame MI5 for that. They couldn't have predicted how deeply unstable he was. Or could they?"

"What are you saying?"

Gervaise sipped more beer. "I'm just telling you a story, Annie, that's all."

"You're warning me off."

"Warning you off what? You're reading too much into what I'm saying. If I'm doing anything at all, Annie, I'm telling you to be very careful, and you can pass that on to DCI Banks the next time you talk to him."

"There's something else," Annie went on. "I don't know what it is, but there's something else. Don't you believe there's something odd about the Hardcastle–Silbert business, something that doesn't quite fit, that doesn't make sense? You do, don't you?"

"You know as well as I do there are always things that don't quite add up. But I would like to point out that, whatever baroque theories you and DCI Banks might have dreamed up, scientific evidence, combined with a thorough police investigation, proved beyond all reasonable doubt that Mark Hardcastle killed Laurence Silbert and then hanged himself. You're not arguing with that, are you. With the facts?"

"No. I'm –"

"Then there is no case to pursue." Gervaise regarded Annie. "Let's say, just for the sake of argument, talking of baroque theories, that DCI Banks had some outlandish idea about someone putting Hardcastle up to it. Showing him fake photos, putting ideas in his head, making innuendos, getting him all riled up, that sort of thing. I went to see *Othello* the other night, and I understand DCI Banks took his girlfriend last weekend. Maybe he got it from there. I knew the play from school, of course, but I hadn't seen it or thought about it for years. It's really quite a powerful story. Interesting, don't you think? Of course, Iago turned a man against his wife, but there's no reason that shouldn't translate into homosexual terms, is there, especially given the element of overkill we sometimes find in gay killings?"

"What?" said Annie. She knew she was on dangerous ground now. She hadn't wanted to reveal the *Othello* theory to Gervaise for fear of being mocked, but now here the woman was quoting it to her. No doubt in order to demolish it in due course.

Gervaise gave her a sideways glance and smiled. "Oh, don't be so disingenuous, Annie. I'm not so green as I'm cabbage-looking, as I believe they say around these parts. Can you think of any other reason why you, or DCI Banks, should think it a case worth pursuing other than that you thought someone put Hardcastle up to it? I'm sure the two of you know as well as I do that our security services have any number of psychological tricks up their sleeves. I mean, even you two don't usually fly in the face of scientific evidence and flout fact. You must have a reason for doing what you're doing, and my guess is that that's it. And as for DCI Banks, well, you probably know as well as I do that if you tell him to do something he does the opposite. I just hope he realizes what happens to spies who go on missions behind enemy lines. Well, am I right? What's wrong, Annie? Lost your voice?"

Banks was in a quandary when he left Sophia's. What should he do? he wondered as he sat in the Porsche down the street, his heart still pounding, hands still shaking. He supposed he could stay at Sophia's house, though it would be unbearable sleeping there on his own after what had just occurred. It was late, but he could also just head home. He'd only had the one glass of wine, and that was some time ago, so he wasn't over the limit. He didn't even feel too tired to drive, though he knew he was distracted. There was always Brian's flat, too, or a hotel.

Sophia had been inconsolable. No matter what he said she couldn't let go of the idea that he had forgotten to set the alarm and someone had been watching and had taken advantage. He supposed, in a way, that was preferable to the truth, that someone from their own intelligence services had done this, perhaps to give Banks a stern message. He also couldn't entirely ignore the fact that he had talked to Victor Morton, Sophia's father, about Silbert, too, and that Victor had spent his working life in the various British consulates and embassies of the world. There had been that strange man at the bar of The Bridge, and all the other strange faces Banks had seen in the street lately. Paranoid? Perhaps. But there was no denying what had happened tonight. Someone with enough gadgetry or know-how to bypass a sophisticated alarm system had walked into Sophia's house and calmly smashed a number of her most treasured possessions and left them in a heap on the living-room floor. Messages didn't get much clearer than that. From what Banks had been able to gather from a cursory look around the whole house, nothing had been taken and no other room had been disturbed; there was just the mess on the living-room carpet. But it was enough. It was more than enough.

Sophia had kept insisting that he go, but he hadn't wanted to leave her alone. In the end, he had persuaded her to phone her best friend

Amy and spend at least the one night at her place. Reluctantly, Sophia had agreed, and Amy had driven over to pick her up. Banks was glad of that. He wouldn't have trusted Sophia not to tell a taxi driver to turn back. But Amy was sensible and strong, and a quick, quiet word in her ear while Sophia was packing her overnight bag was all it took. Banks felt he need have no worries that Sophia would do anything foolish tonight. His dilemma was whether he should stay in London to be around for her tomorrow, in case she had changed her mind about him. For the moment, though, he was about as far in the doghouse as a man could get. Even his feet weren't sticking out.

The woman across the street, he remembered, was a bit of a nosy parker, always at her curtains, lingering a little too long when she closed them at night or opened them in the morning. He got out of the car and went to knock on her door. If she was up to form, she would have seen him coming.

The door opened shortly after his knock. "Yes?" she said.

She was younger than he had imagined from the vague figure he had seen from a distance, and there was an air of loneliness about her, like the shapeless brown cardigan she wrapped around herself, despite the heat.

"I'm sorry to bother you," Banks said, "but it's just that we were expecting someone to come and service the computer across the street. I wonder ..."

"The man and the woman?"

"Yes," said Banks.

"They've already been."

"What time, do you remember?"

"Just after four o'clock. I hadn't seen them before, so I was just a bit suspicious."

"Did they knock?"

"Yes. Then one of them took out a key and they just walked in. It did appear odd, but they didn't act suspiciously at all. They just opened the door and walked in."

"That's all right," Banks lied. "We did leave a key with their company in case we were both out. It was important. They just didn't leave an invoice, that's all."

The woman looked at him as if to say he must be insane leaving keys with strangers. "Maybe they'll post it?"

"Probably. Can you describe the couple for me?"

"Why does that matter?"

"I just want to know if they're the ones I've dealt with before." Banks could tell she was getting suspicious, that his subterfuge was as full of holes as a political manifesto. "I'd like to put in a good word for them."

"Just a man and a woman," she said. "Nicely dressed. The kind of people you'd expect calling in a street like this. Though I must say *she* seems to go in more for the long-hair crowd. Present company excepted, of course."

"Long hair never suited me," said Banks. "Young or old?"

"Young, I'd say. Or youngish. Late thirties, perhaps. About her age. They didn't seem like service people to me. More like debt collectors. Or bailiffs. Is something wrong?"

"No, nothing at all," said Banks, who had never seen a bailiff in his life. He wasn't even sure that they still existed. At least it wasn't Mr. Browne. But then, he wouldn't do something like this himself; he would send operatives. "It's just computers," he said. "You know . . . How long were they in there?"

"Less than an hour, so don't let them over-bill you. I hope they did a good job."

"I don't suppose you'd ever seen them before, had you?"

"No. Why? Look, I'm sorry, but my dinner's in the oven and the cat wants feeding." She started to close the door. Banks muttered goodnight and went back to his car.

Just as he had sat down, his new mobile rang. He had given the number only to Annie, Tomasina and Dirty Dick Burgess. It was Annie calling, he saw, and he owed it to her to answer. She was a part of it all, putting herself on the line for his half-cocked private investigation. He answered the call.

"Alan?"

"Yes. What happened?"

"Don't ask me how, but she found me in the Horse and Hounds."

"What did she say?"

"I don't really know. She told me a story about a young Muslim police officer drummed out of the force after pissing off the spooks. She told me the Chief Constable in particular wanted an end to this business. She told me there was no case to be investigated."

"All to be expected," said Banks. "Anything else?"

"Plenty. She said she'd been to see *Othello* and thought you might have based some theory of events on it."

"She what?"

"My reaction exactly."

"What did you tell her?"

"I didn't need to tell her anything. She was a step ahead of me the whole time."

"Did you tell her about the evidence? Tom Savage? The photos? The Red Rooster?"

"Of course not. But she's no fool, Alan. It's only a matter of time."

"Does she know where I am?"

"I told her you were in London. She's suspicious that she can't get hold of you on your mobile."

"Damn."

"I had no choice, Alan."

"I know. I know. It's not your fault. I just didn't think it would all turn to shit so soon."

"What do you mean?"

"Nothing. It doesn't matter. Just be careful, Annie."

"That's what she said, too. And she told me to pass on the same warning to you. She also said you're the sort of person who does the opposite of what he's told."

"So she knew I'd continue the investigation on my own time. She planned on it all along."

"I wouldn't go that far," Annie said. "But she's not surprised."

"I don't like what's happening."

"There was one more thing."

"What?"

"When she'd finished, Gervaise seemed interested, seemed to think we'd actually got something. She even mentioned that the spooks knew how to use all sorts of psychological weaponry against people."

"Jesus Christ. She didn't tell you to lay off, then?"

"Well, she sort of did. Rather she told me the *Chief Constable* had said to lay off. But in the end she just started rambling on about spies getting caught behind enemy lines. You know what she's like. I think she was just telling us – you specifically – not to expect any mercy if we get caught."

"Annie, you can get out of this right now," said Banks. "Just back off and be seen to throw all your energies into the East End Estate business."

"You must be joking."

"I've never been more serious."

"What are you going to do?"

"I don't know. Come home, maybe. You know, what I could really do with right now is a cigarette."

Annie laughed. "Well, it probably wouldn't be the worst thing that could happen to you. I'm on my third pint of Black Sheep all alone in the snug of the Horse and Hounds."

"I don't know what your plans are," Banks said, "but why don't you call Winsome, stay at her place tonight?"

"You know, I might do just that," said Annie. "I've certainly had too much to drink to drive home, and it would be nice to have the company, if she'll have me."

"I'm sure she will," said Banks. "Give her a ring."

"OK, boss."

"I'm serious. Remember, be careful. Goodnight."

Annie started to say something, but Banks pressed the end-call button. He thought about turning off the phone altogether, then he realized it probably didn't matter with the new pay-as-you-go. It didn't really matter with anything, when it came down to it, he realized. If they wanted to find him, they would find him. Or anyone else he came into contact with. They obviously knew he was still working on the case against their orders, and the mess at Sophia's was an attempt to warn him off. He couldn't even call Brian. They obviously must know that he had a son and a daughter and an ex-wife, just as they knew about Sophia, but there was no sense in bringing Brian openly into the thick of things. Going to see him tonight would simply be marking him out for special attention.

Banks sat with his hands on the wheel. He didn't think he had ever felt so alone in his life. He was beyond even music. There wasn't a song in the world that could alleviate or accompany the way he felt right now. Drink was a possibility. Oblivion. But even that somehow seemed pointless. In the end, he started the car and drove. He had no idea where he was going, only that he had to move on. Bad things happened when you stood still for too long in this game.

13

Banks didn't feel any better at nine o'clock on Friday morning than he had when he had finally fallen asleep at 3:30. After driving around for an hour or so the previous evening, keeping a close eye on his rear-view mirror for any telltale signs that he was being followed, he had checked into the first decent hotel he had seen. He realized as soon as he offered his credit card that if anyone was really serious about tracking him down, that would do it. By then, he was just about past caring.

He had thought of going to Mohammed's B and B, but the idea of waking up in a room like the one Derek Wyman had usually rented when he was in town, or even in the *same* room, was just too depressing. He wanted a room with a shower and a bit of space, somewhere safe to park his car, a decent television set and a well-stocked minibar for numbing the mind and senses. He had got all of this for a little over a hundred and fifty pounds in a place off Great Portland Street, in Fitzrovia, though given the minibar prices, it probably wouldn't turn out to be much of a bargain, after all. At least he hadn't got completely pissed and ended up with a hangover. Physically, he felt OK after a long shower and a pot of room-service coffee.

Over a latte and a cranberry muffin at a nearby Caffé Nero, Banks jotted down a list of things to do that day. Not much remained for him in London, except to try to contact Dirty Dick Burgess again and see whether Sophia would answer her phone.

It would make more sense to head back up to Eastvale today and have another go at Wyman. Surely even Superintendent Gervaise would agree, after hearing Tom Savage's story, that they had enough to arrest him, or at least bring him in for questioning, on incitement or harassment. Annie had done right not to tell her yesterday, but perhaps it was time she knew. If he could convince the superintendent that the business was nothing to do with Silbert and the spooks, but something personal between Wyman and Hardcastle, then maybe she would see the point in trying to find out exactly what had happened.

Banks was about to try Sophia and Burgess again on the pay-as-you-go mobile when it rang. It wasn't Annie this time, or Burgess.

"Mr. Banks?"

"Yes."

"This is Tom. Tom Savage."

"Tomasina. What is it?"

"Some people were here. They were waiting when I got in this morning. They . . . I'm scared, Mr. Banks."

Banks gripped the phone tightly. His palm felt sweaty. "Are they still there?"

"No. They've gone. They've taken stuff . . . I . . ." Banks thought he could hear her sobbing.

"You're still at the office?"

"Yes."

"OK. Stay right there." He looked at his watch. Great Marlborough Street wasn't that far; it wouldn't even be worth taking a taxi. "I'll be over in about ten minutes. Don't move."

"Thank you. I'm not usually so . . . a baby . . . I just don't . . ."

"It's OK, Tomasina. Hang on. I'll be there."

Banks turned off the phone, slipped it in his pocket and hurried out into the street, cursing as he went.

"I'm sorry to disturb you at work," said Annie, "but do you think you could spare me a few moments?"

Carol Wyman turned to the young girl beside her. "Can you cover for me, Sue? I'm just off for a coffee." Sue seemed a little surprised, but she smiled and said OK. They were both standing behind a counter. Two other women were sitting at a desk in the small anteroom surrounded by filing cabinets. From what Annie could see, the office behind was lined with cabinets too. Everyone appeared to be busy. There was nothing quite like the sight of the National Health Service meeting its quotas to get your blood rising, thought Annie.

Carol Wyman grabbed her handbag and ducked under the flap. "There's a nice coffee shop just over the road," she said. "If that's all right."

"Perfect," said Annie. It was nine o'clock on Friday morning, and she was ready for her second cup of the day. It had to be better than the swill they got at the station.

"What's it all about, by the way?" asked Carol as they stood at the zebra crossing in the morning sunshine, waiting for the traffic to stop. The medical centre was an old gabled three-storey building, once a Victorian parsonage, made of limestone and millstone grit with a slate roof. Broad stone steps led up to the heavy varnished wood door. It was set back from Market Street behind a courtyard where the staff parked their cars, wedged between two strips of shops, about a hundred yards north of the theatre on the other side of the street. Handy for Carol to meet her husband after work, Annie thought, though their hours were no doubt very different.

"Just a few routine questions," said Annie as they crossed Market Street and headed for the Whistling Monk. The place was fairly quiet, as it was too late for the pre-work crowd and too early for the tourist coaches. They found a small table by the window. The blue-and-white checked tablecloth was impeccably clean and ironed, and a menu printed on faux parchment in blue italics stood wedged between the salt and pepper shakers.

A young waitress scribbled their orders after apologizing that the espresso machine wasn't working. Annie settled for café American and Carol went for a cup of herbal tea. Both also ordered toasted teacakes.

"Remember the days when all you could get was Nescafé?" said Annie.

"Just the powdered stuff, before all those fancy granules and gold blends," said Carol.

"If you were lucky you might get Cona."

"But it was expensive."

"Listen to us," said Annie. "We sound like a couple of old women. Next we'll be complaining about rationing."

"Now I definitely *don't* remember that," said Carol. They laughed. The coffee and tea came, along with their teacakes. "You've changed your hair since you were over at the house," Carol went on. "It looks nice. It really suits you. Have you ever thought of going blonde?"

"I don't know if I could handle more fun," said Annie. "Still, it's a thought." She blew on her coffee, then added a generous helping of cream. "Actually, it's your husband I wanted to talk to you about."

Carol Wyman frowned. "Derek? Why, what's he done?"

"We don't think he's done anything," Annie lied. "We just need to know a little more about his relationship with Mark Hardcastle and Laurence Silbert."

"I thought that was all over. Your superintendent said so on the news."

"Just tidying up a few loose ends," said Annie, smiling. "Sometimes the job's nothing but paperwork."

"I know what you mean," said Carol, pouring her pale green tea from the rose-coloured pot. It smelled of mint and camomile. "Mine's just the same. And some of the doctors are real sticklers."

"I don't suppose you can read their writing, though, can you?" said Annie.

Carol laughed. "As a matter of fact," she said, "it *is* a problem."

"How long has your husband been directing plays for the theatre?"

"Ages now," said Carol. "I mean, not so much for the theatre, but the Amateur Dramatic Society. They used to put on performances at the community centre, even the church hall sometimes."

"He seems very passionate about his work."

"Oh, he is," Carol said. "Sometimes I think he's more passionate about his work than he is about me. No, that's not fair. He's a good husband. And a good father. It's just that I think he sometimes takes too much on his plate. The teaching certainly wears him down and –"

"I thought he liked it?"

"Well, he does. I mean, something like that, it gives you a chance to make a difference, doesn't it? To inspire future generations." She glanced around the room and leaned forward, lowering her voice. "But a lot of them just don't care. A lot of them don't even bother turning up for school. It's hard when you really care about something, to be constantly surrounded by people who mock it."

"That's what Derek feels?"

"Sometimes."

"It must have made him a bit cynical about it all."

"Well, he gets depressed sometimes, I can tell you that." She took a sip of the steaming tea. "Mmm, that's nice," she said. "Just the ticket."

"Why doesn't he consider another line of work?"

"You try that at forty-two, when you've been a teacher for more than twenty years."

"I see."

"If he didn't have his theatre, I don't know what he'd do. I think it's the only thing that keeps him sane. He loves the new arrangement. You know, it makes him feel just that bit more important to be working in a real theatre rather than a village hall or something."

"I know what you mean," said Annie. "He must feel like a real professional."

"Yes. And he works so hard. Anyway, what is it you want to know?"

"Has your husband ever mentioned going to the Red Rooster pub?"

"The Red Rooster? In Medburn? But that's a chain pub. Derek is strictly a real-ale man. Used to be a member of CAMRA and all. He wouldn't be seen dead in a place like that. Why?"

"It doesn't matter," said Annie, even more curious now. "As I said, I'm just tidying up loose ends. You get swamped with information in a case like this, and you have to sort out the wheat from the chaff."

"I suppose so," said Carol slowly.

Annie could see that she was starting to lose her. Any more questions that implied Carol's husband was up to something, or behaving out of character, and that would be the end of their pleasant little chat. The door opened and an elderly couple stuck their heads around the door and decided the place would do. They said hello and settled down two tables away. "It must have been terrible for Derek when his brother died," Annie said, making an abrupt turn, remembering the photograph in the Wymans' living room.

"Oh God, yes," said Carol. "Derek simply *adored* Rick. Hero-worshipped him. He was just devastated, gutted. We all were."

"When exactly did it happen?"

"Fifteenth October, 2002. I won't forget that date in a hurry."

"I'll bet you won't. Did you know him well?"

"Rick? Of course. He was a lovely fella. You know, you think these SAS chaps are all macho, like someone out of an Andy McNab book, and probably a lot of them are, but Rick was great with the kids, as gentle as could be. And he was considerate. Always remembered your birthday and anniversary."

"Your husband's brother was in the SAS?"

"Yes. I thought he said."

"No." Even Annie knew that the SAS carried out covert operations, and if Laurence Silbert had worked for MI6, he would probably have had some contact with them, might even have ordered missions or at least overseen the supply of intelligence to guide them. This was back in Banks's territory again, but at least *she* was keeping an open mind. She did believe that someone, most likely Derek Wyman, had goaded Hardcastle into killing Silbert and then himself – more likely by accident than design – but she didn't know why. It could just have been annoyance over the theatre, but, on the other hand, it could have had more sinister roots, given Silbert's past.

"Was Rick married?" she asked.

"Not technically, no. Common-law. He lived with Charlotte. Been together for years. He once told me he didn't want to say the vows, you know, till death us do part and all that, because of his job. He thought it might bring him bad luck or something. A bit superstitious, was Rick. But they loved each other so much. You only had to see them together."

"Kids?"

"No." Carol frowned. "Rick once told me that Charlotte wanted children but that he just couldn't do it, given his job, like, the risks, and the kind of world they'd be born into. I think in the end Charlotte just accepted the situation. Well, you have to, don't you, if you really love somebody?"

Annie didn't know; she had never loved anybody that much. "Do you have her address?" she asked.

"No. It was called 'Wyedene,' though. I remember that from when we visited them."

"What was Charlotte's last name?"

"Fraser."

"So Rick was away a lot, was he?"

"I wouldn't say a lot. They had a lovely house in the country. Ross-on-Wye. Charlotte still lives there. He did a lot of training, but he did go on missions, yes. That was what did for him, of course."

"What?" said Annie. "I thought it was a helicopter accident."

Carol lowered her voice again. "Well, that's what they have to say, isn't it? The official line. They don't want people to know what it's *really* like out there. What's *really* going on. Like in the war, they didn't want to give people the really bad news, did they? They made all those propaganda films."

"True," said Annie. "What happened?"

"I don't know the full story."

Annie could feel Carol pulling away again, but she didn't want to let go of this line of questioning. Not just yet. "We never do, do we?" she said. "Even in my job, the bosses hold their cards close to their chests. Half the time we don't know why we're asking the questions we are, following the lines of inquiry we're told to. It's not like it is on television, I can tell you that."

"Well, in this case I really *don't* know. All I do know is that it was a secret mission, not an accident. Something went wrong."

"How do you know that?"

"Derek told me. He'd talked to a couple of Rick's mates after the funeral, when they'd all had a few, like. The funeral was back here, in Pontefract, where they grew up. Anyway, they didn't give much away, either, they're trained not to, but Derek said he got the impression that Rick's mates wanted him to know that his brother hadn't died in some stupid accident, but that he'd died in action, a hero."

Annie didn't know whether this had any relevance at all, but it was something that Derek Wyman had skirted around when they had first talked to him. Perhaps Rick's partner, Charlotte, knew? Annie would never get the SAS to talk to her, especially as she had no official backing on this case, or even a case, come to think of it. They were far more likely to come smashing through her window one night and cart her off to Guantanamo Bay or whatever their equivalent was. But Charlotte Fraser of 'Wyedene' might not be averse to a sympathetic ear, and it shouldn't be too difficult to track her down.

"I realize this is a bit of a cheeky question," Annie said, "and please don't take it the wrong way, but didn't it ever worry you, your husband being close to a gay man?"

"Why should it?"

"Well, some people . . . you know . . ."

"Perhaps if I didn't feel *secure* with Derek it might have done," she admitted.

"But . . . ?"

Carol reddened and turned away. "Well," she said, "let's just say I have no worries on *that* score."

"I'm sorry for asking," said Annie. "How is Derek doing now?"

"Oh, he's all right. I mean, he's still a bit upset about Mark, a bit quiet and moody. Well, you would be, wouldn't you? It's not every day a good friend and colleague goes and hangs himself like that. I mean, someone you've had over to dinner and all."

"How did they go? The dinners?"

"Fine. Except, when we had them over to our house, I overcooked the roast beef the way my mother always used to do."

"Mine, too," said Annie, with a smile, though she couldn't really dredge up a memory of her mother roasting beef. "I meant the conversation. What did you talk about? What did Mark and Laurence talk about?"

"Oh, you know, after a couple of bottles of wine, the ice gets broken, it starts to flow. And Mr. . . . . Laurence told all sorts of stories."

"About what, if you don't mind my asking?"

"I don't mind. I just don't see why it matters. About faraway places. I haven't travelled much. Oh, we've been to the usual places – Majorca, Benidorm, Lanzarote, even Tunisia once, but he'd been everywhere. Russia. Iran. Iraq. Chile. Australia. New Zealand. South Africa. It must have been so exciting."

"Yes," said Annie. "I heard he was a well-travelled man. Did he mention Afghanistan at all?"

"As a matter of fact, he did. It came up when we were talking about . . . you know, Rick."

"Of course. What did he say about it?"

"Just that he'd been there."

"Did he say when?"

"No. I got the impression that he didn't like it very much."

"Dangerous place, I suppose," said Annie. "Is everything else OK with your husband?"

"Yes, of course. Except I think this gang business is getting him down, too."

"It must be," said Annie. "I talked to him yesterday about a couple of his lads involved in that East Side Estate stabbing."

"Did you? He didn't say."

Well, he wouldn't, thought Annie. "It wasn't important."

"Anyway, like I said, you do it because you think you can make a difference, but sometimes . . ." She ran her finger around the rim of her cup. The nail was chipped and bitten, Annie noticed. "I don't know. Sometimes I think maybe Rick was right. What a world to bring children into."

"But yours are doing all right, aren't they?"

Carol's face brightened. "Oh yes. They're a handful, I can tell you that. But I wouldn't have it any other way." She glanced at her watch. "Ooh, is that the time? I really must be getting back now or Sue will be going ballistic."

"I'll walk with you," said Annie.

Tomasina was sitting behind her desk when Banks arrived. She had clearly been crying, as he had heard over the telephone, but she had stopped now. A box of tissues lay on the desk by her hand next to a large mug of milky tea. The mug was white and had little red hearts all over it.

At a cursory glance, the office looked the same as it had on his last visit, as did the reception area. Either Tomasina had already done a good job of tidying up, or her visitors had been very neat.

"I'm sorry for being such a blubberer on the phone," she said. "I could have kicked myself when I hung up."

"That's all right," said Banks. He sat opposite her.

"No, it isn't But you wouldn't understand."

She was full of contradictions, this one, Banks thought. A young beauty, tough as nails, vulnerable, but with another hard centre inside the soft one. And he hadn't spent more than half an hour with her, all told. "Why don't you tell me what happened?" he said.

She drank some tea, holding the mug with both hands. Her hands were shaking. "They came just after I got here, about nine."

"How many of them were there?"

"Four. Two of them searched through everything while the other two . . . well, they called it an interview."

"Did they treat you roughly at all?"

"Not physically, no."

"Did they say who they were?"

"They just said they were from the government."

"Did they show any identification?"

"I didn't get a good look. It was all too fast."

"Names?"

She shook her head. "Maybe Carson or Carstairs, one of them. And the woman was Harmon or Harlan. I'm sorry. It was all so fast, like they didn't want it to register. I should have been paying closer attention, but I was too stunned. They took me by surprise."

"Don't blame yourself. They're well trained in that sort of thing. One of them was a woman?"

"Yes, one of the interrogators. It was interesting, really, because she played the bad cop."

"What were they like, the two who questioned you?"

"Oh, very proper. Nicely dressed. Trendy. He was wearing a dark silk suit and a fifty-quid haircut. Handsome in a Hugh Grant-ish sort of way. She wasn't exactly dressed by Primark, either. Early thirties, I'd guess. The sort of woman Agatha Christie would describe as healthy and blonde. Both a bit posh sounding."

"What did they want to know?"

"Why you came to see me yesterday."

"What did you tell them?"

"Nothing."

"You must have said something."

She blushed. "Well, I said you were my boyfriend's father, and you were in town on business so you just dropped by to say hello. It was the best I could do on the spur of the moment."

"Did they ask if you knew I was a policeman?"

"Yes. And I said that I did, but I didn't hold it against you."

"What did they say to that?"

"They didn't believe me, so they asked all their questions again. Then they asked me my life story, where I was born, what schools I went to, university, boyfriends, girlfriends, where I used to work, how I got into the business and all that sort of stuff. Quite chatty, really. Then they got back to the nitty-gritty, and when I stuck to my story, Blondie started threatening me with prosecution, and when I asked what for she said it didn't matter and they could shut down my business as easy as swatting a fly. Is that true, by the way?"

"Yes. They can do anything they want. But they won't."

"Why not?"

"Because they've no reason to, and those things usually cause more trouble than they're worth. Publicity. They're like bats. They don't like the daylight."

"What about my rights?"

"You don't have any. Didn't you know, the baddies have won?"

"And just who are they?"

"Well, there's a question. These people are ruthless and powerful, make no mistake about it, but their real weakness is their need for secrecy. You're no threat to them. They won't harm you. They just want to know what you were up to, why I visited you."

"How did they know?"

"They must have followed me. That's my fault. I'm sorry. I've been trying to be careful, but it's a crowded city."

"Tell me about it. I know enough about that to realize how difficult it can be to spot a tail, particularly a professional team."

"I still should have been more careful. What were the other two doing while the man and woman were interviewing you?"

"Searching everything, including my handbag. They took some of my files. And my laptop, my lovely Mac Air. Of course, they said everything would be returned when they'd finished with it."

"The Derek Wyman file?"

"Yes."

"Were the photos in it?"

"Yes. I made copies. And my report."

"Shit. Then it won't take them long to work out why I was here. I'm really sorry to bring all this down on you, Tomasina."

She imitated an American tough-guy accent. "'A man's gotta do what a man's gotta do.' Forget it. It's all part of a day's work for the modern girly private detective. But what will they do when they work out the truth?"

Banks thought for a moment. "Probably nothing," he said. "At least, not for a while. Sometimes they're hasty, but usually they like to gather intelligence before acting. That way they already know all the answers to the questions before they ask them. Anyway, they'll be more interested in Derek Wyman now. They'll likely put a tail on him, do a thorough background check, that sort of thing."

"And me?"

"You're no longer of any interest to them. You were just a professional doing a job. They understand that."

"But why?" Tomasina asked. "Why are they doing all this?"

"I don't really know," said Banks.

"And if you did you wouldn't tell me."

"The less you know the better. Believe me. It's to do with the other man in the photo, though. He was one of theirs. First they wanted to hush up what had happened, intimidate everyone involved into just dropping the investigation. I think that was natural instinct, damage control. Now they're interested, though. And that's all I can tell you."

"I see. At least, I think I do." She frowned. "But let me get it straight. Mr. Wyman hired me to take photos of a spy who met another spy on a bench in Regent's Park and went to a house in St. John's Wood. Is Mr. Wyman a spy, too?"

"No," said Banks. "At least, I don't think so."

"Then what?"

"I don't know. It's complicated."

"You're telling me. What if they think *I'm* a spy?"

"I very much doubt they'll think that. They know what your job is."

Neither spoke for a few moments, then Tomasina's stomach rumbled. "I'm hungry," she said. "I think you owe me at least lunch for this."

"Burger and chips?"

She squinted at him. "Oh, I think you can do better than that. Bentley's isn't far, and it's early enough to get a table in the bar."

Bentley's was an expensive seafood restaurant, Banks knew, one of Richard Corrigan's, owner of Lindsay House. With lunch and wine and service, the two of them probably wouldn't get out for under a hundred quid. Still, Banks thought, it was a small price to pay for the guilt he felt at dragging Tomasina into it, though strictly speaking, it was Wyman who had done that. "All right," he said. "Just give me a couple of minutes to make some phone calls."

"In private?"

"In private."

"I'll be outside having a smoke."

When Annie had finished getting her paperwork up to date at the office, it was lunchtime. The Horse and Hounds was out of the question, as was the Queen's Arms, so Annie went to the Half Moon, a pub she had eaten in before, farther down Market Street, with hanging baskets of bright red geraniums outside and a shiny black façade. She went to the bar and ordered a vegetarian lasagna and chips along with a pint of bitter shandy. She was thirsty, and orange juice just wouldn't quench it.

She went outside and sat in the beer garden at the back. There wasn't much of a view, as it was enclosed by walls, but the air was warm and the sun shone on the umbrella that shaded her table. There were a few groups and couples out there already, deep in conversation, so anything she had to say on her mobile wouldn't be overheard.

She missed Winsome, she thought, as she had her first sip of shandy, and she felt guilty about leaving her to handle the East Side Estate business with only Harry Potter. She would make up for it this afternoon, she decided, and from then on she would devote herself to what she was supposed to be doing. Gervaise had been remarkably unthreatening yesterday, but Annie knew that if she went on the way she was, she would be in for a serious bollocking soon, at the very least. She might just find herself in front of the Chief Constable, as she knew she deserved.

What else could she do for Banks, anyway? The next step was clearly to bring Wyman in and question him again in the light of their new knowledge. That might be difficult since there was still actually no case being investigated, and the nature of any charges that might be brought against him were hazy, to say the least. But that wasn't her problem. If it came to anything, it would be up to the Crown Prosecution Service to determine any charges that might be brought. If Banks wanted to come back home, tell all to Superintendent Gervaise, then perhaps they could give Wyman a slap on the wrist, send him home to his wife and get on with their jobs.

That reminded Annie, and she took out her notebook. She had looked up Charlotte Fraser, Rick Wyman's bereaved girlfriend, and found her phone number easily enough from BT. It wasn't unlisted. What she hoped to gain by talking to Charlotte, she was uncertain, but it was worth a try. At least if Wyman knew they'd talked to her before they interviewed him, he might be worried enough to show it if he had something to hide.

Annie waited until she had finished as much of the lasagna as she wanted, then she dialled the number. A voice answered after several rings.

"Yes? Hello?"

"Charlotte Fraser?"

"Who is this speaking?"

Annie introduced herself and explained as clearly as she could why she was calling.

"I still don't quite understand," said Charlotte when Annie had finished. "How exactly can I help you?"

"Well, I don't know that you can," said Annie. "Or will. I know these things are shrouded in secrecy. It's just that I've been getting a few conflicting reports about the death of your . . . of Rick Wyman, and I was wondering if you could help me clear up any misunderstanding."

"How do I know you're who you say you are?"

This was a question Annie had been dreading. All she could do was bluff her way out of it. "I can give you the police station number, the Western Area Headquarters in Eastvale, and you can call me back there, if you like."

"Oh, it's all right," Charlotte snapped. "Why do you want to know?"

It was the other question Annie had been dreading, and the most natural one for Charlotte to ask. She hadn't been able to come up with one good reason why the woman should talk to her, let alone tell her what were probably military secrets, even if she knew them. When in doubt, Annie thought, tell the truth as vaguely as possible. "It's to do with a case we were working on," she said. "It just came up in connection with one of the victims."

"And who would that be?"

"A man called Laurence Silbert."

"Never heard of him."

"Well, I don't suppose you would have," said Annie.

"I'm sorry. I don't mean to be rude or anything, but I was having lunch in the garden with some good friends when you rang, and I –"

"That's all right," said Annie. "I do apologize. I won't keep you long." *If you tell me what I want to know*, her tone implied.

"Oh, very well. But I told you, I don't know this Silver person."

"Silbert," said Annie. That answered one question, anyway. But then why would she know Silbert? "It's actually about your . . . about Derek Wyman."

"Derek? He's not in any trouble, is he?"

"Not as far as I know," said Annie. "It's a little bit complicated but mostly a matter of who said what to whom."

"And what does Derek have to do with this?"

"Well, Derek told us that his brother's death was due to an accident, a helicopter crash."

"That's what was in the papers at the time, yes," Charlotte said.

"But is it true? We've also heard other versions."

"Such as?"

"That he was on a mission and died in action."

"I'm afraid I'm not at liberty to comment on that," said Charlotte. "Surely you ought to have known."

"I guessed as much," said Annie. "But it's hardly breaking the Official Secrets Act, is it? I mean, it's not as if I'm asking you what the mission objective was or the details of its failure."

"As if I'd know."

"Of course. I know you want to get back to your lunch, so do you think you could simply answer me by saying nothing, so to speak? If he really was killed in action rather than by accident, just hang up."

Annie waited, clutching her mobile tightly to her ear. She was aware of the buzz of conversation around her and thought she could hear distant women's voices down the line. Just when she was certain Charlotte was going to speak again, the line went dead. She'd hung up.

14

Banks's wallet was about a hundred and thirty pounds lighter when he walked out of Bentley's with his two companions later that Friday afternoon. But he had eaten the best fish and chips he had ever tasted, and it was worth every penny to see the smile on Tomasina's face. One of the phone calls he had made earlier, while she had smoked her cigarette outside the building, had been to his son Brian, who had not only been available at a moment's notice for lunch, his girlfriend Emilia being away in Scotland filming, but also more than willing to share his father's company with a stranger in need. Or so Banks had put it. When Brian had arrived and joined them just as they were starting on the first glass of wine, Tomasina's expression was a joy to behold and a thing to remember. She had been tongue-tied, of course, and blushed to her roots, but Brian's natural charm had soon worked its magic, and they were all chatting away like old mates by the time the food came.

Now they stood outside the restaurant on Sparrow Street between Regent Street and Piccadilly ready to go their own ways, Tomasina reaching for a Silk Cut, Banks's old brand. For a moment, it made him envious. She offered them around and Banks was surprised when Brian accepted one, but he didn't say anything. If they were being watched, it was from a distance. The street was so short and narrow that Banks would have immediately spotted any suspicious activity.

"Sorry," said Brian to Tomasina, "but I must dash. It's been a pleasure to meet you." He reached into his inside pocket. "We're playing the

Shepherd's Bush Empire next week, so here's a couple of comps and a backstage pass. Come see us after the gig. I promise you it's not as wild and crazy as some people think it is."

"It had better not be," said Banks.

Tomasina blushed and took the tickets. "Thanks," she said. "That's great. I'll be there."

"Look forward to it," said Brian. "Got to go now. See you later, Tom. See you, Dad." He shook Banks's hand and then disappeared in the direction of Piccadilly Circus.

"Thank you," said Tomasina to Banks. "Thank you so much. That was really nice."

"Feeling better?"

"A lot." She shuffled her feet and tucked her hair behind her ears, the way she had done in the restaurant. "I don't really know how to say this properly, and promise not to laugh at me, but I don't really have anyone to, you know, share these tickets with. Do you want to come?"

"With you?"

"Yeah. That's not such a horrible thought, is it?"

"No, no. Of course not. I was just . . . yes, sure, I'd be delighted to."

"It's easiest if you come by the office," she said. "Then we can have a drink after work first. All right?"

"All right," said Banks, thinking of Sophia. He would most likely have gone to the concert with her, and he still would if she was speaking to him again by next week. On the other hand, he didn't want to let Tomasina down right at the moment. She'd been through a lot because of him. Well, he decided, he'd let it lie as it was for now and see how things turned out. It wasn't as if it was a *date* or anything. Tomasina was young enough to be his daughter. Mind you, Sophia was young enough to be his daughter, too, at least technically. Maybe the three of them could go together. Sophia would understand.

"I'd better be going," said Tomasina.

"Office?"

"No. I've had enough of that for the day. Home."

"Where's that?"

"Clapham. I'll get the tube from Piccadilly. See you next week."

Then she gave Banks a quick peck on the cheek and dashed off along Sparrow Street, a spring in her step. How resilient are the young, Banks thought.

The car, with his suitcase in it, was still parked at the hotel in Fitzrovia, and he thought that was probably where he should go to begin the long drive back to Eastvale. The other phone call he had made while Tomasina smoked was to Dirty Dick Burgess, but again he had got no answer.

Banks walked up Regent Street towards Oxford Circus, enjoying the sunshine and the slight buzz from two glasses of white wine, but keeping an eye open as best he could for any sign of a tail. He went into the Bose shop for a couple of minutes and tried out some noise-cancelling headphones he liked. Around Great Marlborough Street, the crowds of tourists got too thick, so he turned right to avoid Oxford Circus altogether. He wanted to call at Borders and HMV, anyway, before heading back up north. He was somewhere between Liberty and the Palladium when he heard an almighty explosion, and the pavement shook beneath him as if there had been an earthquake. High windows shattered and glass and plaster fell into the street.

For a moment, the world seemed to stop, freeze-frame, then it was all sound and motion again, and Banks became aware of people screaming and running past him, confused and terrified expressions on their faces, back towards Regent Street or deeper into Soho. To his left, up the narrow side street, he could see a pall of black smoke mixed with dark orange flames. Alarms sounded everywhere. Without thinking, he ran up Argyll Street, against the panicking crowds, to Oxford Street, and found himself in a scene of carnage that might have come straight out of the Blitz.

There were fires all over the place. The dark, thick smoke stung his eyes. It smelled of burnt plastic and rubber. Plaster dust filled the air, and rubble lay scattered everywhere. Broken glass crunched underfoot. At first, everything happened in slow motion. Banks was aware of sirens in the distance, but where he was, in the smoke, felt like a sort of island separated from the rest of the city. It was as if he had arrived at the still centre of darkness, the eye of the storm. Nothing could survive here.

Wreckage lay everywhere: bits of cars; twisted bicycles; a burning wooden cart; gaudy souvenir scarves and pashminas and cheap luggage strewn over the road; a man lying halfway through his windscreen, still and bleeding. Then, out of it all, a figure stumbled towards Banks, an elderly Asian woman in a bright-coloured sari. Her nose was gone and blood streamed from her eyes. She had her arms stretched out in front of her.

"Help me!" she cried. "Help me. I can't see. I'm blind."

Banks took her arm and tried to murmur words of comfort and encouragement as she held on to him for dear life. Maybe she was better off not being able to see, he thought fleetingly, leading her over the street. Everywhere people were staggering about in the haze, their arms flailing like zombies in a horror film. Some were shouting, some screaming, fleeing from burning cars, and some were just sitting or lying, moaning in pain.

One man lay on the road on fire, thrashing about, trying to douse the flames that consumed him. There was nothing Banks could do for him. He stumbled on and tripped over a leg. It wasn't attached to a body. Then he walked through stuff that squished unpleasantly under his feet and saw body parts strewn everywhere. After he had got the Asian woman out of the smoke and sat her down on the pavement until help came, he picked his way back through the wreckage and the rubble. He found a disoriented boy of about ten or eleven and half dragged him away to the edges of the scene where the smoke thinned, and where he had left the Asian woman, then he went back and guided the next person he saw out of the carnage.

He didn't know how long he went on doing this, taking people by the arm and leading them away, even scooping them up off the road into his arms, or dragging them to the edge of Oxford Circus, where the air was still full of the stink of burning plastic but was at least breathable.

A burning taxi lay on its side and a pretty young blonde in a blood-stained yellow sundress was trying to climb out of the window. Banks went to help her. She had a lapdog held to her chest like a ball of fluff and a Selfridges bag, which was almost too big to get through the window. She got out, but she wouldn't let go of the bag handle, no matter how much Banks tried to pull her away. He feared the taxi might explode at any moment. In the end she pulled the bag free and tottered back into Banks's arms on her high heels. It took only a quick glance in the front to see that the driver was dead. The woman clung to Banks and her bag with one arm and her dog with the other as they edged their way towards the cleaner air, and for the first time, amidst it all, he could smell something other than death: it was her perfume, a subtle musk. He left her sitting by the roadside crying and went back. There was a bendy-bus lying on its side burning, and he wanted to see whether he could help people get out. He could hear the woman wail and the dog start to yap behind him as he walked away.

The next thing he knew the area was full dark shapes in protective gear, wearing gas masks or heavy breathing equipment with oxygen tanks strapped to their backs, some of them carrying submachine guns, and someone was calling over a loudspeaker for everyone to evacuate the area. Banks carried on searching for survivors until a heavy hand rested on his shoulder and pulled him away.

"Best get out of here, mate, and leave it to us," said the voice, muffled by breathing apparatus. "You never can tell. There might be another one. Or one of the cars might go up any moment."

The strong, steady hand guided him gently but firmly past Oxford Circus and around the corner to Regent Street.

"Are you all right?" the man asked him.

"I'm OK," said Banks. "I'm a policeman. I can help." He reached for his warrant card.

The man had a good look at it, and Banks was sure he memorized the name.

"Doesn't matter," the man said, guiding him away. "There's nothing you can do here without the right equipment. It's too dangerous. Did you see what happened?"

"No," said Banks. "I was on Great Marlborough Street. I heard the explosion and came up to see if I could help."

"Leave it to the pros now, mate. And as long as you're sure you're all right, the best thing you can do is go home, leave the medics for the ones who really need them."

Down Regent Street, Banks could see the massed fire engines, police cars, ambulances and armed response vehicles, and the street swarmed with uniforms. The barriers were up already and the whole area had been cordoned off as far down as Conduit Street. He was glad that he could at least breathe now as he stumbled past the barricades into the stunned group of onlookers.

"What happened, mate?" someone asked.

"Bomb, innit?" answered someone else. "Stands to reason. Fucking terrorists."

Banks just walked on through the crowds, oblivious to the questions, back the way he had come he couldn't say how long ago. At first, right in the thick of it with the body parts, the human torches, viscous smoke and walking wounded, time had seemed to slow almost to a halt, but now, when he turned and looked back up Regent Street towards the chaos, he felt as if it had all been over in a flash, a subliminal moment. The emergency rescue worker had been right; there was nothing more he could do. He would only get in the way. He had never felt so useless in his life, and the last thing he wanted to be here was a voyeur. He wondered how the blind Asian woman was doing, and the young blonde with her lapdog and Selfridges bag.

The chaos and carnage faded into the background the closer he got to Piccadilly Circus. He didn't know where he was going now, or care, only that he was moving away from it. His breathing had almost returned to normal, but his eyes still stung. People gawped at him as he passed by, everyone aware now that something serious had happened near by, even if they hadn't heard it themselves. You could still see the smoke spiralling up from Oxford Circus beyond the elegant curved façade of Regent Street, its smell polluting the sweet summer air.

When Banks got past Piccadilly Circus, he knew what he wanted. A bloody drink. Or two. He made his way up Shaftesbury Avenue and turned into Soho, his old stomping ground from the early days on the Met, and finally tottered into an old pub on Dean Street he remembered from years back. It hadn't changed much. The bar was full, and even the smokers had come back inside to watch the breaking news coverage on the large-screen TV in the back. It had probably been used only to show football before, Banks thought, but now it showed images of the carnage around Oxford Circus, less than a mile away. It was all so unreal to him, seeing on the large screen what he had just been a part of only minutes ago. Another world. Another place. That was what it usually was, wasn't it? Didn't these things happen somewhere else? Darfur. Kenya. Zimbabwe. Iraq. Chechnya. Not just up the bloody road. The barman was watching the television, too, but when he saw Banks, he went back to his position behind the bar.

"Jesus Christ," he said. "What happened to you, mate? You look like you've just . . . Oh, bloody hell. You have, haven't you?"

Other people were glancing over at Banks now, some pulling their neighbours' sleeves or tapping their arms and muttering. Banks nodded.

"Whatever you want, mate, it's on the house," said the barman.

Banks wanted two things. He wanted a pint to slake his thirst and a double brandy to steady his nerves. He said he'd pay for one of them but the barman wouldn't have any of it.

"If I was you, mate," he said, "I'd pay a quick visit to the Gents first. It's just behind you. You'll feel better if you clean yourself up a bit."

Banks took a quick gulp of beer before taking the barman's advice. Like most toilets in London pubs, it wasn't much of a place; the urinals were stained ochre and stank of piss, but there was a mirror above the cracked sink. One look was enough. His face was smudged black with smoke, his eyes two staring holes in the darkness. The front of his white shirt was burned and smeared with blood and God knew what else. Luckily, his windcheater wasn't too bad. It was dirty, but then it was navy blue to start with, so it didn't show the stains too badly, and his jeans were just singed and tarry. He didn't even want to think what was on the bottom of his shoes.

About all he could do for the moment, he realized, was a bit of cosmetic work, give his face a good wash and try to cover up his shirt as best he could, which he did by zipping his jacket up almost to the collar. He got the water running good and hot, squirted some liquid soap on to his hands and did the best he could. In the end, he managed to get most of the dirt off, but he couldn't do anything about the look in his eyes.

"That's better, mate," said the barman.

Banks thanked him and drained his pint. When he put his glass down and started working, more slowly, on the brandy, the barman filled up his pint glass again without asking. Banks also watched him pour a large whisky for himself.

"Suicide car bomber, they think," the barman said, gesturing over towards the television set, to which the other customers were still glued. "That's a new one on me. Pulled out of Great Portland Street into Oxford Street, just shy of the Circus. Makes sense. You can't park around there, and only buses and taxis can drive on Oxford Street. Bastards. They always find a way."

"How many injured?" Banks asked.

"They don't know for sure yet. Twenty-four dead and about the same seriously injured is the latest count. But that's conservative. You *were* there, weren't you?"

"I was."

"Right in the thick of it?"

"Yes."

"What was it like?"

Banks took a sip of brandy.

"Sorry. I should know better than to ask," said the barman. "I've seen my share. Ex-para. Northern Ireland. For my sins." He stuck out his hand. "Joe Geldard's the name, by the way."

Banks shook hands. "Good to meet you, Joe Geldard," he said. "Alan Banks. And thank you for everything."

"It's nothing, mate. How you feeling?"

Banks drank some more brandy. He noticed that his hand was still shaking. His left hand was slightly burned, he saw for the first time, but he couldn't feel any pain yet. It didn't look too bad. "Much better for this," he said, hoisting his brandy glass. "I'll be all right."

Joe Geldard moved to the end of the bar to keep an eye on the TV with the rest. Banks was left alone. For the first time, his mind managed to focus a little, come to grips with what had just happened, unbelievable as it still seemed.

Apparently, a terrorist suicide bomber had set off a car bomb just around the corner from where he'd been walking. And if he hadn't decided that the crowds on Regent Street were too much and turned on to Great Marlborough Street at the time he did, he would have walked down Oxford Street, and who knew what might have happened to him? It wasn't courage that had driven him into the flames, he knew, just blind instinct, despite nearly dying in a house fire himself not so many years ago.

He thought about Brian and Tomasina. They would be fine. Both were taking the Underground from Piccadilly Circus. They might find themselves unable to get a train if the service had been shut down quickly enough, but apart from that, they'd be fine. He would phone both of them later, when he'd got himself together, just to make sure. It also entered his head that they might be worried about him, too.

And Sophia? Christ, she often worked at Western House, up Great Portland Street, unless she was off in another studio or out somewhere producing live interviews. She might have wandered down to Oxford Street shopping on her lunch break. She never did, though, Banks remembered. Said she hated it, with all the tourists. On a nice day she'd buy a sandwich at Pret and eat it by the gardens in Regent's Park, or maybe there was a lunchtime concert at the open-air theatre. He'd phone her, though, not least because he wanted a chance to put things right between them.

A wave of nausea came over him and he took a gulp of brandy. It made him cough, but it helped. Glancing over at the TV, he saw helicopter shots of blossoming smoke, and he didn't know whether the sound of sirens came from the scene on the news or from the street outside. A ticker tape was running underneath the images detailing breaking news. The death count was up to twenty-seven, injured thirty-two.

Banks turned to the bar and worked on his second pint. His right hand had almost stopped shaking, and his left hand was staring to throb a bit. When he glanced in the mirror behind the range of spirits and wine bottles, he hardly recognized the face that stared back at him. It was time to make a move.

He realized that first of all he would need new clothes. He had his wallet and both his mobiles, but nothing else. The rest of his gear was back in his car at the hotel. He knew he could get there bypassing Oxford Circus, but he didn't want to. Not only didn't he want to be anywhere near there right now, he also didn't want to drive back to Eastvale, he realized. He would buy new clothes, then go to King's Cross and take a train, come back for the car when he felt better. Sophia had a key – she sometimes liked to drive the Porsche herself – so he could ask her to pick it up and park it outside her house, where it would be safe. Surely she would do that much for him, even if she wasn't talking to him?

Then he realized that all the Underground and mainline stations would probably be closed for a while. It was all too much to contemplate; his brain wasn't fully functioning, and he knew he wasn't going anywhere for a while. The alcohol was slowly calming him down and blotting out some of the horrors of the last hour, so he called out for another pint and told Joe Geldard to have one on him.

15

Annie wondered why Banks wanted her to drive out to his Gratly cottage early on Saturday morning. She had assumed that he would be staying in London with Sophia, at least for the weekend, but obviously not.

All her attempts to phone him the previous evening had been frustrated, as he had been unable or unwilling to answer either mobile. After work, she had simply gone home and watched in horror the events unfold on television after the Oxford Circus bombing. Special anti-terrorist units were already on the move in Dewsbury, Birmingham and Leicester, so it was reported, and there were claims that three people had already been arrested and one mosque in London raided.

The Muslim community was up in arms about the sanctity of their place of worship, but Annie doubted they had many sympathetic listeners, not after the images from the TV screen had seared themselves on people's minds, and Al Qaeda had already claimed responsibility. While Annie tried to respect all faiths, she knew that religion had been used as an excuse for more wars and criminal activities than anything else throughout human history. It was getting harder now, when religious extremism was on the rise, to cling to the sanctity of any system of belief as an excuse for mass murder.

Still, it was a lovely morning for a drive into the dale, she thought, putting the news images aside as her ancient Astra rounded the curves and bounced over the sudden rises. The Leas lay spread out to her right, flat wetlands around the River Swain, which meandered slowly through the meadows of buttercups, cranesbill and clover. Beyond, the dale side rose gently at first, criss-crossed with drystone walls, then more steeply to the higher pasture. The green of the grass turned more sere as it rose to the craggy uplands of limestone outcrops that marked the start of the open moorland. She had her window rolled down and a track from a Steely Dan greatest hits CD, "Bodhisattva," playing on the stereo. Banks probably wouldn't approve, but she didn't give a damn. All was well with the world.

Almost.

Winsome had caught a break on the East Side Estate business when one of the local thugs had let slip that there was a new player on the block, "an Albanian or Turk or something," just up from London, and all the kids who had previously had free rein in what petty dealing of drugs went on were now expected to bow out gracefully, work for him or . . . perhaps get stabbed. They hadn't yet been able to find the newcomer, who went by the name of the Bull, but Annie knew it was only a matter of time. There were also rumours that he had connections and was planning on importing heroin into Eastvale in a big way. Catching the Bull would definitely be a feather in their caps as far as Superintendent Gervaise was concerned, not to mention ACC McLaughlin and the Chief Constable himself, who would be able to appear on television and say they were winning the war against drugs.

Annie drove along Helmthorpe High Street, past the church, pubs and walking-gear shops, then turned left at the school and carried on up the hill to Gratly. She drove carefully over the narrow stone bridge, where a couple of old men stood smoking pipes and gabbing, then a few hundred yards farther on turned right into Banks's drive, pulling up by the stone wall beside Gratly Beck before the driveway ended at the woods. She was surprised to see that his car wasn't there.

Annie had never ceased to marvel at what an isolated and beautiful place Banks had chosen to live in after his marriage broke up. The renovations he had made after the fire had given him a lot more space, but it had all been tastefully carried out in the same local limestone, and the place probably didn't look that much different than it had when it was built – in 1768, according to the gritstone lintel.

Banks answered her knock and took her through the living room into the kitchen.

"Coffee?" he asked.

"Please."

He knew how she liked it, Annie noted. Black and strong. He liked his the same.

"Let's go out to the conservatory," he said.

Annie followed him through the kitchen door. Honeyed sunlight poured in through the glass sides and there was just enough of a breeze through the open windows to keep it from being too hot. That was the problem with conservatories, Annie thought; one warm day and they overheated. In some ways, they were better in winter with an electric fire switched on, flickering fake coals and a couple of elements. But this early in the morning it was perfect. The view up the dale side to the limestone scar at the top, like a skeleton's grin, was stunning, and sheep were dotted all over the hillside. The wicker armchairs, she remembered, were so deep and inviting and had cushions so soft that they were difficult to get out of once you sat down. She sat anyway and set her coffee down on the low glass table beside the morning papers, which hadn't been touched yet. That wasn't like Banks. He wasn't much of a newshound, but he liked to read the music and film reviews and grapple with the crosswords. Perhaps he had slept in. There was some strange orchestral music playing quietly in the background, funereal, discordant in sound, bells and trumpets, tympani, a choir coming and going.

"What's the music?" Annie asked, when Banks sat down opposite her.

"Shostakovich. The Thirteenth Symphony. It's called 'Babi-Yar.' Why? Is it bothering you?"

"No," said Annie. "I was just wondering. It's unusual." It was hardly Steely Dan, but it was quiet enough to keep to the background. "What time did you get back last night?" she asked.

"Late."

"I phoned during the evening."

"Damn battery died on me, and I didn't have the charger."

He seemed more gaunt than usual, his bright blue eyes less full of sparkle. He also had a bandage on his left hand.

"What did you do to yourself?" she asked.

He lifted his hand. "Oh, this? Burned it on the cast-iron frying pan. The doc always told me my diet would kill me. It's nothing. I was going to come back in to the station this morning, but I've changed my mind. That's why I asked you to come out here instead."

"Because you hurt yourself?"

"What? No. I told you, this is nothing. It's something else."

"What?"

"I'll tell you later."

"OK," Annie said lightly. "*Be* mysterious. See if I care. We've got a lead on the East Side Estate stabbing." She told him about the Bull. She could sense his attention drifting as she spoke, so she wound it up quickly and said, "What is it, Alan? Why did you want me to come here?"

"I thought we should talk about Wyman," Banks said. "Given all the new information. We should consider bringing him in."

"New? There's not much, except we now know that he asked for the photos of Silbert to be taken."

"That's enough, isn't it?" said Banks. "Besides, there's more. Much more. Things are getting out of hand."

Annie listened, her mouth opening wider and wider as Banks told her about Hardcastle tearing up the photos, and what had happened at Sophia's house on Thursday evening, and in Tomasina's office yesterday. When he'd finished, all she could say was, "You were down in London yesterday, weren't you? Isn't it terrible? You can't have been far away from Oxford Circus when it happened."

"Just down Regent Street," he said. "They closed all the stations for about four hours. That's why I was so late back. Then I had to take a taxi from Darlington station."

"I thought you took the car down?"

"I left it. Didn't feel like driving. Sick of all the traffic. And I'd had a few drinks at lunchtime. What is this? The third degree?"

"Why didn't you stay with Sophia? The poor woman must have been terrified."

"She's with a friend." Banks stared at Annie, and she thought for a moment that he was going to tell her to mind her own business. A soloist struck up, then the choir joined him and the orchestra came back, loud brass and crashing percussion, staccato rhythms, a gong. It certainly was odd music for a beautiful Saturday morning. Banks appeared to listen for a moment until the music came to a climax and went quiet, almost like a Gregorian chant, then he said, "As a matter of fact, she didn't want me around. She sort of blamed me for what happened, for not setting the alarm."

"Did you?"

"Of course I bloody did."

"Did you tell her that?"

"She was upset. She wouldn't believe me."

"Did you call the police?"

"You know who we're dealing with, Annie. Do you think calling the police would have done any good? For crying out loud, I *am* the police, and *I* can't do any good. Besides, she was dead set against it."

"So did you tell Sophia the truth, who you think it was?"

"No."

"Why not?"

"What's the point in frightening her?"

"To put her on her guard?"

"What do you care, anyway? You don't even like her."

"That's not true," said Annie, smarting. "It's you I'm concerned about. It's always been you."

"Well, you needn't be. Besides, they won't hurt her. Or Tomasina. They could have done that anytime, if they'd wanted. Me, too. No, they've delivered their message, and that's all they wanted to do. For now. They're just trying to scare us off. That's why it's time to bring Wyman in."

"But they *haven't* scared you off. Me neither, for that matter."

Banks managed the beginnings of a smile and said, "What did you find out?"

"A couple of interesting things." Annie told him about her talk with Carol Wyman.

When she had finished, Banks said, "This business with Rick Wyman is interesting. SAS, indeed. You know where they get their orders from, don't you? MI6, I'll bet. This could be the link between Wyman and Silbert's world. I always thought there had to be a lot more to it than professional rivalry. Did you follow up?"

"I talked to his . . ." What on earth did she call Charlotte Fraser? "His *widow*," she decided finally, though it wasn't strictly true. "Of course, she wouldn't tell me anything, but I did get her to admit that Rick Wyman was killed on active duty, not in a helicopter accident during a training exercise."

"Interesting," said Banks. "Very interesting. Now if only we could find out a few more details, such as what the mission was, who gave the orders and who supplied the intelligence, we might actually get somewhere. What if Wyman thinks Silbert was responsible for his brother's death? What if he was? What if it's something MI6 want to keep covered up?"

"Then they'll do everything in their power to prevent you from uncovering it." Annie reached for her coffee. A soloist was singing, bells chiming in the background, then the full choir came in again. "Besides, just how, exactly, do you plan on finding out?"

"Before you arrived," Banks said, "I got a return phone call from a Detective Superintendent Burgess. Dirty Dick Burgess."

"I remember him," said Annie. "He's a sexist, racist, homophobic pig who thinks he's God's gift."

"That's the one," Banks admitted. "I'd been trying to reach him for a couple of days, leaving cryptic messages. He's remarkably resourceful when it comes to this sort of thing. I'm not sure exactly what department he works for these days, but it's connected with counterterrorism, and he's very much in the loop. Made the political transition from Thatcher and Major to Blair and Brown seamlessly."

"Well, there's not a lot of difference, as far as I can tell," said Annie.

"You're too young to remember Thatcher."

"I remember the Falklands War," Annie argued. "I was fifteen."

"Anyway, I didn't hear back from Dirty Dick for a while, and I thought perhaps it was because I'm *persona non grata* with his bosses, or something along those lines. He'd be certain to know, if I was. As it happens, I am, but that wasn't the reason. He's not in London at the moment; he's in Dewsbury."

"Dewsbury," Annie echoed. "But isn't that where. . . ?"

"One of the bombers, or planners, came from? Yes, I know. And that's probably why he's there. The point is, he's agreed to meet me."

"Where? When?"

"This morning, up at Hallam Tarn. It might be our only chance of finding a real link between Wyman and Silbert, this SAS and MI6 business, and maybe of finding out exactly what it was Silbert's been up to these past few years, since his so-called retirement, meeting men on benches in Regent's Park, and so on."

"If there is a link," Annie reminded him.

"Fair enough." Banks studied her. "I know you still think Hardcastle was the intended victim and professional jealousy was the motive. Hold that thought; you could still be right. Wyman did give Hardcastle the photos, and he did react with shock and horror. But bear with me a while longer, too." Banks reached for a pen and notepad from the bookcase beside him. "Have you got any more details about Rick Wyman?"

Annie told him all she knew, which wasn't much.

"Should be able to track him down from that," Banks said. "You're sure about the date of the incident? Fifteenth October, 2002?"

"That's what Carol Wyman told me."

"OK."

"What if there *isn't* a connection?"

"We'll deal with that if and when we get there."

"So what's next? If they're on to Wyman, as you say they must be after ransacking this Tom Savage's files, isn't he in danger now?"

"It depends how much of a threat he is to them. But yes, I agree, we need to act fairly quickly, bring him in and get to the bottom of it."

Annie had lost the thread of the music now, but it alternated between frantic and loud orchestra and solo tenor. Sometimes it disappeared completely. "We need to talk to the super first," she said.

"Can you do that?" Banks asked.

"Me? Jesus Christ, Alan!"

"Please?" Banks glanced at his watch. "I have to meet Burgess soon, and I don't think we should waste any more time. I might have a few more answers in a while, but if we can at least get Superintendent Gervaise's permission to bring Wyman in for questioning over having commissioned the photographs, we're in business."

"But I . . ."

"Come on, Annie. She knows you've been on the case, doesn't she?"

"The *non-existent* case? Yes. She knows."

"Present her with the evidence. Just stress the theatre business and play down the intelligence service angle. That's the only thing that really worries her. She'll go for it, otherwise."

"All right, all right," Annie said, standing up to leave. "I'll have a go. And what about you?"

"I'll be in later. I'll phone for a driver when I'm ready. Bring Wyman in after you've talked to Gervaise and let him stew for a while."

"On what charge?"

"You don't have to charge him, just ask him to come along voluntarily."

"What if he won't?"

"Then bloody arrest him."

"For what?"

"Try for being a lying bastard, for a start."

"If only . . ."

"Just bring him in, Annie. It might get us a few answers."

The orchestra was playing an eerie, haunting melody when Annie left, but the day didn't seem quite so beautiful any more.

When he was alone again, Banks poured himself the last cup of coffee. "Babi-Yar" finished, and he couldn't think of anything else he wanted to listen to. It was almost time to go out now and, tired as he was, this was an appointment he didn't want to miss. Wondering why he bothered with security, he locked up the cottage and struck out up Tetchley Fell to Hallam Tarn.

He hadn't slept a wink the previous night; his mind had still been full of the scenes he had witnessed at Oxford Circus, and he could still smell burning flesh and plastic. Certain images, he knew, would be lodged in his mind forever, and the things he had thought he had seen only fleetingly, a headless figure in his peripheral vision, glistening entrails glimpsed through a film of dust and smoke, would grow and metamorphose in his imagination, haunt his dreams for years.

But in some ways it was the feelings more than the images that affected him. He supposed he must have drifted off to sleep, at least for a few moments now and then, because he remembered those dreamlike sensations of not being able to run fast enough to escape something nightmarish, of being late for an important meeting and not remembering how to get there, of being lost naked on dark, threatening streets, becoming more and more frantic as the hour drew near, of stairs turning sticky like treacle under his feet as he tried to climb them, dragging him down into the abyss, melting beneath him. And when he woke, his chest felt hollow, his heart forlorn, beating pointlessly, without an echo.

After he had left Joe Geldard's pub, he had bought new clothes in a Marks and Spencer's and made his way on foot through the Bloomsbury back streets to King's Cross station. Even from Euston Road, he could still see wisps of smoke drifting in the air and hear the occasional siren. He wasn't sure exactly what time the bombing had occurred, but he reckoned it must have been about 2:30, the heart of a Friday afternoon in summer, when people like to leave work early. It was after five o'clock when he got to the train station, and service was still suspended, though the building had been given the all-clear and had reopened an hour earlier.

Crowds of people milled around the announcement boards, ready for the dash when their gate was announced. It cost him a small fortune to buy a single ticket to Darlington, with no guarantee of when the train would actually leave. The sandwich stalls had all run out of food and bottled water. While he waited, Banks phoned Brian and Tomasina, who were both fine, though shaken at having been so close to disaster. He also phoned Sophia at home and got no answer, as expected. He left a message asking her to pick up his car and said he hoped she was all right. He wasn't going to tell anyone about his afternoon; certainly not now, probably never.

As luck would have it, the first train north left the station at 6:35, and Banks was on it, sitting next to an earnest young Bangladeshi student who wanted to talk about what had just happened. Banks didn't want to talk about it, and he made himself clear from the start. For the rest of the trip, the student obviously felt uncomfortable, no doubt thinking Banks didn't want anything to do with him because he was Asian.

At that point, Banks didn't care what the kid thought. He didn't care what anybody thought. He stared out of the window, without a book or even his iPod to take his mind off the journey and the memories. He wouldn't have been able to concentrate on words or music, anyway. His mind was numb, and a couple of miniature Scotches from the food and beverages cart helped numb it even more.

He had taken a taxi home from Darlington, which was marginally closer to Gratly than York, and that had cost him a fortune, too. The driver's constant chatter about Boro's chances next season had been simply a free bonus. At least he hadn't talked about the bombing; sometimes the North felt far enough away to be another country, with wholly other concerns. All in all, Banks thought, as he paid the taxi driver, it was turning into an expensive day, what with the hotel bill, lunch, new clothes, the train ticket and now this. Thank God everyone took plastic.

The train journey had been slow, with unexpected and unexplained delays at Grantham and Doncaster, and Banks hadn't get home until half past ten. He had to admit that he was relieved to be there and to shut the door behind him, though he had no idea what he wanted to do to distract himself. He knew he didn't want to watch any news reports, didn't want to see the images of death and suffering repeated ad nauseam, didn't want to keep up with the mounting death toll. When he had poured himself a generous glass of red wine and sat down in front of an old Marx Brothers movie in the entertainment room, he didn't really know what he felt about it all.

When he probed himself, he realized that he didn't feel sad or angry or depressed. Perhaps that would come later. What had happened had taken him to a new place inside himself, a place he didn't know, had never explored before, and he didn't have a map. His world had changed, its axis shifted. It was the difference between knowing these things happened, watching them happen to other people on television, and being there, in the thick of it, seeing the suffering and knowing there's nothing, or very little, that you can do. But he had helped the injured. He had to cling to that, at least. He remembered the blind Asian woman, whose grip he imagined he could still feel on his arm, the young blonde in the bloodstained yellow dress, her stupid little lapdog and the bag she just wouldn't give up, the frightened child, the dead taxi driver, all of them. They were in him now, part of him, and they would be for ever.

Yet for all the fear and sorrow, he also felt a deep calm, a sense of inevitability and of letting go that surprised him. It was like the walk he was on now. There was something simple and soothing about putting one foot in front of the other and making slow progress up the hill.

He was climbing Tetchley Fell, following a footpath that crossed several fields, scanning the drystone walls for the stile that led over to the next one. The sun shone in a bright blue sky, but there was a light breeze to take the edge off the heat. Every once in a while, he glanced behind him to see whether he was being followed, and he saw two figures, one with a red jacket tied around her waist by the sleeves, and the other in a T-shirt with a backpack on his back. Banks was panting and sweating when he reached the Roman road that cut diagonally down the dale side to the village of Fortford, in the distance, so he thought he would pause there for a few moments and let them catch up with him.

As they passed him, they said hello, the way ramblers do, then turned left and walked down the Roman road. They could turn off at Mortsett, Banks thought, or go all the way to Relton or Fortford, but they weren't going in his direction. They were just kids, anyway, a couple of students out for a bit of country air. Even MI6 had to have an age limit, surely?

Banks climbed the stile on the other side of the narrow track and carried on through the fields up the hill. The grass grew thinner and browner, and soon he was walking around rocks and through clumps of heather and gorse. They would be in flower soon, he thought, brightening the dull moorland with their purples and yellows. The sheep grew few and far between.

He kept thinking he'd got to the top long before he had. It was one false summit after another. But finally he was there, and had only to totter down the other side of a steep bank to get to Hallam Tarn. It was nothing much, just a hollowed-out bowl of water right at the top of Tetchley Fell, about a hundred yards wide and two hundred long. It was walled in places because children had fallen in and drowned. The body of a young boy had even been dumped there once, Banks remembered. But there was a path around the tarn offering a scenic walk, and today five or six cars were parked in the space at the far end where the road up from Helmthorpe came to a full stop at the water's edge.

Legend had it that Hallam Tarn used to be a village once, but that the villagers took to evil ways, worshipping Satan, making human sacrifices, so God smote them with his fist and the dent he made on crushing the village created the tarn. On certain days, so they said, if the light was right, you could see the old houses and streets beneath the water, the squat, toad-like church with its upside-down cross, hear the blood-curdling cries of the villagers as they whipped themselves up into a frenzy during some ritual ceremony.

Some days you could believe it, Banks thought, as he headed towards the car park, but today it seemed as far away from evil and satanic rites as you could get. A couple passed him on the path, hand in hand, and the girl smiled shyly at him, a blade of grass in her mouth. One middle-aged man was jogging in a tracksuit and trainers, red-faced and sweating with exertion, a heart attack waiting to happen.

Banks reached the end of the tarn where the cars were parked, and then he saw the familiar figure. Standing at the side of the water, throwing flat pebbles that sank rather than skipped, was Detective Superintendent Dirty Dick Burgess. When he caught sight of Banks, he clapped his hands and rubbed them together, then he said, "Banksy. So glad you could come. Who's been a naughty boy, then?"

It was typical that Banks would give her the job of talking to Gervaise, Annie thought, as she pulled up outside the superintendent's house later that morning. Gervaise had been a tad tetchy on the phone – her husband had taken the children to the cricket, and it was her gardening day, she said – but had agreed to give Annie five minutes of her time.

As she drove along the quiet country road, Annie thought about Banks and his odd behaviour earlier that morning. There had been something different about him, and she decided that the rift with Sophia must have been even more serious than he had made out. He had mentioned before how much Sophia valued the various natural objects and works of art she had collected over the years, so it must have really hurt her to witness such wanton destruction. Still, Annie thought, if the silly cow was more fond of her seashells than she was of Banks, then she deserved everything she got.

When Annie pulled up in front of the house and knocked on the door, she heard a voice call, "I'm round the back. Just come down the side." A narrow pathway ran down the side of the house beside the garage and led to the back garden.

The sight of the superintendent in a broad-brimmed hat, baggy man's shirt, white shorts and sandals, with a pair of secateurs in her hand, almost gave Annie a fit of the giggles, but she managed to restrain herself.

"Sit down, DI Cabbot," said Gervaise, a healthy glow on her face. "Barley water?"

"Thank you." Annie accepted the glass, sat down and took a sip. She hadn't tasted barley water in years, not since her mother used to make it. It was wonderful. There were four chairs and a round table on the lawn, but no protective umbrella, and she wished she had worn a hat.

"Have you thought about blonde highlights?" Gervaise asked.

"No, ma'am."

"Maybe you should. They'd look good in the sunlight."

What was all this? Annie wondered. First Carol Wyman had suggested she go blonde, now Gervaise was talking about highlights.

Gervaise sat down. "I suppose you've come to tell me about important developments in the East Side Estate stabbing?"

"Winsome's on the case, ma'am," said Annie. "I'm sure we're expecting a breakthrough any day now."

"Any moment would be better. Even the mayor's getting edgy. And what about *you*, DI Cabbot? What case are you on?"

Annie shifted in her chair. "Well, that's what I came to see you about, ma'am. It's a bit awkward."

Gervaise sipped her barley water and smiled. "Try me."

"You know we were talking, the other day, about Derek Wyman?"

"You mean Banks's Iago theory?"

"Yes."

"Go on."

"Well, what if there's something in it? I mean, *really* something in it." A wasp droned near Annie's barley water. She waved it away.

"Like what?" asked Gervaise.

"Well, I was talking to Mr. Wyman's wife, Carol, and she –"

"I thought I told you to leave them alone."

"Well, ma'am, you didn't exactly spell it out."

"Oh, for crying out loud, DI Cabbot. Maybe I didn't spell it out in words of one syllable, but you know exactly what I was telling you. It's over. Leave it alone."

Annie took a deep breath and blurted out, "I'd like to bring Derek Wyman in for questioning."

Gervaise's silence was unnerving. The wasp droned by again. Somewhere Annie could hear a garden hose hissing and a radio playing "Moon River." Finally, Superintendent Gervaise said, "You? Or DCI Banks?"

"Both of us." Now that Annie had said it, she was gathering courage fast. "I know you've been warned to lay off," she went on, "but there's evidence now. And it's nothing to do with the secret intelligence services."

"Oh, really?"

"Yes. DCI Banks found the private investigator who took the photos of Silbert with the other man."

"A *private investigator*?"

"Yes. He also talked to a waitress in Zizzi's who remembered seeing a man we assume to be Hardcastle tearing up some photos."

"Assume?"

"Well, it was Wyman who commissioned them, and he did tell us he had dinner at Zizzi's with Hardcastle before going to the National Film Theatre."

"But why?"

"To stir Hardcastle up."

"Or so you assume?"

"Well, it makes sense, doesn't it? Why else would he go to all that expense. He wasn't a rich man."

"Why would he want to do it in the first place? He didn't even know Silbert very well, did he?"

"Not well. No. They'd met once or twice, had dinner, but no, he didn't really know Silbert. It was personal, I think. The target was Hardcastle, but when you set things like that in motion you can't always predict their outcome."

"I'll say. Do go on."

"From what I can gather from talking to Carol Wyman, her husband's sick of his teaching job and he's got a passion for theatre."

"I know that," said Gervaise. "He directed *Othello*."

"That's just it, ma'am," Annie rushed on. "He wants to direct more. In fact, he wants it to be a full-time job. But like I said at that meeting when you closed the case, if Hardcastle and Silbert had succeeded in setting up their acting company the way they wanted, there would have been no room for Wyman. Hardcastle himself wanted to direct. Wyman would have been back to square one. That kind of failure and humiliation can really push a man to the limit, hurt his pride."

"And you're saying that's Wyman's motive for killing two men?"

"I don't think he intended to kill anyone. It was just a nasty prank that went wrong. I mean, I'm sure he wanted to hurt Hardcastle, or he wouldn't have gone to all that trouble. I think directing *Othello* just put the idea in his mind in the first place. What he really wanted was to split up Hardcastle and Silbert so that Hardcastle would probably feel he had to leave Eastvale and abandon the theatre."

"I don't know," said Gervaise. "It still sounds a bit far-fetched. And correct me if I'm wrong, but I still don't see that any crime has been committed."

"We'll work something out. People have killed for less – a job, a career, rivalry, artistic jealousy. I'm still not saying that Wyman intended to kill anyone. He may have incited Hardcastle to do what he did. He may have harassed him with the images and innuendos the way Iago did Othello. Maybe Wyman has a certain amount of psychological insight – you might expect it in a theatre director – and he knew what buttons to push. I don't know. All I know is that I think he did it." Gervaise refilled her glass from the pitcher and offered Annie more. She declined. "What do you think?" she asked.

"I suppose there's a certain low-level plausibility to it all," Gervaise admitted. "But even so, we'd never prove it in a million years."

"Unless Wyman confessed."

"Why would he do that?"

"Guilt. If it was a prank gone wrong. If he didn't mean to really hurt anyone. If we're not dealing with a cold-blooded killer. He must have feelings. What happened must be a burden for him. His wife says he's been a bit preoccupied lately. I'll bet it's weighing on his mind."

"All right, DI Cabbot," said Gervaise. "Let's accept that Wyman did cook up some scheme based on his directing of *Othello* to get at Hardcastle, and that it backfired. Are you able to guarantee me that this was nothing at all to do with the intelligence services and with what Silbert did for a living?"

It was as Banks had said, Annie thought. With the intelligence services out of the picture, Gervaise was far more willing to go along with the idea. "Yes," she said.

Gervaise sighed, took off her hat and used it as a fan for a moment, then put it back on. "Why can't things be easy?" she said. "Why can't people just do as they're told?"

"We have to pursue the truth," said Annie.

"Since when? That's a luxury we can ill afford."

"But two people died because of what Wyman did, no matter how he intended it, or even whether he's technically committed a crime. Surely we have to do *something*?"

"I think you'll find that in this matter the law is very much concerned with any criminal offence he might have committed, or lack of one, and I can't think of any."

"We'll leave that to the CPS."

"Hmph. Do you know how much pressure I've had from above to drop this? About the only one who hasn't been on my back is ACC McLaughlin, and that's only because he has no particular liking for the secret intelligence services. But the Chief Constable is adamant. I don't want this on my plate. Bring in Wyman, by all means. Have a chat with him. And if he admits anything that supports your theories, send the file to the CPS and see what they come up with. Just you and DCI Banks make damn sure that there's no room here for things to go pear-shaped."

"Yes, ma'am," said Annie, draining her glass and standing up before Gervaise changed her mind. "I'll do that."

"Where *is* DCI Banks, by the way?"

"He's finishing his holiday at home," said Annie.

"Things not work out in London?"

"I suppose not."

"Well, let's hope they improve. The last thing I want is a lovesick DCI moping about the station. Go on, then. Get to it. I've got to get back to my herbaceous border before Keith and the kids get back from the cricket match and want their dinner."

"This is a bloody godforsaken hole you've chosen for a meeting place," said Burgess as they walked around the scenic footpath.

"It's supposed to be a spot of great natural beauty," said Banks.

"You know me. I'm a city boy at heart. I have to tell you, though, Banksy, Dewsbury is a boil on the arse of the universe."

"It's got a nice town hall. Same architect who designed Leeds, I think. Cuthbert Broderick. Or Broderick Cuthbert."

"Bugger the bloody town hall. It's the mosques that interest me."

"That's why you're up there?"

Burgess sighed. "Why else? It just gets worse, doesn't it?"

"So what's the answer?" Banks asked.

"You tell me. I've been up in Dewsbury for a couple of weeks or so investigating various terrorism-related matters, and now we know that two of the young lads involved in planning yesterday's bombing live there. They're all home-grown these days. We don't need to import our terrorists any more."

"Don't feel so bad. They could have sent you to Leicester."

"Not much in it, if you ask me. Anyway, for what good it'll do, we're searching for a garage, a lock-up somewhere out of the way. Obviously to rig up the car and driver the way they did, they had to have a secure place, out of the public eye. Could be Dewsbury."

"Leicester's closer to London," said Banks.

"What I said, but did they listen?"

"And why not use London as a starting point?"

"It's not the way they do things. It's their policy to use cells. Networks. Contract out. You can't centralize an operation like that. Too many risks involved. Besides, we've got London sewn up tighter than a gnat's arsehole."

"I'd say there were plenty of risks involved in driving a car full of explosives down the M1 from Dewsbury to London," said Banks. "Or even from Leicester. Haven't you ever seen *The Wages of Fear*?"

"Great film. But they use much more stable stuff these days, for crying out loud. It was hardly nitroglycerine."

"Even so," Banks said.

Burgess kicked a stone off the path. "Can you imagine it, though? Some bastard driving a car full of explosives two hundred miles or more knowing he's going to die at the end of it."

"Same as those terrorists on the planes that flew into the twin towers. It's what they're trained for."

"Oh, I know all about their training, Banksy, but it still boggles my imagination. Twenty-two years old, the kid who did it. Bright lad, by all accounts. From Birmingham. Islamic Studies degree from Keele. Anyway, he's wearing an explosive suit wired to a bootful of explosives and he drives two hundred miles to his appointed destination, where he promptly presses the button. The score's forty virgins for him, forty-six dead, fifty-eight injured, some seriously, and seventy-three orphans for London." Burgess paused. "I counted. Do you know, when they raided one of the flats, they found plans drawn up for possible similar attacks on Piccadilly Circus, Trafalgar Square and the front of Buck House, where the tourists all stand and gawp at the changing of the guard?"

"So why Oxford Circus?"

"Just lucky, I guess."

Banks said nothing.

"Hang on a minute, you were in London yesterday, weren't you?"

"Yes," Banks said.

"Were you anywhere near? You were, weren't you?"

"I was there," Banks said. He hadn't planned on telling anyone, but Burgess always had an uncanny knack of knowing these things anyway.

Burgess stopped and stared out over the water. It surface was ruffled by a few ripples caused by the light breeze. "Bugger me," he said. "I won't ask you . . ."

"No," said Banks. "Don't. Thanks. I don't really want to talk about it." He could feel a lump in his throat and tears prickling in his eyes, but the sensations passed. They continued walking.

"Anyway," Burgess went on, "I think I've got a pretty good idea of what you want to see me about. It's to do with these dead shirt-lifters, isn't it? The one who worked for MI6 in particular. The answer's still no."

"Hear me out," said Banks, and told him what he knew about Wyman, Hardcastle and Silbert, along with had happened at Sophia's house and Tomasina's office.

Burgess listened as they walked, head bowed. As his hair had thinned over the years, he had finally gone for the shaved look rather than the comb-over, which some people unwisely chose. He was in fairly good shape, his paunch diminished a little since their last meeting, and he reminded Banks physically a bit of Pete Townshend from The Who.

When Banks had finished, Burgess said, "No wonder you're red-flagged."

"It's not just me," Banks said. "If it were only me, I could deal with it. They go after your loved ones as well."

"Well, the terrorists don't discriminate, either. These are interesting times. Bad things happen. Difficult decisions are made on the fly. No pun intended, Banks, but there's a darkness out there. You should know."

"Yes, and the struggle is to *keep* it out there."

"That's too metaphysical for me. I just catch the bad guys."

"So you're defending their actions? What they did in Sophia's house, Tomasina's office?"

"They're the good guys, Banksy! If I don't defend them, whose side does that put me on?"

"Do you know a Mr. Browne?"

"Never heard of him. Believe it or not, MI5 and MI6 are not my outfits. I work with them from time to time, yes, but I'm on a wholly different detachment. I don't know those people."

"But you do know what's going on?"

"I like to keep my finger on the pulse, as well you know. Can we sit down on this bench a minute? My legs are starting to ache."

"But we've only walked round twice. That's not even half a mile."

"I think the altitude's getting to me. Can we just bloody sit down?"

"Of course."

They sat on the bench, donated by some famous local moorland enthusiast whose name was engraved on a brass plate. Burgess examined the name. "Josiah Branksome," he said in as close an imitation of a Yorkshire accent as he could manage. "Sounds very northern."

Banks leaned forward, rested his elbows on his knees and cupped his head in his hands. "Why did they do it, though?" he asked.

"Because they're fucking crazy."

"No. I mean MI5. Why break Sophia's things and scare Tomasina out of her wits?"

"What makes you think it was MI5?"

Banks glanced at him. "Browne said he was MI5." But when Banks cast his mind back, he couldn't be certain that Browne *had* said that; he couldn't be certain what Browne had said at all. "Why? What do you know?"

"All I'm saying is that Silbert worked for MI6. A whole different kettle of fish, they are. The two don't exactly work hand in glove, you know. Half the time they're not even talking to each other."

"So you think MI6 are more likely to be involved in this than MI5?"

"I'm only saying that it's possible."

"But I thought their brief was working *outside* the country?"

"It is. Usually. But I'd imagine they'd want to investigate the murder of one of their own, wherever it happened. They certainly wouldn't want MI5 to do it for them. Just a suggestion. Not that it really matters. They're all pretty good at dirty tricks. The result is the same."

"So what do you suggest?"

"If you want my opinion, and it's only an opinion based on what little I know of them and the way they operate, I'd say they don't reason; they react. They're not really interested in your girlfriend. Or the private detective. Though I must admit that if she went around photographing an MI6 agent, retired or not, meeting people secretly in Regent's Park, then they might have a justifiable concern for questioning her. But mostly it's just a way of getting a message to you. Look at it this way. One of their own has been killed. There's blood in the water. They're circling. What do you expect?"

"But why not come directly after me?"

"Well, they did, didn't they? This Mr. Browne you were asking about."

"Bloody lot of use he was. He came once, got pissed off when I wouldn't co-operate, and left."

Burgess started to laugh. "Oh, Banksy, you're priceless, you are. Did you expect more? Another polite visit, perhaps? 'Please, Mr. Banks, do cease and desist.' They don't mess around, these buggers. Five or Six. They don't have time. Patience isn't a virtue with them. Don't you get it? This is the new breed. They're a lot nastier than the old boys and they've got a lot of new toys. They're not gentlemen. More like City traders. But they can erase your past and rewrite your life in the blink of an eye. They've got software that makes your HOLMES system look like a Rolodex. Don't piss them off. I tell you in all seriousness, Banksy, do not fuck with them."

"A bit late for that, isn't it?"

"Then back off. They'll lose interest in time. It's not as if there isn't plenty to occupy them elsewhere." He paused and scratched the side of his nose. "I did talk to someone in the know after I got your message, just to see if I could find out what was going on. He was very cagey, but he told me a couple of things. For a start, they're just not sure about Wyman, that's all, and they don't like to be not sure."

"Why haven't they questioned him?"

"Surely even you can work that out for yourself? When this Mr. Browne paid you a visit, and when those people entered your girl-friend's house and broke a few of her things, they were trying to warn you off. They wanted you to shut down the investigation. It's instinct with them, secrecy, second nature. Then they get the photos from the private detective woman, and they start to wonder about this Wyman character. What he might have been up to. Who he might have been working for. What he might know. And more important still, what he might *tell*. Now they're letting you do their job for them, up to a point, watching you from a distance. You could still just let it drop and walk away. Nothing will happen to you or your girlfriend. There'll be no con-sequences. That's another thing, Banksy. People rarely murder each other in this business. They're professionals. If it happens, you can be damn sure there's a good political or security reason, not a personal one. Drop it. There's nothing to be gained by antagonizing them any further."

"But there are still a few things I need to know."

Burgess sighed. "It's like talking to a fucking brick wall, isn't it?" he said. "What will it take to get you off my back?"

"I want to know about Silbert's background, what he did, what they think he might have been up to."

"Why?"

"Because maybe Wyman knows. Maybe Silbert let something slip, pillow talk, perhaps, and Hardcastle passed it on to Wyman in one of their intimate boozy get-togethers."

"But how does that give Wyman a motive to do whatever it is you think he did?"

"I don't know," said Banks. "But that brings me to my next request. Wyman had a brother called Rick. SAS. He was killed in Afghanistan on the fifteenth of October, 2002. According to the press it was a helicopter crash on manoeuvres, but according to other sources I've spoken to, Rick Wyman was killed on active duty, on a secret mission."

"So what? It's standard procedure to downplay your casualties in a war. That's one way of doing it. That and friendly fire."

"I'm not interested in the propaganda angle," said Banks. "What concerns me is that Silbert might have had something to do with the intelligence behind the mission. He was still employed by MI6 in 2002. He and Hardcastle had dinner with the Wymans a couple of times and he mentioned that he'd been to Afghanistan. I'd guess the SAS was after Bin Laden or some important terrorist encampment or cell leader – this wasn't too long after 9/11 – and somehow or other they'd got information on its whereabouts that turned out to be inaccurate, they got lost, or it was better protected than the agent thought. Maybe Wyman *blames* Silbert. I need to know when Silbert was in Afghanistan and why. I want to know if Silbert could have been involved in any of this, and if there's a terrorist connection."

"You don't ask for much, do you? Even if Silbert was responsible for Rick Wyman's death, how on earth could Derek Wyman know about it if it was a secret mission?"

"I don't know. Pillow talk again? Silbert lets something slip to Hardcastle in bed after one of those dinners, and Hardcastle passes it on."

"Crap, Banks. Silbert and his kind are better trained than that."

"But it *could* have happened somehow."

"You're clutching at straws, mate."

"Will you find out for me? You're counterterrorism, you should have an in."

"I don't know if I can," said Burgess. "And if I could, I'm not sure that I would."

"I'm not asking you to break the Official Secrets Act."

"You probably are, but that's the least of my worries. What you *are* asking could possibly bring a whole lot more grief on the intelligence services, including me, who really don't need that right now, thank you very much, as well as on you and all your friends and family. I'm not sure I want to be the one responsible for all that."

"You won't be. It's *my* responsibility. Derek Wyman set in motion a chain of events that ended in the violent deaths of two men. It was a cruel trick he played, if that's all it was, and I want to know why he did it. If it's something do with his brother's death, if there's a terrorist connection, I want to know."

"Why does it matter? Why don't you just beat a confession out of him and leave it at that?"

"Because I want to know what it takes to drive a man to a cold-blooded act like that, something that, while he couldn't be expected to be certain it would end in death, he had to know would at least bring a lot of unnecessary grief and pain into two people's lives. Can't you understand that? You of all people. And don't try to tell me you've never suffered from copper's curiosity. It's what separates the men from the boys in this job. You can have a perfectly good career in the force without giving a damn about why who did what to whom. But if you want to learn about the world, if you want to know about people and what makes them what they are, you have to see beyond that, you have to dig deeper. You have to *know*."

Burgess stood up and put his hands in his pockets. "Well, seeing as you put it like that, Banksy, how can I refuse?"

"You'll do it?"

"I was joking. Look, it's easy enough to find out about Silbert's background – in general terms, without going into any incriminating details, of course – but it might be a bit harder to find any connection with a specific mission. If he was in Afghanistan ages ago, nobody's likely to care about that now, but if it was more recent, that's another matter. They don't talk about things like that, and I don't have unlimited access to files. They'd skin me alive if they knew I was even contemplating something like this. I'm not going to put myself in a position of risk, not even for you."

"What *can* you find out?" Banks said. "What can you reasonably tell me?"

"Reasonably? Nothing. If I was behaving reasonably, I'd walk away from here right now without even waving bye-bye. But I've never been a reasonable man, and perhaps I am as cursed as you are with copper's curiosity. Perhaps it's what makes me good at my job. You say you already know Silbert visited Afghanistan. That doesn't necessarily mean a lot, you know. These people travel widely, for all kinds of reasons."

"I know. But it's a starting place. Can you also tell me what Silbert was up to lately? Who he was meeting in London?"

"You must be joking. I think the best I can do for you is find out if Silbert was working in an area and in a capacity that made it at all likely he could have a connection with SAS missions in Afghanistan in 2002. That shouldn't be too highly classified. Will that do you?"

"It'll have to, won't it? But how can I trust you? You're with them, even if you're not technically with MI5 or MI6. How do I know you'll be telling me the truth?"

"Oh, for fuck's sake, Banksy. You don't."

"I mean, you could be feeding me whatever you want to, couldn't you?"

"And *they* could feed *me* whatever they want *you* to know. Welcome to the dizzy world of the secret intelligence services. Is your phone safe?"

"It's a pay-as-you-go."

"How long have you had it?"

"Week or so."

"Get rid of it as soon as you hear from me. I mean it." Then, muttering "I must be a fucking lunatic," under his breath, he walked back to his car, leaving Banks to sit alone on the bench in the sun.

16

"What's this all about?" Derek Wyman asked Banks after Annie had picked him up and kept him waiting in the interview room for an hour. "It's Saturday. I have to be at the theatre. I've got a play to direct."

"They'll manage without you," said Banks. "They have done before. Remember, when you were in London?"

"Yes, but –"

"You agreed to come here, right? I mean, you came voluntarily?"

"Well, yes. I mean, one doesn't like to be uncooperative. I've got nothing to hide."

"Then we'll try not to keep you too long. I appreciate your attitude, Mr. Wyman," said Banks. "Believe me, our lives would be a lot easier if everyone felt the same way you do. The problem is that most people *do* have something to hide."

"Are you charging me? Do I need a solicitor or anything?"

"You're not under arrest. You're not being charged with anything. You can leave at any time. You're here simply to answer a few questions. I should also tell you that you do not have to say anything, but it might harm your defence if you do not mention, when questioned, something you later rely on in court. Anything you do say may be given in evidence."

"My *defence*? In *court*?"

"It's a formal caution, Mr. Wyman. Standard procedure. To protect all of us. As for the solicitor, that's up to you. Do you think you need one? You're certainly entitled, if you think it would help, in which case you can either drag your own solicitor off the golf course, if you have one, or one will be provided for you."

"But I haven't done anything."

"Nobody's saying you have."

Wyman looked over at the tape equipment and licked his lips. "But you're *recording* this interview."

"Again, standard procedure," said Annie. "A safeguard. It's for everyone's good."

"I don't know . . ."

"If you're at all uncertain," Annie went on, "DCI Banks has already told you that you're free to go. We'll find some other way of doing this."

"What do you mean?"

"DI Cabbot simply means that we have a few questions, and we'd like some answers," Banks said. "This is the easy way. There are other ways. Stay or leave. It's up to you."

Wyman chewed on his bottom lip for a few moments, then he said, "OK. I'll answer your questions. As I said before, I've got nothing to hide."

"Good," said Banks. "Shall we start now?"

Wyman folded his arms. "All right." He looked stiff, tense.

Banks gave Annie the signal to begin the questioning. "Can we get you anything first, Mr. Wyman?" she asked. "Cup of tea, perhaps? Or coffee?"

"Nothing, thanks. Let's just get on with it."

"Very well. How would you characterize your relationship with Mark Hardcastle?" Annie asked first.

"I don't know, really. I mean, I didn't have one. Not in the way you mean."

"Oh? What way do I mean?"

"Don't think I'm not aware of the subtle insinuation behind what you say. I direct plays. I know all about subtle insinuations."

"I'm sure you do," Annie said, "but actually I wasn't being subtle at all. And I wasn't insinuating anything. I was being quite straightforward. You say you didn't really have a relationship, but you were friends, weren't you?"

"Colleagues, really, more than friends."

"But you went for a social drink every now and then, didn't you?"

"Yes, on occasion."

"And you had Mark Hardcastle and his partner Laurence Silbert over for dinner with your family. You also went with your wife Carol to their house on Castleview Heights once. Is that correct?"

"Yes. You know it is. I'm not prejudiced about people being gay."

"So why do you constantly play the whole relationship down? Is there something you're not telling us?"

"No. Everything is just as I said it was."

"But it *was* more than just a working relationship, wasn't it?" Annie went on. "Not only did you go to London with Mark Hardcastle, you went drinking with him on several occasions in the Red Rooster. We just want to know why you didn't tell us about that earlier, when we first questioned you."

"I didn't think it was important where we went for a drink, that's all."

"And perhaps you didn't want to get involved?" Annie suggested. "I mean, it's not unusual for people to want to distance themselves from a murder investigation. It does get rather dirty, and that dirt can sometimes rub off."

"Murder? Who said anything about murder?" Wyman seemed flustered.

"Laurence Silbert was certainly murdered," said Annie, "and we believe that someone deliberately engineered the argument between Silbert and Hardcastle. Perhaps they only expected a falling out and got more than they bargained for, but even that's a bit nasty, isn't it?"

"Maybe. But I don't know anything about it."

"Remember, Mr. Wyman. If you don't tell us something now that you later rely on, it could go badly for you. This is your chance for a clean slate."

"I've told you all I know."

"But you *were* a lot closer to Mark and Laurence than you made out at first, weren't you?"

"Perhaps. It's hard to say. They were a very difficult couple to get to know."

"What were those drinks in the Red Rooster all about?"

"I'm sorry?"

"Oh, come off it, Derek," said Banks. "You know what we're talking about. It's not the sort of place for sophisticated men of the world like you and Mark Hardcastle to hang out. Why go there? Was it the karaoke? Fancy yourself as the new Robbie Williams, do you?"

"There was no karaoke when we were there. It was quiet enough. And they do a decent pint."

"The beer's rubbish," said Banks. "Don't expect us to believe that's why you went there."

Wyman glared at Banks, then looking imploringly at Annie, as if she were his lifeline, his anchor to sanity and safety. "What happened there, Derek?" she asked gently. "Go on. You can tell us. We heard that Mark was upset by something you said and you were calming him down. What was it all about?"

Wyman folded his arms again. "Nothing. I don't remember."

"This isn't working," said Banks. "I think we'd better move on to a more official legal footing."

"What do you mean?" Wyman asked, glancing from one to the other. "More official?"

"DCI Banks is impatient, that's all," Annie said. "It's nothing. Just that this is a sort of informal chat, and we hoped it would resolve our problems. We don't really want to move on to matters of detention, body searches, home searches and intimate samples or anything like that. Not yet, anyway. Not when we can settle matters as easily as this."

"You can't intimidate me," Wyman said. "I know my rights."

"Was it about work?" Annie asked.

"What?"

"Your discussion with Mark in the Red Rooster."

"It might have been. That's what we usually talked about. I told you, we were more colleagues than friends."

"I understand that you were a bit upset about Mark wanting to direct plays himself and trying to start up a professional acting troupe, using paid locals and jobbing actors, attached to the Eastvale Theatre," Annie said. "That you thought it would threaten your position. I can see how that would get to you. It must be the only bit of real job satisfaction you get after a day at the comprehensive with the likes of Nicky Haskell and Jackie Binns."

"They're not all like that."

"I suppose not," said Annie. "But it must still be a bit depressing. You *love* the theatre, don't you? It's the one thing you're passionate about. And here was Mark Hardcastle, already a brilliant set designer, just waiting in the wings to take over directing, too. Artistic director of his own company. It would have been no contest, would it?"

"Mark couldn't direct his way out of a paper bag."

"But he was the up-and-coming star," Banks said. "He had professional theatre experience. He had big ideas. It would have put the Eastvale Theatre on the map a lot more significantly than a bloody amateur dramatic company. You're just a schoolteacher moonlighting as a director. As DI Cabbot says, no contest."

Wyman squirmed in his chair. "I don't know where all this is supposed to be leading, but –"

"Then let me show you," said Banks. "DI Cabbot might want to go gently with you, but I've had enough pissing about." He took some photographs from an envelope in front of him and slipped them across the table to Wyman.

"What are these?" Wyman asked, glancing down at them.

"Surely you recognize Laurence Silbert?"

"It could be him. It's not a very good photo."

"Bollocks, Derek. It's a perfectly good photo. Who's the other man?"

"No idea."

"Who took them?"

"How should I know?"

Banks leaned forward and rested his arms on the table. "I'll tell you how you should know," he said. "They were taken by a young female private detective called Tomasina Savage. On your instructions. What do you have to say about that?"

"That's privileged! That was a private . . . It . . . You can't . . ." Wyman started to get to his feet but banged his leg on the underside of the bolted table and sat down again.

"Privileged? You've been watching too many American cop shows," Banks said. "Why did you employ Tomasina Savage to follow Laurence Silbert and take those photographs? We know you gave them to Mark at Zizzi's and he tore them up as soon as he saw them, but he kept the memory stick. Did he really just go to the cinema with you after that? Or was it all a lie?"

"Can I have some water?"

Annie poured him a glass from the pitcher on the table.

"Why did you pay Tomasina Savage to take those photographs?" Banks repeated.

Wyman sipped his water and leaned back in his chair. For a few long moments, he said nothing, seemed to be coming to a decision, then he looked at them and said, "Because Mark asked me to. That's why I did it. Because Mark asked me to. But as God is my witness it was not my intention that anyone should die."

By six o'clock on Saturday evening Winsome was getting sick and tired of traipsing around the East Side Estate with Harry Potter. It was time to go home, she felt, have a long bath, put on a nice frock and go to the Potholing Club social at the Cat and Fiddle. Maybe have a quiet drink later with Steve Farrow, if he asked her. But they were getting close to finding the Bull.

So far, they had discovered that one of Jackie Binns's recent recruits, Andy Pash, a fifteen-year-old wannabe trying to ingratiate himself with the rest of the gang, had told the Bull that Donny Moore called him a big ugly Arab bastard and said he was going to get what was coming to him. Apparently, Moore had said nothing of the kind – he was neither stupid nor suicidal – but the Bull believed that he had and had gone after him. Nobody had actually witnessed the stabbing – or so everyone said – but they all knew who did it and, as expected, someone had eventually let the name slip.

Now they were going to talk to Andy Pash, and Winsome had the feeling that he might just be the weakest link.

Pash lived with his mother and two sisters on one of nicer streets on the estate. At least there weren't any boarded-up windows or rusted cars parked in the garden. The woman who answered the door, a bleached blonde in a micro skirt with too much make-up, cigarette in one hand and handbag in the other, turned out to be his mother, Kath. If she was surprised to find a six-foot-plus black woman and a detective constable who resembled Harry Potter at her door just after six on a Saturday evening asking to talk to her son, she didn't show it.

"He's up in his room," she said. "Can't you hear the bloody racket? And I'm off out."

"You should be present while we question him," Winsome said.

"Why? He's a big boy. Help yourselves. And good luck. Close the door behind you."

She brushed past them. Winsome and Doug Wilson exchanged glances. "Did she just give us permission?" Wilson asked.

"I think so," said Winsome. "Besides, we're not arresting him. We just want him to tell us where the Bull lives."

Wilson muttered something about "fruit of the poisoned tree," which Winsome was sure he must have got from an American cop program, and they went inside and shut the door. In the living room, a young girl of about thirteen lounged on the sofa watching *The Simpsons*. She had just lit a cigarette, no doubt the moment her mother had gone out of the door.

"Hey, you're too young to be smoking," said Winsome.

The girl jumped. The television was so loud that she hadn't even noticed Winsome and Wilson enter the room. On the screen, Itchy was chopping Scratchy into little pieces again while Bart and Lisa chuckled away. "Who the fuck are you?" the girl said, reaching for her mobile. "Perverts. I'll call the cops."

"No need, love, we're already here." Winsome showed her warrant card. "And mind your language," she said. "Now put that cigarette out."

The girl glared at her.

"Put it out," Winsome repeated.

Casually, the girl dropped her cigarette into a half-empty mug on the coffee table – her mother's, judging by the lipstick smeared on the rim. It sizzled and went out.

"Charming," said Wilson.

It was a small victory, Winsome knew, and as soon as they were out of the way the child would light up again, but with such small victories the war is sometimes won. "We're off up to see your brother," she said. "You behave yourself."

"Lucky you," said the young smoker, turning back to the TV.

Winsome and Wilson climbed the stairs. The noise was coming from the second door on the right, but before they could knock the door across the landing opened and another girl peered out at them. She was younger than her sister, perhaps about nine or ten, a gawky young thing with thick-lensed glasses. She was holding a book in her hand, and though she didn't look scared, she did seem curious as to what was going on. Winsome walked over.

"Who are you?" the girl asked.

Winsome squatted so she could be at eye level with her. "My name's Winsome Jackman. I'm a policewoman. And this is Doug. What's your name?"

"Winsome's a nice name. I've never heard it before. I'm Scarlett. I think I've seen your picture in the paper."

"You might have done," said Winsome. She had last made the headlines after bringing down a suspect with a flying rugby tackle in the heart of the Swainsdale Centre's Marks and Spencer food department. "We've come to see your brother."

"Oh," said Scarlett, as if it were an everyday occurrence.

"What are you reading?" Winsome asked.

The girl clutched the book to her chest as if she feared someone were going to steal it from her. "*Wuthering Heights.*"

"I read that at school," said Winsome. "It's good, isn't it?"

"It's *wonderful!*"

Winsome could see the room behind her. It was reasonably tidy, though clothes lay scattered around on the floor, and there was a bookcase almost full of second-hand paperbacks. "You like to read?" she said.

"Yes," said Scarlett. "But sometimes it's just too noisy. They're always shouting and Andy plays his music so very loud."

"So I hear," said Winsome.

"Sometimes it's hard to follow the words."

"Well, that's a very grown-up book for a little girl."

"I'm ten," said Scarlett proudly. "I've read *Jane Eyre*, too! I just wish they'd be more quiet so I can read."

"We'll see what we can do." Winsome stood up. "See you later, Scarlett," she said.

"Bye-bye." Scarlett shut her bedroom door.

After a swift tap, Winsome opened Andy Pash's door and she and Wilson walked in.

"Hey," said Pash, getting up from his unmade bed. "What's all this? Who the fuck do you think you are?"

"Police," said Winsome, flashing her card. "Your mother let us in. Said we could ask you a few questions. Do you want to turn that down? Off would be even better. Your little sister's trying to read across the hall."

"That little bookworm. She's always got her face buried in a book," Pash complained as he went over to the sound system.

The music was a sort of thumping, pulsating techno-beat rhythm that sounded to Winsome as if it had all been generated by computers and drum machines, though it did have a sort of Caribbean lilt. Most people assumed that Winsome was a reggae or calypso fan, but she actually hated reggae, which had been her father's preferred music, and calypso, which her grandparents had adored. If she did listen to music at all, which wasn't that often, she preferred the "best of" approach to classical music you got on Classic FM. All the catchy bits in one handy package. Why listen to the boring second movement of a symphony, she thought, if all you wanted to hear was that nice theme in the third?

Glumly, Andy Pash turned off the music, which originated from a shiny black iPod seated in a matching dock, and sat on the edge of his bed. It was a small room, and there were no chairs, so Winsome and Doug Wilson remained standing, leaning against the wall beside the door. The first thing Winsome noticed, glancing around, was the bookcases against one wall – or, more specifically, she noticed the rows of traffic cones that stood on them, all painted different colours.

"Quite the artist, I see, Andy," said Winsome.

"Oh, that . . . yeah, well . . ."

"I suppose you know what you've done is theft?"

"They're just traffic cones, for fuck's sake."

"Eastvale Highways Department's traffic cones, to be precise. And don't swear while I'm around. I don't like it."

"You can have them back. It was just a lark."

"Glad you can see the funny side of it."

Pash peered at Wilson and said, "Anyone ever tell you that you look like –"

"Shut up," said Wilson, pointing a finger at him. "Just you shut up right there, you little scrote."

Pash held his hands up. "All right. OK. It's cool, man. Whatever."

"Andy," said Winsome, "have you ever heard of a bloke in the neighbourhood called the Bull?"

"The Bull? Yeah. He's a cool dude."

American television had a lot to answer for when it came to the ruination of the English language, Winsome thought. She had been taught in a mountain village school by an Oxford-educated local woman who had come home after years in England to give something back to her people. She had given Winsome a love of the English language and its literature and inspired in her the desire to go to live in England one day, which had put her where she was now. Perhaps not exactly what Mrs. Marlowe would have wished, but at least she was here, in the land of Jane Austen, Shakespeare, Dickens and the Brontës. It was from her father, a corporal at the local station, that she had got her policing instinct, such as it was. "Know what his real name is?" she asked.

"No. I think it might be like Torgi or Tory or something like that, some sort of foreign name. Arab. Turkish, I think. But everyone calls him the Bull. He's a big guy."

"Does he wear a hoodie?"

"Sure."

"Do you know where he lives?"

"I might do."

"Would you care to tell us?"

"Hey, man. I don't want the Bull thinking I sicced the cops on him."

"It's just a friendly chat we want, Andy. Like the one we're having with you now."

"The Bull don't like the pigs."

"I'm sure he doesn't," said Winsome. "So we'll be especially careful not to oink too loudly."

"Huh?"

Winsome sighed and crossed her arms. Clearly Pash was as stupid as he was obnoxious, which was fortunate for them, or he'd know to clam up. "Andy, did you tell this Bull that Donny Moore, Nicky Haskell's right-hand man, had called him an ugly Arab bastard?"

"Donny Moore is menkle. He deserved everything he got."

"He deserved to get stabbed, did he?"

"Dunno."

"Do you know who did that to him, Andy?"

"No idea. Not one of us."

"What did you have to do to become a member of Jackie's crew?"

"Whaddya mean?"

"You know what I mean, Andy. Usually you have to perform some sort of task, prove your loyalty, your courage, before you can be accepted into a gang. In some places it's got as far as killing someone at random, but we still hang on to the vestiges of civilization here in Eastvale."

"I don't know what you're talking about, man. I don't know nothing about any vestergers."

"Let me try to keep it simple then," said Winsome. "What did Jackie Binns ask you to do to become a member of his gang?"

"He didn't ask me nothing."

"You're lying, Andy."

"I'm –"

"Andy!"

Pash turned away and stared sulkily at the wall. For all his surface bravado, Winsome thought, he was just a confused and scared kid. It didn't mean he couldn't be dangerous, or vicious, but she doubted very much that he would turn out really bad. A dumb, petty criminal, at worst, the one who always got caught.

"OK," he said. "OK. No need to shout at me. Nicky and Jackie, they never got along, right? Then along comes the Bull, and he's, like, bigger than both of them. Jackie thought like maybe it would be a good idea to set them against each other, so, yeah, he said I should tell the Bull that Donny had bad-mouthed him. But I never saw anything. You've got to believe me. I don't know who stabbed Donny, and I ain't no witness to nothing."

"Does the Bull carry a knife?"

"The Bull got a blade, yeah. A big one."

"His address, Andy. The Bull's address."

"I don't know no address."

"Where does he live?"

"The flats. Hague House. Second floor. It's got a green door, the only one there with a green door. Side facing the castle. I don't know the number, I swear it. But don't tell him I sent you."

"Don't worry, Andy. I wouldn't dream of it. But first, I'd like you to come down to the station so we can get down what you've told us all nice and legal, with a solicitor and all."

"Do I have to?"

"Well, let me put it this way. Right now, I'm inclined to be lenient about the traffic cones, but if you start giving us any trouble, I'll arrest you for being in possession of stolen property. Is that clear enough?" said Winsome.

Pash didn't say anything. He just grabbed his jacket from the floor and followed Wilson downstairs.

"Think of it this way," Winsome said. "It'll give your little sister a bit of peace and quiet to read *Wuthering Heights*."

When they left, Winsome could smell cigarette smoke coming from the living room.

"Now let me get this straight," Banks said to Derek Wyman in the hot and stuffy interview room. "You're telling us now that Mark Hardcastle asked you to spy on his lover Laurence Silbert because he suspected that Silbert was cheating on him, right?"

"That's right," said Wyman. "It wasn't meant to go that far. No one was supposed to get hurt. Honest."

"Why not do it himself?"

"He didn't want to be seen."

"Why did you hire Tomasina Savage?"

"Because I simply couldn't get down to London on every occasion Laurence went there. And he knew me, too. There was always a chance he might spot me. I just looked in the Yellow Pages and liked the name. It didn't matter when I found out it was a woman. She did a good job."

"And those conversations with Mark in the Red Rooster?"

"It was somewhere out of the way, that's all. I didn't know the kids from school had started to drink there. Mark was telling me all about his suspicions. No wonder he seemed upset. He loved Laurence."

"Did he also tell you that he had a previous conviction for domestic assault on an ex-lover?"

Wyman shot Banks a puzzled glance. "No, he didn't tell me that."

"So you just decided to help Mark in this out of the goodness of your heart?"

"Well, yes."

"Without any idea of what the repercussions might be?"

"Obviously not. Like I said, I never intended for anyone to get hurt."

"It's not so obvious to me, Derek," said Banks. "What did you have against Laurence Silbert that made you pursue him so aggressively? At the very least, you knew what you were doing might cause him great pain. It clearly caused Mark pain."

"Well, Laurence deserved it, didn't he, if he was cheating on Mark?"

"Were you in love with Mark?"

"Good God, no! Where on earth did you get that idea. I'm not . . . I mean . . . *no*."

"All right," said Banks. "Calm down. We have to ask these questions, just for the record."

"I was only doing what Mark asked. A favour. As a friend. I didn't . . . I mean, what happened is awful. I would never have . . ."

"And you're certain there was nothing else in it for you, that it was nothing to do with the situation at the theatre and that you had no other reason to want any harm to come to Laurence Silbert?"

"No. Why should there be?"

This was sticky ground. Superintendent Gervaise had insisted that they not refer to Silbert's occupation, but Banks thought there was no harm in taking a little digression. "When you saw the pictures and heard Tomasina's report, what did it bring to your mind?" he asked.

"That Mark was right. Laurence *was* meeting another man."

"But they sat together on a park bench and walked to a house in St. John's Wood, where an elderly woman opened the door to them. She might not have been visible in the photographs, but she was mentioned in Tomasina Savage's report. Are you telling me that this looked to you like a man meeting his lover?"

"I don't know, do I?" said Wyman. "It wasn't my business to find out who or what he was, just to report to Mark that he met someone."

"Even if it was innocent? In the sense that they *weren't* having an affair but meeting for some other reason?"

"I wasn't in a position to make those judgements. I just passed the photos on to Mark, told him what the private investigator had seen. Besides, why else could they have been meeting? Maybe the bloke was taking him home to meet his mother?"

"And how did Mark react?"

"How would you expect?"

"He tore them up in anger, didn't he?"

"Yes. You already know that."

"And you just carried on with your evening out together?"

"No. He took off. I don't know where he went."

"But *you* went to the National Film Theatre?"

"Yes."

"So the rest was all lies, what you told us before."

Wyman looked away. "Most of it, yes."

"And did you also know that Silbert was a retired MI6 agent before I told you in the theatre bar?" Banks said.

"No."

"Are you sure about that? You've lied to us before."

"How would I know that? Besides, what does it matter? You already said he'd retired."

"He might have been doing one or two little part-time jobs for his old masters. That would explain the visits to St. John's Wood, not an affair."

"How could I know?"

"Surely Laurence would have let Mark know that his trips were work-related, even if he didn't say what their purpose was? What made Mark think that Silbert was being unfaithful in the first place?"

"I don't know. He didn't say. Just little things, I suppose."

Banks knew he probably shouldn't be asking his next question, that he was courting the farthest reaches of Superintendent Gervaise's wrath, but he couldn't help himself, not now that Wyman had opened the door. "Did Mark give you any reason to believe that Silbert had any-thing to do with your brother's death?"

Wyman's jaw dropped. "What?"

"Derek, I know that your brother Rick died on a secret mission in Afghanistan, not in a helicopter accident. I'm just wondering if there was something extra in this for you, an element of revenge, shall we say, payback?"

"No. No, of course not. That's ridiculous. I didn't even know that Laurence had worked for MI6, so how could I connect him with Rick's death? This is way out of line. I told you, I only did it because Mark asked me to. I haven't done anything wrong. I haven't committed any crime." He checked his watch. "I think I'd like to go to work now. You did say I could leave whenever I wanted?"

Banks glanced at Annie again. They both knew that Wyman was right. He'd been responsible for the deaths of two men, but there was nothing they could do about it, nothing they could charge him with. Whether or not he was lying about Hardcastle asking him to spy on Silbert, it didn't really matter. Whether he had been after revenge, either because Silbert had some direct connection with his brother's death, or because Wyman had something against MI6 in general because of it, it didn't matter. They might never know, anyway, unless Dirty Dick Burgess came up with some answers. Technically, no crime had been committed. Banks still felt deeply unhappy with the result, but he brought the interview to a close, turned off the recorders and told Wyman he could go to work.

Glad to be away from the station and at home for the evening, Banks slipped in the Sarabeth Tucek CD he'd got to like so much over the past few months, poured himself a drink and went out to the conservatory to enjoy the evening light on the slopes of Tetchley Fell. The London bombing still haunted him every time he found himself alone, but it had faded slightly in his mind, become more surreal and remote, and there were moments when he could almost convince himself that it had all happened to someone else a long time ago.

Even though the case was really over, there were still a few loose ends he wanted to tie up, just for his own peace of mind. He picked up the phone and dialled Edwina Silbert's number in Longborough. After about six rings she answered.

"Hello?"

"Edwina? It's Alan Banks here."

"Ah," she said, "my dashing young copper."

Banks could hear her breathe out smoke. He was glad he couldn't smell it over the phone. "I don't know so much about that," he said. "How are you?"

"Coping. You know they released the body? The funeral's next week. If you had anything to do with it, thank you."

"I can't claim any credit," said Banks, "but I'm glad."

"Is this a social call?"

"I wanted to let you know that it's officially over."

"I thought it was officially over last week?"

"Not for me, it wasn't."

"I see. And?"

Banks explained about what Derek Wyman had done, and why.

"That's absurd," said Edwina. "Laurence wasn't being unfaithful."

"But Mark thought he was."

"I don't believe it."

"Why not?"

"I just don't believe it, that's all."

"I'm afraid it's true."

"But Mark knew perfectly well that Laurence was still involved with the service."

"He did? I had thought he might, but . . ."

"Of course he did. He might not have known exactly what he was doing, but he knew the trips to London and Amsterdam were work-related. Why would he ask someone to spy on Laurence?"

"I don't know," said Banks. "He must have become suspicious somehow."

"Rubbish. I think your Mr. Wyman is lying," said Edwina. "I think he did it off his own bat, out of pure vindictiveness. He worked on Mark's insecurity and put his own spin on those photographs."

"You could be right," Banks said, "but unfortunately, it doesn't matter now. I can't prove it, and even if I could, he still hasn't committed any crime."

"What a world," said Edwina, with another sigh of smoke. "Two dear people dead and no crime committed. Was that why you rang?"

"Partly, yes."

"There's something else?"

"Yes. Remember when we talked and you first told me that Laurence worked for MI6?"

"Yes."

"It crossed your mind then, didn't it, that they might have somehow been responsible for his death? Remember, you told me to be careful, too."

There was a pause and Banks heard a tinkle of ice. "At first, I suppose, yes," Edwina said. "When someone with Laurence's . . . history dies in such a violent way, one necessarily has suspicions. They are a devious crowd."

"Was that because of Cedric?"

"What?"

"When you spoke about your husband, you told me he had worked for the Secret Intelligence Service during the war, and that he still had connections. He died in a car crash at the height of the Suez Crisis, when he was involved in some Middle Eastern oil deal. Didn't that set off any alarm bells?"

"I suppose it did," said Edwina. "Cedric was a good driver, and there was no investigation."

"So when Laurence also died under suspicious circumstances, it occurred to you that there might be a connection?"

"I asked Dicky Hawkins at the time of Cedric's death. Of course, he denied it, but there was something in his manner, body language . . . I don't know."

"So you think Cedric might have been killed?"

"That's the problem with these people, Mr. Banks," Edwina said. "You just never really know, do you? And now I really must go. I'm tired. Goodnight." She hung up.

When Banks put the phone down he could hear Sarabeth Tucek singing "Stillborn," one of his favourites. So the Hardcastle–Silbert case, such as it was, was over, even if had been all Derek Wyman's malicious doing. They'd let Wyman walk out, a free man. There was nothing they could charge him with, and no matter what Edwina Silbert thought, no way they could refute his story, though Banks did suspect that there was more to it than he had told them, that what they had witnessed in the interview room was more of a performance than a confession, and that Wyman had simply managed to stay one step ahead and come up with a foolproof explanation when he needed one. Hardcastle and Silbert were dead, Wyman was responsible for their deaths, whether intentionally or not, and he had walked away.

Now that he was finished with Wyman, he could devote more thought to his other problem: Sophia. It couldn't be insurmountable, he believed; there had to be a way of salvaging the relationship; perhaps it was even as simple as just letting a little time pass. Maybe it would also help to convince her that he wasn't responsible if he let her into one or two more details of the case, including his conversation with Burgess. And a present wouldn't go amiss, he was certain. Not a CD, but something unique, something that could become a part of her "collection." He couldn't replace what she had lost, of course, but he could offer something new, something that, in time, would grow into its own story, would acquire its own pedigree and tradition. By finding the right object, he could demonstrate that he *understood*, that he knew how important these things were to her, and that he knew it wasn't just a materialistic obsession. And he thought that he *did* understand. It was a plan, at any rate.

Nearly an hour passed, and Banks had just switched Sarabeth for Cat Power's *The Covers Album*, which opened with a slow, acoustic and almost unbearably sad version of "(I Can't Get No) Satisfaction," when his phone rang. He didn't immediately recognize the voice.

"Alan?"

"Yes."

"This is Victor, Victor Morton. Sophia's father. How are you?"

"I'm fine," said Banks. "What can I do for you?"

"You can tell me what's going on, for a start."

Banks's heart lurched into his throat. Christ, had Sophia told her father about the break-in? Was Victor going to blame Banks, too? "What do you mean?" he asked, with a dry mouth.

"I had a very interesting conversation with an old colleague yesterday," Victor went on. "We met just by chance, in the street, if you can believe that, and he suggested we have a drink together."

"Who was it?"

"His name doesn't matter. It was someone I knew from Bonn, someone I never liked, always suspected of being a bit . . . well, rather like the fellow we were talking about the other day."

"Like Silbert? A spy?"

"Do you have to spell everything out for whoever's listening?"

"It doesn't matter," said Banks. "The case is closed. Hardcastle suspected Silbert was having an affair and hired someone to get the evidence. Official version. It was just plain lover's jealousy, after all, and it went terribly wrong. It's over."

"Well, perhaps someone should tell my colleague that."

"What do you mean?"

"It started off as a pleasant enough conversation – old times, retirement, pension plans and the like – then he started to ask about you, what I thought about you as a detective, how I felt about your relationship with my daughter."

"And?"

"I don't like being grilled, Alan. I told him nothing. Then he moved on, in a roundabout sort of way, started talking about how it is in consulates and embassies all over the world, how you pick up odd bits of information, pieces of the puzzle, things that are usually best forgotten. I simply agreed with him. Then he asked me if I knew anything about a man called Derek Wyman. I said no. Do you know this person?"

"He was the one," Banks said. "The one who Hardcastle asked to get the evidence. But it was nothing to do with secrets, at least not the government kind. As I said, it was all to do with jealousy."

"Well, he harped on about this Wyman for a while, was I sure I didn't know him and so on, then he asked after my 'lovely' daughter Sophia – he actually mentioned her name – how she was doing. I told him fine as far as I knew and got my things together to leave. I'd had enough by then. Just as I was about to go he grabbed my sleeve and told me to be careful. That's all he said. No overt threat. Just 'Be careful, Victor.' Now what do you think that was all about?"

"Melodrama," said Banks, nonetheless feeling his flesh crawl as he tried to shrug it off. "They love melodrama almost as much as they love games and codes."

"Well, I hope so, Alan. I sincerely hope so. Because if anything happens to my daughter, I'll –"

"If anything happens to your daughter, you'll have to get in line. I'll be the first in the queue."

"Just as long as we understand one another."

"We do," said Banks. "Goodbye, Victor."

Banks sipped some wine and stroked his chin, feeling the two days' stubble, thinking over what he'd just heard. Some time later, Cat Power went into a stark and desolate "Wild Is the Wind" and a cloud cast a dark shadow shaped like a running deer as it drifted slowly over the dale side. Banks reached for the wine bottle.

The shadows were lengthening when Winsome and Doug Wilson, along with the uniformed officers they had drafted in and brought up with them as support, approached Hague House. If the Bull was armed, then he might be dangerous. The officers were carrying a miniature battering ram, affectionately known as a "big red door key," which they would use to break the door down if they got no answer. More uniforms were stationed at the bottom of the stairwells, where a small crowd had gathered. Andy Pash had reluctantly given an official statement, which gave them sufficient cause to bring the Bull in as a serious suspect in the Donny Moore stabbing. They had also managed to dig up his real name, which was Toros Kemal – hence the Bull, though Winsome doubted that "toros" meant bull in Turkish – and his criminal record, which was lengthy.

The lifts were out of order, as usual, so they had to climb the stairs on the outside of the building. Luckily, Kemal lived on the second floor, so they didn't have too far to climb. One or two lurkers in the shadows scarpered pretty quickly when they saw the uniforms.

Winsome found the green door easily enough. She could hear the sound of a television from inside. Andy Pash had let slip that Kemal was living with a young woman called Ginny Campbell, who was on the council list as the only tenant. She had two young children by another man, so there was a potential hostage situation and they would have to be careful.

"Step back a bit, ma'am," said one of the uniformed officers. "We'll take care of this part."

"Be our guest," said Winsome. She and Doug Wilson stepped back towards the stairwell, about twenty feet away.

The officer rapped on the door and bellowed, "Toros Kemal. Open up. Police."

Nothing happened.

He knocked again, his colleague beside him with the battering ram at the ready, itching to use it. People were starting to appear in their doorways and at their windows.

Finally the door opened and a tall man stood framed in the doorway, stripped to the waist, wearing only a pair of tracksuit bottoms and trainers. He rubbed his head as if he had just woken up. "Yeah, what is it?"

"Mr. Kemal," said the uniformed officer. "We'd like you to accompany us to the station for questioning in the matter of the stabbing of Donny Moore."

"Moore. Don't know him," said Kemal. "Just let me get my shirt."

"I'll accompany you, sir," one of the officers said. They went inside. The other officer lowered his battering ram, clearly disappointed, relaxed and shrugged at Winsome. Sometimes things were easier than you thought they'd be. Winsome was standing by the stairwell, Wilson behind her, when Kemal came out with the uniformed officer. He was wearing a red T-shirt.

"I've gotta tie my laces, man," he said in the doorway, and knelt. The officers stepped back, behind him. In less than a second, Kemal had a knife in his hand, pulled from a sheath strapped to his lower leg. The officers took out their extendable batons, but they were too slow. The Bull wasn't hanging around. Winsome was blocking his way to the stairs, and Wilson was hidden behind her. The Bull came charging straight for her as if he'd just come into the ring, building up a head of steam, letting out an almighty yell with his arm stretched out, mouth open, pointing the blade directly at her as he ran.

Winsome felt a chill run through her, then her self-defence training took over, pure instinct. There was no time for anything else. She stood her ground, readied herself, let him come to her. She grabbed his outstretched knife arm with both hands, let herself fall on her back and, using the impetus he'd built up, wedged her feet in his solar plexus and pushed with all her might.

Kemal was travelling fast enough that it all happened as one seamless, choreographed movement. There was a gasp from the crowd below as he flipped heels over head in the air, then his back bounced against the flimsy balcony, and he disappeared over the edge with a scream. Winsome lay on her back on the concrete now, gasping for breath. She had long legs, she had pushed hard, and his momentum had been considerable.

In just seconds, Doug Wilson and the two uniformed officers were standing over her, muttering apologies and praise. She waved them aside and stood up gasping for breath. She felt lucky. One minor misjudgement and she would probably have had a knife through her chest. They should have handcuffed and searched Kemal before bringing him out. Well, it would all go down in the reports, and bollockings would be freely handed out. For the moment, Winsome was just happy to be alive. She turned and looked over the balcony, down at the courtyard. The Bull wasn't so lucky. He was lying on his back in a very twisted way, a darkening stain spreading slowly around his head.

Wilson was already on his mobile for an ambulance, so the best thing they could do now was get down there. In the melee, the woman Kemal lived with, Ginny Campbell, had come out of her flat, and she was hanging over the balcony, a baby clutched to her breast, looking down at her lover's body, crying and screaming, "You've killed him! You've killed him! You filthy murdering bastards!" The crowd were picking up on her outrage, too, calling out insults. Winsome didn't like the way the mood was quickly changing.

Before things got any worse, she phoned the station for back-up, and slowly the four of them made their way down the stairs to see what, . if anything, they could do for Toros "the Bull" Kemal.

17

The rain started to come down hard on Sunday morning and it was still pouring on Monday when Banks took the newspapers and his second cup of coffee into the conservatory. It had started as it usually did, with a light pattering on the glass roof, then soon it was running down the windows in thick slithering torrents, distorting the view of the dale outside like a funfair mirror. That was the way Banks had been seeing the world lately, too, he thought, as through a glass darkly: Hardcastle and Silbert, Wyman, Sophia, the bombing – dear God, most of all the bombing – all of it nothing but a distortion of the darkness he was beginning to believe lay at the centre of everything.

The weather suited Banks's mood well enough. The music, too. Underneath the noise the rain made, Billie Holiday was singing "When Your Lover Has Gone" from one of her last performances, in 1959. She sounded as if she were on her last legs.

He had slept hardly at all the past three nights. The images seared in his mind's eye wouldn't go away; they only became more distorted. He had seen death before in all its gruesome forms. As a young patrol officer, he had been called to road accidents, six-car pile-ups on the M1, with body parts strewn over a radius of almost a quarter of a mile. He had even been in his own house when it had been set on fire, though he didn't remember much about that as he had been drugged at the time.

But none of that was quite the same as what had happened on Friday. This had been different, and most of all, like the fire at his house, it hadn't been an accident. Someone had done it deliberately to inflict as much as pain and suffering as possible on innocent people. He had met criminals who had done that before, of course, but not on this scale, in this *random* way. And none of the murderers he had ever met before had been more than happy to blow themselves to smithereens along with everyone else, women and children included. More than once, he had wondered how the people he had led out were doing: the Asian woman, the young boy and the pretty blonde in the yellow dress. Perhaps he could make some inquiries and find out.

The music had finished and he needed more coffee, so he went first to the entertainment room and put on something a bit brighter and instrumental, a lively, jazzy string quartet called Zapp, then he refilled his mug in the kitchen. Just when he had settled down to see whether he could concentrate on the crossword, his telephone rang.

He was tempted not to answer, but it might be Sophia. One day soon, he thought, he should invest in a telephone that displayed the caller's number. Of course, that only helped if they didn't withhold the number and if you recognized it. Most of Sunday he had contemplated phoning Sophia, and every time his telephone rang he had hoped it was her. But it never was. Brian rang once. Annie phoned with more details about Winsome's latest death-defying escapade. Tracy, his daughter, made her weekly report. And Victor Morton had rung, of course. But that was all.

This time it *was* her.

"Alan, I moved your car. You're lucky the police didn't impound it. Things are still crazy around there. Anyway, it's just down the street. It's safe now. I put my key in the glovebox. Do you know you left your iPod in there, too?"

"Yes," said Banks. "How are you?"

"I'm fine."

"You sound a bit . . ."

"What?"

"I don't know."

"I'm fine."

"I'd like to come and see you. I've still got some free time and things have quietened down up here."

"I'm glad to hear that, but I don't know. I'm really busy this week."

"We've always worked around that before."

"I know, but . . . it's just . . . I don't know."

"What don't you know?"

"I think I just need some time, that's all."

"Time away from me?"

She paused, then said, "Yes."

"Sophia, I *did* remember to set that alarm."

"Then how did someone just manage to walk into my house and break my things without alerting the police?"

"The people who did it are very adept," Banks said. "You have to believe me. They can get in anywhere." He hadn't told her that before, hadn't wanted to frighten her, but as it turned out, he needn't have worried.

"I don't know what's worse," Sophia said. "You not setting the alarm, or these paranoid delusions you've got about the secret service. Do you seriously believe what you're saying, or is it some kind of elaborate excuse you've just come up with, because if it is —"

"It isn't an excuse. It's true. I told you about them before. Laurence Silbert was a retired MI6 agent. Semi-retired."

There was a pause at the other end of the line. "Anyway, it's not even that. I don't want to argue."

"Me neither. What is it, then?"

"I don't know. It's all been too fast, that's all. I just need some time. If you care at all about me, you'll give me some time."

"Fine," he said in the end, exhausted. "Take your time. Take all the time you want."

And that was that.

The rain continued to fall and Banks thought he could hear thunder in the distance. He thought about Sophia, how she would get emotional during thunderstorms. She would make love like a wild thing, and if she was ever going to tell him that she loved him, he would have bet it would be during a thunderstorm. But that wasn't likely to happen now. They had been living together in so many ways, yet they lived so much apart. No wonder it all seemed too fast for her.

"I'm sorry for disturbing you, honest I am," said Carol Wyman, opening the door to Annie, "but I'm really beside myself."

She looked it, too, Annie thought. Hair unkempt, no make-up, dark circles under her eyes. "It's all right," Annie said. "What's the problem?"

"Come in," Carol said, "and I'll tell you."

The living room was untidy, but Annie managed to find a place to sit on the sofa. Carol offered tea, and at first Annie declined. Only when Carol insisted and said she needed a cup herself did she agree. She had driven all the way in from Harkside to Eastvale and was stopping at the Wymans' on her way to Western Area Headquarters, where Superintendent Gervaise wanted the whole team assembled at twelve o'clock for a meeting in the boardroom. As she waited for Carol to make the tea, Annie glanced around the room and noticed that the photograph of Derek Wyman with his brother was missing, as were several others.

"What is it?" Annie asked, when Carol brought the tea and sat next to her.

"It's Derek," she said. "I don't know where he is. He's disappeared. Derek's disappeared."

She started crying, and Annie put an arm around her shoulder and passed her a tissue from the box on the coffee table. "When was this?" she asked.

"He didn't come home last night, after the evening performance. I haven't seen him since he went out for the matinee at two o'clock. He usually comes home for his tea between performances on a Sunday, but yesterday he didn't." She gave a harsh laugh. "You haven't locked him up or anything without telling me, have you?"

"We wouldn't do that," said Annie, moving her arm away.

"At first I just thought maybe he'd grabbed a sandwich or something instead of coming home for tea – he sometimes does – then gone with his mates for a few drinks after the play, but . . ."

"Did he phone or anything?"

"No, nothing. That's not like him. I mean, Derek's not perfect – who is? – but he wouldn't do something like that. He knows my nerves aren't good. He knows what it would do to me." She held her hands out. "Look at me. I'm shaking."

"Did you phone the police station?"

"Yes, this morning. But they wouldn't do anything. They said he was a grown man and he had only been missing for one night. I told them about Saturday, when he was there talking to you, like, and that he'd been upset ever since, but they didn't even know he'd been at the station. That's why I phoned you. You gave me your number. You said I should ring."

"It's all right," Annie said. There was no way the Monday morning desk officer would know that Wyman had been in the station on Saturday afternoon; he hadn't been arrested or charged, so his name wouldn't appear on any of the weekend arrest or custody records. They had simply questioned him and let him go. "You did the right thing. Have you any idea at all where he might go? Any friends or anything?"

"No. I've already phoned all his colleagues at school and from the theatre. They don't know where he is, either. They said he didn't show up for last night's performance."

"But he was there for the matinee?"

"Yes. It ended about half past four. Maria said he left the theatre, and she just assumed he was coming home for tea. But he never turned up. I don't know where he went."

"Does he have any relatives near by?"

"An uncle and aunt in Shipley. But he wouldn't go there. He hasn't seen them in years. And he's got an aunt in Liverpool, but she's in a home."

"So he disappeared after the Sunday afternoon matinee?"

"That's right."

"Is his car gone?"

"As far as I know. It's not parked on our street, at any rate."

"You'd better give me some details." Annie noted down what Wyman had been wearing, along with the make, colour and number plate of the car he was driving.

"Something must have happened to him," Carol went on. "I think it was something to do with those people who came."

"What people?" Annie asked.

"Late yesterday afternoon, while Derek was at the theatre. A man and a woman. They were something to do with the government. Anyway, they were a bit abrupt. Pushy. Wanted to know all sorts of things, personal things. Wouldn't tell me why. And they went through the house from top to bottom. Took some stuff with them. Papers, photographs, Derek's computer with all his school and theatre work on it. They gave me a receipt, mind you." She showed it to Annie. It was a sheet of paper listing the items taken. The signature was illegible.

"They took those family photographs, too, from the sideboard?"

"Yes. They do work for the government, don't they? I haven't been stupid, have I? I haven't been burgled? I don't know what's going on any more."

"No," said Annie. "They are who they say they are." Not that that helps at all, she thought. "You haven't been stupid. Did Derek know about this visit?"

"He can't have done. He was at the matinee."

Unless he'd been on his way home and seen them from the end of the street, Annie thought. That might have caused him to do a runner.

"His mobile wasn't working," Carol went on. "Maybe it was the battery. He's always letting the battery run down. Maybe he's seeing another woman?"

"Don't jump to conclusions," said Annie, hardly sure what was the worst conclusion Carol Wyman could jump to: that something had happened to her husband, or that he had run off with another woman.

"But what can have happened to him?"

"I'm going to the station to report him missing and see about initiating a search," said Annie. "If I do it, they'll have to listen. In the meantime, if there's anything else you can think of, don't hesitate to phone me again." Annie stood up. "My boss might want to have a word with you about those two people who came to visit."

"The government people?"

"Yes."

"Why? Do you really think they have something to do with all this?"

"I don't know anything at the moment," Annie said, "but I shouldn't think so. There's probably a simple explanation. Let me get working on it." She paused. "Carol, you seem . . . well, you're in a dreadful state. Is there someone . . . ?"

"I'll be all right. Honest. You go. Do what you have to do to find my Derek. The kids are at school. I thought it best to send them off, just like normal. There's Mrs. Glendon next door. She'll stay with me for a while. Don't worry."

"Just as long as you're OK. I won't be far away, remember. And if you hear anything . . ."

"I'll phone you right away. Oh, I do hope he's all right. *Please* find him for me."

"Don't worry," said Annie. "We'll find him."

There was more than a little tension in the boardroom, Banks sensed, as the Major Crimes squad congregated around the impressive varnished oval table under the disapproving stares of the Victorian wool barons whose portraits in oils hung on the walls. Rain snaked down the broad sash windows and hammered against the slates on the roof, dripping from the blocked gutters and gurgling down the old drainpipes. So much for summer.

"Right," said Gervaise, standing and leaning forward with her palms resting on the table. She was in true fighting form; it was time to chuck around some blame and see where it stuck. "I notice that DI Cabbot hasn't seen fit to join us yet, but let's get straight down to business. It's wrap-up time. We'll start with you, DS Jackman."

Winsome almost jumped. "Yes, ma'am."

"That was a very stupid thing you did on Saturday evening, wasn't it?"

"But ma'am, in all fairness –"

"In all fairness, you should have taken more back-up and you should have stayed out of the way until the suspect had been subdued and handcuffed. You knew he was big and probably armed with a knife. It's no good blaming uniform branch for this one, though the two officers involved will be disciplined if it is deemed appropriate."

"But ma'am, we had no reason to think he'd go crazy like that."

"Where drugs are involved, DS Jackman, you should realize that it's folly to try to predict what someone will or will not do. Toros Kemal was high as a kite on methamphetamine. Given the reason you wanted to talk to him, you should have known to expect something like that. There are no excuses."

"No, ma'am." Winsome looked down. Banks noticed her lower lip tremble.

Gervaise let a little time pass, then she turned to Winsome again and said, "I hear your fancy footwork was quite a sight to behold. Well done, DS Jackman."

Winsome smiled. "Thank you, ma'am."

"But don't even think of trying a trick like that again. We don't want to lose you. How is our wild man?"

"Well," said Winsome, "I did call by the hospital yesterday, and he's out of danger. As a matter of fact, he was awake, and when he saw me, he ... well, ma'am, he said some rather rude words. Words I'd not care to repeat."

Gervaise laughed. "I'm not surprised."

Winsome shifted in her chair. "Anyway, he's got a broken collarbone, broken arm, broken leg and a minor skull fracture, along with untold cuts and bruises."

"Not least to his ego," said Banks.

"Well, maybe that was why he swore at me," Winsome said.

Gervaise turned to Banks. "Now, DCI Banks, make my day and tell me I have no reason to fear any more fallout from this Hardcastle–Silbert business you've been probing against my orders."

"No," said Banks. "It's over. Derek Wyman admitted to watching Laurence Silbert and hiring a private investigator to take photographs of him with whoever he met. When we questioned him yesterday, he told us that Hardcastle asked him to do it. He'd become suspicious of Silbert's frequent trips to London, thought he'd found a lover. It was jealousy, pure and simple. Wyman didn't tell us earlier because he felt guilty about what happened and he didn't want to get involved."

"I see," said Gervaise. "And do you believe him?"

"Not entirely," said Banks. "Edwina Silbert assured me that Mark Hardcastle knew her son was still working on the occasions he visited London and Amsterdam, so why would he ask Wyman to follow him?"

"I suppose he *could* have become suspicious over something," Gervaise said. "You know, found a monogrammed hankie, someone else's underwear in the laundry basket, whatever. Then he might have begun to think that Silbert was using work as an excuse to cover up an affair. And maybe he was."

Banks looked at her. "You've got quite an imagination, ma'am," he said. "And it's entirely possible. But it doesn't matter what we believe. There's nothing to charge him with."

"So these half-baked theories of yours about Othello and Iago were exactly what they appeared to be? Half-baked?"

"So it would seem," muttered Banks. "If his confession is to be believed."

"And the involvement of the secret intelligence services was purely tangential?"

"Up to a point. Silbert was still engaged in intelligence work in some capacity – I'd hazard a guess that this man he was meeting in London was the mysterious Julian Fenner, Import-Export – but it now turns out that none of it has any relevance to the murder-suicide."

"You're sure of this?"

"Well, you can never be entirely certain with these people," Banks said, echoing Edwina. "But yes, ma'am. As sure as we'll ever be."

"So I can tell the Chief Constable and whoever's been on *his* back that it's all over?"

"Yes," said Banks. "Though I would imagine the Chief Constable is well aware of that already."

Gervaise looked at him suspiciously but didn't follow up on the remark. "Right. Well, I hope you've learned a lesson from the whole sorry affair."

"Yes, ma'am," said Banks.

At this moment, Annie Cabbot rushed in and sat down, distracting Gervaise's attention from Banks. "Ah, DI Cabbot," she said. "So good of you to join us."

"Sorry, ma'am," said Annie. "I was out on a call."

"What kind of call?"

"Missing person," she said, glancing towards Banks. "Derek Wyman's disappeared."

"Why would he do that?" Gervaise asked. "I thought you said he was off the hook. You let him go."

"He is," said Banks. "And we did." He turned to Annie. "When did this happen?"

"Yesterday afternoon. He left the theatre after the matinee and didn't turn up for the evening performance. And there's another thing."

"Yes?" said Gervaise.

"You're not going to like this, ma'am."

"I don't like anything I've heard so far. Better tell me, anyway."

"Two people went over to Wyman's house yesterday afternoon. A man and a woman. They scared the sh—, the living daylights, out of his wife, took a few photographs and papers and went away. Said they were from the government."

"*Shit!*" said Gervaise. "This was just yesterday?"

"Yes. I told you you weren't going to like it, ma'am."

"Reminding me of what you told me doesn't help your cause in the least, DI Cabbot," snarled Gervaise.

"Could he have got back from the matinee in time to see these people enter his house, or come out of it?" Banks asked Annie. "Do you think they picked him up and spirited him away?"

"It's possible," Annie said. "The timing's close enough."

"But DCI Banks just assured me this mess was over and done with," said Gervaise.

"Well, it was," said Annie. "It might still be. I mean, maybe he's just . . . I don't know . . . another woman? Or he's done a runner? These things happen. Just because he's missing it doesn't have to mean that MI6 carted him off to one of their secret interrogation camps."

"There are no such places," said Gervaise.

"Very well, then. One of their secret *non-existent* interrogation camps."

"Very clever. Don't let your imagination run away with you, DI Cabbot."

"Have these government people had access to any of our case files?" Banks asked Gervaise.

"Not through me," she answered. "Or through anybody else in this office, I shouldn't imagine."

"Has the Chief Constable been around much lately?"

Gervaise paused. "A bit more often than he usually is. What are you trying to suggest, DCI Banks? Is this connected with that innuendo you made earlier?"

"I think you know, ma'am. You might not like to admit it, but you know. They took an interest in this from the start, at least as soon as they realized I wasn't going to stop investigating. They've been following me around. Annie, too, perhaps. They probably know what we know. Given that we didn't tell them, I'm wondering how they found out. It's my bet they went straight to the top. The Chief Constable's ambitious, and he has political aspirations."

"Do you know what you're saying?" said Gervaise. "And you're not also suggesting that the government is responsible for Wyman's disappearance, are you? I mean, this isn't some little tinpot South American dictatorship."

"You don't have to look that far south when it comes to citizens disappearing," said Banks. "But I don't know. I'm just calling the facts to your attention, that's all."

"But why on earth would they be interested in a bloody schoolteacher cum amateur theatre director?"

Banks scratched his scar. "Because he hired a private detective to take photographs of Silbert meeting a man on a bench in Regent's Park," Banks said. "And because we're interested in him. It seems logical to assume that this wasn't anything to do with an affair of the heart, but that those activities were part of Silbert's post-retirement covert work. There's also the brother."

"Brother?"

"Wyman's brother, Rick. He was SAS. He was killed on a secret mission in Afghanistan in 2002. The Ministry of Defence covered it up. Called it an accident during manoeuvres. Silbert has visited Afghanistan. There's a chance that he might have been involved on the intelligence side, and Wyman might have found out about it through Hardcastle, blamed him for Rick's death."

"Oh, this just gets better and better." Gervaise glared at Banks, breathed out heavily, ran her hand over her hair then filled a glass with water from a pitcher on a tray beside her. The rain continued to hammer on the slates and windows. "What a bloody great start to the week this is turning out to be," she said. "I think we'd better discuss this later, in my office, when we've got a bit more information in, don't you?"

"Yes, ma'am."

Gervaise got to her feet. "I suppose we ought to count our blessings as well as lick our wounds," she said. "Even if Derek Wyman has gone and thrown a spanner in the works, at least we've got Donny Moore's assailant and maybe done a little bit towards keeping more heroin and methamphetamines off the East Side Estate. Maybe that saves the weekend from being a total disaster."

"And don't forget, ma'am," Doug Wilson spoke up. "We've got the traffic cones back, too."

Gervaise gave him a withering glance.

Banks had dug out his old portable CD player, in the absence of his iPod, and he listened to Laura Marling's *Alas, I Cannot Swim* on the train down to London that Monday evening. He needed his car back, and despite what had been said on the phone, he believed that if he could just see Sophia for a few minutes, he could convince her to stay with him. Beyond that, he hadn't thought. Annie was heading the search for Derek Wyman, though they were hardly combing the moors just yet, mostly running through the list of old friends and relatives dotted about the place. So far nobody had seen any trace of him.

It was after five o'clock when the train he had caught in Darlington earlier pulled out of York. On his right, the Yorkshire Wheel, a mini-version of the London Eye, was turning forlornly, deserted in the rain that had been falling steadily since the heavens first opened on Sunday morning. Already there was talk of flooding in Wales and Gloucestershire.

A group of four teenagers had the table just down the aisle from Banks, and they were already well into the ale. They sounded as if they had been on the train since Newcastle. Banks fancied a drink himself, but he decided to lay off. After all, there was always the chance that he might have to drive straight back to Eastvale.

The landscape and the stations drifted by as he gazed out of the window: Doncaster, Grantham, Newark. Peterborough, where he had grown up. He thought about his parents, away on a Mediterranean cruise. Since they had inherited his brother's money, they hadn't changed a great deal about their lives, Banks thought, but they had taken to cruising with a vengeance, much against his expectations.

He also thought of Michelle Hart, a detective inspector in the local force, and an ex-girlfriend of his. She had moved to Hampshire, he'd heard, Portsmouth, and as the train passed the flats down by the river where she used to live, it brought back memories. He could also never pass by Peterborough without thinking of his old boyhood friends Steve Hill, Paul Major and Dave Grenfell. Graham Marshall, too, of course, who had disappeared and then turned up buried in a field years later, and Kay Summerville, the first girl he had ever slept with. He had bumped into her just a few years ago when he was back home for his parents' wedding anniversary, and she was clearing out the house after her mother's death. They had repeated the experience. Later, they had promised to get in touch, but both knew they never would. Their moment had passed, and they were luckier than most in that it had passed twice, and passed well. Moments are often all you get. You can watch them walking away. The rest is crap. Let go with both hands. No regrets.

But Sophia was a different matter. He didn't want to let go of her.

His pay-as-you-go vibrated discreetly in his pocket. He didn't like mobile conversations on trains, his own or other people's, but he wasn't in a quiet coach, so it wasn't against the rules. He took his earphones out and answered it.

"Banksy?"

"Ah, Mr. Burgess."

"Right. I'll keep this brief. Are you listening?"

"I'm listening."

"Laurence Silbert operated strictly in Cold War territory, primarily Berlin, Prague and Moscow. Got that?"

"Yes."

"His only visit to Afghanistan was in 1985, when the Russians were there. It was a joint operation with the CIA. I think we can say almost certainly that it was probably to do with supplying backing to the anti-Russian Taliban forces. This particular bit of knowledge isn't classified, by the way – though the details are – but I'd prefer it if you'd keep it under your hat."

"Of course."

"Basically, Laurence Silbert was a Cold War warrior. He never had anything to do with the situation in the Middle East, except insofar as it impinged on the Cold War. He spoke Russian, German and Czech, and those countries were the primary areas of his operations."

"What about after his retirement?"

"I said I wasn't going to tell you about that, but I'd say it was pretty obvious, wouldn't you? If I can put two and two together, I'm sure you can, too. We all know the old KGB and Stasi agents have turned up in one form of organized crime or another, or have become 'businessmen,' as many of them like to call themselves. They're operating quite openly in the West now. Silbert was part of that world for a long time, in the old days. He knew all the players, their strengths, weaknesses, trade routes, hiding places, the lot."

"So they're using his old knowledge?"

"Yes. I'd say so. Just a guess, mind you."

Banks made sure to keep his voice low. "Why all the secrecy about it? The Regent's Park meetings. The house. Fenner's phone number. The Townsends. I mean, we're all fighting the Russian mafia. Why didn't he just go to Thames House or wherever and have a chat with them when they wanted to pick his brains?"

Banks heard Burgess chuckle down the line. "That's not the way they do things, Banksy. They like games and codes and passwords and things like that. Basically, they're like little kids at heart. When he was ready for a meeting, Silbert would ring a phone number they gave him, an untraceable number, as I'm sure you discovered, and all he'd get would be a line disconnected message, but they'd know he was ready. They'd also know if anyone else phoned the number, too, which I assume is one of the things that tipped them off to your meddlesome presence in the first place."

"Maybe," said Banks. "Julian Fenner, Import-Export. I certainly wasn't trying to hide anything."

"It may have been better if you had. Anyway," Burgess went on, "they clearly didn't want anyone to know that they were using him because the other side, of course, also know exactly what and who Silbert knows, and they would be able to change any plans or routines or personnel accordingly."

"Is that all?"

"I can't think of anything else. Can you? And don't forget what I said about the phone. Dump it. You owe me, Banksy. I must get back to bugging Muslim MPs now. Bye-bye."

The phone went dead. Banks switched it off and put it in his pocket. He'd dispose of it later, in the Thames perhaps, with all the other secrets that had been dumped there over the years.

18

It was a muggy evening on the London streets. The rain had stopped by the time Banks was walking down the King's Road at about half past eight, but a kind of heavy mist hung in the air, enveloping everything in its warm humid haze. The street still maintained its usual aura of busyness, of constant motion and activity. It was one of the things Banks loved so much about London, and one of the things he loved to escape from by going back to Gratly.

The street lamps made blurred halos in the mist, and even the sounds of the main street were muffled. Banks had sensed an odd mood as he made his way on the tube and by foot. London was still in shock from Friday's bombing, but at the same time people were determined to get on with life as usual, to show that they weren't going to be intimidated. There were probably even more people out and about than you would normally find on a humid Monday night. They needed to stand up and be counted. Banks felt a part of that, too. But most of all he wanted to find Sophia.

He turned into her street, which was considerably quieter, and felt his chest tighten as he rang her doorbell. No answer. He had a key, but there was no way he was going to use it. Besides, he had no reason to go in if she was out. He had deliberately not phoned her to say he was coming, too, in case she reacted badly and tried to avoid him.

She was probably working. Often her job demanded that she attend evening events – readings, openings, premieres – so he decided to pass the time in their local wine bar, just around the corner. Like other cafés and bars he had passed on his way, it was crowded. Not many establishments had tables out on the pavement along the King's Road – there simply wasn't that much room – so the inside tables were all taken, and knots of people stood around where they could find a bit of space, leaned on pillars, held their glasses and talked.

Banks went to the closest section of the bar, where he was able to wedge himself between a couple of noisy, animated groups who had probably come for a drink after work and stayed too long. Nobody paid him any attention, including the bar staff. Angie, the blonde Australian barmaid, was engaging in her favourite pastime – flirting with the customers.

Then, through the crowd, Banks saw a profile he recognized sitting at one of the tables. *Sophia.* She was unmistakable, her smooth cheek, the graceful curve of her neck, her dark hair tied up and held in place by that familiar tortoiseshell comb, one or two loose strands, curling like tendrils over her shoulders. She was in half-profile and would be able to see him only if she turned around. But she wasn't going to do that.

Opposite her sat a young man with lank, longish fair hair and the kind of scruffy beard you get after not shaving for four or five days. He was wearing a light green corduroy jacket over a black T-shirt. Banks hadn't seen him before, but that didn't mean much. He knew that Sophia had many friends in the arts he hadn't met. He was just about to walk over when he noticed Sophia leaning in towards the man, the way women do when they're interested. Banks froze. Now more than ever anxious not to be seen, he edged away from the bar towards the exit, without even having ordered a drink. The next moment he was wandering down the street, heart pounding, not quite sure what to do.

There was a pub just down the King's Road called the Chelsea Potter, and in a daze Banks wandered inside and bought a pint. There were no seats left, but there was a shelf running below the front windows, where he could rest his drink. From there, he could see the end of Sophia's street. He decided that if she went home alone, he would approach her, but if she went with the man from the wine bar, he would head back to Eastvale.

Someone had left an *Evening Standard*, and he started reading an article on the aftermath of the bombing, keeping one eye on the street.

They had a photograph of the young blonde in the yellow dress – she was a model, it said, and one of the survivors. She had told the reporter how terrible it was, but she didn't mention anyone rescuing her. She didn't mention clinging on to the Selfridges bag, either, only that her darling dog Louie had survived, too.

Banks had been in the pub perhaps an hour and a half, had long ago finished the newspaper article and was into the dregs of his second pint of Pride, when he saw Sophia and her friend turn into her street. There were still plenty of people around outside, so he left the rest of his drink and crossed over, just part of the crowd. From the corner, he could watch them approach Sophia's front door. They stood for a moment, chatting, then she put her key in the lock. She paused for just a moment, turning the key, and glanced down the street to where Banks's car was still parked. Then she opened the door. The man put his hand on the small of her back and followed her inside. Banks walked away.

Annie cursed the rain as she walked around the parked car. The way the wind blew slantwise rendered her umbrella close to useless, and in the end it was easier just to close it and get wet. She was wearing a waist-length leather jacket, which she had treated with waterproofing spray, her jeans, which she hadn't, and her red PVC boots, which would keep out anything. Only her hair was getting seriously wet, and that was now short enough to dry in seconds. She thought about what Carol Wyman had said about going blonde. Maybe she would.

For the moment, though, she was looking at Derek Wyman's 2003 Renault, which was parked in a lay-by across from the Woodcutter's Arms, a couple of miles outside the village of Kinsbeck, about twenty miles south-west of Eastvale, over the moors from Gratly and Helmthorpe.

A local patrol car had discovered it about an hour ago and called it in. Now Annie and Winsome were on the scene, shooing away the sheep. The patrol officers, a couple of surly buggers by the name of Drury and Hackett, which sounded to Annie like a bad comedy duo, were leaning against their car smoking, clearly eager to get on their way back to whatever pub they spent their shift in. Annie wasn't going to make it that easy for them. They had already made it quite obvious that they didn't like taking orders from two plainclothes female officers, one of them black.

No crime was suspected, at least not yet, so Annie had no reason to preserve the scene, but she was aware that a forensic examination of the car might become necessary if the situation changed. Still, there were certain things she needed to know. She tried the driver's door, but it was locked, as was the other side. There was no way she was going to force her way in. Wiping off the rain and glancing through the window, she could see that the keys were gone, and there was nothing out of ordinary in the interior on a cursory examination in poor light conditions. No obvious blood. No signs of a struggle. No cryptic messages scrawled on the windscreen. Nothing. She turned to PC Drury. "It's an unusual place to leave a car, isn't it?" she said. "Any ideas?"

"I was thinking maybe he might have run out of petrol," said Drury. "Want me to check?"

"Good idea," said Annie, perfectly happy to let the man do what was clearly man's work and dig out a dipstick to measure the level of fuel. When he had finished, Drury seemed very pleased with himself, so Annie knew he must be right.

"Nary a drop left," he said, "and not a garage for three or four miles."

"What about in the village?"

"Closed a year back."

"Do you think he may have walked to the garage to get petrol?"

"Possible," said Drury. "But if it was me, I'd have gone to the Woodcutter's and phoned and enjoyed a pint while I was waiting." He pointed down the road, in the opposite direction from the village. "The garage is down the road that way. You can't miss it." Then he checked his watch. "Though I doubt it'll be open at this time of an evening."

It was after eight o'clock. Annie knew that most businesses kept short hours in this part of the country. "Why don't you go down there and check for us?" she said. "Wake them up if you have to." She gestured over to the pub. "We'll be in there."

Drury glared at her, but he had a word with his partner, who stamped out his cigarette. They got in their patrol car with exaggerated slowness and drove off down the road.

Winsome and Annie walked into the welcome shelter of the lounge bar, which was deserted apart from an old man and his dog by the empty fireplace, and two farm labourers enjoying their pints at the bar. Everyone looked around.

"Evening all," said Annie, smiling as she walked up to the bar. The farm labourers gawped at Winsome and edged away to give them room. "Thank you," Annie said. She turned to the barman. "Two Cokes, please."

"Want ice in them?"

Winsome shook her head.

"In one of them," Annie said. "Nasty night out there."

"Seen worse," the barman said.

"My colleague and I are from Major Crimes, Eastvale," Annie said, flashing her warrant card. "We're here in connection with that car parked over the road."

"Been there since yesterday, it has," said the barman.

So Derek Wyman clearly hadn't just gone down the road for petrol. Or if he had, something had stopped him from coming back. But there was nowhere else to go. It was all open countryside around there as far as Annie could tell – the pub was as close to the edge of the moors as you could get. Sheep came and grazed right beside it and nosed around the parked cars. Annie didn't know whether any buses ran along the B road outside, but she doubted it. If Wyman had disappeared into the wilds, she would have to wait until tomorrow to get a search organized; the light was already bad, and soon it would be getting dark.

The barman handed her the drinks and she paid. "Yesterday, you say?" she said. "Any idea what time?"

"Well," said the barman, scratching his bald head, "at a guess, it'd probably be about the time the bloke who was driving it came in." The farm labourers snickered.

Ah, thought Annie, a true Yorkshire wit. This area had a surfeit of them, if Drury and Hackett were anything to go by. Must be something in the water. Or the beer.

"Did he look anything like this?" Annie asked, taking Wyman's photograph from her briefcase.

The bartender scrutinized it. "Aye," he said finally. "I'd say he looked a lot like that, yes."

"So this was the man?"

The barman grunted.

"I'll take that as a yes, shall I?" Annie said. "What time was he here?"

"About seven o'clock Sunday evening."

Annie remembered that Carol had told her the matinee finished at half past four. It certainly didn't take two and a half hours to get from Eastvale to here, so he must have been somewhere else first, maybe just driving around aimlessly, unless the MI6 pair had been chasing him. "How long did he stay?" she asked.

"Two drinks."

"How long's that?"

"Depends on how long a man takes to drink them."

Winsome leaned over the bar. "Would you prefer to shut the place up and come to Eastvale to answer these questions, because that can be arranged, you know?"

That shocked him. The farm labourers laughed, and he blushed. "Hour and a half, maybe."

"What state of mind was he in?" Annie asked.

"How would I know?"

"Try to remember. Was he upset, jolly, aggressive? Did he appear flustered? What?"

"Just kept himself to himself, like. Sat in the corner over there and drank quietly."

"What else was he doing? Did he have a book? A newspaper? A mobile? Magazine?"

"Nowt. He just sat there. Like he was thinking or something."

"So he was thinking?"

"Looked like that to me."

"How would thee know, tha's never done it," said one of the farm-hands. The other laughed. Winsome shot him a warning glance, and they shifted uneasily on their feet.

"Did he say anything?" Annie asked. "Did he talk to you or anyone else at all?"

"No."

"He wasn't with anyone?"

"I already said he was sat by himself."

"Did anyone come in and talk to him?"

"No."

"What about after he'd gone? Did anyone come looking for him, asking about him?"

"Only thee."

"Did you see where he went when he left?"

"How could I? I was working behind the bar. You can't see the road from here."

"OK," said Annie. "Any idea where he might have gone?"

"How would I know?"

"Guess," Annie said. "Is there anywhere near here a traveller might go and spend the night, for example?"

"Well, there's a youth hostel up the lane."

"There's Brierley Farm, too, Charlie, don't forget," said one of the farmhands.

"Brierley Farm?"

"Aye. They converted the barn for bed-and-breakfast a couple of years ago. It's half a mile back towards Kinsbeck. You can't miss it. Big sign outside."

"Anything else?"

"Not near by. Not that you'd leave your car here and walk to."

"He'd run out of petrol," Annie said.

"Bert's garage closes at five o'clock on a Sunday," said the barman, "so he'd have no joy there."

At that moment the door opened and everyone looked around again.

"Oh, how jolly," muttered Annie to Winsome. "It's Dreary and Hackneyed again."

"That's Drury and Hackett to you, ma'am," said one of them, with a weighty pause before the "ma'am."

"Any luck?" she asked.

"No. He wasn't there. They were closed, anyway."

"Right," said Annie, finishing her Coke. "I think it's a bit late to start sending out the search parties on the moors tonight, but we can make a start by doing a house-to-house of the area – the youth hostel and Brierley Farm being first on our list. All right, lads?"

"But we've got our patrol route to cover," one of the officers protested.

"Want me to clear it with your superior?" Annie asked.

"No," the officer mumbled. "Don't bother. Come on, Ken," he said to his partner. "Let's start with Brierley."

If truth be told, Banks probably hadn't been fit to drive, he thought as he pulled up outside his Gratly cottage at some ungodly hour in the morning. But all he knew was that he couldn't stay in London. After he had tossed his pay-as-you-go mobile into the Thames, he felt that he had to get away.

The drive home hadn't gone too badly. He had wanted loud, raucous sixties rock and roll, not mournful torch ballads, so he set his Led Zeppelin collection on random. The first track that came on was "Dazed and Confused," which just about said it all. The rest of the drive had passed in a sort of aural slide show of guitar solos, memories and surges of anger alternating with resignation. He was probably lucky to be alive, though, he thought. He didn't really remember the M1 at all now, just the loud music and a swirling haze of red brake lights ahead and the glaring headlights coming towards him on the other side.

As he drove, he second-guessed himself, told himself he should have gone over to Sophia and her friend in the wine bar, should have confronted them on the doorstep, punched the bloke on the nose. Too late for all of that. He had done nothing, and this was where it had led him.

He had also tried to convince himself that it was all innocent, just a drink with an old friend, but there had been something about the body language, the ease between them, the chemistry, which made him doubt it, and he couldn't shake the image of Sophia in bed with the young man, the bed where *they* slept, with the semicircular stained-glass panel above the window and the net curtains fluttering in the breeze.

When he finally shut the door behind him, he felt exhausted, wrung out, but he knew he wouldn't be able to get to sleep. Instead of trying, he poured himself a large glass of wine and, without turning any lights or music on, went to sit in the conservatory.

So this was how it felt to have your heart broken, he thought. And, damn it, it really *did* feel like something was broken. He could feel the pieces inside him grating against one another. It had been so long that he had forgotten the sensation. Annie hadn't broken it when they split up, only bruised it a bit. He and Michelle had simply drifted apart. No, the last time he had felt anywhere near like this was when Sandra had left him. He put his feet up and took a deep breath, reached for the bottle on the table at his side and refilled his glass. He hadn't eaten since lunchtime, and his stomach growled, but he couldn't be bothered to go and see if there was anything in the fridge. He didn't think there was, anyway. It didn't matter. Rain pattered on the glass. The wine would soon take the edge off his appetite, and if he drank enough he would find sleep. Or oblivion.

19

"So just what the bloody hell is going on?" Superintendent Gervaise asked Banks in her office on Tuesday morning at an "informal" meeting over coffee. The rain was still pouring down, Derek Wyman was still missing, and Banks's head was pounding. Oblivion had finally come to him in the wee hours of the morning, but not before he had downed enough red wine to give him a headache even extra-strength paracetamol couldn't touch.

"We think Wyman might have made it to a town," said Banks. "Harrogate, Ripon. York, even. Maybe hitched a lift or caught a bus. From one of those places he could have gone anywhere. Could even be abroad. Anyway, Annie and Winsome are concentrating on checking the bus and train stations. We've also got his picture in the paper and it's coming up on the local TV news this evening. We've got uniforms checking supermarkets and men's outfitters within a thirty-mile radius in case he needed a change of clothes. His credit and debit cards are covered, too. If he uses them, we'll know where."

"It's the best we can do, I suppose," said Gervaise.

Banks finished his coffee and poured himself another cup from the carafe.

"Rough night?" Gervaise asked.

"Just tired."

"OK. What are your thoughts?"

"Something obviously put the wind up him," said Banks. "Maybe Mr. Browne got the thumbscrews out."

"There's no call for flippancy. It was expressly to avoid something like this happening that I told you to lay off over a week ago."

"With all due respect, ma'am," said Banks, "that wasn't the reason. You told me to lay off because MI6 told the Chief Constable, and he passed the message on to you. Your hands were tied. But I'd hazard a guess that you knew damn well that the best way to get me asking questions on my own time was to tell me to lay off. Just like MI6 did eventually, you let me do the dirty work for you while keeping me at arm's length. The only thing you didn't expect was for Wyman to do a runner."

Gervaise said nothing for a moment, then she allowed a brief smile to flicker across her features. "Think you're clever, don't you?" she said.

"Well, isn't it true?"

"You may think that, but I can't possibly comment." She waved her hand. "Anyway, it doesn't matter now. For better or worse, we're here. The point is what are we going to do?"

"We're going to find Derek Wyman first," said Banks, "and then we'll work on calming everyone down. I know it sounds impossible, but I think we should just sit down and thrash it out with MI6, or whoever we can get to talk to us, and settle the matter one way or another. It doesn't matter whether Wyman upset the apple cart because of his brother or because he was angry with Hardcastle. He still hasn't broken any laws, and it's about time everyone knew that."

"You think it's that easy?"

"I don't know why it shouldn't be. Get the Chief Constable to invite his pals to the table. He's in with them, isn't he?"

Gervaise ignored his barb. "I don't think they're concerned right now about *why* Wyman stirred up Hardcastle and Silbert," she said, "but how much and *what* he knows about matters of a top-secret nature."

"I don't think he knows anything," said Banks.

"You've changed your tune."

"Not particularly. I wondered before, speculated perhaps, but I've had a chance to think it through. I've got a contact who does know about these things, and he told me that Silbert had nothing to do with

Afghanistan except for some joint mission with the CIA in 1985, and that his recent work involved the activities of the Russian mafia."

"You believe him?"

"About as much as I believe anyone in this business. I've known him for years. He's got no reason to lie. He would have simply told me he didn't know or couldn't find out." Or, knowing Burgess, to fuck off, Banks thought.

"Unless someone fed him misinformation."

"Who's paranoid now?"

Gervaise smiled. "Touché."

"What I'm saying," Banks went on, "is that we might never know for certain, just the way Edwina Silbert doesn't know for certain that MI6 killed her husband. But she thinks they might have. They might also have had a hand in Laurence Silbert's murder, too. Maybe he was a double agent and that's why they wanted rid of him? We'll probably never know. Despite all the scientific evidence, I still don't think it's beyond the realm of reason that someone in their dirty tricks brigade got into the house and killed him. You saw as well as I did how useless those local CCTV cameras were when it came to covering the area we were interested in. But if that is the case, there's no evidence and there never will be. I'm sick of the whole damn business. The point now is to stop all this before it gets worse. If Wyman hasn't found shelter, a change of clothes, food and water, do you realize that the poor bastard could die of exposure out there? It's got cold as well as wet. And for what? Because a couple of jumped-up boy scouts in suits have ransacked his home and scared the shit out of him the way they did with Tomasina Savage?"

"But what if Wyman's working for the other side?" Gervaise asked.

"The Russian mafia? Oh, come off it," said Banks. "What use would a puny schoolteacher like Derek Wyman be to a bunch of neckless ex-KGB agents? And why would he hire a private detective if he was in with them? They'd have their own surveillance people to follow Silbert. Besides, if they were involved, they would have broken Silbert's neck or pushed him in front of car. Shot him, even. They don't care. I will admit that what happened smacks of British secret service silliness, or the Americans, with their exploding cigars for Castro – it's all a bit Pythonesque – but the Russian mafia . . . ? I don't think so."

"When did you become an expert all of a sudden?"

"I'm not an expert," said Banks, straining to rise above the pounding in his head. "I don't pretend to be. It's just common sense, that's all. I think we all left a little bit of our common sense at home on this one, including me."

"Perhaps," said Gervaise. She glanced at her watch. "I've got a meeting with the Chief Constable in half an hour. I'll put your idea to him. I doubt that he'll go for it, but I'll try."

"Thank you," said Banks. He topped up his coffee and carried his cup and saucer back to his own office, where he stood by the window looking down on the market square for a while. His head pounded and waves of nausea drifted through his stomach. His own fault. He could still hardly believe it. When he thought about it, yesterday evening on the King's Road had the same surreal dreamlike quality as what had happened at Oxford Circus. But perhaps he could do more about last night. At the very least he could stop running and confront Sophia. Maybe she would have an explanation. Maybe he would believe it.

Rain slanted across the square and bounced on the cobbles. Deep puddles straddled all the intersections and people skirted them to avoid getting their feet wet. The sky was an unrelenting grit grey and none of the forecasters could see an end in sight to the dreadful weather. Banks thought of Wyman, alone and frightened out there somewhere, hoped he was dry and sheltered in some cosy bed-and-breakfast, despite all the trouble he had caused. This business had started with a suicide; he hoped it wouldn't end with one. When his phone rang, he hoped it might be Sophia calling to explain or apologize. Instead, it was Tomasina.

"Hello," she said. "I had a hard job tracking you down. That phone number you gave me doesn't work any more."

"Oh, sorry," said Banks. "It was only temporary. I never thought. It's at the bottom of the Thames."

"That's wasteful. Lucky I know where you work."

"Lucky I'm actually here," said Banks. "What can I do for you? No more problems, I hope?"

"No, nothing like that. They haven't returned my files yet, though."

"Give them time. So what is it?"

"Well, actually, it's a bit awkward," Tomasina said.

"Go on."

"Well, you know that concert, the Blue Lamps at the Shepherd's Bush Empire?"

"Yes." It had slipped Banks's mind momentarily, but now that she mentioned it, he remembered. It was a big gig for Brian, and he knew he should try to be there. "Friday, isn't it?" he said.

"That's right."

Banks had been intending to spend the weekend with Sophia, but now he realized he probably wouldn't be doing that, barring some sort of miracle. Still, he could always find somewhere to stay. Brian and Emilia had a pull-out sofa. "You can still make it, I hope?" he said.

"Oh, yes. It's just that, well, I was in the pub last night, and I ran into this old friend from uni. He's really crazy about the Lamps and, well, we'd had a few drinks, you know how it is, and I said why didn't he come with me, you know, to the concert, because I had tickets. You don't really mind, do you, only I thought you'd be able to get another ticket from Brian easily enough, and we could still meet up for a drink and get together backstage later and all that. I'm sorry."

"Whoa, slow down," Banks said. "You're calling off our date, is that it?"

Tomasina laughed nervously. "It wasn't really a *date*. Was it?"

"What else?"

"Well, it's not as if you don't have a girlfriend or anything. I mean, look, if you *really* insist, I know I promised you first and I can tell him –"

"It's all right," said Banks. "I'm only teasing. Of course you should take your friend. I might not even be able to make it, anyway."

"Pressure of work?"

"Something like that," said Banks. "Anyway, the two of you have a great time, OK? And if I'm not there, say hello to Brian from me."

"I will. And thank you."

Banks put down the phone and looked out of the window at the rain again. He could hardly see the dale sides beyond the castle.

Darkness came early that night, and by ten o'clock it was pitch black outside Banks's Gratly cottage, and still raining. There would be no sitting on the wall by the beck tonight, Banks thought, tidying away the remains of his takeaway vindaloo. He had eaten it in front of the TV, drinking beer and watching *No Country for Old Men* on DVD. The movie was about as bleak as he felt. He knew he was feeling sorry for himself when even the memory of Tomasina ringing to cancel their trip to Brian's concert felt like a betrayal.

There had been no progress in the search for Wyman that day. Annie had rung from Harrogate to say she had got nowhere there, and Winsome had reported the same from Ripon. The local forces were helping all they could, but resources were still limited. If they didn't find him soon, it would be time to concentrate on the moors again, maybe drag Hallam Tarn.

Several times over the course of the evening Banks had been on the verge of ringing Sophia, but every time he had backed off. She had wanted time, she said, and she also seemed to have another relationship she wanted to pursue. Often the two went together. When a couple split up, Banks knew, the odds were that one of the partners had found someone else, even if that someone were only the excuse to leave, and the new relationship didn't last. It had happened with Sandra, and she had married the bastard *and* had a child with him. It hadn't been like that with Annie, though. She hadn't left him for someone else; she had just left him.

Had he misinterpreted the situation last night? Had it really been perfectly innocent? How would he ever know if he didn't ask her?

He switched to red wine, poured himself a generous glass and went through to the conservatory. He was just about to go ahead and ring her when he thought he heard a noise out in the back garden. It sounded like the click of the latch on the gate. He held his breath. There it was again. Something, or someone, out there in the bushes. He was about to pick up a kitchen knife and go outside to see what was happening when he heard a light tapping at the conservatory door. He couldn't see any sort of shape through the frosted glass because it was so dark, but there was definitely someone there. The tapping persisted. Eventually, Banks walked over and put his hand on the handle.

"Who is it?" he asked. "Who's there?"

"It's me," a familiar voice whispered back. "Derek Wyman. You've got to let me in. Please."

Banks opened the door and Wyman half stumbled in. Even in the darkness, it was clear that he was soaked to the skin.

"Bloody hell," said Banks, switching on the table lamp. "Look at the state of you. The spy who came in from the cold."

Wyman was shivering. He just stood there in the doorway dripping.

"Come in," said Banks. "I ought to put you over my knee and give you a bloody good spanking, but I think I can find you a towel and some dry clothing. Drink?"

"A large whisky wouldn't go amiss," Wyman said through chattering teeth.

They went through to the kitchen, where Banks poured him a healthy shot of Bell's, then they went upstairs and Wyman dried himself off in the bathroom while Banks dug out some old jeans and a work shirt. The shirt was fine and the jeans were a bit short, but they fitted around the waist all right. Finally, they went back to the conservatory. Banks refilled his wineglass.

"Where've you been hiding?" he asked, when they were sitting down.

Wyman kept the towel around his neck, as if he had just run a race or finished a football game and come out of the shower. "Moors," he said. "I used to do a lot of walking and caving around here. I know all the spots."

"We thought you'd gone to Harrogate and taken the train to distant parts."

"It crossed my mind, but in the end it was too risky. Too open. I thought they'd be looking for me at the stations." Wyman held the glass to his mouth and gulped. His hand was shaking.

"Steady on," said Banks. "Slow down. Take it easy. Have you eaten anything?"

Wyman shook his head.

"I've got some leftover vindaloo," Banks said. "At least it's fresh."

"Thanks."

Banks went into the kitchen, warmed up the vindaloo and half a naan in the microwave and put it on a plate for Wyman. He ate fast, much faster than anyone should eat vindaloo, but it didn't seem to have any adverse effects.

"You said 'they,'" Banks said.

"Pardon?"

"You said you thought 'they' would be watching the stations, not us, not the police."

"Oh, yes."

"Would you like to tell me why you ran?" Banks asked. "The full story."

"I saw them at my house," Wyman said. "The spooks. I was on my way back for tea after the Sunday matinee. They were carrying stuff out. The computer. Papers. Boxes. They don't do that for nothing."

"How did you know who they were? It might have been us."

"No. They'd already talked to me once. Warned me what to expect."

"When?"

"The day before, Saturday, just after I left the police station after talking to you. They were waiting in the square in a car. Put me in the back seat between them. Man and a woman. They wanted to know why you were talking to me, what connection I had to Laurence Silbert's murder. They think I'm hooked up with the Russian mafia, for God's sake. When I saw them at the house, I just panicked."

"They must have got to Tomasina's file on you," Banks said.

"Tom Savage? What do you mean?"

"They raided her office on Friday morning, took most of her files. They obviously had to read through them all, and you're a 'W.' It must have taken them until Sunday, then they came back for you, but you weren't there."

"How did they find her?"

"Through me, I'm afraid. You dropped her card down the back of the radiator at Mohammed's, and he found it."

"You went to Mohammed's? You didn't tell me this before, when you interviewed me."

"There's a lot I didn't tell you. You didn't need to know."

"And now?"

"It might help you to understand what's going on and why."

Wyman paused to digest this. He put his empty plate on the table and sipped some more whisky. His hand seemed to have stopped shaking. "They knew I'd been to Russia."

"That wouldn't be hard to find out. As soon as they knew I was interested in you they'd check you out, but Tomasina came into the picture later. When were you in Russia?"

"Four years ago. Moscow and St. Petersburg. I was a bloody tourist, for crying out loud. I saved up for years for that trip. Went by myself. Carol wasn't interested. She'd rather lie on a beach in Majorca. But I love Russian culture. I love Chekhov, Dostoevsky, Tolstoy, Tchaikovsky, Shostakovich –"

"All right," said Banks. "You can spare me the cultural catalogue. I get the picture."

"They told me they knew about my visit," Wyman went on. "They wanted a list of people I'd met and talked to while I was there."

"What did you tell them?"

"The truth. That I couldn't remember. I didn't meet anyone. Well, I did, but no one . . . you know. I went to museums, galleries, the Bolshoi, the Kremlin, walked the streets."

"And?"

"They didn't believe me. They said they'd be back. Warned me about some of the things they could do to me if they thought I was lying. Lose me my job. Turn my family against me. It was awful. When I saw them at the house on Sunday, I just panicked and took off. But I ran out of petrol. I had a drink or two and tried to think what to do. I realized they'd be searching for my car, so I set out on foot. I've been living rough, up on the moors, ever since. Then I thought of you. You seemed a decent enough bloke when we talked. I thought if anyone could sort this mess out, you could. I haven't done anything, Mr. Banks. I'm innocent."

"I'd hardly call you innocent," said Banks. "How did you know where I live?"

"The fire a while back. It was in the local paper. I remembered the place from my walks, when the old lady lived here."

"So what do you think I can do for you?"

"Get it sorted. Tell them the truth, with a solicitor and other people present, in the police station. I don't trust them. I don't want to be alone with them again."

Nor did Banks. And he had told Gervaise that he wanted to set up a meeting. Perhaps it would be best to take Wyman in. It might give MI6 an extra reason to turn up at the table. With any luck, the matter could be settled once and for all. "Why don't you tell me how it really happened first?" Banks said. "All that about Hardcastle asking you to spy on Silbert, it was crap, wasn't it?"

Wyman hung his head. "Yes. Mark never asked me to check up on Laurence. He never suspected for a moment that he might be seeing someone else. It was me who suggested that. It was all me."

"Why did you lie when we interviewed you?"

"It seemed the easiest way to explain it without making myself look too bad. There was no way you could prove I was lying. There was no one to contradict me."

"But you're telling me the truth now?"

"Yes. I've got nothing left to lose, have I?"

Banks poured Wyman another tumbler of whisky and himself some more wine. The rain continued to slither down the windows of the conservatory, and a drainpipe gurgled by the door. "Why did you do it, then, if it wasn't Hardcastle's idea?"

"Does it matter?"

"It does to me, especially if it was nothing to do with the Russian mafia or your brother's death, either."

"Rick? I told you before, I don't know anything about that. I didn't even know what Laurence did for a living. How could it have been anything to do with Rick?"

"Never mind," said Banks. "Carry on."

"I wasn't interested in Laurence Silbert. I knew nothing about him, really, just that he was some rich bloke who'd taken a shine to Mark. He was just a means to an end. Mark loved him. That was who I wanted to hurt, the smug bastard. Mark."

"Are you telling me this was all about the bloody theatre, after all? Your directing career?"

"You don't understand. He was going to wipe out my job. With a professional acting troupe there, he was going to end up artistic director of the whole bloody show, and getting well paid for it in the bargain, and I was going to be stuck teaching the likes of Nicky Haskell and his mates for the rest of my bloody days. And he delighted in letting me know. He even used to bloody *tease* me about it. I put hours of work into those plays. They were my *life*. Do you think I was just going to stand around and have it all taken away from me by some Johnny-come-lately?"

"I don't believe this," said Banks, shaking his head. "For *that* you destroyed two lives?"

Wyman drank some whisky. "I never intended for anyone to be destroyed. I just wanted to cause a rift, so maybe Hardcastle would bugger off back to Barnsley or wherever and leave us all alone. It started as a bit of a lark, really, thinking about *Othello*. Then I wondered if you really could do that, you know, drive someone around the bend through innuendo and images. Mark *was* a bit jealous about Laurence's frequent trips to London or Amsterdam, whether they were supposed to be business trips or not. I thought I could use that. Mark told me about the flat in Bloomsbury, and one time I was in London at the same time Laurence was there on a business trip I went and watched the flat. That was when I saw Laurence come out. I don't know why, but I followed him, saw him meet a man on a park bench and go to a house in St. John's Wood. I didn't have my camera with me. You know the rest."

"And you hired Tom Savage because you couldn't get down there as often as Laurence Silbert did?"

"That's right. I told her I'd ring her and give her an address when I wanted her to follow someone and take photographs. She did a terrific job. Mark went spare when I showed him them at Zizzi's. I didn't expect him to tear them up, but he did. Naturally, the photos weren't enough in themselves, I had to embellish a bit on the sort of things I thought they were going to do to one another when they got upstairs. But the hand on the back was a lovely touch. If it hadn't been for that, it might have looked innocent."

A harmless gesture. Again, Banks wondered about Sophia. Was that all her friend's gesture had been last night? And was he doing his own embellishment? He put her out of his mind. That was for later.

"I never expected what happened next. You have to believe me. I've been a wreck ever since. Ask Carol. Poor Carol. Is she all right?"

"You should ring her," Banks said. "She's worried sick about you."

"I can't face that just now," said Wyman. "Give me a bit of time to get myself together."

Banks finished his wine. "Look," he said, "as far as I can tell, technically, you've created a hell of a mess, caused two deaths and wasted a lot of police time, but you haven't committed any crime. It's down to the CPS to make the final decision on that, of course, but I honestly can't see what the charge would be."

"You've got to take me in," said Wyman. "We've got to get it sorted before I can go home again. I don't want them coming to my house again. Carol. The kids. I'm willing to accept whatever punishment you think I should have, but I want you to help me get them off my back. Will you do that?"

Banks thought for a moment. "If I can," he said.

Wyman put his tumbler down and got to his feet. "Now?"

"We'll ring your wife from the station," Banks said.

As they walked out to the car, Banks thought he had probably had too much to drink to be driving – a can of beer with dinner and a couple of glasses of wine in the fairly short time Wyman had been there. He was also in a pretty shaky emotional state. But it *was* almost midnight, and he didn't feel at all impaired. What else was he going to do? Send Wyman back to wander the moors in the rain? Give him a bed for the night? The last thing Banks wanted was Derek Wyman skulking around the house in the morning. He could do that perfectly well himself. He knew he wasn't destined for sleep tonight, anyway, so he might as well take the silly bugger to the station, get him off his hands for good and go back to nursing his broken heart over another bottle of wine. It was unlikely that MI6 would turn out for a meeting in the middle of the night, but if Wyman was too nervous to go home, Banks would be more than happy to put him in a cell for a night then arrange for a solicitor to attend in the morning to thrash it all out.

There were no street lights on the road to Eastvale, and only Banks's headlights cut through the darkness and the steady curtain of rain ahead, the windscreen wipers beating time.

Then he noticed the distorted glare of someone's headlights in his rear-view mirror, too close and too bright for comfort. They started flashing.

"Shit," said Banks. He realized that they must have been watching his place, either hoping he would lead them to Wyman, or that Wyman would fetch up there looking for help after they'd put the wind up him. *Parasites.*

"What is it?" Wyman asked.

"I think it's them," Banks said. "I think they were staking out my house."

"What are you going to do?"

"It seems as if they want us to stop." Banks readied himself to pull over at the next lay-by, which he knew was a good half-mile ahead. He was still driving quite fast, definitely over the speed limit, but the car behind was still gaining, still flashing its headlights.

"Don't stop," Wyman said. "Not till we get to town."

"Why not?"

"I just don't trust them, that's all. Like I said, I want a solicitor present the next time I talk to them."

Banks sensed Wyman's anxiety and felt a little surge of paranoia himself. He remembered the callous brutality these people had shown at Sophia's, a brutality that he was certain had led to what happened between him and her. He also remembered stories he had heard, things Burgess had said, how they had frightened Tomasina and Wyman, and that it was still possible they could have been responsible for Silbert's murder. He remembered Mr. Browne's veiled threats. And he didn't like the way they had tried to warn him off one minute and then use him the next.

Call me paranoid, Banks thought, but I don't want a confrontation with MI6 out here in the middle of nowhere, in the middle of the night, with no witnesses. If they wanted to have it out, they could bloody well follow him to Eastvale and have a nice cosy chat in the security of the police station, with a mug of cocoa and a solicitor present, just the way he and Wyman wanted it.

But they had other ideas. As soon as Banks overshot the lay-by and put his foot down, they did the same, and this time they started to overtake him on the narrow road. The Porsche was powerful enough, but they were driving a BMW, Banks noticed, and weren't lacking in power themselves. There was a corner coming up, but they obviously didn't know about that when they started to edge to their left, about half a car length ahead. No doubt they intended to bring Banks to a smooth halt, but either because of the rain or not knowing the bends in the road, or both, they misjudged terribly, and Banks had to turn the wheel sharply to avoid a collision. He knew this part of the road well, so he braced himself as the Porsche broke through a section of drystone wall and flew over the steep edge.

Banks was strapped in the driver's seat, and he felt the jolt of the seat belt as it absorbed the impact. Wyman, in his distracted state, had forgotten to fasten his belt, and he shot forward through the windscreen, so he lay half on the bonnet, his lower half still in the car. For some reason, the airbags hadn't been activated. Banks unbuckled his seat belt and staggered out to see what had happened.

Wyman's neck was twisted at an awkward angle, and blood pumped all over the bonnet from where a large sliver of glass had embedded itself in his throat. Banks left it there and tried to hold the wound closed around it, but he was too late. Wyman shuddered a couple of times and gave up the ghost. Banks could feel him die right there in front of him, feel the life go out of him, his hand resting on the dead man's neck.

Banks fell back against the car's warm bonnet, slick with blood, looked up to the heavens and let the rain fall on his face. His head throbbed. Disturbed by the noise, a few sheep baaed out in the field.

Two people were walking down the slope towards him, a young man and a young woman carrying torches, the slanting rain caught in their beams of light.

"Bit of a mess, isn't it?" the young man said when they got to the Porsche. "Nice car, too. Not quite what we had in mind at all. We only wanted to talk to him again. Find out what he was doing putting a tail on one of our men. You should have stopped when we flashed you."

"He couldn't tell you anything," said Banks. "He was just a bloody school teacher."

The man shone his torch on the bonnet of the Porsche. "Dead, is he? We'll never know what he was up to now, will we?"

Banks could think of nothing to say to that. He just shook his head. He felt dizzy and weak at the knees.

"You all right?" the young woman asked. "You've got blood on your forehead."

"I'm fine," said Banks.

"We'll take it from here," she went on. "This is what we'll do. My friend is going to phone some people. They're used to cleaning up situations like this. We'll have your car back outside your cottage again by tomorrow morning, as good as new." She paused and looked at the Porsche. "Make that the day after tomorrow," she said. "It can sometimes be hard to get replacement parts for foreign cars. We'll make sure they fix the airbags, too."

Banks gestured towards Wyman. "What about him?"

"Well, there's nothing anybody can do for him now, is there? Best let us take care of it. He was distraught over what he'd done. He went walkabout and either he jumped or he fell off a cliff. We don't want any fuss, do we? I'd just go home if I were you. Walk away."

Banks stared at her. She was pretty in a slightly hard-faced sort of way, but her eyes didn't flinch; there was no milk of human kindness in them. "But he didn't do anything," said Banks.

"Maybe not," the woman said. "Mistakes get made sometimes. It doesn't matter. Let us deal with it now."

"But you killed him."

"Now, wait a minute," said the young man, squaring up to Banks. "That rather depends on your point of view, doesn't it? From what I could see, you were driving way too fast. You've obviously been drinking. And he wasn't wearing a seat belt. You should have had your airbags checked, too. They malfunctioned."

"And you wouldn't know anything about that, would you?"

"Don't be ridiculous. If we wanted you both dead, you'd be dead in much easier circumstances to clean up than this. It was an accident. Besides, don't forget he was responsible for the death of one of our best men, and if you'd had your way he'd simply have walked away. Hardcastle never asked him to put a tail on Silbert. The whole thing was his own twisted, crazy plan."

"How do you know?"

"What?"

"I can understand you probably got the transcripts of the interview. The Chief Constable would have given you those. But how did you know that was all a lie, that Wyman . . . ?" Banks paused as the truth dawned on him. "You bugged my cottage, didn't you? You bastards."

The man shrugged. "You're away a lot. Access isn't a problem."

Banks looked towards Wyman's body again. "So *this* is your idea of justice?"

"I'll admit it's sloppy," the man said, "but it's justice of a kind. Look, Silbert helped us bring down some pretty big players – sex traffickers, drugs dealers, killers for hire. He even helped us put some terrorists behind bars. And this piece of scum you're defending so eloquently basically killed him."

"Are you sure?"

"What do you mean?"

"I'm still not convinced," Banks said. "Oh, Wyman stirred Hardcastle up all right, but you lot could still have killed Silbert. Wyman just makes a good scapegoat because he's so full of guilt."

"Why would we do that? I've already told you Silbert was one of our best men."

"Maybe he was a double agent. What about those Swiss bank accounts? People led me to believe that agents feather their nests when they're in the field, but who knows? Maybe he was playing for both sides."

"Then maybe the other side killed him. Whatever happened, you'll never know, will you? Anyway, this is ridiculous, and it's getting us nowhere. We need to move fast."

"So what are you going to do?"

"What do you suggest?"

"I don't believe this."

"Believe it. The best thing you can do is –"

But he never got to end the sentence. Banks felt the urge begin in his solar plexus, and the next thing he knew his fist was connecting with the man's jaw. It happened so quickly the man never had a chance, no matter what fancy martial arts he had been trained in. Banks heard a satisfying crunch and felt the jolt run all the way up to his shoulder. He could also sense that he'd probably broken a knuckle, maybe two, but the pain was worth it to vent some of his anger – anger about Wyman, about Sophia, the bombing, Hardcastle, Silbert, the Secret Intelligence Service. The man crumpled and fell like a sandbag to the earth. Banks cradled his right hand in his left and bent double with pain.

"Carson," the woman said, bending over him. "Carson? Are you all right?"

Carson groaned and rolled over in the mud. Banks kicked him hard in the ribs. He groaned again and spat out a tooth.

Banks was just about to kick him in the stomach when he realized that the woman was pointing a gun at him. "Stop it," she said. "I don't want to use this, but I will if I have to."

Banks glared at her, realized that she meant what she said, then took a few deep breaths. He looked at Carson again and felt no desire to inflict any more pain. He leaned back on the car and caught his breath, still cradling his right hand.

"The truth is that none of this happened," the woman went on. "We weren't even here. You'll get your car back as good as new. His body will be found at the bottom of a cliff, and nothing changes. You can tell all the stories you want, but I guarantee you that nobody will believe a word you say. If necessary, we'll give you a legend that will land you in jail for the rest of your days. When we've finished with you, even your family and your closest friends will never want to talk to you again. Do I make myself clear?"

Banks said nothing. What was there to say? Any insults and threats of retribution he might want to make would just be empty bluster in the face of the power these people had. He knew he'd had all the satisfaction he was going to get from the punch he'd landed. Carson was still groaning through his broken jaw. Banks's knuckles were throbbing in synchronization with his head.

The woman held her gun in one hand and her mobile in the other. Both hands were perfectly steady. "Walk away," she said. "Do it. Now."

Banks's legs were still a bit wobbly, but they worked. He didn't say anything, just made his way up the slope to the road. The night was a dark wet cloak around him. There was only one place he wanted to be now, only one place left for him to go. A little unsteady at first, but gaining strength and momentum as he went, Banks started the long walk home. He wasn't sure whether the wetness he felt on his face was rain, blood or tears.

ACKNOWLEDGEMENTS

I would like to thank everyone who read the manuscript and offered suggestions for improvements – in particular, Sheila Halladay, Dinah Forbes, Carolyn Marino and Carolyn Mays. There are also many others to thank for their hard work and support – my agents Dominick Abel and David Grossman; Jamie Hodder Williams, Lucy Hale, Kerry Hood, Auriol Bishop, Katie Davison and Kate Howard at Hodder; Michael Morrison, Lisa Gallagher, Sharyn Rosenblum, Wendy Lee and Nicole Chismar at Morrow; and Doug Pepper, Ellen Seligman, Ashley Dunn and Adria Iwasutiak at McClelland & Stewart. Also thanks to all the sales reps and booksellers who work so hard to get the books out there, and to you for reading them.

I would also like to offer a special thanks to Julie Kempson for her help with the technical and legal matters. Any mistakes, it goes without saying, are entirely my own.